The Upstart

Also by Piers Paul Read

GAME IN HEAVEN WITH TUSSY MARX

THE JUNKERS

MONK DAWSON

THE PROFESSOR'S DAUGHTER

The Upstart

Piers Paul Read

J. B. Lippincott Company
Philadelphia and New York

U.S. Library of Congress Cataloging in Publication Data

Read, Piers Paul, birth date
  The upstart.

  I. Title.
PZ4.R285Up [PR6068.E25]   823'.9'14   73–653
ISBN–0–397–00966–6

In each one of us there is a sinner and a saint. The one and the other develop, each on his own plane. The one and the other, not the one or the other. Both at the same time. While the saint develops—if the man is a saint—the sinner in him develops on the imaginative plane. . . . If the man is a sinner—that is to say, if the sinner gets the better of the saint—the saint develops as best he can on the imaginative plane (a yearning for holiness). That is why a sinner who is converted never starts from scratch. He has made some progress during his life of sin.

—JULIEN GREEN, *Diary*

Part One

1

In the spring of 1937 a curate was admitted to the Charing Cross Hospital in London for the removal of a stone from his bladder. Sponging his puny body, and clipping the stitches on the fringes of his groin, there was a nurse who spoke with a soft and pleasant Yorkshire accent. The curate and the nurse fell in love. The healthy, buxom farmer's daughter formed a passion for the clergyman's gentility, and the bloodless cleric had the aberrant spirit to think of his hand under her starched skirts. The couple were later married and I was their only child.

The first two years of my life were spent in a parish in South London. In 1941, my father joined the army as a chaplain and we moved into married quarters in Aldershot. For a short period he served with the Coldstream Guards in the Western Desert, where his only achievement was to make the acquaintance of Colonel Sir Edward Metherall, Bart., the man who owned the village of Lasterby and the land farmed by my mother's brother in Yorkshire. Then, after only one engagement against the Germans, he returned to England with "shell shock" and spent the rest of the war ministering to the spiritual needs of the new recruits at Aldershot. In 1951, however, he was offered the parish of Lasterby by his old comrade in arms, Sir Edward Metherall, who had the living. There was some discussion in our family, which I remember, of the advantages and disadvantages of taking up this offer. I myself was all in favor of going north, having spent some holidays with Uncle Ernest and my cousins Sam and George on the farm; to my mother and father, the proximity of Uncle Ernest was somehow a disadvantage. I did not at that age understand why.

It was decided in the end, however, that the offer should be accepted, and at the beginning of the summer of 1951 we moved north.

The village of Lasterby lies on the southern rim of Ryedale. It had then around three hundred inhabitants and has now less than half that number. The church had been built in the fifteenth century; the rectory had been rebuilt by the Church Commissioners in 1910. Before that there had been, so I understand, a fine sprawling house built of the local stone and roofed with russet pantiles, but the building had fallen into disrepair and was thought too large in any case for the shrinking stipend of the rector. It had therefore been demolished to make way for the present house, which was built of imported granite that did not crumble and roofed with slate that did not crack. It was, as a result, the only ugly house in Lasterby, but it did not spoil the village because it was hidden away at the foot of the hill which rose to the south at the "top end."

From here to the east there was a mile of straight country lane with hedges and trees on either side. The trees were part of an irregular avenue which led to Lasterby Hall. To the left, over the tops of the hedges, there was a view across Ryedale to the North York Moors, which rose in the distance, a mauve horizon, clear and close in some weathers and in others hidden by the mist and drizzle. At the end of the avenue there were the great gates of Lasterby Hall. The road, which had hitherto been straight, swung off to the right, free and winding, toward Malton. Through the gates, which were huge and rusty and could never have been closed, the drive continued the straight line of the road. There was a lodge house to the left of the gate and, beyond this, a screen of trees and bushes which opened out after fifty yards or so to give a view of the house and park.

The first time I saw Lasterby Hall was before we came to live in Yorkshire—a time when I was on holiday at the farm

—and it was not from the vantage point of the drive but through a gap in the hedge shown to me by my cousin Sam. It had impressed me immensely because of its large size: there were seventeen windows in two rows on the south front and all these windows were white. I asked Sam, who crouched beside me, to explain this phenomenon, and he said that the windows were white because the shutters were closed behind them, and the shutters were closed because the family was away.

"Who lives there?" I asked.

"The Metheralls."

"One family?"

"Aye, and servants and things."

I did not see the house again until I was invited there as the rector's son, and on that occasion the windows were black again—but the event needs some introduction.

I was out in the garden kicking rotten cabbages with Sam and George when my mother called me in. I knew at once that it was for something unpleasant because she used her refined tone of voice and called me by my full name, Hilary, itself an inspiration of her gentility from which I suffered much in life.

I came into the kitchen. She looked flushed and excited. "You're to put on your suit," she said.

"Why?" I asked.

"You're asked to tea at the hall."

"Are Sam and George going?"

"No."

"Why not?"

"She didn't ask them, did she?"

"Who didn't?"

"Lady Metherall."

"Why didn't she?"

"Why should she?"

"If they're not going, then I'm not going neither."

"You'll do as you're told."

"Then I'll go as I am."

By now my mother was angry. "Don't be so daft," she said.

"But why do I have to go?" I asked.

"I told you. Because Lady Metherall's asked you."

"What a bugger," I said.

A slap. "And don't you go talking like that, you cheeky boy."

"Why not? Sam does."

Sam, who was a year older than I was, had come in behind me and was standing at the kitchen door.

"Don't you go using those words, Sam," said my mother.

"What's wrong w'bugger?" Sam asked.

She made a swipe at him; he ran off. "I'll tell your dad on you," she shouted after him, and then added, in a more controlled tone of voice, "I'll tell your father."

When I came down in my suit she brushed my hair and straightened my tie.

"I don't know the way," I said.

"Yes, you do," she said. "And anyway, I'll drive you to the gates."

"And what do I do then?"

"You follow the drive up to the house."

"And which door do I use?"

"The front door, of course," she said, biting her lip and speaking in a most unconvinced tone of voice.

When I reached Lasterby Hall, the front door was by no means as evident as my mother had implied. The house is a square of ashlar stone with its principal floor raised from the ground. Above this there is one other story; beneath it, the kitchen and a hallway with an interior staircase, both added in the middle of the nineteenth century. The original means of entry to the main floor was up an open staircase in the center of the east front which started in two arms and then joined up into one, a typically Palladian construction which led to a recessed portico with giant, unfluted Ionic columns.

[12]

It seemed to me then that the doors at the top of these steps were what one would think of as the front door, so I climbed them and, not finding a bell or a knocker, tried to turn the handles and push them open to let myself in. It appeared, however, that they were locked and the glass in their upper halves rattled as I pushed at them. I tried to peer in but the reflection of the sky behind me made it difficult to see anything at all. I saw a figure pass across the enormous room into which these doors would open if they opened at all. The figure made some gestures and then disappeared.

I tried the doors again but then heard a voice beneath me shout, "Down here!"

I went to the top of the Palladian staircase and looked down. There, looking up at me, was a boy of exactly my age but with blond, curly hair.

"Are you the vicar's son?" he asked.

"Yes," I said.

"I'm Mark Metherall," he said. "I live here."

"I'm Hilary Fletcher," I said, going down the steps toward him.

"Hilary?" he asked. "Isn't that a girl's name?"

"It can be," I said, blushing, "but it's a boy's name too."

He led me toward a door which was under the arch beneath the steps.

"Aren't you related to Sam Cartwright?"

"He's my cousin."

"Hattie says that when they killed the pig at Baxton's, Sam Cartwright picked up its eye and threw it at her."

I said nothing.

"Did he do that?"

"He might have done."

We went into the hallway, which had a barrel-vaulted ceiling and a bowl on a table filled with dried rose petals. The floor was paved with squares of white unpolished marble. To the right a large flight of stairs led upstairs. We climbed these stairs, which were shallow and wide, and came up into the great hall—an immense room with a huge fireplace, a carved

[13]

stone mantel, a painted ceiling, large windows looking out onto the park, and the glass doors through which I had first tried to enter the house.

"We never use those doors," said Mark. "In fact, we don't really use this room."

On the far side of the hall we went under a large arch and past another, smaller staircase; then we turned left into what was called the small drawing room, though it was six times the size of the largest room in the rectory.

There, around the fireplace, stood what seemed to me to be an immense crowd of people, though there were in fact only eight, of whom five were children around my age. I glanced first at the man, who was tall and heavy and had a mustache, then at the plump lady who wore an apron, then at the thinner of the two women who came toward me.

"Come in," she said in a brisk tone of voice; and then, almost in the same breath, but looking over my shoulder at Mark, she added, "Tell Mrs. Hugill that we're ready."

Mark left the room; Lady Clare Metherall took hold of my hand. "Come and meet the others," she said, drawing me toward the fireplace. "This is Harriet, Mark's sister."

A girl a little younger than I was looked at me with a sulky expression but said nothing. I studied her face for signs of where the pig's eye might have hit her but there was nothing.

"This is Caroline," Lady Clare went on, "and Pips and Joss and Simon."

"How do you do?" I said to this row of children.

"And you're Hilary, aren't you?"

"Yes," I said.

"And that's what you're called?" she asked. "You haven't got a nickname?"

"No," I said.

"Shall we call you Hilly?" asked Harriet.

There were guffaws from the other children. I blushed since this was just what my mother sometimes called me.

"Don't be silly, darling," Lady Clare said to her daughter,

and then, turning to me, she added, "We call her Hattie, you see."

The insolent expression remained on Harriet's face. "Have you brought me a present?" she asked.

I blushed very deeply indeed. "I didn't know . . ."

"Don't be silly," said Lady Clare. "You weren't meant to know and you weren't meant to bring a present. Hattie's had quite enough."

"But it is my birthday, Mother," said Harriet.

"You'll spend your birthday in your bedroom if you aren't careful," said Lady Clare, after which Harriet was silent.

I sat down on an armchair and looked at the room around me. I was not yet of an age to appreciate the regency furniture or the swirling Turner on the wall. I noticed, however, the tidiness of everything and the photographs in silver frames of Mark and Harriet when they were much younger, and of Sir Edward in dress uniform.

Mark returned and said that tea was ready, and we went into the dining room where sandwiches and cakes were laid out on a long table. There were snappers, and a birthday cake with eleven candles which Harriet blew out in one go.

I would have enjoyed the party more if I had not felt so ashamed for not bringing a birthday present.

Two days later it was Sunday, and for the first time since we had been at Lasterby the whole Metherall family took their place in their pew.

After the service was over, Mark and Harriet came up to me on the path which led from the church.

"When are you going to come and see us again?" Mark asked.

"Well, I don't know . . ." I began.

"Mother," Harriet shouted to Lady Clare, "can Hilary come over this afternoon?"

"I should think so," said Lady Clare, looking at me without a smile, "but you'd better ask Nanny."

Harriet skipped back to the plump woman who had worn an apron at her birthday party and returned a moment later to say that it was all arranged. "Can you walk down?" she asked.

"Oh, yes," I said.

Before lunch that Sunday, my mother and father went for a drink at the hall and I went to tea in the afternoon, but while their visits to the older Metheralls were to remain spaced every seven days, mine became more frequent. There were also days when Mark and Harriet came to tea at the rectory. One thing, however, was always clear: I never went to tea at Lasterby Hall without an invitation, delivered either by the telephone or by casual conversation between our mothers meeting in the village street. Nor would my parents go for a glass of sherry before lunch on a Sunday unless Sir Edward asked them after the morning service; and there were occasions, especially during the shooting season, when the invitation did not come. Thus my parents would know that there were grand guests at the hall—sporting baronets or London intellectuals—for whom they were thought un-suitable. And if it was my invitation to tea that did not come, I would know that some of the many cousins of the Metheralls had come to stay.

All the same, I saw a good deal of my new friends, and my admiration of them grew with this greater familiarity. Though I myself was a proud child, my pride was secret, whereas they made an exhibition of theirs, flaunting it before their parents and servants alike. In Mark it took the form of perpetual politeness. Even at the age of twelve, be-fore he had gone to Eton, he acted with unnatural correctness and charm. It was all part of his self-possession and confidence which, together with his fair, curly hair, his even features, his blue eyes and, later, his height, gave him an aura of natural authority. This did not reflect his true character, for he was too amiable to be decisive and it was usually Harriet who chose what we should do on those summer afternoons.

Like her brother she had blond hair, but hers was straight

and fine. At the age of eleven when I met her she had large eyes which looked with unblinking haughtiness on everyone, a thin, rasping voice, spoiled little gestures, thin little lips and a neat little dress.

Her effect upon me was great from the very first, and for some time the word "hilly" made me blush. Having suggested this abbreviation to my name, however, and having got a good laugh from her friends at my expense, Harriet never thereafter called me Hilly or anything other than my full name, Hilary. Nor did I call her anything but Harriet—though her family called her Hattie—except once, when she blushed, but there were other circumstances surrounding that incident which may have accounted for it.

The similarity of the letters starting our first names did not go unnoticed, and when we had nothing better to do we would intertwine our initials thus:

on the page of an exercise book or drawing pad, the doodling thereby producing something like a television aerial.

It was not love, however, which led to this intertwining of our initials but the imitative spirit in both of us, for we had often seen Mark lying fully stretched on the floor of the day nursery at Lasterby Hall with pencils, crayons, even watercolors, designing the most intricate intertwining of *his* two initials:

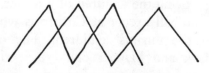

One afternoon, when we were all there drawing our initials because it was raining outside, I thought that our television aerial would go nicely on top of his roofs, and so while Mark was out of the room I drew our initials on the side of his first M and put a chimney pot on the other side to balance it. When he returned and saw what I had done to his drawing he was very angry but did his best not to show it. He liked to be controlled, and anyway Harriet was on my side.

There was no question but that Harriet, of the three of us, had the strongest character. There was only one other child in the neighborhood who had a character as strong as hers, and because of this she was fascinated by him, which gave me, indirectly, some hold over her, for this other was my cousin, Sam Cartwright.

He was about a year older than both Mark and I and had a reputation in the village for daring and toughness—or, in the language of our parents, mischief and cheek. I myself had admired him for a long time for climbing trees, finding birds' nests, or leading George and me to abandoned quarries. What frightened me but fascinated Harriet was the way he could drown a kitten or strangle a chicken with no compunction. "A useful lad to have around a farm," my uncle Ernest used to say, who was himself gentle and loath to drown kittens or wring the necks of his poultry.

Sam, of course, was aware of the power his ruthless nature gave him over others, and the incident of the pig's eye, which he had picked up and thrown at Harriet, was partly to encourage her admiration and partly to avenge himself for the telling-off he had had the day before from Sir Edward's gamekeeper, who had caught him poaching.

Now such were the conventions of the countryside that Sam and George, being the children of a tenant, could not be asked to tea at the hall except at Christmas when there was a party for all the tenants' children. The only children with whom Mark and Harriet could properly be friends were the sons and daughters of neighboring landowners like Pips Slingsby, Simon Grant-Carrington or Joss Plunkett, who had been at Harriet's birthday party, but all of these lived seven to ten miles from Lasterby and so had to be fetched and carried by their parents whenever they were invited. The parents had to be asked in for a drink; thus for Mark to see Joss Plunkett involved Sir Edward and Lady Clare in a visit from Brigadier Plunkett or Mrs. Plunkett, something they would normally do their best to avoid.

It was in this context that I was so useful to them, for not only did I live within walking distance but I was the rector's son, and the rector's son could quite properly be asked to tea at the hall. My close relationship to the sons of a tenant farmer was overlooked, for the Metheralls were English and tolerant and would never pursue a prejudice beyond a single generation.

What they overlooked, their children regarded as my prize asset, for while they could never go to tea at the farm, and my cousins could never come to tea at the hall, I could go to tea at both and ask both to come to tea at the rectory. I was, as they say, acceptable to both sides—the man in the middle who could bring the two sides together and organize a time and a place where we could all meet to play rounders, "he," go quarry climbing, fight or disturb Lizzie Harrison's rabbits so that the mother ate her young. We were also known to take cattle barriers from the beck and make them into flagpoles and, on mischief night, take gates off their hinges and ring the church bells.

Most of our pranks and games were organized either by Sam or by Harriet, for in the fields around Lasterby and the barns of the farm there were no distinctions of class, only of character. Sam and Harriet were decidedly the leaders. They made up their minds about what we should do and we followed them. Mark and I were next in rank; we would make suggestions and even go off on our own if we did not like what Sam and Harriet had decided. George, Fred Plowman and Lizzie Harrison (the children of the farm laborers who were asked to tea neither at the hall, the farm, nor the rectory) were the ordinary soldiers who did as they were told without question.

Though there was no overt pact between them, Sam and Harriet were content to share the bossing. Each had apparently decided that it was best not to fight for supremacy; both were unsure which of them would come out on top. Sam may have had the obvious advantages—he was older and exceptionally tough—but Harriet had such a talent for nasty and acute observations that Sam, like the nanny and all the Metheralls, would rather not have her comments. Like all of us, he was a little afraid of her. I believe that the only one who was not was Lady Clare, from whom she had inherited her waspishness, but this woman had her mind on higher things and did not give the time to soften her daughter's nature.

The summer came to an end and I started school in the village with Sam, George, Fred and Lizzie and all the other children except the Metheralls, for already at that age Mark went to a private boarding school and Harriet to a private day school in Malton—the Academy of Madame de Pollande, a name which was abbreviated by local ladies to "Madame's." The founder of this school to which all the daughters of the gentry were sent was now dead; she had been a Mademoiselle de Pollande who, in the 1920s, had been governess to the children of the greatest of our local landowners, the Earl of Barton. At the insistence of the Countess, she had retired early; at the insistence of the Earl, she had remained close at hand—a compromise quite acceptable to both the spouses and to the general opinion of the county.

I knew little about Mark's preparatory school because he never talked about it, but I could tell from the dread with which he looked forward to going back at the end of the holidays, and from the stunned look on his face when he returned at Christmas, that he was unhappy there. I even overheard Lady Clare tell my mother that Mark had never "settled down." This did not stop my mother from doing her best to persuade my father to take me away from the village school and send me, if not to a boarding school, at least to the Academy of Madame de Pollande, which also taught boys. My father refused, not because I was happy at the village school and quite well taught, nor because he liked to have me at home, but because the money he had set aside for my education would only just be enough to send me to a public school from the age of thirteen onward.

Often, when my father refused her something, my mother would return to the subject at some other time and gently pester until he gave in. On this occasion, however, she accepted completely what he said, for she realized how important and how fragile were the plans for my secondary education.

I lived a year at Lasterby before the start of that grim passage of my life. It was certainly the happiest year of my childhood and perhaps its only happy year. It was divided into seven parts—three terms and four holidays. In the term I saw much of Sam and George. After school we would either play at the pond end of the village or go back to the rectory to tea. Before the dark evenings of the winter had started, I would sometimes walk back with them to the farm —a mile and a half from Lasterby—and have tea with Uncle Ernest. In winter when it was dark by four or five in the afternoon, it was thought that I should not walk back to the rectory alone, though Sam and George were allowed to take the same walk in the opposite direction if they had tea with us; but they were two whereas I was only one.

I appreciated this adult reasoning and had no great wish to walk alone the mile and a half in the dark, but against this was set my great affection for Uncle Ernest and the superiority of the tea served at the farm. It was made by Mrs. Bosomworth, who had been Uncle Ernest's housekeeper since my aunt Maud had died. It consisted of her own bread, scones and drop scones; her own muffins, flans, pies, tarts, and short-bread. There was cream to go with the flans and pies and butter and jam to go with the rest. There was also a main dish of eggs and bacon or fried fish, as often as not with dinnertime's potatoes fried up again. Uncle Ernest drank tea; we drank milk with a little tea in it to make it warm and a lot of sugar to make it sweet.

Tea at the rectory was similar only in the beverages offered to us, though the milk was thin and the tea was weak. Moreover, my father would insist that we drank either milk or tea because the mixture we had at the farm was "sickly" and "offended against the integrity of the thing." There was also shop-bought ready-sliced bread spread with margarine.

Tea at the farm was eaten in the kitchen; at the rectory it was eaten in the dining room, which smelled of stale food and table polish. There was to eat, besides the bread and margarine, either Swiss roll or cake or biscuits—all bought from the shop.

Once, after my mother had been with me to tea at the farm, she thought she would make some bread for our tea. After all, she said, she had done it as a girl. The loaf she made the next day was a success—quite as good as Mrs. Bosomworth's—but my father took against it. "It is quite uneconomic," he said, "in our developed, industrial society, to reverse the process of the specialization of labor." He extracted from my mother the confession that the cost of the flour, milk, yeast, butter and heat from the stove equaled and probably exceeded the cost of a ready-sliced loaf. "And anyway," said my father, "baking makes you sweat."

Since the facts, related simply like this, make my father out to be an unpleasant man, let me say in his defense that his stipend was small; that he worried constantly about money, not without reason; that my mother did sweat a great deal when put to any exertion. I myself liked her to do it. I loved the smell that mixed with that of her cheap scent and soap, but those related less biologically to this natural woman could not be expected to take the same delight in the odor and the sight—above all, not a man as fastidious as my father. There may once have been a day when her smell had attracted him; perhaps it was that which, as she leaned over him to remove the stitches, had first made him think of her in terms of pleasure and affection. If that was so, it was a short-lived aberration, for as early in my life as I can remember, my mother did her best to limit the flow of her perspiration and my father did what he could to save her from exertion.

On the question of the two different teas—one which to this day splits the British nation in two—I might add another factor which should be taken into account. Tea at the farm, like tea at the farms and cottages round about, was the last meal of the day; while tea at the rectory, like tea at Lasterby Hall, was not. The former was served at half past five or six, after a hard day's work in the fields; the latter was served at half past four to show, if nothing else, that those who took it were beyond a hard day's work of any kind. Later in the day—at a quarter to eight at the rectory, at eight fifteen at the hall—there was another meal called supper or dinner, a matter of soup, meat, vegetables and pudding. Thus, while in the short term it was better to take tea at the farm, in the long term you got two meals if you took tea at the rectory. That is to say, I did. If Sam and George had tea with us they were unlikely to eat much else that day, because Mrs. Bosomworth had to get back to the village.

On the other hand if I went to tea at the farm and came home before seven forty-five I would sit at supper with my parents and let what was offered there follow what had been given at the farm down my gullet. My father, suspecting that I had stuffed myself at Uncle Ernest's table, would look over his spectacles and ask me if, in view of my previous and recent meal, I should like to be excused the mince my mother had set before us. I would reply that I had only had a cup of tea at Uncle Ernest's and so would like my mince. It pained me that my father should grudge me the mince, for even if I had owned up to the bacon and egg and gone without my share he would not have eaten it and neither would my mother. It pained me, too, to lie to him, though I did so early on, but he was someone who had to be told lies to be saved from irritation—irritation caused by his own most unnecessary principles, such as that his son should not eat both bacon and egg at the farm and mince and turnips at the rectory.

I say mince and turnips; it could as well have been stew or boiled fish. We had nothing fried because of my father's digestion. Even so, these boiled dishes were not well cooked. My mother's heart was not in their preparation. She was, by nature and upbringing, a cook of flans, tarts, pies and home-made bread. While her strong and stubborn mind would never let her abandon her genteel habits of dinner at a quarter to eight, she was in her heart one of those for whom dinner is at midday and the evening meal is tea. Thus, for Sunday lunch she could do a fine roast beef and Yorkshire pudding; it was in her bones to do so. But asked to cook the same food for a dinner at night and it would result in dried-up meat and soggy pudding. Habits of childhood die hard, and habits of many generations die harder still.

During the holidays there was a third choice—tea at the hall —which was always set up a day in advance by an invitation; for instance, "Mother says, would you like to come to tea tomorrow?" Now tea at Lasterby Hall was like in kind to tea at the rectory in that it was not the last meal of the day. It was brought up to the day nursery, a drab room with worn linoleum on the floor and the scratchings and draw-ings of several generations of Metheralls on the walls, and was attended by Lady Clare; as often as not, Sir Edward would "look in for a cup." Sir Edward's presence was inci-dental, but I would say that he enjoyed the event more than his wife, even though her presence was more deliberate. It had to be deliberate, just as his could be incidental, for on all other occasions Lady Clare avoided the company of her children while Sir Edward would leave the library or the estate office on any pretext to chase his children or take them pigeon shooting in the park.

During the term I went only occasionally to tea at the hall and then only at weekends. I came to value these occasions because already at that age I liked to be alone with Harriet—not because I loved her but because I looked up to her—and Harriet, knowing the position she held in my estimation, took it upon herself to use her authority and educate me in the ways of the country.

Her favorite pejorative term, learned from her mother, was the word "common," by which she did not mean the low and vulgar language and behavior of Sam but the subtler gaffes of someone from a town. She was especially delighted with me because, on first coming to Lasterby, I condemned myself every time I opened my mouth and she was able to correct me. I learned, for instance, that it was wrong to call the red coat of the huntsman *red*, because it was *pink*. A white horse was not *white* but *gray*. I learned also to say "What?" in place of "Pardon?" but stopped short of calling my mother "Mother," as she did, and continued to call her "Mummy" even though it was quite clear that Harriet thought this common. It was somehow beyond me to pass on to my mother what I learned from Harriet, but I was tormented every time she said "Pardon?" when Harriet was there—and soon I was tormented whether Harriet was there or not.

There arose a matter, however, in which a habit of hers was revealed to me not as something common but as something wrong. It was Harriet who put me right, with some smugness and the unspoken suggestion that there was something common about the error: it was my mother's, my father's and my own use of the term "Lady Metherall" to

[25]

describe the wife of our benefactor, the mother to Harriet. For we had not understood that Lady Metherall was an earl's daughter and should therefore be addressed as Lady Clare Metherall. To be called Lady Metherall pained Lady Clare, according to Harriet, because an earl's daughter was so much more than the wife of a baronet who, from mere title, could as well be the wife of a knight bachelor. Of course Lady Clare had never said anything about it, nor had my mother discussed, other than in her own home, the vulgar familiarity of those in the village who referred to Lady Metherall as Lady Clare. And those in the village never mentioned to my mother that Lady Metherall was not Lady Metherall but Lady Clare Metherall because they were delighted to see her make a fool of herself. They thought she was stuck up.

When my mother discovered her mistake—when I told her about it—she was so appalled that she had to sit down. It was certainly for her the worst moment in her life, the worst day, the worst week, the worst month. She only recovered her self-possession by the end of that month by sowing the ground, both stony and fertile, with so many "Lady Clares" that this worst moment of her life was, as it were, buried in them.

My poor mother. If she had stayed at home and never gone nursing in London she would not have made such a mistake. And if she had been on better terms with her brother Ernest, he might have enlightened her, even if he had been unable to explain why Lady Clare was not Lady Metherall; but he was firmly in the camp of the rural fools, so far as she was concerned, and he led the band of those who thought his sister stuck up.

My father, of course, had always called Lady Metherall by that name and on odd occasions continued to do so, but no one expected him to do otherwise.

The fact that the earldom of which Lady Clare was a daughter was a recent creation did not matter. She loved it, and as deeply as she loved it I was humiliated. Her children too, especially Harriet, had learned to disregard their father's baronetcy, which went back two centuries into history, for the earldom. It was the foundation on which the dazzling and intricate structure of their snobbery was built. Like their mother they believed that the English upper classes were better; indeed, the mother believed it so strongly that her face had taken on the expression of a Norman knight in the Bayeux tapestry. She was, however, no fool. She had an intellect and a liberal education and was better equipped to write a book than many of those who do so. If she did not write one it was because she thought it an unsuitable occupation for a woman in her position—for "people like us," as she said—whereas embroidery was acceptable. She made dozens of cushions and chair covers, none of them any good. Her mind was always on Sartre, Jung, seating arrangements and social justice; moreover she had no sense of color.

Her chief quality, after her arrogance, was her spasmodic timidity. She was so shy on occasions that she removed her mind from the company of others, which meant that she often did not reply to questions or greet people when they came into the room. This led "people like her" to consider her snooty—above all the local buffoons, what one might loosely call the lesser gentry—especially when they caught glimpses of *Being and Nothingness* or Frantz Fanon with marked pages next to the bowl of dried rose petals on the table in the entrance hall. She only came alive for her own friends, her London intellectuals with advanced views, and for her husband's friends who were earls and above.

Those who thought she was snooty still came to her house, however, because they loved Sir Edward. He was their kind of chap, even if he yawned a little in their company. He shot at their birds and asked them to shoot at his alongside the dukes and fellow baronets. Moreover they had all been to Eton as he had, and their sons all went to Eton as Mark was to do; they had all been in the army, too, and still addressed themselves as Captain this and Brigadier that and wrote postcards to Sir Edward as Colonel Sir Edward Metherall, Bart., D.S.O., M.C. They must often have thought, as I did later, how strange it was that this likable country baronet should be married to Lady Clare. What sort of marriage of minds could there be when one was so empty and amiable and the other so incisive and full of philosophy and psycho-analysis? The answer to this riddle, like the answer to the riddle of so many marriages, could only be given by someone who had known them well at the time of their courtship. I would guess, however, that her beauty—her lovely, Nor-man-knight face and her tall, gracious, forthright body—would have been enough to explain it. And I dare say that Sir Edward liked the idea of a clever wife; moreover the war was approaching—life might be short.

On her part—well, she was fifteen years younger than he was. It is easy to see that a girl of twenty might be won by a man of thirty-five, whatever the differences in their charac-ters. Perhaps, in spite of her intellect, she admired his mili-tary figure. He was, at any rate, of her class.

2

When I was thirteen there came into effect the scheme, devised by my father with great care and entailing, both before and after, great sacrifice, which was to provide me, his son and only child, with a private education. Put another way, I was to be saved from the ordinary schooling provided by the state to which Sam, George, Fred and Liz-zie were inevitably consigned. It was ensured that thence-forth my education should in some sense be better than theirs, though better in what sense was never explained to me and it would have been hard to do so.

As that second summer at Lasterby came to an end, I

found myself reluctant to leave my cousins and village friends but excited that I was to do the same sort of thing as Mark and Harriet, but Mark in that year went to Eton for the first time while I, at less than half the cost, went to Newton College in Staffordshire. The school still exists today. It would be described as a minor public school and could only exist in a country where a sense of social superiority is placed on the highest altar of human achievements, for that alone is what it was able to instill in its one hundred and thirty pupils.

It was housed in the mansion of a nineteenth-century industrialist once set in the countryside; the town had spread and surrounded his estate and so the owner had bought another house yet farther from his factories and sold his parkland at a profit to make red-brick homes for his men. It was, therefore, in this dark, damp and ugly house set in an industrial suburb that I was to grow up, left in the charge of unqualified amateurs, the quacks of education, who neither loved their pupils nor tried to improve them but saw in their fees an easy and age-old confidence trick permitted by the law. The wet sheets, foul food and bullying were passed off as Spartan disciplines which built the character. Learning was induced by terror and order kept by a gang of bullies recruited from among the worst of us and given the title of Prefect. Those who were not prefects formed a class of surly plebeians, often in open revolt and then savagely repressed with the prefects' cane or the masters' ferule. Always there was resistance, and from the start I formed part of the maquis; all I gained from my time at Newton College was a lasting love and knowledge of painting and sculpture, taught by the timid art master, and the friendship of my companions in the secret opposition—Eric Feber, Caspar Abbot, Johnny Hume and a Persian called Qazvini.

In my first term I wrote many tear-stained letters to my parents, begging them to take me away from Newton, but of course they would not. To my father the suffering was just part of the painful process of character building which he paid the school to provide. He himself had been to a similar school and saw all the unpleasant practices as part of an initiation ceremony into the middle classes.

My mother, I believe, suffered to see me suffer, but the only alternative to Newton College was Malton Grammar School, or the Ryedale Secondary Modern, to which Sam and George were sent, and she would rather have seen me dead than a pupil at either of these institutions. I believe that even if she had known the effect my attendance at Newton would have on me, and all that followed from those developments, she would still have kept me there.

It brought two immediate changes to my life when I returned home for the Christmas holidays. It put a distance between me and my cousins Sam and George, and it gave me a well-justified feeling of resentment against my parents which, in the case of my father, coaxed my incipient dislike for him into open hatred.

To take the last case first, my father was not, in most people's eyes, an especially nice man. He was small in stature and mentality. He was introverted and constipated, a pedant, and possessed of a sense of humor peculiar to himself. He had a colorless face and wiry hair which he had cut so short that the back of his head was shaved to the scalp. This close-cropping of his head was intended, originally, as a measure of economy, but he would never let it grow long so he had it cut as often as anyone else. Since he would only go to the barber at the Station Hotel in York, because that was where Sir Edward and others of his kind went to have their hair cut, his economy was in fact an extravagance.

It was not for his hair that I hated him, however; it is merely a physical aspect that I pick on to give a picture of the man. Let me add, to fill out this picture, that unlike my mother he was almost odorless. If any smell came from him at all it was likely to be that of soap or book dust. He had a large number of books, most of them by Anglican theologians of the nineteenth century. He must have been the only man who still read them.

I know to this day the content of many of these works because they were served up, uncooked and undigested, on Sunday after Sunday, in his long sermons. He would take two or three days each week preparing these long discourses and was always proud of them. "I think Sir Edward will appreciate my use of Hare," he might say one Saturday at supper; or, at lunch on Sunday, "I think Sir Edward took my point about Froude."

"Yes, dear," my mother would reply—knowing as well as I did that Sir Edward had been asleep during the passage in question. My father never noticed Sir Edward's snooze, for when he was preaching this normally reticent man was so carried away by his rhetorical training that his eyes looked heavenward and so missed Sir Edward's closed eyes and lolling head.

As a child I had admired my father's performance in the pulpit and at the altar; later I watched it contemptuously, amused that his normally pursed lips should become fat and full as the words of the psalms fell from his tongue like rich cake or overripe plums. His usual voice, which was mean and thin, changed into the deep, ringing tones of the Church of England; better trained than an actor's, his voice echoed with exquisite, measured sounds—and meanings as dull and empty as the mind in which they were conceived.

It is not from indulgent impiety that I describe my father in this way. He emptied the church of Lasterby at a faster rate, even, than the churches were emptying elsewhere in the country. None of the farmers or farm laborers bothered to come. Uncle Ernest came now and then for my mother's sake, and occasionally he dragged Sam and George along too. Mrs. Christie, the nanny, came with the Metherall family, and Sir Edward's old nanny came too. There was also a widow, Mrs. Potter, who attended regularly, but only because she was paid to clean the church and put flowers on the

[*31*]

altar. There were one or two others who came irregularly, but the average congregation—the audience for my father's wit and learning—was seven.

My father bothered the farmers and farm laborers as little as they bothered him. There were no visits to the sick and infirm, no jumble sales or bazaars. He wrote his sermons; they plowed their fields. They nodded their heads at him; he raised his hand to them. Their only use for him was for weddings and funerals, which he conducted with his usual empty style.

His only friend, therefore, was the man who had brought him to Lasterby in the first place, Sir Edward Metherall. It was a most difficult friendship to analyze. Why the amicable country gentleman—a friend to dukes, a hero of the Desert war—should take to a "shell-shocked" padre and friend to no one was an unsolved mystery of human behavior. Whatever its cause, however, the friendship was real. In the year I went to Newton, the drink before lunch on a Sunday was upgraded to cold meat on a Sunday night, and on Wednesday evenings at twenty to six Sir Edward would appear at the door of the rectory and, forgoing his usual pink gin, for there was no gin in the house, would take a glass of dry, medium or sweet sherry with my father.

I never knew what they talked about; perhaps about the sherry, for my father considered himself an expert on the wine and could talk about it at length. (I dreaded this because Harriet had said that talk about wine, especially about sherry, was common. "Men shouldn't drink sherry, anyway.")

The friendship between the two men was, in an odd way, reflected in my mother's feelings for Lady Clare and Lady Clare's feelings for my mother. Indeed by this second year at Lasterby my mother and Lady Clare had formed a girlish friendship and talked to each other about cooking and children. I have never since seen Lady Clare come down to this level with anyone else. I dare say that it took her great effort of will to do so, but either she saw this farmer's daughter as a test for her liberal principles or she realized that she would inevitably see much of this woman, who could never rise to Sartre and Jung, and so might as well descend to her domestic preoccupations.

Bear in mind, too, that the country is a lonely place—especially in winter with its early darkness—and those like my parents and the Metheralls were all the more isolated for the artificial limits they set to their acquaintance.

I returned after my first term at Newton and was kissed by my mother. I somehow shrank from this embrace, which surprised me, since I had always liked to be held by her before. My father never kissed me anyway and made no attempt to do so now, but he asked me questions about the school which I hardly answered. I had asked them to remove me from the school; they had refused. Thus my heart hardened against them. If I had dared, I should have asked that all future contracts between us should be in writing since there no longer existed an unwritten contract in my heart.

My mother noticed the change in me. "You're not so jolly now, Hilary," she said. "What's got into you?"

I hated her weakness in asking that question. She knew the cause of my solemnity as well as I did. On another occasion, sensing my withdrawal from her hugs and embraces, she said, "Don't you love your mother any more?" On a third occasion, most dishonestly of all, she said, "Getting too grand for us, are you, now you're at public school?"

Perhaps I should have attempted to reason with my parents about Newton, but I was at the age of thirteen when all is emotion and nothing sense. The damage was done, anyway, and even now I do not believe that my objections would have brought about any change.

"How's Sam?" I asked my mother, at breakfast on the first day of the holidays.

"Oh, we don't see so much of him now you're at school."

I thought I would walk down to the farm that morning. I

found Sam with Uncle Ernest emptying sacks of pig meal into metal bins. My uncle gave me a kind look—a glance as if to see if I was injured. "Now then," he said.

I bit my lip to stop myself crying, because Uncle Ernest's sympathy, and the sight of his weather-beaten, grizzled skin, revealed to me the depth and width of my misery; that he could understand so easily what my own parents would not accept was a certain sign that I was condemned to a full sentence at Newton College.

Sam, who had not looked at me when I first appeared, now said, "What's it like, then?"

"Not too bad," I said, to counteract my feeling of wretchedness.

Sam nodded, his eyes on the sacks.

"Be off w'you, then," Uncle Ernest said to his son.

"No, I'll stay," said Sam, picking up another sack and cutting at its opening.

"Go off and play w'Hilary."

"I'd rather work," said Sam.

"I can help," I said.

"It only takes two," said Sam. He looked up and I saw in his eyes a look of confused resentment which I could not at that time interpret.

Uncle Ernest turned to me. "Go and tell Mrs. B. that we'll be in for t'lowance in a minute."

I went down, out of the fold yard, and along to the farmhouse. Mrs. Bosomworth, when she saw me, smiled and said, "Well now, Hilary. A little gentleman, are you, now?"

I gave her a kiss as I always used to, but that embrace, like my mother's, was suffocating and sickly and I was glad to be free of it.

"They're coming in for lowance," I said.

"All right, then," she said. "I'll have it ready."

I wandered out of the kitchen, and as I reached the door I saw Sam approaching. When he came up to me he did not look at me but said, "Come on, then."

[34]

"What?" I asked.

"Let's do summat."

"Oh, I don't know," I said. "I'd better be getting back."

Sam glanced in the direction of the fold yard and then at me. "I'll walk w'you," he said.

We set off up the track toward the road.

"What's it like, then?" Sam asked again.

"School?"

"Aye."

"Not . . . well, not especially nice."

"Do you play football?"

"No. Rugger."

"Not football?"

"No."

We reached the road. Sam hesitated, then decided to come with me a bit farther.

"Where's George?" I asked.

"With Fred in t'village."

I nodded.

Sam stopped in the middle of the road. "I'd better get back now," he said.

"All right," I said.

"I'll be around," he said as he turned.

"All right," I said.

As it happened he never came to the rectory that holidays, nor in the Easter and summer holidays that followed. And from that time on I only went to the farm when my mother was going there too.

I was not lonely, however, because on the third day of the holidays the telephone rang with an invitation to tea at the hall. Mark was back from Eton, and Harriet came back from her boarding school the day after, when I also went to tea with the Metheralls. Indeed it soon became accepted that I went there almost every afternoon, except when their cousins were staying.

Harriet no longer showed her old interest in Sam. She and

Mark both seemed to take it for granted that we now played alone together and never met up with the group from the village. Our haunts around Lasterby Hall were distant enough from theirs in the village for our two groups never to come into contact with one another. Indeed I now saw more of Joss Plunkett and his sister Caroline than I did of my cousins Sam and George. At first I felt unhappy about the more frequent visits of the two Plunketts but later welcomed them, for though Joss was at school with Mark, Mark clearly thought him feeble and treated him as such.

At this age the advantages of some of the facilities offered by Lasterby Hall became evident. While the barns and machinery of the farm had been fine for hide-and-seek, the hall had a billiards table in a billiards room which Mark and I were now allowed to use. There was also ping-pong in the stables and, for his fourteenth birthday, Mark was given a go-cart with a two-stroke motor on which we could drive, one at a time, up and down the drive from the house to the gates and from the gates to the house.

The arrival of the go-cart was of some importance in the shift of power away from Harriet. We no longer obediently followed her to the horses, or sat cleaning tack, or helped her build jumps in the paddock. She was left to do that with Caroline Plunkett, who shared Harriet's banal passion for horses.

It was on Caroline Plunkett, as she lifted a saddle onto a pony's back, that I first noticed the ghastly swelling of a breast. It was spring and I was in an observant mood, having studied the moss which grew on the tiles of the stable roof. Mark was having his turn on the go-cart. Harriet and Caroline were saddling up. My eye fell from the roof onto Caroline's shoulder, and from there to the shape beneath her stretched jersey. I opened my mouth to say something—as if to point out a great boil which the bearer of it had not noticed—but then realized what it was and looked away.

I watched Harriet closely from then on to see when her

flat chest would break out like Caroline's, and sure enough, when she returned after the summer term, there were slight signs of the same affliction. Thus started for her the humiliation of puberty, and in time it came to us all. Down grew thicker on Mark's and my upper lips; our voices croaked and cracked and then broke altogether.

Harriet, I know, felt some dismay at the advent of the go-cart and her own cumbersome bosom. The company of the servile Caroline Plunkett did not make up for our defection. It was not that we were totally free of her authority. She was, for one thing, better than both of us at ping-pong —her thin legs standing taut and astride, her sharp eyes watching the little ball, her hand flicking and pushing and the bat hitting it at difficult speeds and spinning it to impossible corners of the table. And still she had the time and presence of mind to brush back the hair which fell over her face.

She was bad at billiards but made sure not to play. She was always careful not to appear at a disadvantage and to retain her influence over us where she could. She had in her favor the habit in all of us of falling in with her suggestions, and she retained a sharp tongue whereas Mark was as amiable as ever. He never teased her about her bosom, for instance, as he might have done; one could tell from the way she blushed at the mention of breasts or brassieres that it was a vulnerable area for her. I myself did not pursue it because I still felt from the earlier years a strong but unspecific emotion when it came to Harriet. It was not love but had something to do with the components of love—fear, mystery, prurience, admiration—that many men feel for women in general or, on occasions, for one woman in particular. It was only because of these feelings that I did not tease her as I did, say, Caroline with talk of her "bloody udders" and "fat dugs."

These coarse remarks were the extreme extent of our adolescent sexuality. From what I have read about the early initiation of other children, it would seem that we were prudes. There was no sexual exploration or experimenta-

[37]

tion, and when the rabbits rutted or a cock jumped on a hen we would all look away. Sniggering at farts was the nearest we got to sin.

Thirteen, fourteen, fifteen, sixteen. We grew up. I now talk in the plural because Mark and Harriet had become for me like a brother and sister. We went off to different schools each term, but we wrote letters to each other—letters which for me were like portholes looking out at the sky from a deep cabin on the long voyage of a prison ship.

Sir Edward and Lady Clare became like an uncle and aunt. I still called them by their proper titles—as Mark and Harriet called my mother and father the Rev. and Mrs. Fletcher—but I became closer to them than to my real relatives on the other side of the village. Certainly, Sir Edward never listened to what I said, and Lady Clare always maintained a slight reserve, especially when it came to the visits of her nephews and nieces—her brother the earl's children—but these visits were rare. On the whole in the holidays I went to the hall every day, my mother and father went for a cold supper on a Sunday night and Sir Edward looked in for a glass of sweet, medium or dry sherry on a Wednesday before supper.

The only irregular event in these years was the birth of another child to Lady Clare. It was when Harriet, Mark and I were only vaguely aware of how such things came about, and none of us sufficiently informed as to how this in particular had occurred after so great an interval. She was certainly only thirty-six years old and still fecund enough to bear a child, but it would appear that the pregnancy was as much a surprise to her as it was to her husband and her neighbors. If it had happened to any other woman there would most certainly have been gossip and sniggering behind her back, but Lady Clare's probity was so evident that the suggestion of any irregularity was absurd.

The baby, Martha, did little to interfere with the life of her brother and sister except that they were frequently chased out of the day nursery by the nanny, whose powers of every sort had been so adventitiously restored. And soon after the birth the summer holidays came to an end and we all returned to school.

It was at about this time that certain conventions arose both at Newton College and at Appledore, Harriet's school, which caused a further shift in our relationship. It became, in both institutions, a matter of some prestige that one should be corresponding with a girl friend or boy friend. Thus it was that the letters between Harriet and myself, formerly the exchanges of companions, became somewhat awkward billets-doux.

I began the process of risking "My dear Harriet" instead of "Dear Harriet" at the start of my letters and was immediately rewarded with "My dear Hilary." Then "love from Hilary" became "with much love" and even "with all my love," and each increase in the currency of affection was reciprocated, though the reciprocation was not always exact. Thus my "with all my love" might be countered with her "with much, much love." "My dear Harriet" was occasionally answered by "Dear, dear Hilary." She liked repetition whereas I preferred the possessive pronoun; later the fashion for repetition must have left Appledore because she returned to "My dear Hilary."

Of course the whole thing was put on. Our feelings for one another had not changed. They remained comradely. It was just that we were for each other the most suitable candidates for the posts of boy friend and girl friend. Who else could I have chosen? Certainly not Caroline Plunkett. Nor would Harriet have chosen Joss. And in any case, we already wrote to each other and so were saved the embarrassment of opening a correspondence.

There was no question, however, when we met again in the holidays, of continuing with looks and gestures what had been started with words on paper. Just as the substance of our letters had been as banal as before, so our activities in the holidays returned to what they had been: I played billiards with Mark and rode on the go-cart while she went riding with

Caroline Plunkett. But when anything came up which involved pairing off—and such things did increasingly come up as we grew older—we always assumed that we would make up a couple.

By now I was used to the changes that had taken place in her body, and their effect on her personality made her increasingly attractive to me. Her assertive manner now seemed less arrogant and more an expression of her vitality. Vitality was her greatest quality, for she was not otherwise a great beauty. She had grown to be tall with slender legs, but she had plum cheeks and a turned-up nose whose nostrils dilated when she breathed, like those of a horse that had been ridden hard. It was, inexplicably, exciting to watch, seeming to mean that the health in her lungs spread out with the oxygen in the blood to every part of her body. She epitomized the expression "to glow with health." Her ears, her fingers, her teeth— all glowed with health and gave her an attractiveness of a positive, primitive kind. I may have imagined in my ignorance that a healthy girl was the more sensuous. Or would it be more accurate to admit that I hardly thought in these terms at all? Certain idealized legs and bosoms may have passed pleasurably through my mind, but her breasts, when I thought of them, came more into the category of mushrooms. I was also as aware of the unattractive details of her appearance as I was of the attractive whole—crumbs caught between her teeth, small hairs seen up the dilating nostrils, and sediment from slumber caught in the corner of her eyes.

Nor were the situations in which we found ourselves romantic or suggestive—ping-pong, the ponies or tea in the day nursery—until a possibility presented itself with Lady Clare's pronouncement that we were to go to our first Pony Club dance.

The Pony Club was the cadet force for the Hunt. The Hunt itself was considerably more than a chase across fields after a fox. It was the institution of the local ascendancy, the club which you joined if you belonged to or believed in the ascendancy or merely adhered to its system. Thus farmers belonged to the Hunt who did not hunt but adhered to the system by paying rent to the landowners and treating them as their social superiors. Like most subordinates, the farmers despised the landowners and laughed at them behind their backs, but they cooperated because if they forgot their place the laborers might forget theirs.

Being more than an organization for hunting, the Hunt had members who did not hunt or even ride horses. Sir Edward, for example, did not hunt, and neither did Lady Clare; but they belonged to the Hunt, they subscribed to it, and twice a year they took a party to the Hunt Ball.

Harriet at that age did go hunting, and cubbing in the summer, but she did not go to the Hunt Ball because she was not yet seventeen. Nor did she go to the Hunt dances (for the farmers). She was eligible, however, for the Pony Club dances—so was Mark, so was I—and we were all members of the Pony Club, though Mark and I had more or less ceased to ride.

Lady Clare had asked my mother two weeks before the first of these Pony Club dances whether I would go with Mark, Harriet and the two Plunkett children. My mother accepted for me and paid for the ticket out of her housekeeping allowance. Both she and I were excited at the thought of it until, two days before the dance, Mark took me up to his room at the hall to show me his new dinner jacket.

I said nothing as I looked at this black suit of clothes, for I was too proud to admit that it amazed me. Its lapels were faced with satin and the seams of the trousers were decorated with an embroidered stripe. There was a separate waistcoat, and in the drawer there was a special white shirt with a pleated front and a black tie. At the bottom of the wardrobe in his room, still in the box, there was a pair of brand-new patent leather shoes. All this Mark showed me with a certain nonchalance.

"Are you wearing this on Wednesday?" I asked.

"Oh, yes," he said, "one does."

He then looked embarrassed, as if he had guessed what I was now considering—that of this equipment for a Pony Club dance, I possessed only the black socks.

I returned home that evening perplexed almost to panic at the thought of my own best suit—a dull gray flannel—among the black dinner jackets, and the contempt that Harriet would feel for me, and the derision of all the other guests. I remember the weather of that evening—warm and damp with spring, yet the grass still brown from winter—because for many years the same sight of the same trees in the same weather evoked the same sickness and despair.

It may be thought that I exaggerate my feelings—or that I was a fool to have had them. But what else would a boy of sixteen feel at the prospect of exclusion from the circle of his only friends? Exclusion it would be, because I made up my mind on the walk home that on Wednesday I would pretend to be sick.

My mother anyway could not distinguish mood from condition and assumed from my behavior that evening that I was sickening, for I sat at supper without eating anything or saying a word. Even my father looked at me—which he rarely did—but thought the oddity of my behavior uninteresting and certainly not grounds for speculation about my health.

He was right to the extent that by the next morning I had made a recovery. What made me so much better was the thought that a dinner jacket could always be bought for me.

I suggested this to my mother.

"A dinner jacket," she said, as if slightly uncertain of what that might be.

"Mark has one, and he says that everyone will be wearing one."

My mother bit her lip. "I'll ask your father," she said.

She went into the study, interrupting the composition of a sermon, which she rarely did but was a good omen for my purposes, showing that she took the matter as seriously as I did.

I waited in the hall and heard a few phrases from my father's shouting. "He's got a suit, hasn't he?" was one of them; "Nonsense!" another; and "Good God, woman, I'm neither a bishop nor a millionaire!" the last.

My mother came out of the study, looked at me, said nothing and went into the kitchen. I followed her and she said to me, "We'd better go to York this afternoon."

Few words were spoken at lunch, and when it was over and we had cleared up the dishes my mother and I set off in the car. "I've no idea how much they cost," my mother said as we drove through Flaxton, "but I've a little money set aside and I'd like you to be dressed like the other boys."

Unfortunately it turned out that the sum my mother had saved was insufficient for our purpose. She did not tell me exactly what it was, but I imagine it was around fifteen pounds, while the cheapest dress suit was twenty-two pounds fifteen shillings. There was one shop which would have hired us the whole set but had nothing of my size in stock. To have fetched one from London would have taken four days.

All we bought in York, then, were the pleated shirt, the black bow tie and the patent leather shoes, and these took six of the fifteen pounds.

On the way home my mother tried to persuade me that these, with the gray suit, would look perfectly all right, but her voice had no conviction and my silence showed her that I too was unconvinced, so that when we reached the garage and she pulled up the handle of the brake she sighed and said, "I don't know, Hilary."

We did not discuss it with my father at supper. After supper Mark telephoned to ask where I had been that afternoon.

"I went to York with my mother," I said.

"Well, Mother was looking for you," he said.

"What did she want?"

"I've no idea." There was the sound of voices in the background; then Mark said, "Hattie wants to know whether you're coming over tomorrow afternoon."

"I don't know," I said, "I'm not feeling so well."

"You've got to be all right for the dance."

Harriet evidently snatched the telephone from Mark. "Hilary?"

"Yes?"

"Don't you dare get ill."

"I won't if I can help it."

"And you've got to promise to dance with me."

"Yes."

"If ever I'm a wallflower, you've got to drop everything and come and ask me to dance."

"All right."

"And if I'm dancing with someone ghastly and I make a face, you've got to come and rescue me."

"All right."

"Come over tomorrow and we'll discuss it. I don't want there to be any excuses from either of you two boys."

"I'll come over if I'm feeling up to it."

That night I tried on the pleated shirt and black bow tie with my gray suit and compared my appearance in my imagination with Mark's appearance in his dinner jacket. It was a poor comparison, and so the next morning I was worse and stayed in bed.

My mother brought me my breakfast on a tray, the boiled egg and the toast laid out on a napkin just as they had been when I had had measles or influenza. She knew quite well that it was a diplomatic illness, but she joined in the charade. "What a pity," she said. "What with the dance tonight and dinner with the Metheralls beforehand . . ."

"It can't be helped," I said.

"You don't think you're well enough . . . just for the dinner?"

"I might be."

[44]

"Well, we won't ring up the Metheralls until lunchtime."

At eleven o'clock that morning a car drew up outside the house. My bedroom door was ajar, and I went to it to listen to whoever it was that was paying a call. I was afraid for a moment that my mother had taken the charade too far and had called the doctor, but it was the haughty voice of Lady Clare that came up to me from the hallway.

"I know it's a little early for the jumble sale," she was saying to my mother, "but I've been clearing out some cupboards and there's this pile of clothes which might do for the bring-and-buy."

"Well, yes," said my mother, clearly confused by this unusual visit from Lady Clare and her reference to a jumble sale.

"I don't know if you think they're any use," Lady Clare went on. "No one seems to buy secondhand clothes any more. But this dinner jacket, for instance. . . . Edward wore it as a boy and soon grew out of it so it's hardly been used."

"It's in very good condition," said my mother. "I'd say it might do for Hilary. . . ."

"How is poor Hilary?" Lady Clare asked. "Mark said he'd been feeling ill."

"Oh, he's much better this morning," said my mother. "He's staying in bed until lunchtime, just to get rested for the dance."

"I do hope he's well enough to come. Hattie's absolutely counting on him to look after her."

Lady Clare refused a glass of sherry, which was all my mother could think to offer her, and returned to the front door and her car with a few last remarks about my health and the weather.

As soon as she had left, my mother came into my room. "Look at this," she said. In her hands she held the dinner jacket.

She laid it on the bed beside me and I touched it without saying anything.

"Try it on," she said.

I jumped out of bed and put the coat on over my pajamas. It was too big.

"I'll take up the sleeves," said my mother, "and you'll look beautiful."

It was thus that I came to own a dinner jacket, and I have never loved another material possession as much as I loved that suit of clothes. This was not just from my need of it; it was fine in itself, well tailored and in excellent condition, though over thirty years old. On the inside of the inside pocket there was the name of the tailor in Windsor who had made it, presumably while Sir Edward was still at Eton. Its style was old-fashioned, the lapels having wide wings as if belonging to a double-breasted suit, though the coat was joined by only one button. It had a waistcoat which itself had lapels, descending in an elegant curve from the collar to four small, closely set buttons at the waist. These buttons caused me some worry when I came to dress, because I had been told that the last waistcoat button should always be left undone but it seemed that there were rather too few for this. By this time my mother had taken up the sleeves of the jacket, but because of the position of the pockets she had left the hem as it was.

The trousers too had been taken up. For some reason these had a double stripe, were extremely wide—almost a divided skirt—and were designed for a high waist and braces so that when they were on they were almost visible over the top button of the waistcoat.

I have never felt more glamorous than I did that evening. Even the sour remarks from my father about my looking like a teapot in a tea cosy did not dilute my jubilation. My mother was as happy as I was, straightening my tie and brushing my shoulders right up to the last moment when she dropped me off at Lasterby Hall.

"You must thank Lady Clare," she said as I opened my door.

"I will," I said.

This was the first time I had been to dinner with the Metheralls, and I was as much in awe of this as I was of the dance itself. Their butler, Mr. Todd, was dressed in a black suit I had never seen him wear before, and he opened and closed the door for me as I came into the hallway and then led me up the stairs to the large drawing room as if I might not know the way.

"Master Fletcher," he said as I entered the room, which contained, after all, only Sir Edward, Lady Clare, Mark and Harriet, all of whom knew quite well what I was called.

The formal behavior of Mr. Todd was an indication that for that evening we were all to behave in the same way; indeed Sir Edward, who wore a plum-colored velvet smoking jacket, offered me a drink as if I were a different person to the boy who came to play with his children, and Lady Clare, in a long dress, made conversation with such deliberateness that I felt myself blush with confusion. It was as if we were all on stage but I did not know my lines.

The Plunketts came—parents and children—which made things easier, for the Brigadier and Mrs. Plunkett seemed to know just how they were required to behave. At dinner, which was served by Mr. Todd, I sat between Harriet and Caroline, and the conversation descended to a more familiar level. "If you leave me alone for one second," Harriet said to me, "I'll never forgive you."

When the party that were to go to the dance were all getting their coats, I went up to Lady Clare and thanked her, stuttering, for the dinner jacket.

"I'm so glad it was of some use," she said vaguely. "It does suit you most awfully well."

The dance itself, held in another country house about ten miles away, was a disappointment to most of us but less to me than to the others. I was less inclined than the other boys to stand in a group and talk, largely because they all went to Eton and I did not. I therefore danced—with Harriet, Caroline and two or three other girls. Since it was somehow humiliating for them to stand in a group in a way it was not for the boys, they were all grateful for my company, which gave me a sense of power, and with the sense of power a feeling of elation. There was too a wine cup which went to my head and led me to ask impertinent questions—one girl her age, another the end she chose to lie in the bath, a question which a boy at Newton had told me was audacious. This treatment produced giggles and blushes and eyes which followed me around the floor.

Harriet, who was occasionally left standing, was angry with me for letting it happen but angrier still with her brother. "That pig Mark," she said. "He hasn't danced with me once."

"He prefers talking to his friends," I said.

"He can talk to them any time."

I remained with her now until the end of the party, dancing, drinking or sitting on a sofa watching the others dance and drink. My chief observation of the evening, which I did not convey to her, was that every young man wore a dinner jacket.

3

One day that Easter I was walking toward the village from the hall with Mark and Harriet and we passed, walking the other way on the other side of the road, Sam, George and Fred Plowman. I had not then been to the farm for more than a year and I was astonished to see what louts the three of them had become; indeed, I only recognized them when they were ten yards away and as we passed I merely nodded. Sam and George did not even nod to us, but when they were twenty or thirty yards beyond us, I heard Sam shout out, "Fuck y'!"

I turned and saw him glaring at us with an expression on his face I could in no way interpret.

"Don't take any notice," said Mark in a sensible, controlled tone of voice.

I did as he suggested and we walked on in silence; the others, too, went on their way.

After a minute or so, Harriet said, "What did he mean?"

"Don't let's discuss it," said Mark. He looked neither at Harriet nor at me but straight ahead. We continued to walk in silence beside him until Harriet peered across at me and said, "They're your cousins, aren't they?"

"Sam and George are, yes," I said, and I blushed. A moment later came shame and humiliation.

"We can't help our cousins," said Mark.

"I know," said Harriet, "but it's funny all the same . . . to think that they're Hilary's *first* cousins—I mean, as close as Jojo and Bet are to us."

She was referring to the children of her uncle the earl for whom I was thought unsuitable. I have seen them since and can say that she was right—that she and Mark did look like their cousins whereas Sam and George were unrecognizable as mine. In truth of course the difference between us was only superficial. They both worked at the farm now and hard labor had matured them—and the open air had wizened their skin—while I had remained in the classroom so the skin on my face and hands was soft; but in size and shape we were much the same—heavy-boned, with round faces—whereas Mark Harriet, Jojo and Bet all had long jaws and sharp noses. Their natural expression was a sneer whereas mine, like my cousins', was one of wariness and cunning. Their gestures were languid and careless as if phantom footmen and housemaids were at hand to pick up what they dropped and tidy what they disarranged, whereas I set things right myself and took pride in practicality. At sixteen and nearly fifteen neither Mark nor Harriet could mend a fuse, sew on a button or peel an apple, whereas I had made fitted bookshelves for my bedroom.

Harriet's remarks about my relationship to Sam and George—the "yobs," as we called them—had a confusing and contradictory effect on me, and I took advantage of their sauntering gait to walk ahead a little lest they see the turmoil in my expression. The immediate emotion which afflicted me was strong resentment that any of Sam's coarseness should rub off on me—though my resentment was more against him for being my cousin, which he could not help, than against Harriet for making the connection, which she need not have done. The very existence of Sam and George scraped the skin off the bone of an anxiety which always lay at the back of my mind—my consciousness that I was different from the Metheralls in some intrinsic way, and that the difference was of a sort which made me inferior. What riled me was that the flaw lay in my mother, for while my father's origins were equally insignificant, he did not have relatives at hand, nor did he lapse into the local patois when he became angry. At the same time, however, I rebelled against any rejection of my mother because I loved her intensely and believed in her domestic qualities. The warmth and comfort of her kitchen compared well to my mind with the chilly spaciousness of the little drawing room or the day nursery at Lasterby Hall.

My love of my mother and the simple values she represented may have been strong, but in time it appeared that my own urge to the ways of the Metherall family were stronger still. When I showed Harriet the bookshelves I had made in my room, she snorted and said that "do-it-yourself hobbies" were for people who lived in the suburbs, and from then on, if ever I practiced carpentry, it was as a secret vice and I made sure that Harriet never saw what I had made.

If I had lived in the eighteenth century the issue which perplexed me could have been more clearly expressed: I should have worried as to whether I was a gentleman. Since now this word was put at the entrance to any public lavatory, the question was more complicated, though in essence it may have remained the same. If I had lived anywhere but deep in the English countryside, I dare say it would not have existed at all, but as it was I pondered a great deal over whether I was essentially the same as the Metheralls but superficially different, or superficially the same and essentially different.

Though I never went so far as to be ashamed of my mother, I had, as I have said, abandoned my visits to the farm. I felt that if I was to be a friend to Mark and Harriet, I could not be seen in the company of their tenants. It was a feeling certainly shared by Mark and Harriet.

Thus, by the time I was seventeen, I adhered in every way to their values. I dressed as much like Mark as my mother could afford; I used their language, saying "orf" for off, and expressed their sentiments on politics and shooting, though I was as far from the use of a twelve bore as I was from the vote. I learned to dance an eightsome reel and dutifully wore my dinner jacket to Pony Club dances, private parties and dinner at Lasterby Hall. It came to a point that I was so much like them that my anxiety was almost quietened. I felt sufficiently secure, at any rate, to let my fears withdraw again to the back of my mind.

This complacency was upset by the sudden appearance of the family of the Earl of Barton.

The earl was a middle-aged Conservative peer who lived twenty-five miles away in a house twice the size of Lasterby Hall and twice as grand with twice as much land attached to it. He had a son and two daughters, the son being called Alexander and bearing the courtesy title of Viscount Amotherby, and the daughters, Elizabeth and Mary Ferris-Gaskell, having the same prefix as Lady Clare. I give them their full titles because their full titles were the cause of a perception concerning Lady Clare, for in early summer I was asked to dinner at Lasterby and it was there, in the large drawing room, that I was introduced by her to these three children of my own age as *Mr.* Fletcher simply so that she could then call them *Lord* Amotherby, *Lady* Elizabeth and *Lady* Mary Ferris-Gaskell.

It may seem a small sin, that she liked so much to use a

title—we all like to play games that we are equipped to win—but it was offensive to those who did not have one.

When we sat down at table I was placed to the left of Lady Clare and therefore opposite Alexander Amotherby, who sat to her right. On the other side of me was Lady Elizabeth, who throughout dinner ostentatiously faced away from me and talked to Mark. I was therefore forced to join in the conversation of the other two, though they seemed equally reluctant to talk to me.

Alexander Amotherby did not know Lady Clare very well and he had mistakenly assumed that, because Sir Edward was chairman of the local Constituency Association, she too was a Conservative. It was not an assumption she did much to correct from the drift of her answers to his early conversation. I knew, however, that she was not, for political argument had always been one of the favorite pastimes at nursery tea. Mark usually took his father's side, while Harriet, like her mother, was a liberal. She argued strongly for the abolition of hanging, the liberation of homosexuals, the better treatment of blacks and the social acceptance of Jews as vehemently as her mother, though she hardly knew what they were.

Her mother, of course, could speak with more authority, for in her London circle she certainly came across Jews, blacks and homosexuals—if not murderers—and she was a victim, so I later discovered, of that curious pattern of psychological behavior which takes hold of women from the upper classes whereby the idea of a man who has been or might be persecuted evokes images of bull whips and gas ovens which have a markedly erotic effect and puts the force of sexual passion into their enlightened campaigns.

No issue was more divisive at that time than the previous autumn's invasion of the Suez Canal Zone by the French and British armies. It was a Dreyfus affair in which members of the same family had stopped speaking to one another and members of Parliament had voted against the actions of their own government—some against sending the soldiers in, some against taking them out. It was on this subject that Alexander Amotherby and Lady Clare were having a conversation.

"If a man votes against the government," said Alexander Amotherby, "the Constituency Association has got to make sure they get him out."

Since this could apply to either type of rebellious member, Lady Clare merely said, "Yes, perhaps."

"The whole system would fall apart if they didn't," said Lord Amotherby. He leaned back in his chair and then went on talking in his yawning, Etonian voice. "I mean to say, we work to put him in, don't we? He's elected to support the government; he can't then go and vote with the Opposition."

"Perhaps not," said Lady Clare.

"To my mind," said the eighteen-year-old viscount, "they're little less than traitors, anyway . . . the whole lot of them."

There was becoming less and less doubt as to which group in the controversy he was referring to, but Lady Clare, who in the presence of her family and the rector's son was the very prow of the Opposition, merely said, "I can see why one might think that."

"And what about those," I asked, "who voted against the withdrawal? Waterhouse, for instance, and Amery?"

Alexander Amotherby gave me a quick glance. "Quite different," he said.

"Why?" I asked.

He looked at me, flushed and angry, as if my very question placed me in the camp of the traitors. "They may have betrayed their party," he said, "but they didn't betray their country at the same time."

I shrugged my shoulders and looked at Lady Clare as if to say that it was now her turn. She knew, of course, what Alexander Amotherby could not know—that I was arguing against the position I usually adopted in the day nursery, which was, like Mark's, in favor of the invasion. For an instant her eyes met mine; then they looked away.

"Do your sisters hunt?" she asked, turning toward Alexander Amotherby.

This episode with Lady Clare was, I think, what turned her against me. She might pretend that it was from politeness that she had forborne to argue in favor of her principles, but I knew that it went deeper than that—and she was aware of what I knew. It was as if I had found her naked in the arms of her lover, snobbery; and while being no friend of her legitimate spouse, liberalism, I could hardly admire her disloyalty.

I realize, in writing this, that her explanation for her behavior may sound more convincing than mine, for no one likes to spoil both food and their digestion with a raucous argument, and why should Lady Clare be afraid to disagree with this insolent boy when she herself was the daughter of an earl and almost twice his age? The answer is that this daughter of an earl had a daughter herself.

It was in this context that I retained some value for Lady Clare. There were, it so happened, many girls in the neighborhood and not so many young men. Every brother seemed to have two sisters and there were few with none. It was because of this—my gender—that I continued to be asked to dinner at the hall, and it was because of this that I went with Mark and Harriet to the Hunt Ball.

I will not say that all choice in the matter was left to Lady Clare. Mark and Harriet still liked to spend their time with me and I still seemed to have a certain influence over Harriet. Indeed the situation which developed was paradoxical, for while the old embarrassment at finding ourselves alone persisted, it became a convention that we did things together. On a trip to the moors, for instance, we would sit together on the back seat of the car while Mark would sit next to his mother or my mother or whoever was driving.

If, once on the moors, we went for a walk, clambering over the heather and fern beside the rivulets running south, we might be in a group of four or five but two of us—myself and Harriet—would remain closer together than any of the others and move in relation to one another's movements. If I chose to climb over a stream in one particular place, Harriet would follow my example and cross at the same spot. This might mean a helping hand but the hand never lingered. It let go as soon as it could, finding the touch of the other—its texture and heat—awkward, even unpleasant.

If we had been two molecules under a microscope, the scientist studying us would have been hard pressed for a hypothesis. The two cells moved toward one another and moved in relation to one another but they did not move closer together and they did not join. At a vital moment, nature seemed paralyzed; at a certain distance, attraction and revulsion seem to equal each other.

I remember once when we did find ourselves alone together in the saddle room at Lasterby that Harriet watched me with a look of some sort of curiosity in her eyes. I could not interpret it then and I cannot now. I am sure that the look was not an invitation. It might have been a challenge. I am as convinced now as I was then that the attraction and repulsion, equally matched, existed in both of us. If I had made some affectionate or carnal gesture she might have accepted it—but then I should have been a different person had I done so.

The proximity that we did achieve had a side effect, a vague estrangement between Mark and myself. There was nothing deliberate or dramatic about it, but it is a sad truth about human nature that love must be exclusive to be convincing, and as I came nearer to Harriet I moved farther from Mark.

He also moved a certain way from me. As he entered into the elite of Eton and drank the intoxicating punch of schoolboy despotism, he became less interested in his life at home. Indeed he was bored by it and liked best to talk of school affairs with Alexander Amotherby, who had recently left Eton, or Joss Plunkett, who was still there.

We still liked one another, of course, and treated one another as friends. We both passed our driving tests around this time and thenceforth went to the cinema together in Malton. Harriet came with us and I sat between the brother and the sister, but on the whole I inclined toward Harriet while Mark's patrician features faced the screen.

He had become by now quite handsome—over six feet three inches tall with broad shoulders, wavy blond hair, blue eyes and this patrician face: an eagle nose, a way of tilting his head backward, and a languor directing his eyes downward as if the person or object beneath his gaze was not worth much effort by the muscles of his eyes.

My appearance contrasted with his in that I was a few inches smaller, my hair was brown and my face was most energetic in concealing my feelings with an all-purpose smile. Just as camels develop humps for the storage of water, so those who must live off their wits develop their wits as I had done, while those like Mark who have no need of wits are quite happy without them. All that he did possess— appearance, inheritance and membership of Pop—left him contented with his lot in life.

My position in the sixth form at Newton College was also a contrast to his at Eton. Cunning and good humor were not qualities appreciated by our headmaster but were of use in the resistance to the thugs and bullies he put in authority over me. They were chosen as prefects because they were thought to have qualities of leadership, but since, in our last year, they were our contemporaries, the sham we had always suspected was proved to be true. As in a corrupt state, the criminals who could not be controlled were given the name and uniform of the police. Churston, Ranskill, Gerrard and Totton —the crude and stupid boys—were made prefects, while those who had any delicacy, sensitivity or kindness in their character—including Hume, Feber and Qazvini—were not and had to suffer under them. That we were the same age as our persecutors made it worse. We held for them no kind of respect, and they in their turn used their authority to pursue the meanest feuds left over from preceding years.

My life at Newton was so unpleasant and dull that I have no wish to live it over again by describing it; nor, however, do I wish either to exaggerate or understate the nastiness of that institution. It was better, I dare say, than a concentration camp but it was worse than prison, and when, finally, I went to prison I suffered little from the experience because its conventions were all familiar to me. The only subject which I enjoyed was art—partly because the art master, though fusty and pedantic, treated his pupils with some kindness and respect. It was considered an unimportant subject—the lessons were "extra" and in one's spare time—but the art room was a refuge, and though I soon discovered that I had no particular talent, I spent as much time as I could sketching, painting or studying reproductions of the work of Goya, Titian, Rubens and El Greco.

I could never escape for long. A bell would ring and I would jump up for some sport or lesson in the vile institution outside.

This, then, was the reason why my life at Lasterby—my life with the Metheralls, for they were the substance of my life at Lasterby—was so important to me. I longed for the holidays and I dreaded the start of a new term. The academic year which began in the autumn was to be my last. It seemed long but I had done well enough in the summer's examinations to be thought a suitable candidate for Cambridge University. To be clever at Newton, of course, was not necessarily to be clever by the standards of the world at large, and while the school continued to enter its pupils for Oxford and Cambridge, it rarely got them in. My hope lay in my adequate academic record together with my father's connections with Selwyn College, where he had himself been an undergraduate. I was determined to work hard, both as a distraction from the miseries of school and because Cambridge had the same place in my mind as the dinner jacket. Mark, I knew, was trying for Cambridge.

The one difference to me this term was that Harriet had

left school, with no academic qualifications but some wise advice. "Never marry a man," she was told, "who asks his gamekeeper to dinner." She came away with friends, however, who with the same advice set about the same thing, finding a husband who would not ask his gamekeeper to dinner. For this purpose they went to London and were presented at court—that is, they were debutantes, following the old though vulgarized convention of their class. By now it had lost the participation of the British head of state, but it would take time for Lady Clare and her kind to follow their monarch and abandon their season. It was part of Lady Clare's liberal affectation to denigrate this ritual and despise those who took part in it, yet she obeyed the promptings of her class instinct and did for her daughter what had been done for her. She opened up their terraced house in Belgravia and, with Harriet, Sir Edward, Martha and the nanny, went to live in it. There she entertained other mothers and other daughters doing the same thing. With them she drew up a list of young men and women who were suitable for a dance through one of a combination of qualities, birth and money being the desirable prerequisites. No imagination was shown in the choice they made. Lady Clare, reader of Jung and friend to intellectuals, included on her list the same young stockbrokers and Guards officers as the most thick-necked dowager. The dance was to be held at Lasterby in June, and almost the only guest on her list with neither prerequisites nor qualifications was the rector's son.

Harriet described all these plans to me in the letters she continued to send from London. The reading of these letters was the happiest moment of my day at school, especially as she seemed to include me in her vision of the year ahead. In January she was to go abroad for some months—probably to Paris, to stay with a family and learn French. Perhaps, she suggested, I might come out and visit her at Easter? I could take her up the Eiffel tower.

She would return in May when the season would begin.

There was Queen Charlotte's Ball in London where she would have to wear a long white dress. She hinted that she might ask me to accompany her to that, but she could not be sure since her mother might have other ideas. "It'll be awfully boring going to all those parties after that," she wrote, "and I'm trying to get you invited to as many as possible so at least I'll know someone, but I don't see why *my* dance shouldn't be fun."

Harriet's letters did not only provide occasions of happiness when I read them and reread them, they were my entire and only inspiration for the future. I worked hard—my entrance examinations were in December—because I thought she might take pride in me if I won a place at Cambridge, and it was at home at Lasterby a week or so after Christmas that I heard that my hard work and my father's connections with Selwyn College had prevailed over my middling intellect and the unqualified teachers of Newton College. Before that day was over, however, and before I could convey the news to Harriet, my triumph was countered by a disaster.

It was on that evening that I was to go to a Hunt Ball with the Metheralls at the invitation of Lord Barton, in whose house the ball was to take place. My invitation had come through the Metheralls and it was phrased thus: Would I like to come "to make up the party"? It may be thought that I was oversensitive to read much into this choice of words, but I suspected then and I know now that the Bartons and those like them use words with the care of a poet, and the phrase "to make up the party" was designed to make it clear to me that their invitation was not to be taken as an overture of friendship but as the submission of a contract in which their interest was to balance the sexes and mine to taste crumbs from their table.

I accepted, of course, and saw my mother fluster and blush as much as she had done when I was first asked to the Metheralls—in her heart probably more so because the Metheralls were always a known quantity whereas the Bartons to her had the awesomeness of myth. She spent that afternoon ironing the pleats of my shirt and pressing the trousers of my evening clothes and brushing away at the coat. My shoes were polished and my socks laid out as well as any young duke's, and I lay in my bath at half past six as if that was just what I was. I shut out the old toothbrushes beneath the mirror over the basin and the broken bumps of plaster where damp was coming through the walls. I wrapped myself in a dream of aristocratic hedonism and persuaded myself that the small and worn gray towel beside me was white and six foot square.

What neither my mother nor I had foreseen was that since the summer when I had last worn my dinner jacket I had grown, and that in the process the shape of my body had changed. It was now less like that of the young Sir Edward than it had been before. I was taller and thinner. Even the shirt was loose around my neck, the trousers were now short and the hem of the jacket did not come down to the base of my buttocks. There had been little of substance anyway to fill the jacket and now there was less, as if the tea cosy had lost its stuffing. My appearance, therefore, was almost ridiculous. I could see that and so could my mother. We managed to lower the trousers by adjusting the braces but it was too late to do anything about the jacket. There being no full-length mirror in the house I was less aware of my odd appearance than my mother, whose expression was a little perplexed. We were both persuaded, I think, though we never said it, that the technical correctness of my attire would make up for its sartorial confusion: that with a black tie and black shoes it would be a uniform among a hundred other uniforms and so go unnoticed.

My mother dropped me at the hall, wishing me a good time. I walked in beneath the steps and went up to the small drawing room where I was to join the Metheralls before proceeding with them to Castle Barton. Only Sir Edward was in the room, sitting by the fire reading *The Times*. It was something of a shock for me to see that he was not wearing a dinner jacket, as I was, but was dressed in a tailcoat cut away at the waist, a wing collar, white waistcoat and white tie.

I had never seen one of these costumes before and decided now that it was something worn by members of the older generation. I could not conceal from myself, however, the meaning of Sir Edward's glance as he laid down the paper and got up to give me a drink. I had become expert at interpreting these glances and this expressed what he felt so often, a pained embarrassment at the disorder of the world.

From this glance I was filled with fears, and as I sat down gripping a glass of gin and tonic Mark came into the room wearing a white tie and tails, his shirt held together by exquisite ruby studs. He glanced at me too and blushed. "Hello," he said.

"I seem to be in the wrong sort of clothes," I said.

"I shouldn't think it matters," he said without any confidence in his voice.

"Oh, no," said Sir Edward from the other side of the room, where he was studying one of his English watercolors. "There are sure to be one or two others . . ."

I realized by now of course that this Hunt Ball was in some way which was beyond my understanding more important than the usual Hunt Ball where a dinner jacket might be sufficient. The appearance of Lady Clare and Harriet in long dresses with low necks, and their hair elaborately prepared, confirmed this knowledge. Like Mark, Harriet had apparently been given access to the family jewels, and laid on the live flesh of her bare bosom were the dead stones of a necklace— a delicate, beautiful group of amethysts. Lady Clare wore diamonds, which were duller, in my eyes, but doubtless more valuable.

I felt grateful to Harriet, who was so taken up with her own appearance that she did not notice mine. Lady Clare, on the other hand, looked momentarily upset—whether at the

[*61*]

culpability of my ignorance or at the failure of the tact and foresight she herself had shown two years before, I do not know.

We now set out in Sir Edward's car for the drive to Barton Castle. The conversation was inconsequential; no one mentioned my attire but I thought of nothing else and cowered in dread of what was to come.

We were met at the door of Barton Castle by Lord Barton's butler, who was dressed, like me, in a black bow tie. Lord Barton, Lord Amotherby and the three or four other men who were there all wore white tie and tails. It was then—as we entered the drawing room—that Harriet noticed my omission and directed at me a look of such contempt that it prompted me to cry or leave the room, but the years at Newton had taught me to hide my feelings and bear humiliation. There was no outward change in my behavior.

There were sixteen at the dinner table. I was placed between Mary Ferris-Gaskell and another girl who never told me her name. They talked to me and I talked to them as if nothing was wrong, but I felt all the time like a dwarf or a cripple. There was an imagined odor coming off me which caused them to breathe shortly with their noses half turned away. Both girls were dull and stupid but their instinct was enough to sense that I reeked of social inferiority—the worst kind of social inferiority, the genteel, aspiring kind. I was nothing honest like a keeper or a farmer but an intruder who pretended but was caught out, if not by his accent then by wearing the wrong costume to the Hunt Ball. They talked to me because they were brought up to be polite, but their reserve was intense lest I should feel that they liked me and should later ask them to dance.

Harriet sat opposite me, two places to the left. She never let her eyes look in my direction—not while eating or when she rose to withdraw with the other women. I stood as they left and then moved up the table to sit nearer to my host. The port was passed around *from right to left*. . . . How futile it had been to learn that so well if I could not wear the right suit of clothes.

Lord Barton let his bulging eyes rest on me as if studying a common fish served on a plate with a salmon. He was a grander, nastier man than Sir Edward—a bloated, adulterous Whig to whom the sight of this cod, improperly dressed, was half an affront and half a curiosity. He stopped his bleary, wandering gaze on me but then appeared to have decided that I did not merit a thought or comment and so turned to Sir Edward and asked after a friend they had in common. Alexander, Mark and the others started on Eton, and there was another conversation at the other end of the table. I sat on the edge of it all, passing the decanter obediently when it came to me but saying nothing.

The worst aspect of my humiliation was my fear that the Metheralls, who had introduced me into Castle Barton, were just as humiliated as I was. Perhaps Lord Barton himself would feel humiliated by my presence in his party. I thought of going up to him or Sir Edward when we rose to join the women—to apologize and suggest that I go home—but I did not, for out of my humiliation, as I sat in silence drinking port, there came the defense that nature provides in the mind. I began to feel a contempt for them to throw back at their contempt for me. The spirit of revolt first suggested to me by Harriet's disdain for Sam and George grew in the artificial warmth of Castle Barton, and by the time the paying public had arrived, all the men without exception wearing white tie and tails, my mind was filled with defiant thoughts and fantasies and, as if to reflect them, my hands were in my pockets.

For an hour or so after the ball had started I stood alone in the hall of Castle Barton, moving from the bar with a glass of champagne to the base of a pillar, and then back from pillar to bar. Around me the county moved and talked and paired off to dance, shouting at one another in their caricature accents, looking indeed like caricatures of themselves. Men in pink tail coats had faces as red as the material; others in mauve tail coats (the uniforms of a Gloucestershire hunt) had matching noses. The women were either scraggy or had necks like swollen tree trunks. Like peahens their clothes were dowdy and their voices screeched above the hubbub in the drawling, haughty accent of the gentry.

Every now and then I caught sight of members of my party—Alexander Amotherby with Harriet, say, or Mark with Elizabeth. They made quite sure that they did not see me. There were others, too, whom I had met on odd occasions—the Lord Lieutenant, and the Plunketts—none of whom came up to me in my corner.

After a time, however, the champagne which I had been drinking, together with the wine and port I had drunk at dinner, changed my mood from bitterness and resentment to a reckless enjoyment of my situation. I left my pillar, and my glass on its base, and set out in pursuit of Mary Ferris-Gaskell, intent on asking her to dance. I did so in what I thought of as a spirit of inquiry; if I asked her to dance would she succumb to her repugnance and refuse or obey the promptings of her upbringing and accept? I found her in a group of others I did not know. I went up to her, greeted her and asked her to dance. Without a word she came away with me to the ballroom, where we danced. I tried to make conversation but she only gave replies of a single word and never met my eyes. It may have been that she did not have the wit and intelligence to make much conversation anyway, but at the time I was sure that it was my appearance and origins which inspired her taciturnity. Even now I do not doubt but that that was the reason for it.

As soon as the dance was finished, the girl nodded to me in token thanks and left me. She was in her own home and must have known a dozen ways to escape from me. It was not, however, that I wanted to pursue her. My courage was still up. I decided to find Harriet.

I saw her with Alexander Amotherby and an older couple. I watched her face as she saw me approach—her eyes still avoiding mine until the last moment, when they looked at me with an appeal that was now too late and would anyway have been useless in my present mood.

"Now then, Hattie," I said, imitating a Yorkshire accent so the two others should take it for the normal sound of my voice.

She blushed. "Hello," she said.

Alexander introduced me without looking at me. Then the four of them continued their conversation. I listened for a while and then interrupted to ask Harriet to dance. She hesitated and then looked at Alexander as if to see if he would help her, but he continued talking to the other couple so there was nothing she could do but accept my invitation.

"You're not being very nice to me," I said when we were dancing.

"Don't be silly," she said. "Of course I am."

"You might have told me," I said.

"What?"

"About the white tie and tails."

"How was I to know?" She looked petulant. "I don't know about men's clothes."

"Then Mark should have told me."

"I know. He's a fool. It just didn't occur to him."

"I'm sorry if I've embarrassed you," I said, with as much sarcasm as I could manage.

She looked at me. "It's not your fault, I suppose."

"I realize," I continued, "that it's humiliating for you to be seen dancing with me. . . ."

"Don't be so silly," she said again. "Of course it isn't. And anyway, Mother said that I ought to dance with you."

I said nothing more, and when the music for that dance ended I left Harriet on the ballroom floor and went to get a drink. I was angry with her for what she had said and knew that if I slipped into sobriety my anger would turn into despair. I returned to my pillar and spent the rest of the evening waiting for the Metheralls to decide that they wanted to go home, for I had no other means of returning to Lasterby.

[65]

Every now and then I sauntered to the door of the ballroom and watched the dancing. The champagne stimulated images in my mind of dirt and violence smashing into the lights and silks and music. I loathed the arrogance, condescension and stupidity of the roomful of snobs—I ridiculed the archaism of this living museum which parodied the life of a hundred years ago—but my eyes were still amazed by the spectacle before them, and one scene in particular delighted me: Harriet Metherall dancing an eightsome reel, weaving in and out among four tall young men all dressed in white tie and tails.

It was among other things the small privileges of dress accorded to the French nobility and denied to the bourgeoisie which brought on the revolution of 1789. My humiliation over the tailcoat had, in a small way, the same effect on me. I now took against the Yorkshire gentry—and then the entire English upper class—though this enmity remained hidden in my mind. When, from then on, I came across the local buffoons who lived nearby—the landowners, the brigadiers, the masters of fox hounds, the justices of the peace or the self-styled gentleman farmers—my face retained its usual expression, which wavered between deference and familiarity, but my heart seethed with hatred and my imagination was crammed with schemes for their downfall and humiliation.

My dreams were varied and often contradictory. In one I would return to Yorkshire richer and more powerful than any of them and buy Lasterby or Castle Barton from their bankrupt owners; in another I would lead a socialist revolution and, like Hindenburg, be given a confiscated estate by a grateful government. Beforehand, of course, there would be a succession of Hunt Balls disrupted by the armed agents of the People. The effete white tie and tails would be stamped under by bloodstained khaki. The reels of film turning in my imagination were old and melodramatic—I was Robin Hood or Jesse James—but their themes were real to me, these fantasies necessary to my self-respect.

[66]

In all plots of this kind there is a heroine who, in her crinoline, submits to the brutality of the hero. My heroine, even after her behavior at the Hunt Ball, was Harriet. I remained angry with her for what she had said, and for her embarrassment, but she showed some shame and regret the next day by walking to the rectory and staying to tea. Like all girls, she was eager to be thought well of, whatever devious schemes she had in her mind, and I was sufficiently inexperienced to mistake her attempt to put things right as a gesture of affection toward me. Thus she regained the position which she had never lost as the girl in the crinoline. Indeed, she was the only escape from my increasing loneliness and isolation. I began to think of her as a prisoner of her class and an exception to it—a sheepdog among the poodles, a changeling, perhaps Sir Edward's bastard by a country girl. How else could there be such health among the wanness and inbreeding of her kind?

Also at that time I began to feel toward her what is called desire. The crinoline came off—the film was changed from adventure to romance—and I lay aching as I imagined her limbs and mine entwined together.

The village had always sniggered about my friendship with Harriet. On frequent occasions we had been asked—at the shop, say—"Are y'courtin'?" We had always ignored this vulgar impudence and had been embarrassed by it, but now I wanted the suggestion to become the truth. As Harriet sat at tea in our drab drawing room, her long legs in seamless stockings crossed and tucked under her, I wondered to myself how to set about some kind of declaration of love. My mother flustered around, bitter with regret that Harriet's visit had not been foreseen so that scones could have been baked and more genteel clothes put on, and we made general formal conversation.

"When are you going to Paris?" I asked.

"On the twelfth."

"That's next week. . . ."

"We're going to London tomorrow."

"Are you looking forward to it . . . to Paris?"

"Quite."

"If you're there at Easter, I might pay you a visit."

She smiled at me. "I wish you would."

"Do you really?" I asked intensely. Courting, or so I thought, meant the asking of intense questions with hidden meanings.

"Yes," she said—with no hidden meaning. She might even have added "Why not?" but it never came.

"How long will you be there?" I asked.

"Until the middle of May, I think. I'd better give you my address." She opened her bag and took out a pen and two pieces of paper, on one of which she wrote her address and then handed it to me.

"Who's Madame Vignon?" I asked.

"I don't know. Some old bag who takes paying guests. Cecily Hammond's going to be there too."

"Who's she?"

"Oh, a girl from school."

"Is she nice?"

"She's all right. Better than nothing, anyway. It'd be awful to be stuck with just a family of frogs."

When my mother left the room to fetch more hot water for the teapot, I leaned forward and said to Harriet, "I thought that since I've got a place at Cambridge . . ."

"Have you? Well done," she said.

"I found out yesterday."

"Mark hasn't heard yet."

"He's sure to get in."

"He should do."

"I thought," I said again, "that since I've got a place I might as well leave school."

"You mean . . . not go back?"

"I don't see much point, do you?"

Harriet looked blank. "No," she said. "I suppose not. I mean, you don't like it much, do you?"

"No."

"I think Mark's going to stay at Eton. . . ."

"That's different."

"Yes."

"I haven't told my parents yet," I said, "but I'd like to travel."

"That's a much better idea than going back to school."

"It's because of that . . . I mean, I'm sure to be passing through Paris."

"Oh, good. Then you must come and see me. Perhaps you can stay with the Vignons. I don't know, though, if paying guests can have unpaying guests." She laughed.

"I could stay at a hotel."

"Will you have enough money?"

"I thought that my father might give me the school fees he won't have to pay now."

"Of course," said Harriet.

"And if he won't, I can get a job somewhere and save up some money."

"Oh, do," said Harriet, "and come out and see me."

My mother returned with the hot water and a dainty array of biscuits on a plate which were declined by Harriet, to whom she offered them, but this did not dispel the happiness I felt at that moment—the possession in the faded, tasteless, pretentious confines of my parents' drawing room on a dark afternoon of this tall girl who looked at me and smiled at me and asked me to visit her in Paris. It was at this moment that I understood that I loved her and all I lacked was the courage to tell her so.

When the time came for her to go it was too dark to walk, so I drove her to the hall.

"Give my love to Mark," I said as we reached the gates.

"All right," she said. "It's a pity we won't see you before we go . . . but I'll see you in Paris."

I was due to return to Newton College in ten days' time but by now—especially after this conversation with Harriet—

I was determined I should not do so. I knew, before approaching my father on this matter, what the issues would be. Against the plan would be his distaste for changing anything that had already been arranged, for doing what was not at that time commonly done, and for proposing something as vague as "traveling."

In favor there was only one point but one which I knew would carry great weight, the saving of two terms' school fees. I had suggested to Harriet that this saving might be used as funds for my journey, but I knew that such a claim to the entire sum would deprive me of my best argument. I was therefore prepared to compromise.

My father was poor, certainly, as most clergymen are poor, but he was also mean. He savored certain luxuries for himself such as a glass of sherry each evening, though he offered my mother none. He hated to see her spend money on clothes yet insisted on a respectable appearance. The area of expenditure he thought the least necessary was his son. I had rarely had new clothes—Sir Edward's dinner jacket was not the first bundle of castoffs from the hall—and when I went to Newton each term I had always to take an overnight coach from York to Birmingham because it was cheaper than the train.

I presented my case, therefore, as one of common sense and economy. My father sat in his armchair—we were in his study—eying me oddly as if wondering what I was doing there, but gradually he understood what I was suggesting and his face began to show what I had predicted—the strains and stresses of the advantages and disadvantages.

He was doubtful at first that the school would remit the fees. I pointed out that he had not yet paid them for the terms ahead and could hardly be forced to do so if I was not there. Then he suggested that the university would object, but I told him, truthfully, that I had mentioned the idea to the Senior Tutor at Selwyn College when up for my interview and he had called it a good one.

Then we came to the kernel of the question: how much of the saved school fees would I need for my travels?

"Half," I said.

"That would be what?"

"Around a hundred and forty pounds."

He winced. "But you aren't going round the world, are you?"

"No. Just to the Continent."

"I should have thought that fifty or sixty pounds would do you for that."

"I had thought of going away for several months . . . long enough to learn a language."

"You could get some sort of tutoring job, couldn't you?"

"Possibly, but I'd have to get there, and get back, and have some money in reserve."

We settled, as I knew we would, on a hundred pounds—and this was conditional on the school's acceptance without compensation of my removal from their care. Newton College did later try to extract the fees for the spring term, but before that wrangle had come up I was already abroad with a hundred pounds in traveler's checks.

4

There were four projects in my mind for the months ahead. The first and the least important was to learn a language that might be useful to me later in life. The second was to try and earn enough money to equip myself with a new dinner jacket and white tie and tails upon my return to England; I wished to be well prepared for Harriet's dance and Queen Charlotte's Ball. My third objective was to do something or go somewhere which would impress Harriet; and my fourth—related to this—was to gain some sexual experience. It did not seem wrong or inconsistent to me to wish to be initiated by someone other than Harriet; indeed, I sensed most strongly—or perhaps I had read it somewhere—that my virginity was not a mark in my favor but rather a disadvantage in the eyes of a girl of her age.

I crossed the North Sea from Harwich to the Hook of Holland and from there took a train to Munich, stayed in a hotel near the station and then trudged around the city on the squeaking snow looking for a job. I spoke few words of German, but my disability was not this but the visitor's visa in my passport. After ten days I had already spent half my money, and to save what was left I started to live off hot sausages and bread bought on the street. I knew no one in the city and made no friends but on one occasion fell into conversation with a French student in a café who told me that my best chance was to try the hotels in the skiing resorts.

I therefore left Munich and took a train to Zermatt, in Switzerland, and there quite quickly found a job as a porter in the Mont Cervin Hotel. Though my duties were of the most menial kind, I fulfilled my first two objectives: I learned some German and saved all the money I earned, for my board was free. Though my salary was small, I cleaned cars in my spare time and ran errands for the hotel guests to augment it.

I wrote to Harriet in Paris telling her what I was doing but suggesting that the job was grander than it was. I hoped to impress her by suggesting that I had discovered in myself a talent for skiing, though I never in fact had the time to try it.

The question of sexual experience was more difficult. A homosexual encounter would not have been difficult; indeed, it might have been difficult to avoid if I had not had considerable practice at deflecting the advances of both boys and teachers at Newton. Unfortunately the women in the hotel were either plain, brisk peasants who worked in the kitchen and had neither the time nor the inclination to seduce me or elegant guests whose languid eyes were more likely to alight on the skiing instructors than on the lowest flunky in the hotel.

I had read *The Confessions of Felix Krull*, however, and

had hopes . . . and toward the end of the season a woman came to the hotel who had dogs; and I was given the concession, as it were, of looking after them. They were three Salukis, and I fed them and took them for a walk in the afternoon. They slept in her suite, which was against the hotel's regulations, but Frau Kohner was an established guest and the exception had long been made.

She was one of those indeterminate European women whose faces are too brown from the sun. She could have been Dutch, German or Swiss. Certainly she had a Swiss passport, for I saw it once on the table in her room where she had left it and discovered that she was aged only thirty-two when I had thought she was forty. She was handsome, fastidiously preserved (which was why I had thought she was older) and athletic. She spent all day on the slopes, drank a cocktail with the hotel manager, dined alone and went early to bed.

Each evening I returned the Salukis to her room at six o'clock as she had instructed. She was then usually in the bath, having just returned from skiing, and on the second day she carried out a long, shouting conversation from there—first in German, which I barely understood, and then in English, which she spoke quite well—about the food I was giving the dogs. It appeared that their breath smelled of fish and I was not to give them tinned food but scraps from the kitchen or fresh meat.

On the fourth day she emerged from the bathroom swathed in a towel and thanked me for successfully changing the dogs' diet so that they no longer smelled of fish. She did not look at me, so I thanked her and withdrew. On the fifth day she emerged from the bathroom without the towel—in other words, naked. She did not look at me and I thought for a moment that she had not realized I was there, but she said, as she lay back on the bed, "Were they good, my puppies?"

"Yes," I said, and would have turned and left but I had never seen a naked woman before and was sufficiently startled to remain where I was, standing more or less at attention by the door.

[73]

She lay back on the bed, lifted her knees to her chest and called to her dogs, calling them "my puppies" in English, presumably for my benefit. They jumped up onto the bed and started to sniff around her face and lick her body. I understood, now, why the fishy smell had been so unattractive, for one dog at least licked her lips while the other two were directed by her hands toward the lower orifices of her body and the cries of "my puppies" became more languorous and less specific sounds. The dogs, however, were either not in the mood or not well trained or were as fastidious about smell as she was, for they jumped off the bed and started to chase each other around the room.

Frau Kohner sat up and for the first time looked at me. "It is nice, you know," she said, "when they do it properly."

I nodded.

"You should try it."

I had not meant to seem to agree with what she had said, for I did not believe that canine tongues on my naked body would be a pleasant experience. My reaction, indeed, to the sight had been nearer to horror than to envy, but at a primitive level it had excited me and in my mind I realized that this might be a chance of experience. When, therefore, the naked Frau Kohner began to unbutton my bellboy's uniform, I did not object, and when it was off I overcame my modesty and lay on the bed while she whistled for her dogs. By then, however, the dogs had laid down by the window and would not obey her. She gathered up one of them into her arms and dropped it onto the bed beside me, but far from licking me it jumped off the bed again, whereupon Frau Kohner shrugged her shoulders and said she would simulate the dogs to give me an idea of what it was like.

That evening, and on other occasions while she was a guest at the hotel, she did what the dogs would not do, but she also taught me more straightforward forms of sexual behavior. When she left she gave me a kiss and a tip of two thousand Swiss francs, which I accepted for looking after the dogs.

[74]

I was thus provided with the money and the experience to go to Paris, and at the beginning of April I gave in my notice to the hotel and left Zermatt. I spent a night in Zurich and bought two new suits of clothes, one made of gray flannel, the other of a thick tweed. From my hotel in Zurich I telephoned a hotel in Paris and booked a room. I was still only eighteen but I had learned from my work in Zermatt the most effective tone to adopt with the staff of hotels—a blend of condescension and familiarity—so that I felt I might be taken for a young milord on the Grand Tour.

I sent a telegram to Harriet to say that I was on my way to Paris and then caught the express from Zurich. When I arrived I went straight to the hotel and once in my room asked for the number that Harriet had given me.

A voice answered in French; I asked in English for Miss Harriet Metherall.

"Ah, oui, Harriet," said the woman who had answered.

In a moment I heard Harriet's cautious voice. "Hello," she said. "Who is it?"

"Hilary," I said, my confidence suddenly leaving me and my bluff voice croaking back into its usual tentative tone.

Harriet, on the other hand, seemed to become more relaxed when she gathered who it was. "Oh, Hilary, hello. Where are you?"

"I'm in Paris."

"When did you get here?"

"This morning."

"How nice."

"Did you get my telegram?"

"Your telegram? Oh, yes. Yes, I did. This morning."

"Could we meet?"

"I should think so," said Harriet, "but I'd better ask Madame Vignon. Hold on."

She went away. I heard voices but could not make out what they said; then she returned.

"When?" she asked.

"I hadn't thought. When would it suit you?"

"You see . . . I'm not meant to go out in the evening."
She sounded embarrassed.

"Could you come to tea?" I asked.

"Tea? Yes, I'm sure I could. Where?"

"At my hotel."

"All right. Where is it?"

"The Saint James and Albany, rue du Rivoli."

"Rue *de* Rivoli."

"I'm sorry, yes. Rue de Rivoli. Tomorrow afternoon?"

"Yes. What time?"

"About four."

"Yes. Good. I'll see you then."

It became evening and I lay back on the comfortable bed
in my hotel room studying the molding around the edge of
the ceiling and I began to imagine that Harriet was there
beside me, learning from me what I had learned from Frau
Kohner. My thoughts, however, were not all pornographic or
my intentions all dishonorable. My feelings for Frau Kohner,
in retrospect, were as much of disgust as of delight, and I
wanted from Harriet what I had never had from her—kisses
and caresses of simple affection. The joy I dreamed of was
from dallying—the leap from friendliness to intimacy, from
comradeship to love. If I had no more specific intentions it
was because it did not cross my mind that lovers once joined
ever parted.

Far from slight, my attitude toward Harriet involved my
whole destiny, and if there was a way other than the sexual
method by which I might have possessed her I would
gladly have taken it. As it was, it seemed the best and only
fashion both to take, hold and keep, and it coincided with the
nagging appetite of my sexual nature.

It had as much to do with a place as with a person. Though
I did not at this time admit it to myself, I had hated both
Munich and Zermatt, and London as I had passed through it
had seemed too large to comprehend. I decided that the world

beyond Lasterby was entirely unpleasant, too complicated and impersonal; yet the rectory was the opposite to that, too familiar and predictable, the repository of the mother whom I pitied and the father whom I despised. The only home I recognized was Lasterby Hall—not the house in particular but its whole world of beauty, space, intelligence and graciousness. Like paradise it was an invented memory, something to which I longed to return but had never in reality possessed. To have Harriet would be to have it all, in the past as well as in the future. It was thus that my feeling for her was no simple love but all the same a real, sincere and desperate emotion.

Later that night I went out and ate dinner in a cheaper restaurant than that of the hotel. Then I wandered around the streets smoking a cigar, a habit I had picked up in Switzerland, looking in shop windows and at the stills outside the cinemas. I was approached by a woman, presumably a whore, but I had had more than enough experience and on the eve of my meeting with Harriet I was disgusted to be reminded of what I had done in Zermatt. I returned to the hotel and tried to read but could not. I took a bath and went to bed.

The next morning. . . . I do not know how the time passed. I dressed with great care in my new Swiss tweed suit —*Englische art*—and while eating breakfast downstairs tried to read a French newspaper. Then I went out to buy a present for Harriet and settled on expensive chocolates. I ate lunch at the hotel with a bottle of wine, went back to my room, fell asleep, awoke in good time but feeling and looking somewhat crumpled.

When Harriet arrived I was sitting in the foyer of the hotel. I noticed that there was another girl who came in with her but at first it did not occur to me that they were together. After saying hello and kissing me on the cheek, Harriet introduced her as Cecily Hammond.

[77]

"I hope you don't mind my crashing like this," said this companion, who was heavy and haughty and heightened the delicacy and grace of Harriet's appearance, "but we went shopping together. . . ." She looked at Harriet and giggled.

I too looked at Harriet. She had not changed. She was dressed more elegantly than usual with a pearl necklace over her pink cardigan, but that was natural enough. We sat down.

"You look different," she said to me.

"How?"

"It's that suit, I suppose. And you're so sunburned." She wrinkled up her nose.

"Where have you been?" asked Cecily Hammond.

"In Switzerland."

"You lucky thing," she said.

"Oh, he wasn't really skiing," said Harriet. "Just working in a hotel."

"A job before going up to Cambridge," I said.

She nodded, but clearly I had sunk in her estimation.

I ordered tea for the three of us.

"It's a funny hotel, isn't it?" said Harriet.

"I came here because of Felix Krull."

"Who's he?" she asked, with little interest, as if he was certainly another porter in the hotel in Zermatt.

"It's a book," I said.

"Oh, yes. You wrote something about it in your letter."

"Yes."

There was a silence. Cecily giggled again and Harriet looked reprovingly at her.

"What do you do all day?" I asked.

"Oh, well, we have lessons in the morning," said Harriet.

"What lessons?"

Cecily giggled. "Madame Vignon tries to teach us French," she said.

"I've become rather good at it," said Harriet.

"And what do you do in the afternoons?" I asked.

"We either go shopping, or to a museum. . . ."

"With Madame Vignon?"

"No. She goes to sleep. Jean-Pierre sometimes takes us . . . if he's not working."

"Who's he?"

"He's Madame Vignon's son-in-law. He lives in the flat beneath hers."

"He's smashing," said Cecily.

"Oh, no," said Harriet. "I don't think he is. He's awfully greasy, really." She smiled to herself.

The tea came and we chose cakes.

"What are you going to do now?" Harriet asked me.

"I don't know," I said. "I thought I might stay here for a bit and try and learn some French."

Harriet frowned slightly. "I shouldn't," she said.

"Why not?"

"Well, I don't think Paris is very nice, really. It's all right out by the Bois where we are, except it's boring; but in the middle it's so noisy and expensive and the Parisians are so nasty." She was not looking at me as she said this.

"Perhaps you're right," I said, attempting to ingratiate myself by agreeing with her.

"You'd be very much on your own, too," she said. "I mean, you don't know anyone here, do you?"

"Only you."

She glanced at Cecily. "We wouldn't be much company. Madame Vignon's a real old chaperon. She won't let us out at night with anyone unless Mother and Father write a special letter. Not even Alexander. He had to . . ."

"When was he here?" I asked.

"A few weeks ago. He had to ring up Lasterby from Madame Vignon's flat to be allowed to take me out."

"I could write to your parents."

"They're away at the moment," she said, and looked away from me.

I shrugged my shoulders. I was hot in my thick casing of Swiss tweed. "Don't you go to the theater, then?"

"Oh, yes," said Cecily. "But either Madame Vignon takes us or Jean-Pierre."

"It's as bad as being at school, really," said Harriet. "I can't wait to get back to England."

"When are you going back?" I asked.

"In May," she said.

Cecily Hammond stood up. "I'm just going along to Smith's," she said, "in case it closes."

"It won't," said Harriet, who appeared not to want her to leave.

"It might," said Cecily. "I think they keep English hours. I'll be back in a minute." She giggled and left us.

I offered to fill Harriet's cup with tea but she did not want any more. The gesture was to give me time, for I saw that she would leave me soon (she looked at her watch) and not so much as a corner of my imaginings had been touched by the reality of this tea party.

"I missed you in Zermatt," I said, the panic I felt giving a breathless tone to my voice.

Harriet looked embarrassed. "Yes, well, so did I . . . miss you."

I glanced at her bosom and legs as if lust might give me courage. "I had hoped to see quite a lot of you here."

"I *know*," said Harriet. "Isn't it a nuisance?"

"There's no way. . . ?"

"Not really, no." She sat up straight in her chair. "I'm so cross with Mother for landing me in this, but I suppose I'd better see it through."

"Yes."

"It's not long now."

"You'll be back in May?"

"Yes."

"At Lasterby?"

"Yes. There's my dance, you see."

"For your dance," I said, thinking of my planned visit to a tailor, "does one wear tails or a dinner jacket?"

"Oh, goodness, not tails," she said.

"And for Queen Charlotte's Ball?"

She blushed. "Well, tails, I suppose . . . but you needn't

bother, because . . . well, Mother asked Alexander to come with us."

After this I said nothing more of a personal nature and did not take the chocolates out of their bag and give them to Harriet. I talked about Zermatt; she talked about Paris. It was a relief to both of us when we saw Cecily come back into the hotel.

"Ah, there's Cecily," Harriet said, standing. "I'm afraid we ought to go."

I stood up.

"It wasn't shut," said Cecily.

Harriet looked at me, her head lowered, her blue eyes visible only through their lashes. "You will go on writing, won't you?" she said. "I love getting your letters."

"Yes," I said.

"Will you go back to Lasterby?" she asked.

"I should think so. There's a lot of reading to do for Cambridge."

"Well, I'll see you there in May."

"Yes."

"Thank you so much for tea."

"Yes," said Cecily, "thanks awfully . . . and I am sorry . . . I mean, crashing like that."

"It was nice to meet you," I said.

They left. I sat down and paid the bill. I then went to my room, packed my suitcase and threw the chocolates into the wastepaper basket. I took the night train for England.

I was tired now of solitude, and of hotels and foreign languages, so I returned to my parents' house at Lasterby and set about my reading list in a methodical manner, starting with Herodotus. I would rise late in the morning, after my father had finished his breakfast and was either sitting solemnly on the lavatory or already at his sermon in his study. I had to face him at lunch and again at supper, but I usually avoided him at tea by taking a long walk in the afternoon.

There was no one at Lasterby Hall—Sir Edward and

[*81*]

Lady Clare were on a Hellenic cruise—but my walks often went that way, not so much to the gates as down a track from which one could view the west side of the house. It was now as dead as when I had first seen it with all its windows white. I wish my feelings had been as lifeless, for the sight of the house evoked thoughts and memories which ravaged me, yet I took the same walk, day after day, as if afraid that the pain would fade from these emotions.

I wrote long poetic letters to Harriet, full of suppressed affection. She wrote back—short dull letters of a dutiful sort which started "Dear Hilary" and ended "with love." If she had not been so eager to behave well, I dare say she would not have written at all. Certainly if I had read the words with any detachment I should have realized that I might count myself lucky just to be her friend—that I was an idiot to love her when my love was not returned—but I did not read her letters for their sense. I treasured them as objects, as if the paper and envelope were part of her which could respond to caresses and possession.

It is often the case that men and women who are normally sane and objective refuse from an instinct of self-preservation to accept a truth that would destroy them. A bankrupt continues to live as if he is a millionaire. A woman's lover is invisible to her doting husband. In just this way I would not recognize Harriet's indifference, and while suffering from her absence I assumed that she would return from Paris with her love for me in full bloom.

Had there been anyone to whom I could have confessed my feelings, I might have been brought gently down to earth, but my father would have been embarrassed by any confidences and would anyway have thought Harriet too good for me. Indeed, he had heard from Sir Edward that Alexander Amotherby had been to see Harriet in Paris—ringing up, even, to ask if he might take her out—and he tattled about it with my mother like an old woman. My mother took part in this gossip, though she threw a sympathetic glance in my direction. She knew me well and it may be that she pitied me just as I pitied her.

The only person besides my mother who understood my situation, and then only in an oblique way, was my uncle Ernest. I had met him out walking one afternoon and he had asked me back to the farm for tea. I accepted his invitation but was nervous of seeing Sam. As if sensing this, my uncle told me before anything else that Sam and George were in Malton.

"How are they?" I asked.

"Grand."

"What are they doing?"

"Both still working on the farm."

"Will Sam take it over?"

Ernest spat onto the track which led down to his farm. "I hope so," he said.

"Is there any reason why he shouldn't?"

"Aye." He paused and then said, "I've talked to Sir Edward about it, but they won't agree."

"To what? To Sam taking it over?"

"I wanted to make Sam tenant now, like, you see, while I'm still alive, but they want to wait till I'm gone and then have him bid along with all the others."

"But you've farmed it all your life," I said.

"But they're the landlords, aren't they? If they won't let our Sam take it on, there's nowt I can do aboot it."

Mrs. Bosomworth was there with tea and she fussed over me. "It's years since we've seen you here," she said.

"He gets a better tea up at the 'all," said Ernest.

I blushed. "This is the best tea in the world," I said.

My uncle smiled at me. "And you should know," he said. "You've been traveling, haven't you?"

"Yes," I said.

"Where did you go?"

"To Germany, Switzerland . . . and then to Paris."

"Did you see Miss Harriet?"

"Yes . . . yes, I did."

"How was she, then?" he asked.

"Fine."

"She's a lovely girl," said Mrs. Bosomworth, with an emphasis directed at my uncle.

"She's pretty enough," said Ernest, with a sour look on his old face.

"She's all right," said Mrs. Bosomworth.

It was not difficult to see from her defensive tone, and from my uncle's reluctance, that there had been conversations on the subject before. I made no comment myself but let the cleanliness and simplicity of the kitchen waft over me. I thought of how nice it was to sit in a room with hams hanging from the ceiling and a view from the window into a modest garden. It made me happier, too, to hear my uncle's doubts about Harriet—even if these doubts were only the offshoot of his fears for me.

No such sympathy came from my father. The feelings of other people—even those of his wife and son—were beyond the range of his imagination. As I had grown older I had not come to like him any more. Indeed, the more I learned and experienced, the more I appreciated the fraudulence of his life and character.

Many sons, I have discovered since, despise their fathers, but at that time I imagined I was alone in doing so. At Newton, where one's mere presence was reason enough to detest one's parents, the discussion of them was a taboo, so it was not until much later that I realized what my friends' feelings were on this subject. Earlier in my life the only comparisons I could make were with Sam and George and Mark, all of whom loved their fathers as much as their fathers loved their sons.

I saw nothing unusual in this, since both my uncle Ernest and Sir Edward were likely objects of filial affection and respect, whereas my father was not only disliked by me but by almost everyone else. Except for the odd case of Sir

Edward, I can think of no one who liked him—least of all my uncle Ernest. This did not lead me to pity my father because it did not lead him to pity himself or take any measures to make himself likable. I dare say that he did not notice that he was friendless. He cared for the friendship of only one person—Sir Edward—and, this accomplished, he saw no need for further human contact. I believe that Lord Barton and the Dean and Archbishop of York were the only other people in Yorkshire for whom he would have bothered to expend a smile or some conversation.

Until I went away to Newton I did my best to please my father. If he noticed these attempts, he paid no attention to them. At the age of six or seven (this was before we moved to Yorkshire) I made an ashtray out of clay for a church bazaar which later he used in his argument with my mother against the very idea of a sale. "This ashtray, for example," he said. "You can't expect people to pay money for rubbish like this."

As my mother explained to me later, he had forgotten that I had made it. Her heart was soft and it excreted pity like a well-functioning gland, but she always cooperated with the nasty side of my father's character and as such made it possible. A favorite trick of his, when I was around fourteen or fifteen years old, was to refer to some Anglican theologian whose work he had been reading that morning and then ask me for a comment on the man's ideas. I would confess that I had never read it, nor heard of the writer, upon which he would scoff at my ignorance and look to my mother for a scornful smile to support him. And she would smile and say, "Really, Hilary, what do they teach you at school if you've never heard of Fenton Hort?"

It can easily be imagined, I think, and may already have been surmised, that my upbringing by this loveless pedant and his pitiable sow left me with no affection for the concept of God. To tell the truth I preferred God to Jesus, for the nearer my father's exposition came to the human, the more sickly it seemed to me. God had the advantage of being an idea, and ideas went better with my father's dusty mind. It was an idea, all the same, which I did not consider until I was fourteen and then did so only to reject it.

The historical figure of Jesus was a different matter. My father pronounced his name slowly, allowing the echo of the first syllable to reach our ears before speaking the second, which he emphasized. He made him out to have been a man rather like himself. Certainly I could see my father turning to his mother and saying, "Woman, what is that to me?" And "Let the dead bury the dead," always seemed a phrase which might well have come from my father's lips, since he was as reluctant to perform funerals as he was to take on any other of his parish duties. My father, like Christ, might have soberly recommended the hacking off of limbs lest they offend their owners; indeed, I often saw him eying me as if I was no more than a collection of potentially damning limbs and organs. The long hours he himself spent in his armchair may have been to humble his limbs and let them wither, as well as to avoid exercise and the immorality of the world outside his study.

I was later to discover that there are aspects of Christ's character out of keeping with my father, but as a child I did not notice them. The rector of Lasterby would never have consorted with publicans, nor would he suffer little children to come unto him. And had he the power to perform miracles, it would have been more readily in the service of Sir Edward and Lady Clare—to rid their dogs of fleas, for example—than to cure the maimed or the sick of the village.

It was many years, however, before I could return to the Bible and form from it my own picture of Christ. For throughout my childhood and adolescence, whatever wisdom it might have contained was sieved through the tight mesh of my father's personality, and its words were heard in his tone of voice. Nor could I, like the farmers and villagers, avoid his homilies by not going to the services. Week after

[*86*]

week I was his captive audience; in consequence I was quickly bored with the Christian religion and then, being unable to escape what bored me, increasingly averse to it until my reaction to the smallest whiff of its doctrine or values was one of hysterical disgust. Like a psychologist's rat, I shied automatically at the least intimation of Christian injunction. I grew to loathe such words as meekness, chastity and humility, and at eighteen was already determined to be assertive, lascivious and proud.

This revolt took place in the secrecy of my mind, though now I see that it fitted in with my behavior at Newton, where it was the prefects who led the school in prayer. It surprised me, however, that as I left my childhood and saw more of the world I discovered that my egotistic intentions were shared by almost everyone else. I was not so undemocratic as to take exception to this; indeed, I was happy that "there are liars and swearers enough to beat the honest men and hang them up." Nor did I think myself bad in any way. Wickedness had meant doing what irritated my father—sliding down the banisters, playing hide-and-seek in front of his study window or eating both high tea at the farm and supper at home. It was, in other words, his interest against mine. As soon as I understood this I accepted it and in the same way made my interest my good. I adopted thereby what I later discovered was the most generally accepted ethical system, for many kinds of morality are preached but all have in common their identity with the behavior of the preacher. The rich want freedom; the poor want justice. The repressed enjoin chastity; the lecherous call for free love. It seemed to me quite sensible that we should cut our coat according to our cloth like this, and I respected my father more when I came to understand how his belief in Christ provided him with a modest but comfortable life of complete idleness.

In the same way my own morality changed with my circumstances, and while others whose values change just as swiftly and radically as mine affect not to notice their volte-

[87]

faces, I was happy to admit to mine and even congratulate myself on the adaptability of my moral system.

At eighteen, sitting in my room at Lasterby reading history books, I was by nature and circumstance poor, cunning, ambitious and lustful. Thus I formed out of my early reading convictions which were agnostic and radical—almost revolutionary—with an especial belief in revolutionary heroes, leaders of the people such as Cromwell, Robespierre, Bonaparte, Garibaldi and Lenin. I was most sympathetic, in reading about the French Revolution, toward the peasants who burned down the feudal *manoir* with its lord inside and then guillotined his wife and children. I need hardly add that with my mind's eye I watched it fall on the necks of Lady Clare, Mark and the baby Martha. And I also commended Napoleon where his contemporaries had criticized him for executing the duc d'Enghien, because I saw in that cocky royalist an Alexander Amotherby of his day.

In those weeks I did as much as I could to absorb myself in my work but my concentration was not so great that I was not elated by the first of May, not as May Day or a sign of spring but as the start of that month which would see the return of Harriet.

By then Sir Edward and Lady Clare were back from their Hellenic cruise and my parents had resumed their regular visits to the hall, my mother returning with Lady Clare's "love," then her "interest that I had visited Harriet in Paris" and, in mid-May, her "looking forward to seeing me when Mark and Harriet get back." But then, just as I began to suspect that each ringing of the telephone might be she, my mother told me that Sir Edward and Lady Clare had left for London.

I had so well imagined the return of Harriet to Lasterby that I could not believe the implications of what my mother said. I took my walk that afternoon down the lane which gave views of the front of Lasterby Hall—and sure enough, its windows were again white. Then, despite the calm nature of that warm day, a panic entered into me. I remembered their house in London and the season of parties and dances to which Harriet was committed. There was no reason at all why she shoud return to Lasterby until it was over, and by then I would certainly have been forgotten for an officer in the Guards.

As I walked I stamped in puddles, as if this somehow expressed the mixture of misery and rage which I felt. Love of all sorts is a disease, but if it is returned it can run a course and burn itself out; if not, if frustrated, it remains in you forever, festering the spirit. If only to cure myself of my affection for Harriet, I had to see her, yet Yorkshire now seemed the worst place to do so. I had some money, certainly, and might go to London, but London frightened me. I knew no one there, had nowhere to stay and could think of no particular excuse for calling on the Metheralls in Belgravia.

I had momentarily forgotten, of course, that Harriet herself was to have a dance, but I was reminded of it when I got back from my walk because my invitation to it had arrived by the afternoon's post. I saw it on the hall table as I came in and took the large, heavy envelope up to my room. There I sat on my bed and pulled open the flap of the envelope, which was neither licked nor sealed but tucked into the main body. Before removing the invitation, however, I turned the envelope around to look at the address, *Hilary Fletcher Esq., The Rectory, Lasterby, York.* It was written in neat, girlish handwriting and in blue ink. It could have been Harriet's handwriting but I doubted it.

I removed the invitation from the envelope. It was only slightly smaller than the envelope which contained it and was made of thick card, almost a millimeter thick. Around it was wrapped a piece of paper which was not simply to protect it but had printed on it certain information about trains from London to York, connections from York to Malton, and also a sentence: "Please state if you would like to be included in a house party."

I now looked at the invitation itself. On the top of it was written, in the same hand as had written the address on the envelope, *Mr. Hilary Fletcher.* Beneath this was printed "Lady Clare Metherall, At Home, Tuesday 4 June 1957. Dancing. 10:30 o'clock. R.S.V.P. Lasterby Hall, Lasterby, York," all of which was spaced out in an elegant manner so that "Lady Clare Metherall," for example, and the "At Home," all had a line to themselves. The "10:30 o'clock" was tucked down in the left-hand corner of the card, and the "R.S.V.P." was in the right-hand corner. The whole thing was printed in copperplate, a fancy style designed to look a little like handwriting. It was also engraved, which is to say that the words took on a third dimension and stood out from the surface of the card. All this, as I had learned from Harriet, was the only way to do these things.

When I had finished studying this invitation I placed it on top of the mantelpiece of my bedroom as I had seen done with invitations in the little drawing room at Lasterby. The piece of paper which had surrounded the invitation I put aside on my desk. I then lay down on my bed, wondering whether to answer the invitation at once or to wait a day or two, the first course seeming polite but the second somehow more worldly. I decided upon answering it now and then sending it later, so I jumped off my bed, went to the desk and took a piece of my parents' writing paper out of my drawer. I felt ashamed that the address was only printed on the paper, not engraved, and sensed that the irregular edges were somehow common. It was better, all the same, than an ordinary piece of paper, so I wrote my acceptance in the manner I had been taught by Harriet: "Mr. H. Fletcher thanks Lady Clare Metherall for her kind invitation for Tuesday 4 June 1957, and is pleased to accept." I wrote the date at the top—the date of two days' time—and went back to lie on my bed and think of the great ball at Lasterby.

A week later I was told by my mother that she had offered to give a dinner party for the dance and that her offer had been accepted. Nearer the time we were told whom we were to have: the doctor from Muscoates and his wife, their daughter Isobel, a dreadful spotty girl of my age, and a solicitor from Kirkbymoorside with his wife. It was clear to me—though not to my mother and father—that the least desirable guests had thus been thrown together lest the odor of the middle class should spoil the other parties.

Harriet was up at Lasterby for only one weekend before her dance. She came to church on the Sunday morning, dressed neatly in a tweed skirt. I sat throughout the service with my eyes on the altar but my whole attention on her person on the other side of the aisle. Her hair was caught in the sunlight; even a man not in love with her could mistake her for an angel or the goddess Diana.

After the service in the porch she asked me if I would like to come to tea that afternoon. As if to test the strength of her invitation I hesitated. The test failed. Before I had time, even, to give a definite answer, she said, "Well, we'll see you at the dance, anyway."

"Yes," I said, wondering how I might go back on my hesitation and accept the invitation.

"It's awfully nice of your mother to have a dinner party," Harriet said.

"Not at all."

"I'm sorry giving you such ghastly people. . . ."

"That's all right."

"You will come early, won't you?"

"What time?"

"Well . . . not later than eleven."

"All right."

She smiled a false smile. I thought then that its falsity was especially for me but in thinking about it later decided that it was a common mark of her class, something she must have picked up in London.

She started walking down the path between the gravestones toward the gate. I walked with her.

"How are you enjoying London?" I asked.

"Oh, it's exhausting."

"Do you go to other dances?"

"I mostly don't go to bed before three or four in the morning. . . . You get used to it though."

"Are they . . . are the other people nice?"

"I've made a few friends."

"Girls?"

"Oh, yes. The men are ghastly."

We reached the Metheralls' car, in which Sir Edward and just said but still could not think of any way to make it clear that I had changed my mind, that I had not meant to hesitate.

"Will there be a lot of people?" I asked.

"We've asked four hundred," she said, "but only about three will come."

"Four hundred . . ."

"It's not a lot. Cecily's asked six. . . . By the way, she wants to ask you."

"That's nice of her."

"It is, rather, isn't it?"

We reached the Metheralls' car, in which Sir Edward and Lady Clare were waiting for their daughter. As Harriet got in, Lady Clare wound down her window and said, "You must come over when Mark gets back."

I was later told that Harriet's dance cost Sir Edward more than four thousand pounds, a large sum in those days. The expense lay first in the caterers, who provided cold tongue, beef and ham salads for those guests who had not stuffed themselves sufficiently before coming and, after midnight, breakfast of coffee, toast and bacon and eggs. Besides that there was champagne or any other drink served in the great hall, and in one or two other places around the house, a band in the ballroom, and a jukebox in the old kitchen which had been made to look like a nightclub——all this for around three hundred guests, most of whom were bored by it all because they had been going to the same sort of dance two or three times a week every week for the space of the season.

The money might have been better spent on the starving masses of Africa and Asia, perhaps, though eight of the guests at least were greatly impressed by the display of conspicuous consumption—the eight who had dined at the rectory.

Of those who received us in the great hall (the doors which were never used were opened for that occasion), Lady Clare looked the best. Never had her Norman-knight face looked better, the mask of an actress playing her finest role. Harriet, though bedecked and bejeweled, looked dowdy. I imagine that she was tired. She gave me her false smile as I shook her hand; for a moment it opened into a genuine expression—almost an appeal—and then closed again almost at once. And without further words than the original "hello" she moved her attention to Dr. Potter, who was behind me.

One thing our party had in common—besides its middle-class character—was that we knew almost no one else among the three or four hundred guests. Of the eight of us, I was at an advantage for I knew the Barton family—though it became clear in the course of the evening that they did not know me—and Cecily Hammond and Caroline Plunkett, who were both quite prepared to excuse my shortcomings for the sake of a dance.

"Isn't Harriet looking lovely," said Cecily, with whom I danced first.

"Yes," I answered.

We kicked each other's feet so she said, "Hey, don't dance. . . . I mean, let's just shuffle."

I had not realized that she was such a lumpish girl, but she jogged up and down in time to the music and grinned at me.

"Why didn't you stay in Paris?" she asked.

"There didn't seem to be much point."

"We had a spiffing time."

"I thought you were . . . well, rather hemmed in at Madame Vignon's."

Cecily giggled. "Oh, I don't think we minded, really."

"Harriet seemed to."

"She *seemed* to, yes." Cecily giggled again.

"Didn't she mind?"

"How should I know?" She looked at me knowingly—but I did not know what the knowing look meant and thought that to confess my ignorance would betray gaucheness and immaturity so I said nothing.

"Look," said Cecily. "there's Alexander."

There indeed was Alexander Amotherby. Cecily tried to catch his eye while we danced, but he ignored her just as he ignored me.

We returned to the great hall, drank some champagne, met up with Caroline Plunkett, drank more champagne with her, and then I asked her to dance since my mother was in sight with Isobel Potter.

Caroline Plunkett did not like me, nor did I like her, but we were old enemies and though she was the right class for this dance she was not a debutante and so knew equally few of the guests. She was therefore glad of a partner, and her gratitude expressed itself in a certain civility and odd attempts at conversation.

While the aim of my overall strategy for the evening was to dance with Harriet and even walk out with her into the garden, there to kiss her, my tactics at this early stage were to keep clear of my parents and avoid dancing with Isobel Potter. Thus, after dumping Caroline Plunkett, and made brave by the champagne, I asked some quite strange girls to dance with me who, not knowing my origins, and left standing for most of the dance, were happy to be my partners.

There was one girl besides Harriet who was particularly tall and beautiful, and it became my tactical ambition to dance with her. She was pointed out to me by one of the other debutantes as a possible "deb of the year" called Amanda Richardson, and I thought that if Harriet could see me dancing with her it would make me somehow more attractive to her. This Amanda Richardson, however, was never to be seen standing in a gaggle by the fireplace in the great hall. She was always dancing or disappearing into the garden with some suave young man, a bottle of champagne and two glasses held in the fingers of his left hand. Eventually, however, I saw her with Mark and went up to them. Mark introduced me, affably enough, and I asked her to dance. She looked startled, then embarrassed, and then looked around as if Mark was waiting for her; but he smiled and waved his hand as if to say that he did not care if I took her from him, so she had no alternative but to comply with my wishes.

Once on the floor of the ballroom, I could think of nothing to say to her and she made no attempt to think of anything to say to me.

"Do you know many people here?" I asked her.

"Yes," she said.

"Are you a friend of Harriet's?"

"Yes."

"Do you know her well?"

"I haven't known her for long, if that's what you mean."

"Did you meet her . . . at this sort of thing?"

"No. At a tea party."

She had a cold look, this Amanda Richardson, and she may have been stupid; more likely, however, she was that kind of vain, ambitious beauty which cannot meet with anything which does not feed its narcissism. She sensed that I was worthless but could not spoil her composure by spurning me as she would have liked to do.

My next question, as it happened, succeeded in ruffling her. "Do you know Alexander Amotherby?" I asked.

She looked at me sharply. "Yes. Why? Do you?"

"Yes," I said.

"Why do you ask?"

"For no particular reason," I said, smiling.

She looked irritated now, but with nothing to lose I pursued the question. "Do you know him well?"

"Quite well."

"Do you live up here?"

"No."

"Where do you live?"

"In London and in Berkshire."

"He lives up here."

"I know."

I asked these questions only because it seemed to upset her, and any reaction was better than none. But then the music for that dance came to an end.

"I think I'd like a drink," said Amanda Richardson.

We went back to the great hall, where she saw the Alexander Amotherby we had been discussing. She went up to him silently like a dog that has found its master. He greeted her but ignored me so I moved away to find myself another glass of champagne.

After two glasses, one after the other, I went after Harriet. It was past one in the morning and I was afraid that if I did not find her now I might not get to dance with her at all. For some time she was not to be seen, either in the ballroom or the dining room or the discothèque or the great hall. I even glanced into the small drawing room where Sir Edward and Lady Clare sat with some of their grown-up guests, though not with my mother and father, who had already gone home.

At last I saw Harriet come in from the garden. To judge from the expression on her face and the more or less friendly way in which she greeted me it had not been a pleasant excursion.

"Hello," she said. "Are you having a nice time?"

"I am, yes," I said. "Are you?"

"Oh, yes."

She introduced me to the young man beside her, but as if he too had not enjoyed their walk he took my presence as an excuse to leave her.

"Who's he?" I asked.

She smiled. "Awful, don't you think?"

"He certainly looked it."

We walked into the great hall.

"Would you like a drink or would you like to dance?" I asked.

Harriet thought to herself and then said, "Have you tried the discothèque in the old kitchen?"

"No."

"Nor have I. Will you take me down?"

"Yes, certainly."

I was happy and excited as we went down. Her friendliness encouraged me to ignore all the evidence that her feelings toward me were only of a vague friendship. I even anticipated the kiss that she would give me, and the muscles of my arms flexed as they prepared to hug her forever.

When we started to dance, however, in the semidarkness, to the slow beat of the jukebox records, she kept her body at a definite distance to mine, and I found that I was abashed at finding myself suddenly with one hand holding her hand and another around her waist. She was much more solid than I had imagined her, and my fingers on her back sank into a layer of plumpness beneath her skin. This strange consistency to her body—together with her unusual appearance, with her hair done up behind her neck and her body covered in a long beige dress like stale icing—made me confused and unsure. I put slight pressure on her back to pull her toward me, but either she consciously resisted it or was too solid to be moved by such ambiguous gestures. I did not dare risk any less equivocal movement and so decided to test my ground in

[97]

conversation. I saw, in the corner of the room, a couple entwined together, dancing, except that their steps had stopped, their arms around each other, their mouths half open, their lips pressed together.

"Some people," I said to Harriet, nodding to this couple, "some people are enjoying your dance."

She giggled. "Yes," she said. Then the couple broke apart and we could see that it was Amanda Richardson and Alexander Amotherby. Harriet saw this as well as I did and the expression on her face changed quickly from amusement to fury; then as we continued to dance, I felt her body shake and saw that she was crying.

"Oh, dear," she said, "oh, dear."

"What's the matter?" I asked.

"Oh, it's nothing," she said, but her tears continued.

We left the discothèque and went out by a door known to us but not to the other guests which led to the kitchen yard. There she broke loose from me and walked a few yards away with her back turned and still crying.

I waited until she had stopped before going up to her again.

"I'm sorry," she said. "It's just that I'm so tired . . . and this dance . . . it's been such a strain."

"Yes," I said.

The cold tone with which I said this made her look up at me and realize that I knew quite well what had made her cry.

"I'm sorry," she said again—but she did not sound it. Then she added, "For God's sake don't you make things more difficult." She wiped away the tears from her eyes. "Oh, God, I'd better go up and do my face again."

She looked at me, then left and went in at the back door. I did not follow her but walked around to the front of the house and from there back along the lane toward the rectory.

A mixture of alcohol in my blood and the secrecy of the darkness now undid my inhibitions and I started to cry just as she had done. I saw a car approaching and was afraid that my tears would be seen and that I would be recognized; from the light of its headlamps as it passed I noticed mud on the trousers of my new dinner jacket.

In time, however, the exercise and the fresh air did me good. By the time I had reached home, my tears had stopped —and my love for Harriet had stopped too. I now loathed her along with all the rest.

Part Two

Part Two

5

In October I went to Cambridge and it was a sign of
my estrangement from the Metherall family, which had taken
place in the course of the summer, that I made no arrangements to travel with Mark, who was going to the same university town from the same parish in Yorkshire. I was soon
to discover that while Cambridge University presented a
uniform exterior of privilege to those outside it, for those
within there were many subdivisions of snobbery, and Mark
and I went each to our own proper place—he to Trinity, the
college for the sons of landowners, founded by a king in 1546;
I to Selwyn, the college for the sons of clergymen, founded
by public subscription in 1882.

Besides Mark Metherall I knew only one other undergraduate at the university, Eric Feber, who had been a contemporary of mine at Newton—not one of my closest
friends, like Qazvini, nor one of my particular enemies. He
had been by far the cleverest boy in the school but was given
no credit for it because he was a Jew. Newton would have
preferred to exclude Jews altogether, but it could not afford
to turn away any fee-paying pupil and indeed did well out
of the aspirations of Jews as well as the ignorance of for-
eigners like the parents of Qazvini.

I hesitated before going to see Feber—I would rather have
made new friends than take up with him—but halfway
through the first term I felt such acute loneliness that I looked
him up in his rooms in Caius. He was affable; he seemed almost pleased to see me. He made tea and we toasted bread on
the grill of his gas fire. Everything he said confirmed that his
personality had changed as little as his appearance; that his

intellect—his brilliance at French and German—had not provided him with either the detachment or the cynicism to
escape from the snobbery inherited from his parents and
nurtured at Newton. He told me, for instance, that he had
only been admitted to Caius as a possible rowing Blue when I
knew quite well that he could not row and, with such a puny
body, was never likely to do so; but I knew too that he
would dearly love to be a rowing Blue—a tall Adonis, ef-
fortlessly superior, a member of the Pitt Club with a beautiful
sister, a great fortune, an Eton education and titled parents
living in a country house. He would have liked to be
Mark Metherall, but fate had made him short, corpulent and
the son of a bankrupt jeweler in North London.

I knew all about him that he wanted to conceal, which may
be why he accepted me so readily as a friend. We had other
things in common besides our school days. He had as little
money as I did. We both had to live off the state grant of
around three hundred pounds a year, though I had fifty
pounds left over from Zermatt with which I intended to buy
some clothes. Eric gave me a quick education in elegance.
Under his instructions I bought tight-fitting flannel trousers
with no pleats and no cuffs, half a dozen heavily striped
shirts, slip-on shoes and a Shetland pullover. I became, like
him, something of a dandy. Mark, when I saw him in the
street, wore the same old clothes, though they were, as they
had always been, better cut than mine.

Eric, who dressed well and lived flamboyantly, supple-
mented his income by playing poker—mostly with his friends
at Caius—for five-shilling stakes, winning or losing up to
twenty pounds in an evening. I do not think that he cheated,
but he was good at the game and played with others who
were not. Since this was his pastime and he was as yet my
only friend, I was eager to join in, and he taught me the game
but would not let me play until he felt I had mastered not
only the written rules but his own unwritten regulations.
"Chaps like us should never bet on a bad hand," he would say.
"We haven't the money. Only bluff if you're sure you can go

on and on and on." Or, "If you've got a good hand, don't bet heavily on it until you've lured everyone in. Then raise them gently or you'll frighten them off."

The first game in which I played was held in Kings in the rooms of some aesthete who had recently read Huysmans. The windows were blacked out with scarlet curtains and there were dim lights with deep purple shades. The table was bedecked like an altar with a joss stick burning in the place of incense. Our host served us with whisky and oysters and then we played cards. I soon felt sick with what I had eaten and half an hour later vomited into the lavatory at the end of the passage outside his room. By that time I had lost around eight pounds, so the moment bent over the lavatory bowl was unhappy in all respects. But having rid myself of the whisky and oysters I felt better, returned to the table and started to win. Perhaps the nausea had spoiled my concentration for now, freed from it, I stuck to Eric's advice, dropping out at once if my hand was weak, raising gradually if it was strong. By the end of the evening I was seven pounds up; Eric had won over twelve. The aesthete and his companion had lost but they seemed happy enough, as if losing at cards was one of their affectations.

After this, however, I disregarded a further piece of Eric's advice—"Conserve your capital, dear boy"—and spent some of my winnings on a pair of Chelsea boots. Later in the week when I played again, in Eric's rooms, I won again, but only four pounds. I won again—ten pounds—at the next game and spent five of them on two more shirts. I also offered three to Eric toward the champagne he had served to the players in his rooms.

Eric would not accept this contribution. "You can't afford it," he said, stroking his gray jowls with the finger of his right hand which wore his gold signet ring.

"Of course I can," I said. "You know how much I won last night."

"But you keep buying shirts and shoes," he said.

"I've kept at least a third of what I've won."

"What does that amount to? Ten or twelve pounds?"

"I'd say I'd thirty pounds to play with."

"That's nothing," he said. "You could lose that at one hand."

"It's not likely."

"Not for five-shilling stakes. . . . But we've got to move on."

"What do you mean?"

"There are men in Trinity and Magdalene who play for one-, five-, even ten-pound stakes. We've got to get in with them, dear boy, and leave those five-shilling nobodies behind."

Later in the term we decided not to play at the same table, for there had been occasions when we had won off one another, and such was our affinity by then that this seemed to spoil the game. Moreover, Eric had made contact with richer players.

When Selwyn College had been founded, its aims were stated in its charter as being to give a university education "with economy combined with Christian training based upon the principles of the Church of England." My first experience of these principles came soon after my arrival. It was at the hands of that fellow, a Dr. Miller, who had been as an undergraduate a friend of my father and was now of sufficient authority in the college to secure me a place and his own offices as my moral tutor. He was a plump, gray-faced, unhealthy-looking man with a soft voice and handshake, whose kindness made me immediately uneasy. I owed much to him, however, and he was *in loco parentis;* I could not therefore obey my qualms and avoid him until he gave me good reason to do so.

This happened soon enough. I had been to tea with him on a number of occasions, but at the end of my third week he asked me to his rooms after hall for "a glass of port." I had done this once before and there had been other young

Christians present, but this time I found myself alone with him in his smelly, ill-lit rooms. I sat down on the sofa. He poured me a glass of his port and then settled himself on an armchair. He talked to me of his friendship with my father—of how they had been so young—too young and immature for their friendship to develop into fulfillment. How delighted he was, he said, to see my father again in me. How much he hoped that the friendship might be continued into the next generation.

He rose and filled my glass and then filled his own. The alcohol had had no effect on me, but it put blotches into his face and a heavy look into his eyes. He returned to his chair and continued to talk about human friendship, full and entire, of the mind and of the body. . . .

He rose and filled his glass for a third time—mine was still full—and after ridding himself of the decanter came and sat down beside me and, with passion obscuring the meaning of a sentence involving Christ, friendship and Christian friendship, lunged at my groin and drew my hand toward the same area of his body.

I was no fool when it came to the antics of faggots and so I stood up and left, with my host and moral tutor weeping, apologizing and drunk on the floor. But however experienced I might have been in dealing with such a situation, my abhorrence remained strong, and this incident not only confirmed my contempt for the Church of England but led to a repugnance for the brick buildings of Selwyn College. I now went there as little as I could.

Indeed there was little I liked about my life at Cambridge except the poker games and perhaps the city itself, and as the term proceeded my behavior came to reflect these preferences. After the end of a game, at three or four in the morning, I would climb out of the college where it had been held, walk back to my lodgings and sleep until eleven or twelve the next day. I had bribed my landlady not to report me, and to seal her complicity she would make me a pot of tea whenever

I chose to rise. I would drink it, read the morning paper, work a little to prepare some semblance of a weekly essay and then walk down into the town again to have lunch with Eric and exchange accounts of the previous evening's poker games.

In the afternoon, if it was fine, I would walk along the backs—those flat lawns and gardens bordering the river Cam behind the colleges—which induced in me a calm bordering on happiness. If it was wet I would either work in a library or go to the Fitzwilliam Museum and study the collection, for I retained my love of painting and sculpture and was now able to educate myself more fully in art than I ever did in history, which was my ostensible subject of study.

At half past four or five I would meet Eric and some other poker-playing companions for tea at a small café in Trinity Street, where the evening's games would be arranged.

This pleasant life continued until one day in early December I arrived in Eric's rooms for lunch. He was sitting over his gas fire, and when he turned to greet me I could see that his face was unusually pale and could tell from his voice that his nose was congested. Since he then told me that his head and limbs all ached I told him that he obviously had influenza and had better go to bed.

"Can't, dear boy," he said.

"Why not?" I asked. "I'll call a doctor."

"No, please don't."

I shrugged my shoulders. "You'll get pneumonia," I said.

Eric now went whiter still, for he was a hypochondriac. "Why," he said—not to me, but to the heavens—"why does this have to happen today of all days?"

"What's wrong with today?"

"It's tonight, dear boy, tonight. I'm on to the really big boys. Billy Cade's asked me to play at Magdalene."

"Who's Billy Cade?"

"Billy Cade? My dear Hilary, you must know who Billy Cade is."

"I'm afraid I don't."

"Eldest son of Lord Purves? Committee member of the Pitt Club? Need I say more?"

"My dear Eric," I said, "my congratulations." (I had taken to speaking to Eric in his own florid style.)

Eric gave a shrug of mock modesty and returned to face the fire. "It's nothing, dear boy, it's nothing," he said through his cold.

"But how can you play with a fever?" I asked.

"I don't know, but I must. If I don't go tonight, I won't get asked again."

"If you do go, you'll give them all flu and certainly won't get asked again."

Eric did not reply to this. His silence was a sign that he could not refute me. I went into his kitchen to see if he had anything to drink and to let the idea that had formed in my mind stew for a while. I found some sherry and took it back into his living room with two glasses.

"I'll go, if you like," I said.

Reluctantly, as I sipped his sherry, Eric agreed to let me go in his place—"But only this once, dear boy, only this once."

The rooms of Billy Cade were not unfamiliar to me, since their atmosphere approached that of the small drawing room at Lasterby Hall. They were paneled—which started them at an advantage to the rooms of most other undergraduates —but William Cade had brought certain furnishings with him: a leather sofa, an armchair, two oil paintings of sporting scenes, a number of prints, a photograph of his parents in their Coronation robes in a silver frame and a corner cupboard for his glasses and decanters.

I had never met Billy Cade before, nor the two others who were to play, but again their type was familiar. All three were wearing crumpled smoking jackets—but then so was I, because Eric had discovered what the form was in games of this sort and had lent me the costume he had so carefully prepared for himself.

Billy and his friends seemed unconcerned that I had arrived in Eric's place. They offered me a glass of port, which I accepted, and talked a little among themselves and then sat down at the card table drawn up in front of the fire.

Billy Cade eyed me. "We play for five-pound stakes," he said.

"Fine," I said.

"With no limit."

"Of course not."

"How much would you like?" He opened a leather box which lay on the table. It was filled with ivory disks each with £5 engraved on it.

"Give me . . . two hundred." I succeeded, I believe, in sounding casual, though this sum represented rather more than I had in my bank.

Billy Cade drew out forty of the ivory chips and pushed them over toward me. The two others took out only twenty each. Billy took out thirty for himself.

The game started. I played cautiously and lost my ante on five or six succeeding hands. I then bet on two pairs and won their antes only, because no one had bet against me.

The game went on unadventurously like this for an hour. At one point Billy and one of the others bet against each other, and the friend, having lost steadily before, was forced to take out another twenty chips. Billy won the round—more than a hundred pounds—and the friend took out yet another twenty chips. There followed two more cautious hands; then I won around seventy pounds on a full house.

At this point we changed the game to stud poker: one card down, the rest up, no second deal and betting on each card. I won on a pair of tens showing and a third ten concealed. I now had more than fifty chips in front of me. I lost ten of them in the next two hands, just one chip on each card to stay in the game. The second friend had had to draw out more money; only Billy was winning.

At this point I saw that my money might be milked away if I had half a dozen mediocre hands, and since the second and third cards of the hand I was playing at that moment were both hearts I decided to go for a flush. It was impossible, of course, that I could have one, since my first card had been a ten of clubs—but they were not to know that. I thus raised on the third card to twenty-five pounds and on the fourth, also a heart, put on another twenty-five. All the players matched me; thus there were now two hundred and forty pounds out in front.

My fifth card was also a heart. The other three players glanced at me; I felt that my face was flushed. Billy, next to the dealer, opened with a single chip, though neither his hand nor the other three could do better than three of a kind. I followed with twenty chips, a hundred pounds. My only chance was to frighten the others out. I succeeded with the next two players, but when it came to Billy he paid in ninety-five to see me and then raised me by another hundred.

I should at this moment have cut my losses; he was betting heavily that my flush was a bluff and could clearly afford such perversity. I should have dropped out but I was at one and the same time confused and angry—confused at the size of the stake and angry that this sneering Etonian should be so sure that my hidden card was not a heart. Thus I bought more chips and met his hundred and raised him by two hundred. At this point he hesitated but then in his turn bought more chips. I believe that if he had raised me I should still have gone on, but from caution or, more likely, condescension, he put in only two hundred pounds to see me. There was thus one thousand and fifty pounds on the table, of which four hundred and sixty had come from me, and I had now to turn up my ten of clubs and see it all pass into the hands of Billy Cade.

No one said anything. One of the friends gave a short laugh, but the rest of us were silent. We went on to the next hand. I still had twelve chips left and I played carefully with them for the next hour or so, which was as long as our game lasted. When we broke up I had eight chips—that is to say, I had lost not only my original two hundred pounds but two hundred and twenty pounds on top of that.

Billy was the only one who had won; the other two, after counting their remaining chips, drew out their checkbooks and so I drew out mine. They wrote in theirs; I looked at Billy.

"How . . . " I began.

"Four hundred and twenty pounds," he said.

"I know. How should I make it out?"

"William Cade will do."

I wrote out a check for four hundred and twenty pounds to William Cade, knowing quite well that I had only around one hundred and eighty pounds in the bank.

I walked back to my lodgings from Magdalene—a distance of about two miles—and as the damp East Anglian cold entered me so did the despair. My situation was quite comfortable so far as the law was concerned, since gambling debts could not be collected through the courts, so when my bank returned my check to Billy Cade there would be nothing he could do about it. It was, however, a debt of honor. For myself, I would happily stand dishonored in the eyes of those Magdalene swells, but my dishonor would be shared by Eric, who had sent me in his place. It would finish me in poker-playing circles but it might also finish him—unless he paid my debt, but that I dared not ask him to do. Now that he had reached the fringe of high stakes and high society, his "capital" was most precious to him. I felt that he would never forgive me if I deprived him of it, and his animosity—the animosity of my only friend—was not something that I could contemplate.

I took off the clothes he had lent me—carefully folding them—and went to bed. I hardly slept at first and only dozed toward dawn. When I awoke, and as I drank my tea, I was still in a state of nervous panic.

That morning I went down to Caius College to return Eric's clothes to him. He was in bed when I went in—his influenza as bad as ever—but he raised himself up on an elbow and, after thanking me for returning his jacket, asked me how the game had gone.

[*112*]

"All right," I said.

"Did you win?" he asked.

"About even."

"That was lucky." He lay back on his bed. "I was worried."

If he had been less ill he might have noticed my dissimulation.

"It was a risk sending you," he said. "They're a different kettle of fish, those chaps. . . . They've got capital; you need capital to beat them. They'll raise you to heaven just to amuse themselves."

"No, well, you needn't have worried," I said.

"Good," he said, sighing. Then, "Did they talk about another game?"

"No," I said.

"I'll go round and see Billy Cade when I'm better," Eric said.

I asked him if there was anything he wanted. He said that there was not so I left.

I had made up my mind either to get the money or to leave Cambridge. It had struck me as a simple choice. I could not let my check bounce and then remain to see Eric's face, day in, day out, whether he forgave me for what I had done or not.

Quite calmly I made a list of every possible source from which I might obtain two hundred and forty pounds. I knew that the bank would not lend it to me; I knew that my father would not, even if he could. My mother's savings did not exceed the usual fifteen pounds. If my father's friend, my moral tutor, had the money, he would probably lend it only in exchange for services rendered. There remained only one other possibility.

I walked down from Caius to Trinity and asked at the porter's lodge for the rooms of Mr. Metherall. I was directed to them, across the Great Court toward the river, and I walked in their direction. As I passed through the passage which exists in all colleges, with the kitchens on one side and the hall on the other, I met Mark passing the other way.

"Mark," I said at once, in case he might decide not to recognize me.

He stopped with a look of surprise. "Hello, Hilary," he said. "What are you doing here?"

"I came to see you."

"I was just off to a lecture."

"It's about something specific," I said, "and it's quite important."

His amiable eyes brightened a little as if something specific and quite important was more interesting than what he was used to from me. "All right," he said. "Let's go back to my rooms."

We did so. He did not put his arm around me but hovered in a friendly way and asked after my mother and father. He also said what a pity it was that we had not seen more of each other that summer. "We were up in Scotland most of the time," he said.

As we climbed the stairs to his rooms, I looked down at his face. It had lost some of its soft plumpness and now expressed a more forthright personality.

"Are you liking Cambridge?" he asked me as we entered his rooms.

"Yes," I said.

"So do I."

He lit his gas fire and then stood with his back to it with his hands in his pockets. "Have a drink?" he said.

"No, thanks."

"What's up, then?"

"I wondered," I said, "whether you could lend me some money."

He blushed very deeply and suddenly. "I don't really do that sort of thing," he said.

"It'd be until the start of next term," I said. "Around two hundred pounds."

Something suddenly occurred to him. "It wasn't you . . . I mean, did you play poker with Billy Cade last night?"

"Yes."

"You were a fool to try and bluff him."

"I know."

There was a pause. Mark looked at his watch. "I think I might still go to that lecture," he said.

"Can't you lend me the money?"

"I could but I don't think I will."

"There's no other way I can get it."

"You borrow from banks and from Jews, Hilary. Not from your friends."

At this I almost cried and Mark, perhaps seeing it, turned and knelt to turn out the gas fire. I waited, my hands behind my back, the fingers of one hand clutching at the fingers of the other.

He stood up. "Come on," he said. He held his door open and I walked out in front of him. We walked in silence to the gates of his college.

"Don't you ever go to lectures?" he asked as we stood for a moment in Trinity Street.

"Sometimes," I said.

We then walked off in opposite directions, and I left for London that afternoon with all my belongings in two suitcases and all my money in my pocket.

In leaving Cambridge I left everything; it was as if I had stepped out of my own skin. Above all I had abandoned my identity—as undergraduate and rector's son—and exchanged it for the anonymity of one among ten million rootless, friendless urban vermin scurrying around the vast acreage of somber streets. I lived in rented rooms in Camden Town, then in Chelsea, then in Fulham, and took odd jobs: delivering for one store, packing for another. I made no friends, largely from choice; I had no wish to befriend the other packers and delivery boys for I loathed poverty and did not want to console myself for my present plight with the simple pleasures of a pint in the pub with junior representatives of the lumpen proletariat. Nor was I unhappy to be alone, for the effect of my solitude was to fuse my rancor and bitterness into a vengeful nihilism—and nihilism is a mood that can be enjoyed. Like some great love, it became the inspiration of my life. Without it I should certainly have gone under.

I had written to my mother that I had left Cambridge and come to London to "study art," but it was never my intention to do that or to enter any profession. My acrimonious frame of mind was such that the idea of becoming a doctor, a lawyer or an accountant disgusted me. I would not take advantage of a society which put Mark Metherall, Alexander Amotherby and Billy Cade at the top, even if it offered me a place only a few rungs farther down; nor, on the other hand, did I see myself working for wages for the rest of my life.

I therefore decided to become a criminal—or, more specifically, a burglar. The newspapers were then full of the increase in crime and the fall in the rate of detection, and London was at one and the same time so impersonal yet so bloated with the rich and their possessions that there seemed no outrage in the contemplation of theft. If, in this city, "all men are either carrion or crows," I saw no reason why I should not take my pickings.

I was determined not to start precipitately in my chosen career nor to gamble on good luck. Thus for some weeks I spent my free time in libraries and bookshops and read all that I could find on housebreaking and burglary. Alone in my bed-sitting room I collated the material gathered from these studies and reached certain conclusions. It became clear, for example, that such was the volume of crime that petty theft would draw less attention from the police; that a man who worked alone was less at risk than one who worked in a gang because most cases of detection and arrest followed "tip-offs" from within the criminal fraternity. Skill, speed and planning were the ingredients of success; violence, greed and impetuosity were the most likely causes of failure.

It was difficult to be a criminal without some contact with others—there had to be a fence for the stolen goods—but I thought that if I kept my burglaries on a modest scale the chances of detection were small. After all, many thousands of secondhand goods changed hands each day in London—in the Portobello Road or Petticoat Lane markets—without the seller presenting a certificate of ownership and provenance.

Another precaution which I knew was essential was a cover, for nothing more quickly betrayed a criminal than evidence of an income without an apparent source. I decided therefore that I would, after all, become a "painter," and with what remained of the sum of money that I had brought with me from Cambridge I paid the first month's rent on a studio in Fulham. It was little more than a hut between two houses, but I stocked it with canvases and paint and even put the paint onto the canvases in formless smears somewhat in the style of Jackson Pollock. I was also a painter who experimented with sculpture—in my case, unfinished constructions of glass, wire, metal and wood—for the construction of which many different types of pliers, cutters (of wire and glass), hacksaws and blowtorches were required.

My landlady, who lived in the house next to the studio, came one afternoon to visit me. When I opened the door I was wearing jeans and a shirt covered with paint, and I made the poor woman stand for a good ten minutes looking at my smears and piles of junk. At the end of it she shrugged her shoulders and said that she would never understand modern art.

Four months after my arrival in London I was ready for my first job. I had chosen—almost arbitrarily—a house in Paulton's Square in Chelsea which seemed to be temporarily unoccupied. There were no milk bottles outside the door, but I had watched from a hired van in both the morning and evening and had not seen anyone enter or leave. I had walked past it a dozen times and even rang the doorbell without getting a reply. At night there were no lights, and I thought I could conclude that the owners were away.

There was no sign of an alarm on the outside of the house, and though I could not see the back I felt sure that there would be no closed circuits, pressure pads or direct lines to the police. The house was not grand enough. I therefore waited until ten in the evening on a Saturday night, then parked my van outside the house, waited until the pavement was empty and slipped out of the van and down to the basement door. I rang the bell and waited, studying the entrance. The windows were barred and the door had a Yale lock. There was no reply to the bell, so I took out of my bag a brace with an inch center bit: in less than five minutes I had drilled six holes through the door around the lock. I then punched the lock out onto the floor, put my hand through the hole, opened a bolt underneath where the lock had been and opened the door itself.

If a policeman had walked by during the few minutes when I was doing this I might have been discovered, but the basements of London houses are an instance of poetic justice. Built beneath the level of the ground with little air or light they were considered good enough for the servants who occupied them; now they are good enough for thieves whom they shield from the eyes of passers-by. They muffle any noise that might be made in forcing a window or a door and permit the use of the heaviest tools to cut or bend bars and force locks.

After entering the house, I waited, motionless, for the sound of someone else's movements. After two or three minutes there was still silence so I went into the kitchen, which seemed to have been recently refitted, and opened every drawer and cupboard in search of silver. Unfortunately the owners of this house had French cutlery with wooden handles which was then becoming fashionable—and, to judge from an empty cupboard lined with green baize, had removed any valuable silver in their possession. I took two sugar bowls, wrapped them in tissue paper and dropped them into the canvas bag that was attached to my belt.

The front room on the ground floor was a dining room. Here there were two silver candlesticks on the table—reproduction plate and consequently of little value. There were prints on the walls—scenes of ancient Rome, mostly by Rossini but one by Piranese. I cut out the back of the frame of the Piranese, removed the print, rolled it up and put it in my bag.

The back room seemed to be used as a nursery. There was an old television, worth two or three pounds at most. There were more prints on the stairs—of no value—and a bathroom on the half landing. The drawing room went across the front of the house on the first floor. I stood in the doorway, studying its furnishings by the light of my torch before proceeding into the room. There was always the danger of being seen in front of the windows by a passer-by. I could see at once that there was quite a lot to be taken from this room—bric-a-brac, mostly, but some of it quite valuable. My bread and butter was now to depend upon the passion of the middle classes for covering every available surface in their houses with little knickknacks that they had "picked up" or "bought for a song." If they did not collect them, I could not steal them, nor could I have passed them on. Luckily, however, almost every house had something, ranging from Victorian paperweights and Coronation mugs in the homes of young couples to Maillol bronzes and Henry Moore maquettes in the houses of the very rich. Even the most modern young couple—an architect, say, or an advertising executive—would sin against his functional credo and dot his bare, hard-edged surface with mobiles, stringed figures or pilfered Grecian heads.

The objets d'art in this house in Paulton's Square were perfect for my purposes, neither worthless nor of immense value. There was a dainty array of antique enameled snuffboxes, some nineteenth-century miniatures, a jade ashtray, some pieces of crystal and polished marble, a silver inkstand, a mother-of-pearl tear jar. . . . This is not an exact inventory; there were other things, all of which I wrapped in tissue paper and put into my canvas bag.

The pictures on the wall showed some taste and discrimination in the owner of the house. (I presumed them to be of the husband's choosing while the bric-a-brac belonged to the wife.) There were some watercolors by Jongkind; a horse by Degas, drawn in charcoal; a Vuillard pastel and a watercolor of a nude woman that I took to be a Jules Pascin but was not sure. These were just the sort of thing that I would not be able to pass on—the chances were that they were photographed—but I removed them from their frames all the same, placing tissue paper between each one.

By the time I had finished there was nothing left in the drawing room which was either of a size that I could carry or of worthwhile value. I went up to the next floor: a bathroom, a dressing room and the owners' bedroom. I quickly went through the husband's suits but found nothing in the pockets. Then the wife's dressing table: if she had valuable jewelry, she had removed it. There was, however, a pretty antique brooch and a pearl necklace, both of which I took and put in my pocket. Next, in its own box, I found a small piece of pre-Columbian jewelry which would also be difficult to pass on but which I put in my bag all the same.

There was a small bookcase in the bedroom where the husband, who I gathered was an auctioneer or a gallery director, had an incipient collection of rare books. I could not take them all and did not know enough about them to pick out the most valuable, so I took three or four at random.

Finally I went up to the children's rooms at the top of the house. Like good bourgeois, they had only two, a son and a daughter, the son, so far as I could make out, around fourteen years old and the daughter a year or two older. The boy's room contained nothing except a stamp collection but one without a penny black or anything else of value that I could recognize. I therefore went into the daughter's room and sorted through her jewelry, ornaments and bric-a-brac, emptying her drawers of cardigans, blouses and underclothes and taking anything that might be worth more than a pound or two.

By the time I had finished I had spent more than an hour in the house—an unprofessional length of time—and had chosen more to take away with me than would fit into my bag. I therefore took a suitcase as well, which I found in the room of the daughter. It took me half a minute to load the goods into my van and another quarter of an hour to have them hidden away in my studio. Within a week I had sold all but the most valuable of the things I had stolen and was two hundred and seventy pounds better off.

I was not as yet so free from the moral atmosphere of my upbringing that I did not develop in my own mind an apologia for the profession which I now practiced with increasing regularity and skill. I believed, with Proudhon, that all property was theft; that every man had as much or as little right to what he could take and hold from other men; that the so-called right to private property was an ethic invented by the rich to deter the poor from reclaiming more systematically what the capitalist has stolen in the first place either by paying them too little or by charging them too much.

This is not to say that I had thrown in my lot with the masses. For one thing, they would not want me—my middle-class aroma would have been as repugnant to them as it was to those at the other end of society—and for another, I did not want them. Their need was for general justice; mine was for personal revenge. I wished not to balance the scales but to tip them the other way and see the rich not only disgorge their glut into my pockets but suffer and starve thereafter. For this reason I robbed only private houses, for if I could not ruin their owners by pillaging their houses I could at least make them suffer; whereas the robbing of shops, offices or warehouses, while easy enough, was too impersonal to fulfill my purposes because everything I might steal from such premises would be restored by an insurance company, and the insurance company itself repaid by an adjustment to the general premium. Only by taking what an individual bourgeois prized and loved could I satisfy my loathing for him.

It was by indulging this passion that after six or seven months of successful burglary I had amassed a hoard of objects too valuable to be hawked in the usual way in the streets of Notting Hill or the East End; indeed, my stock of jewelry, snuffboxes, statuettes, reliquaries, teapots, tankards and paintings—including the Pascin and a Courbet—had reached a size when a raid on my studio would have solved the riddle of half a dozen robberies in the West End of London. I therefore decided to extend my outlets and selected for the purpose a fifteenth-century German madonna, about eighteen inches high and carved in alabaster, which I had taken from a house in Hampstead and was worth, from a study of prices at Christie's and Sotheby's, around five or six hundred pounds. I took it around to some antique shops to ask if they were interested in buying it. I dressed for this excursion in a check tweed suit and behaved like a man who has recently set up in the antique trade. I also adopted my usual slight disguise—greased-down hair, horn-rimmed spectacles and small deposits of eye shadow to add lines to my face.

The statue was one of the most recent things I had stolen and, to judge from the pedantic neatness of the house from which it was taken, likely to have been photographed by the owner or his insurance company and the photograph circulated to dealers. Thus if I was offered anything like its value but told to come back, or if the dealer retired from behind his counter for more than a minute—and this happened with the first half dozen I tried—I knew that the shop was honest and thus unsuitable for my purposes.

My hope was for an immediate offer of a quarter of its value with no disappearances but the immediate presentation of used five-pound notes, for this would be a sure sign that I had found a fence who could handle it. On the second day of my attempts in this direction I went to the shops around Westbourne Grove—an area which looks dishonest and smells of crime—and chose a dingy business on the Ledbury Road for my first attempt. In its window was displayed a wooden figure of a saint, quite clearly carved a few months ago and artificially aged with acid.

Encouraged by this fake, I went in. A thin-faced man looked up from the counter to greet me. "Can I help you?" he asked.

"That statue," I said. "The one in the window."

"Yes?"

"What . . . well, what sort of date is it?"

"Well, sir," he said, standing and coming toward me, "I'm afraid we can't be absolutely sure, but we place it somewhere between 1520 and 1530."

"Indeed," I said.

"We know that it's an authentic Riemenschneider," he said.

"And how much are you asking for it?"

He looked at me uneasily. "Are you in the trade?"

"Yes."

"I thought so. . . . Well, we'd put a trade price of seven hundred and forty pounds on it."

"I see," I said. "And would you . . ."—I took my canvas bag from under my arm—"I was wondering if you might take this . . . in part exchange, as it were?"

I took out my madonna and unwrapped the cloth in which it was swathed. He looked at it, then at me—sharply—then at the statue again. He must have recognized it immediately.

"It's certainly very fine," he said, dropping his dealer's drawl and reverting to a kind of cockney.

"It saddens me to have to sell it," I said.

He laughed. "Of course it would be hard to offer much for an immediate sale."

"I'm afraid I'm only interested in an immediate sale."

"Of course, of course," he said. "But without time to find a buyer . . ."

I said nothing.

"Would you wait a moment, please, while I consult my partner?" he said. "If you'd just wait a moment."

He turned and went through a door into the back of the shop. I started to wrap up the madonna again, ready to leave, but almost at once he reappeared with a squat, jovial Persian whom I recognized at once as Qazvini.

"My God," he said, "it's Hilary." And with the oriental flourish I had almost forgotten, he stepped forward, embraced me and kissed me on both cheeks.

The face of the Dickensian rascal behind him twisted with surprise. "So you know him, you know him?" he kept repeating.

"Know him?" said Qazvini. "Why . . . why, he's my brother." He embraced me again.

His partner looked unconvinced since Qazvini was short and dark with black hair while I was tall and almost fair; nor had I any trace of Qazvini's Persian accent. He could hardly deny, however, that we were somehow related so he simply said, "What about the statue?"

"The statue, of course," said Qazvini. He turned to me. "My dear boy, you're mad. There's a photograph of that madonna in every shop in London."

"I know," I said. "I was looking . . . well, for a fence."

Qazvini laughed. "I should have known that you'd turn up in the same business sooner or later."

He led me into the room at the back of the shop while his partner remained in the front. There, beside an armchair, he had a pot of Turkish coffee—the same copper pot, I believe, which he had in his study at Newton—and from it he filled a cup and gave it to me.

"Is this your shop?" I asked.

He glanced at the door through which we had come, then held out his hand, opened his fingers and wobbled them. "We're sort of in partnership," he said. "But now you tell me, right from the start, what you've been doing since you left Newton . . . or rather, since you failed to return."

"Since I left . . . well, that's quite a long time ago. I took a job in Switzerland and then went up to Cambridge . . . but I couldn't take it there so I came here and . . . well, as you can see . . ." I glanced down at the bag containing the madonna.

"Are you on your own?"

"Yes."

Qazvini sipped his coffee and grinned at me. "If you hadn't walked in, how would we ever have found you?"

I shrugged my shoulders. "I didn't realize that you were still in England."

"I go back from time to time . . . import-export, you know." He laughed and I laughed with him, the first time for months that I had laughed—almost the first time since I had last laughed with Qazvini.

"What's happened to the others?" I asked. "Caspar and Johnny?"

"They're around . . . in fact, you must come back and see them."

"You're still in touch with them?"

"Indeed I am. We all live in the same house."

"Have you been together since school?"

"More or less."

I sipped my coffee. "I like your mustache," I said.

"Do you?" He smiled and stroked this new decoration to his round face.

I relapsed at once into the friendship with Qazvini I had felt during the bad years at Newton, and the same occurred when I met Caspar Abbot and Johnny Hume with Qazvini that evening. It may seem improbable that someone who had been without friends for two years should have ever had any,

[*125*]

and more improbable in view of the fact that since then I have made no other friends of the same sex. The truth is that while I am not especially open or accessible, we had found ourselves at Newton in the same wretched situation over a number of years, and like veterans of the trenches we had forged bonds in our common misery which were never broken. It is my belief that all friendship is superficial which is not based on some common experience—and the larger the experience, the greater the friendship. Indeed there is a feeling among those who have known great suffering or great joy that they can only be appreciated and understood by those who have shared their experience.

I had made the mistake, upon leaving Newton, of thinking that my friends there would pass with that passage of my life. I had thus never thought to seek them out again. I now realized that childhood, rather than preparing one for life, is one's life in its essence and that years of maturity would be spent in blowing on its embers until finally there was only ash.

I have given a brief description of Qazvini's physical appearance, saying that he was squat and jovial. His squatness, however, did not make him unattractive nor his joviality exclude cunning. He was always sensitive to the expectations of others and, as if to fulfill them, played the role of an Oriental with slight exaggeration. He was indulgent and loved food, women and sweetmeats. He smoked Turkish cigarettes, drank Turkish coffee and sat on large cushions.

His father was a civil servant in Iran. So far as I could make out, he was corrupt and made millions in bribes and blackmail. Whether to keep his son in safety or from admiration of our system, he had determined to give him an English public school education. Somehow he had been misinformed, and thinking that Newton was Eton or Harrow, he had sent Qazvini there.

Qazvini had hated it as much as the rest of us but when it was over was sufficiently anglicized to want to remain in

England. Under the pretext of studying law, he had done so. His father was happy to pay for the son to pursue such a respectable profession and did not discover until much later that his son was really as criminal as he was.

Qazvini's specialty lay in making and selling fake antiques abroad—to Germans, Italians or Libyans. At the time I met him he had just started to extend his interests to cover stolen goods, a trade of quite a different sort but complementary to the other. Through a network of friends and cousins he seemed to have contacts all over the world, above all in those countries like Lebanon and Venezuela where collectors of works of art had few scruples about the provenance of their acquisitions.

He laughed easily and sat back at every opportunity in a way I envied because I could never do it myself.

In the house in Blenheim Crescent which he shared with Caspar and Johnny, he had the largest room, which was natural enough because he paid the rent. The room was thickly furnished with carpets and hangings and looked like the inside of a bazaar. He never slept alone but the girls were never introduced to his friends—not from pudeur or possessiveness but because Qazvini considered their company an unnecessary intrusion into our comradeship. I envied him his nonchalance in this respect as much as I envied him his easy nature but was led to believe that it was usual for a Moslem. "Women have no souls," Qazvini would say, "and in the order of creation they come lower than cows. Why then should we treat them better than we treat cows?"

This was an attitude I admired and adopted as my own.

Johnny Hume was quite different from Qazvini. He came from Nottingham, where his father manufactured oil dipsticks and mattress springs. Like most high-minded sons of small capitalists, Johnny was a socialist. His thin face on its long neck looked with sincerity into a noble future. He too, however, had been crippled by the experience of Newton and seemed unable to do more about the socialism he believed in

[127]

than talk about it to his old school friends and propose schemes for the redistribution of our ill-gotten gains.

He had inherited from his father a practicality which was most useful in the enactment of more complicated crimes. When we started, as we now did, to work as a group, he came with me to steal the goods that Qazvini would later dispose of. He had done little before I met him and was good only at breaking and entering, though he was able to disarm the most complex alarm and deterrent devices, such as infrared beams or a Chubb R. F. Volurada. It was then up to me to decide which objects were to be taken.

The last of the group with whom I lived in Qazvini's house was Caspar Abbot. More than any of the others, he had changed since I had known him at school. There had always been a delinquent look in his eyes, and now the impression had spread to his whole appearance and demeanor. His hair had grown down to his shoulders—and being fine and dirty, it followed the shape of his skull like a rat's skin. His eyes never met anyone else's, not even those of us, his friends, who stood by him. His clothes were filthy and without any style; he wore what was at hand when the clothes on his back disintegrated or were carried off by the vermin which inhabited them.

While we all tolerated Caspar for the sake of the old days, none of us liked what he got up to. I have to concede that his criminality shared some common inspiration with mine— the difference being that while I indulged a detestation for the rich, he was possessed by a general misanthropy, a spirit of perversity which took delight in any harm that could be done to any human being outside our group.

He was indifferent to comfort, possessions or material gain, and he was equally indifferent to the comfort, possessions and material conditions of others. Thus he found robbery uninteresting—at best an excuse for winding or kicking someone weaker or less agile than he was. His specialty, though I knew little about it, was blackmail, which he liked not for the pay-off but for the suffering it caused his victims.

His only pleasure was pederasty, and for this he would sacrifice the squalor of his appearance. Every six months or so he would cut and wash his hair, buy six clean shirts and a gray suit and take up some post as tutor to a boy in the country whose parents were afraid he would not pass Common Entrance into a public school.

It was no surprise to me that the pretensions of middle-class parents blinded them to the extent that they would admit someone so evidently unwholesome as Caspar to their homes, and it was just punishment for the parents, if not for their child, that the tutor would leave their boy a little cleverer and totally corrupt.

At first I would not believe the stories of these escapades which Caspar told us upon his return, but one should never underestimate the skill of a degenerate bent on seduction, and soon enough the tales would be shown to be true by the appearance at Blenheim Crescent of the thirteen- or fourteen-year-old boys, on their way from country home to boarding school, for a few hours of affection and debauchery with Caspar in the basement.

Qazvini and Johnny were as disgusted as I was by these activities of Caspar, but we stood by him and permitted them because he was one of us.

It was some weeks after meeting my school friends again before I moved into their house. I did so then—taking the top floor—because I found I was spending most of my time there anyway. With the basement, the house had five floors; we shared the ground floor—ate there and talked to each other—and then had two rooms each where we left each other alone. I kept on my studio in Fulham and went there every so often to paint on some canvases and destroy others. I had a party there for Caspar, Johnny and Qazvini to celebrate my twentieth birthday, and at this party it was decided

[*129*]

that Qazvini should use one of his outlets, the Persepolis Gallery in Cork Street, to deal in my art.

The day after this I went to York and had lunch with my mother at the Station Hotel. It was the first time that I had seen her for two years. My father was not present and he was not mentioned; nor were the Metheralls. I could tell from the way my mother looked at me that my prosperous appearance and confident manner impressed her. She asked me why I had not told her that I was such a success as a painter. "We don't hear about these things up here," she said.

I smiled and answered that I would send her a gouache to hang in the rectory.

"Oh, do, Hilary," she said. "I'd love that."

After lunch I took a train back to London. She came onto the platform with me. "I do wish you'd come home sometime," she said. "I know you've no reason to, but I do wish you would."

I did not answer but kissed her and left; on the train I reflected on how glad I was to return to the filthy air and cluttered streets of London.

7

One day in the spring of 1963 Qazvini told me that he had made contact with a collector in Hong Kong who would like to buy anything we could lay our hands on of the T'ang dynasty and would pay two thirds of the market price. He was aware, of course, of our probable sources and even suggested himself certain pieces belonging to a Mr. James Patterson who lived in Richmond.

Johnny was at that time distracted by his political activities, and I therefore decided to take this on myself. I made the usual preparations, studying the house from front and back and watching it for the movements of its inhabitants.

Mr. Patterson seemed to leave the house every morning at nine; his Mercedes was brought to the door by a chauffeur who did not live in the house. Later three children were taken to school in a Renault, either by a tall, blond woman of around thirty whom I took to be Mrs. Patterson or by a younger woman, a Dutch or German *au pair*. Just after that—on a weekday—a cleaning woman would arrive. She would leave around lunchtime; so, occasionally, would Mrs. Patterson. The lunch hour might have been the time to enter the house, but the *au pair* was usually there. Also the house, though set back from the street, faced other houses and had no basement.

At the back it went down to the river, and I decided that it might be easiest to approach it by boat—but for that I would need the cover of darkness. The only protection against burglary seemed to be a Banham alarm, most probably fitted to a direct line to Scotland Yard. I knew how to deal with these, however, but wanted a night when the house was empty because I might have to make some noise removing the glass or smashing the frames of a window.

I was entitled to expect the entire family to go away for a weekend and sure enough, one Friday, the chauffeur put two suitcases into the Mercedes when he came to fetch Mr. Patterson in the morning, and in the afternoon the children were pushed into the Renault with another suitcase and driven away by the *au pair*. Mrs. Patterson left the house around six, presumably to join her husband at his office and drive straight from there to the country. By ten they had not returned, so I drove the van to a position by the river where I had prepared a boat and set out onto the river.

Navigation in the darkness was more difficult than I had anticipated but I had not far to go and had studied the landing facilities in daylight. At around half past ten I was up into the garden with my equipment and by a quarter to eleven I was in the house.

I was almost certainly the only person there. An empty

house has a particular atmosphere which was almost enough to convince me, but—still wary of gambling—I checked all the same by going into every room. This survey also informed me that all the T'ang pieces were to be found in the drawing room and dining room, which were both on the ground floor.

I set about removing them immediately, for though I was reasonably sure that the house would now be empty for the weekend I nevertheless disliked the place and wanted to leave it as soon as I could. There was something unpleasantly incongruous about the beautiful statuary and vases in the home of what appeared to be a vulgarian. The house had clearly been decorated by a professional—I could tell from the impersonal taste—but every now and then there were such objects as a mink-covered ice bucket which betrayed to me the taste of crude, new money. There was also a study littered with expensive toys—tape recorders and a high-fidelity gramophone with gigantic speakers boxed in teak. There were telephones everywhere: two lines in the study and four extensions in the drawing room alone.

By the time I had finished in the drawing room and dining room I had in the bag a figure of a lady, a Hsing-yao white ewer, a glazed oviform pottery jar, a set of five standing figures of musicians, a glazed pottery figure of a Fereghan horse and a blue glazed ewer—all T'ang—and a bronze figure of a horse which was Chou dynasty. The market value for these pieces was around thirty thousand pounds; our profit therefore would be twenty.

I might have contented myself with this—and indeed had no intention of bothering with the Scandinavian silver or worthless modern paintings on the walls—but I did want to take a look around the lair of someone as apparently distasteful as Mr. Patterson. I therefore left my bag and tools by the window through which I had entered and climbed to the children's rooms at the top of the house.

As I had previously observed, the children were all under

ten and all boys. It did not surprise me—given the character of the parents as betrayed by their house—that the rooms were characterless and empty. I therefore left their few possessions, went down and entered the parents' bedroom and was about to open the drawers of the wife's dressing table when I heard the front door being slammed shut.

There was a pause; then the light was switched on in the hall. I went quickly to the door of the bedroom and looked over the banisters. There I saw Mrs. Patterson standing by the door removing her coat. I stepped back so that she could not see me and wondered what to do, but as I did so she switched on the light in the landing where I stood. With no time to form a plan—and worrying more about the discovery of my tools and the Chinese pottery than about the discovery of myself—I went back into the bedroom. As soon as I had done so I realized that it was the worst course of action to have taken in the circumstances, for if she was coming up the stairs the chances were that she was coming to her bedroom. I looked into the bathroom which led off the bedroom but saw that it had no place to hide nor a window through which I could escape. I had just time to draw the curtains of the bedroom window and stand behind them before she entered the room. My reason for standing there was so as to be able to examine the chances of escape through that window, but again it was quite clear that it would not be possible. The height was not so great, but there was no gutter or trellis to aid a descent and the paved terrace below would have given me at least a broken ankle if I had jumped.

Moreover the noise I would have made would have alerted her, for I could hear her moving about the room. My only chance, I decided, was to remain where I was; and if she discovered me—say by coming to open the window—I could knock her on the head or tie her up, both things I had never done before but was quite prepared to try.

There was an opening of a quarter of an inch between the two curtains through which I now watched Mrs. Patterson.

I was immediately optimistic because she had removed her necklace and was cleaning her face. I imagined that she would soon be in bed and asleep. I worried only that the husband might be following her and reach the bedroom before I could escape. It would not be so easy to overpower him; my only chance would be to run for it.

Mrs. Patterson was tall, as I have said, and more beautiful than I had thought her when watching the house from my van. She was thin but not scraggy with good bones in her face and long legs. What I noticed at once about her as she walked to and fro in her bedroom was the vulgar quality of her attractiveness. There was nothing gracious or patrician about her and yet her appearance was unmistakably English.

She went into the bathroom but left the door open, so I could not take the opportunity to escape. When she returned she was half undressed; she wore a shift but had taken off her stockings. Before removing any more of her clothes, however she crossed to a chest of drawers beside the bed and removed some object from the top left-hand drawer. I could not at first see what it was that she had in her hand. She bent over it, there at the chest of drawers, and blew on it as if warming it. Then I heard a click like that made by the cocking of a pistol and saw as she turned that it was indeed a pistol—or, rather, a revolver—that she held in her hand. I immediately assumed that she had discovered my presence and was about to shoot me—or make me her prisoner while she called the police. Certainly she walked toward the window but did not look at it and, when level with the bed, fell onto it and lay there, breathing heavily, the gun in her hand by her side.

In a moment she moved her legs apart and proceeded to make use of the revolver—assisted by her other hand—in a manner that I could never have imagined and would never have believed had I not seen it for myself. I was immediately reminded of Frau Kohner and her dogs and decided that women, though perhaps without souls, were as ingenious as they were odd. I had to concede to Mrs. Patterson that her gun, being inanimate, was a good deal more obedient to her desires than had been the dogs of Frau Kohner, and its efficacy more pronounced, for within seconds it had her gasping and writhing and quite soon had completed her purpose.

What it had not done, and could not do, was complete mine —for in watching Mrs. Patterson on her bed I had felt re-emerge in my body specific desires which, since the days with Frau Kohner, I had kept so controlled that I had thought them extinct. I had since then seen many pretty women in the streets, in films or in magazines, but their figures and faces had left me more or less unmoved. Mrs. Patterson, on the other hand, had presented an entire tableau which had skittled my inhibitions, and quite forgetting my situation I emerged from behind the curtains and was on top of her before she could lift her head in surprise.

Not that she did lift her head in surprise. She gave a kind of interrogatory murmur, blinked, stared into my face, then closed her eyes and entered into the spirit of what I was doing—though it did not escape my notice that judging from her reactions I was considerably less efficacious than the revolver had been, the revolver which she still held in her hand.

Later she pointed it at me. "Who the hell are you?" she asked.

I sat up. "Your lover," I said.

"Fuck you."

"What?"

"Are you paid for this sort of thing?"

"No."

"James hired you. . . . He did, didn't he?"

"Your husband?" I laughed. "Does he normally hire people for this sort of thing?"

"He'll do anything." She hesitated. "There's no reason why I shouldn't shoot you, though, is there? If I said you'd raped me?"

"There's no reason, no, except that the gun isn't loaded."

"Of course it's loaded."

For some reason I had assumed it was not. "Then wasn't all that . . . dangerous?"

She blushed. "Were you watching? Yes, of course you were. Well he can't divorce me for that."

"No."

"But he can for you, I suppose."

"Is he . . . by the way . . . on his way home?"

"No."

"Are you sure?"

"He's gone with the children."

I nodded and considered her—first of all her appearance where she sat half naked, looking alternately at me and at her toes; then her accent which, like Eliza Doolittle's, was too good to be true.

"Are you sure he didn't hire you?" she said.

"I'm sure."

"I'm sure he does hire people to spy on me."

"Why? Does he want to divorce you?"

She shrugged her shoulders. "I suppose he couldn't have done . . . well, tonight. He couldn't have hired you tonight because he thought I was going to be with him."

"Why aren't you?"

"We had a quarrel . . . oh, we're always quarreling. Anyway, I hate the country."

"So do I."

Her eyes swung off her toes and onto my face. "Who the hell are you, anyway?"

"I was robbing your house. You interrupted me."

"Well, don't take anything of mine."

"It was . . . well, the Chinese stuff."

She smiled. "That, yes. He'll be furious."

"Hasn't he insured it?"

"Yes, of course. But it's his pride and joy. He'd rather you stole me than his beloved vases." She smiled again. "I suppose you have, in a way, stolen me."

We now introduced ourselves. I called myself Brian Brown and she told me that her first name was Pamela. "It's a horrible name so don't make it worse by calling me Pam." This was something she must have said to everyone because she spoke in a dead, automatic tone of voice.

"All right," I said. "I'll call you Pamela."

She sat up. "I'll go down and make some tea."

"I'll come too," I said.

"No. Wait here."

She put on her dressing gown and disappeared. It was a measure of how much I already trusted her that I lay back on the bed and closed my eyes. It was the first gamble I had taken since the poker game in Cambridge, but there are occasions when one concedes that deceit of a certain quality deserves to be taken as truth, and such is the intimacy established by making love that I could not believe that she would either call the police or leave the house.

In ten minutes she returned with a tray on which were placed, on fine embroidered mats, a teapot with a floral design, matching cups, milk jug, a sugar bowl and a hot water jug. The sugar was in lumps and there were tongs for placing it in the cup.

I cannot, even now, explain why, but I was immensely moved by the sight of this daintiness. It brought me near to tears.

"Let's get into bed," she said. "I love having tea in bed. It's *ever so* cosy." She blushed. "It's awfully nice, don't you think?"

This was the only occasion upon which she made a mistake of this kind. She put the tray on the bedside table and got in beside me.

"The only thing is, it makes you want to go to the loo in the middle of the night."

She poured me out a cup of tea and I asked for one lump of sugar, though I never normally took any, to see if she would use the tongs. She did.

She poured herself out a cup but did not drink it. "Would you mind," she asked, "if I made a telephone call?"

"Not at all," I said.

"It's not to the police," she said. "I thought you might think it was if I rang up from downstairs."

"Why didn't you?"

She looked at me and smiled. "Oh, you're quite attractive, you know. I'd hate to see you languish in prison." She picked up the telephone.

"Who are you ringing, then?" I asked as she dialed.

"Just James."

I sat quietly while she spoke to her husband. "Did you get down all right? . . . Yes. . . . Are the children asleep? . . . Yes. . . . I'm sorry. . . . Yes. . . . Come back tomorrow. . . . Yes, of course I do. . . . A bit lonely. . . . Good night."

She put down the receiver and started to drink her tea.

"I hope he won't be back too early tomorrow," I said.

"Oh, no," she said, smiling. "He's been dying to sleep with Helga for ages. Now's his chance."

Before we went to sleep we made love again. My rival, the revolver, was back in her husband's sock drawer, but I still felt inadequate in its place. The next morning she made me breakfast and served it as daintily as she had the tea the night before. At nine I left by the garden door with all my tools and my bag full of chinoiserie. She helped me down into the boat and then returned to the house to telephone the police.

Besides living a modest, almost monkish existence, I always kept exact accounts of what I gained from crime and invested my profits—ostensibly those from painting—so that my money should never be idle. In my accounts for the financial year ending 5 April 1963, my profits from burglary continued to show an increase; and though the market was unsteady throughout that period, my investments on the whole did well. I was already quite a rich man, though only twenty-four years old, but I continued to live in a humble, unpretentious style both from choice and for fear of attracting too much attention.

My only extravagances were some well-cut suits to wear when I met Pamela Patterson for lunch at Wilton's or the Ritz. It was to take me only a short time to discover that she loathed to meet anywhere more ordinary—and it is some indication of what I came to feel for her that I was prepared to sit and eat in these nests of plutocratic worms. Having had little experience of love, I did not recognize its symptoms until I was possessed by it. I thought at first that it would merely be pleasant to see her again and so telephoned, quite prepared to ring off if her husband answered, as I had done so often before for different reasons. She answered, however, and reluctantly agreed to meet me for lunch, "After all," she said, "I've nothing better to do."

I thought this a cool response—in view of what had occurred when we had last seen each other—but it is a symptom of love that even the most unpleasant qualities become objects of one's passion. Indeed it is often those which fire the love, for, when thinking back about it, I dated mine from the sight of those dainty mats and sugar tongs.

When I met Pamela for the first time after our accidental encounter, she behaved as if we had never met before. I had to woo her all over again and might well have been too shy and unsure of myself to do so had I not possessed the memory of how she had once behaved toward me. I would occasionally allude to that evening, which would bring a blush to her otherwise expressionless face. "Oh, that . . ." she would say, or, "That. . . . Well, yes . . . it was different."

Our conversation was always continuous so long as we talked about her. Though she would profess interest in other subjects, she could find nothing to say about them; and her ear would be easily distracted when I was talking about anything except her. I was happy, however, that we should do this for she presented me with a riddle: who was she and why did I love her?

The mystery lay in her diction and demeanor, for she had erased all traces leading back to her past with the broom of adopted mannerisms, customs and clothes. The English language has great variety, and none greater than in the vocabulary and vowels of the different classes; but the slow, exact manner in which she spoke betrayed none of her origins, for like an actress she had learned the lines of a daughter of the upper middle classes. She never said *dinner* when she meant *lunch,* or *tea* when she meant *supper.* She would wrestle with the temptation to eat a *pudding,* never a *sweet* or a *dessert;* and when lunch was over, she would wipe her lips with a *napkin,* never with a *serviette.* If she wished to wash or urinate, she would ask for the *lavatory* or *loo,* never the *toilet.*

What gave her away was the delivery of these lines, for their correctness did not give her confidence and she had to reflect before opening her mouth not just on what she said but on how she said it. Her unspoken explanation, as it were, for this slow, halting behavior was enigma. She cultivated an air of mystery, and considering that there was so little to be mysterious about she managed it very well.

In the course of our lunches I plumbed the shallow depths of this mystery, for while hugging her enigma she could not resist talking about herself. The kernel of her personality lay in her origins—as anyone might have guessed—for she came from Slough, one of the more characterless suburbs of London, where her father had been manager of a dry-cleaning store. Why this should give a girl a twisted mind may be difficult to understand for those unacquainted with the significance of a town such as Slough within the structure of English class prejudice, for it is in the very middle which, in view of the polarization that takes place—to the aristocracy at one end and the proletariat at the other—is an empty center which faces its inhabitants with a negative social identity. The middle is despised by either end.

As I got to know her better, I came to love her more—though I cannot see why one should have led to the other. She barely returned my affection; I knew all the time that I was no more than a counter in some game, and that there would come a time when she would flick me off the board.

I would spend many hours analyzing my love, insisting to myself that she was only an attractive girl whose enigma was no more than the tension between unnecessary fears of inferiority and improbable aspirations to superiority. For, dissatisfied with her husband's wealth, her own beauty and the house and children they shared together, she wished to be respected for her mind. Only a greater fool than she was could have done so. The fascination lay not in her intellect but in that face, which at one moment was that of a princess and the next was that of a barmaid. I sat, as it were, in the front stalls watching her perfect performance as a *grande dame* from a mysterious land which might have been Shangri-la but was Slough.

It was fortunate that her egotism was such that she never asked me questions about my own life. She said in her "salonnière" voice that my paintings were really quite good and she seemed to have forgotten that it was I who had stolen her husband's collection of T'ang. She only alluded to it to say that he had not really liked it. "He only collected it because someone told him at a dinner party that they were the most perfect things made by man, or something like that. He didn't really like them. He just liked owning them. It's the same as his attitude toward me. He just likes to feel he owns me but he doesn't love me and I don't love him."

"But what about the children?"

"Yes . . . perhaps he loves them . . . but that's because they're part of him, isn't it?"

I found it difficult to understand why, if she hated her husband as much as she professed to do, she did not leave him.

"Who with? Where could I go? Back to my mother in Slough?"

"You could come and live with me."

She gave me an odd look and then laughed. "With the children?"

"If you like."

"Could you afford it?"

"Yes."

She laughed again and said nothing else. I did not pursue the subject and think now that it was wrong ever to have brought it up, for while I was sincere in my offer I was repeating a mistake I had made on the only prior occasion when my feelings had been involved—the mistake of being more *serious* than the other, of overloading a flippant heart with dismal glances and breathless protestations of eternal love.

Or was it just that she did not believe I was rich enough to keep her out of Slough? She had only seen my shabby studio in Fulham, and my rooms in Blenheim Crescent would not have reassured her. She had certainly noticed my attempts to lunch at less expensive restaurants and may well have misinterpreted my motives for doing so. Certainly at one point she said, "How can you do so well out of painting when you've never had an exhibition?"

"The Persepolis Gallery have my pictures."

"Why don't they give you an exhibition, then?"

"I sell well enough without one. . . . And anyway, there are my other activities."

She understood what I meant by my other activities but said only, "That's very insecure."

I agreed with her and when I next saw her was able to say that I would be having a show of my paintings at the Persepolis Gallery in the following month.

It was absurd, of course, not to have done this before, for if Pamela Patterson was curious about this omission, how much more curious might the Inspector of Taxes or the police have been had they bothered to investigate. I therefore quickly daubed two dozen canvases with oil and two dozen sheets of paper with poster paint, had them framed and hung them in Qazvini's gallery.

Qazvini was amused by this exercise and spent much of his time organizing and advertising the exhibition, for it was in his interest as much as in mine to have a respectable front. Our plan was to put high prices on the paintings—three hundred pounds for the gouaches, a thousand for the oils—and during the exhibition stick red spots onto their frames to show that they had been sold. Afterward we would destroy half the canvases and pay my profit from the Patterson burglary through the gallery account.

Pamela came to the opening of the exhibition—believing that Hilary Fletcher was my *nom de pinceau*—and brought with her her husband and half a dozen of their friends. From the way she behaved with me in front of them I could guess that she was deliberately exhibiting a relationship with someone outside their circle, and her husband put on that expression of boredom and irritation adopted by an upper-class ox when his nose is put out of joint.

Qazvini put three red spots on three pictures during the first hour of the opening. By the end half the pictures had red spots, and it was not until the four of us—Qazvini, Johnny, Caspar and myself—were sitting in a restaurant that Qazvini confessed that half of the sales had been genuine.

"It all started with Patterson," said Qazvini. "He bought one of those big oils . . . gave me a check there and then. . . . It was rather awkward."

[*143*]

We all laughed and let Qazvini order the best wines and most expensive dishes.

"The beauty of our profession," I said to them all, as I took the wrapper off a cigar, "is the inexhaustible variety of ways by which fools can be parted from their money."

The proof that what I said was true lay in the subsequent success of the exhibition. By the time it closed six weeks later, two thirds of the paintings had been sold and all but the three to genuine buyers.

In defense of the imbeciles who bought them let me say that, while I had no positive gifts for painting, I did possess some negative talent. My daubs were so careless that they had spontaneity; and for want of anything else to guide my hand I had arrived at some balanced form. The result was somewhere between Mathieu and Appel—canvases with figures like Chinese or Japanese characters, but colored and undisciplined.

I do not know why James Patterson should have been persuaded by his wife to buy one of my paintings; I imagine it was an aspect of their close but unsatisfactory relationship that he should demonstrate the power of his money. Certainly it was his purchase that set the ball rolling, for he had a reputation among his colleagues and acquaintances for great astuteness in art. He was, of course, as philistine as they were, but his T'ang collection, until it was stolen, had risen in value at a faster rate than the best of equities, as had certain other of his investments in art; thus, when he bought a "Hilary Fletcher," the Gadarene swine, possessed of the same minor demon of greed and blind to the true aesthetic value of anything, followed him over the cliff and made my reputation.

Whether Pamela thought of me as a genuine painter or not I do not know; perhaps in her benevolent, megalomaniac woman's mind she thought that she knew that I did not know about myself. I might have discovered the truth of the matter one way or the other if our adulterous liaison had not ended soon after the vernissage.

I was still only twenty-four years old and though hardened in some ways I was soft in others. Above all I was soft about Pamela—tremulous, tender, considerate. I should have learned from her love of the revolver that kindness and solicitude were not what she wanted.

She began to invite me to her dinner parties—to introduce me to "people who could be useful"—and then take me into the corner of her drawing room and talk to me in soft, intimate tones. When I told her that I thought this provocative and indiscreet, she laughed and said nothing. I saw the effect this behavior was having on her husband, but I was too naïve to realize that it was the "desired effect." He grew increasingly jealous and treated me with alternating warmth and coldness as if, like a pricked bull, he could not decide between force and guile.

I liked Pamela's dinner parties—for all the emotional sideshows—and the people I met there who were not, certainly, the *haut monde* but a likable circle of social adventurers with pretensions so brittle and obvious that they convinced only each other and themselves. None of them would ever have been asked to Lasterby Hall.

I might even have been mellowed by their company had I not been so uncomfortable about my position in the household. I had as few scruples about sleeping with another man's wife as about stealing his T'ang figures, but I was irritated nevertheless by the untidiness of the situation. I would have liked Pamela to leave him and could not understand why she did not. Perhaps she remained with him because of their children. Though she normally appeared indifferent to them there was an occasion when she betrayed some unease. They were away with their father and the *au pair* girl in the country and I had spent the night with Pamela at Richmond. She had taken me on a tour around the house and when in the bedroom of her youngest son, seeing his cot and small shoes on the floor, she had turned to me and said, "No, don't let's look in here. It makes me feel so guilty."

"Why guilty?" I asked as we went down the stairs again.

"I don't know."

On the Wednesday after this she telephoned me at my studio and said she had to see me at once. I could tell from her tone of voice that she had reached some resolution, and when she arrived I said to her, "Have you come to chuck me?"

"How did you guess?" she asked, her face as expressionless as ever.

I studied her penciled eyebrows and shrugged my shoulders.

"James has found out," she said.

"How?"

"I had to tell him."

"Why?"

"He told me about Daisy."

"Who's Daisy?"

"You met her once."

I frowned, I believe, or looked irritated. "What about her?"

"He's been having an affair with her."

"Do you mind?"

"Of course I do."

"Why? If you don't love him . . ."

"Of course I don't love him, but it's humiliating."

I sniffed.

There was a silence. She twisted the gloves she held in her hands, a token of gentility which pained me so much I had to look away.

"He wasn't in the country last weekend. He was at Claridge's, with her."

Pamela did look angry.

"How did you find out?" I asked.

"Helga . . . the *au pair*. She told me."

"Why?"

"Pique."

"Did she have an affair with him too?"

"Yes. But I don't care about that. It's Daisy; she's my best friend."

"Why," I asked, "if he confessed, did you have to confess as well?"

"I had to, don't you see? It was only fair."

"And what did he say?"

"He was furious . . . he hit me."

There were no bruises, or if there were she had successfully concealed them with cosmetics.

"He's known for a long time," I said.

"Not for sure."

I turned toward my canvases.

"I'm sorry," she said.

"Never mind."

"I'll never forget, I promise."

"No. I won't either." I still had my back to her.

"When it's blown over, perhaps we'll see each other again. You know, lunch and so on."

"Yes." I turned and smiled. "After all, you've nothing else to do."

She smiled too and then left.

8

The absence of Pamela Patterson from my disorganized days had more effect on me than I would have thought likely. Somehow I could not make the transference of love to loathing which had made my first rejection easier to bear. And then that early passion had been largely of the mind, whereas Pamela had left the most specific memories of gestures and caresses which it pained me to dwell on yet which I could not forget.

Why could I not hate her? It was the tea mats and sugar tongs, those traces of her genteel past in Slough. Like me she was an *ancien combattant de la guerre des classes*, and I pitied her too much to detest her. Nevertheless I did not thank her that now I writhed under the torturing disease of sexual frustration and found it impossible to return to my former chastity.

"Tell me," I said to Qazvini one afternoon as we sat drinking Turkish coffee on the cushions spread out over the floor of his room. "Those girls who come in and out of your room. Do they do it for love or for money?"

Qazvini gave me a quick, shrewd look from his oriental eyes and then laughed. "My dear Hilary . . ." he said.

"Well?"

He stopped laughing and shrugged his shoulders. "Why do women do anything?"

"Come on," I said. "Do you pay them anything?"

"Pay them?" he said, readjusting his position on the cushions and puffing at the marijuana he had taken to smoking from a pipe. "No, I don't pay them, not just like that. They do it for love and money. Haven't I told you that women are more like animals than human beings? Does a cat stay with you because it loves you? Or because you give it saucers of milk? Or because you stroke its back? It's a combination of all three, and women are the same."

I sighed.

"There's a girl coming round this evening," Qazvini said. "You can have her, if you like."

"Who is she?"

"She's not at all bad."

"Are you tired of her?"

"My dear boy, I'm not passing her on. No. It's just that I've something else—something more in my line—coming up just at the same time."

"All right," I said, "but if it's you she's expecting . . ."

He made a gesture of brushing aside my objection. "She's just run away from home. She'll take what she gets. She's got no friends and nowhere to live, except that flat of mine in Westbourne Grove. . . . If you're at all nice to her, she'll do what you like."

"What shall I do?" I asked. "Shall I take her out to a restaurant?"

"Good heavens, no," said Qazvini. "Kindness but also contempt. Women form an image of themselves from the way they're treated. Treat them too well and they take themselves too seriously. It's like letting a dog sleep on the sofa."

That night Qazvini sent the girl up to me; she was called Jane. I was nervous but impatient and set to work on her at once, to which she made no objection. I then sent her out for fish and chips, and she returned and made tea without having to be asked. After we had eaten she sat down beside me on the bed and laid her head against my shoulder. It surprised me that a girl of that age should prefer this treatment to her life at home, but she came from Westbourne Grove whenever I called her during the next six weeks and was sorry to go when I kicked her out.

I did so because she was clinging and insignificant. Her body served its purpose but I felt ridiculous rutting at it and incomprehensibly dissatisfied afterward. The girl that followed was equally obliging and equally banal. Her body was neat and all in place like a clever invention of the Japanese. The only characteristic of any originality were her thick lips and cow eyes, both of which irritated me. I bullied her and hit her but she had no spark to be summoned up so I sent her on her way and went out to find another.

Some of my girls of this period were from Qazvini, others were not. None of them lasted more than a month, though I learned to discern and develop preferences. I liked working-class slags and girls who were indelibly whores. Middle-class girls who were kind and clinging and would have made excellent wives I only liked for the pleasure of knocking them around, tormenting them and loading them with humiliation until their patience and understanding were finally ground out of them.

I mention the indelible whores because it soon struck me that Qazvini ran the flat in Westbourne Grove as a brothel. Many of the girls who lived there at his expense—there were usually six or seven in residence—moved on or were thrown out when he had finished with them, but a few stayed on. I wondered why they were allowed to do so and was eventually told by Qazvini that they were partners in an enterprise. He wanted to expand this line of business but because of his extravagance was short of capital so I went in with him. We did up the flat in a plush style and put good double beds into the bedrooms.

The three girls who became permanent members of our staff were Carol, Sue and Alice. All were middle class but none of them was docile. Carol and Sue had both been married; both had had children whom they had left with their husbands. When business was slack, or one or other of them had a spare half hour or was laid up with clap, I would sit and have tea with them or they would make me lunch or supper. I was never the lover of any of them, which was why I remained their friend.

They were older than my usual girls—all three around thirty—and their skin was looser on their arms and bodies, but because of their age and experience there was great skill in their sexual behavior which I watched through the two-way mirrors which were fitted in one of the rooms. Alice especially was able to judge the preferences and moods of her customers and perform with a range from masochism so convincing that one feared for her life to sadism so brutal that one feared for the life of the customer. In between these extremes she could act out the most lighthearted fantasies or lend herself as casually as she would eat an apple.

She was also extremely beautiful—tall, thin and cheerful. All three were good-natured. I believe that the only thing that had made them whores was the tedium of the married state. It was always easier to recruit women who had been married, though their juniors were often girls Qazvini had discarded. The business of pulling the tentacles of these pathetic creatures off oneself—and then throwing them to the public—was irksome and often made me feel that it was not worthwhile.

[*150*]

The girls were not all Qazvini's; I soon developed my own knack of picking them up and pulling them in. Like training horses or handling dogs, it is largely a matter of confidence and experience. Nor was it difficult, with London full of seventeen-year-old runaways with nowhere to live and no way of earning their living, or girls who were freshly divorced and looking for the easiest way to make the most money. They were all already halfway to prostitution. There was only one girl who went the whole way from virgin to whore at my instruction, and she later became as competent and successful as Carol, Sue or Alice.

It happened in the following manner. I was removing a set of four George II candlesticks made by Paul de Lamerie in 1739 from a house in St. John's Wood when the daughter of the house returned unexpectedly. It was a Sunday afternoon and the kitchen where I stood was half dark. I stepped into the hallway at the bottom of the stairs as I heard the front door close, ready to depart by the basement. Unfortunately the girl came straight down the stairs and found herself face to face in the obscurity with the intruder. She had half taken off a fur-trimmed cape, as she came down the stairs, and was frozen in that position when she saw me. My hand covered her mouth before she could melt and scream or make any other sound. I whispered threats in her ears and, as I removed my hand, she said nothing but breathed quickly—in fact she panted—with her continuing fear. Having handled her in this way, I regarded it as almost automatic that I should handle her further, which I did, on her parents' bed. It had apparently not happened to her before and I cannot say that I enjoyed it any more than she did. To me at that time she was just another cunt—and another set of frightened eyes.

I left the house after I had finished with her and might never have seen her again had we not run into each other at the north end of Sloane Street three days later. This was the danger of London. It may have had ten million inhabitants but the middle classes tended to congregate in certain small areas. When I saw the girl I could think of nothing better to do than to smile at her and say hello. She stopped but did not scream or even look around for a policeman. "You," was all she said.

I thought it safer to walk with her for a little until we were clear of policemen or a crowd. "Well," I said, "how are you?"

She did not reply. Her thin, intellectual face looked straight ahead; indeed, I believe she was wearing spectacles that afternoon, though she has never worn them since.

"Why?" she asked. "Why did you do that to me?"

"It was love at first sight," I said.

"And the candlesticks?"

"That . . . er, no. I had been fond of them for quite some time."

"Did you know that Daddy hadn't insured them?"

I shrugged my shoulders. "How could I be expected to know that?"

She said nothing.

"And," I asked, "did you tell your parents what you lost?"

She blushed. "No."

"And the police?"

"No."

"Good girl."

She did not reply to that either, and I felt that the least I could do was offer her tea.

We walked down Knightsbridge to a small Viennese café opposite Harrods. There we drank our tea and ate cream cakes. I watched as her eyes widened at the sight of this confectionery like a greedy child's, and then later as her clean tongue licked the cream from her lips.

"What's your name?" I asked.

"Rosamund Hallet."

"And what do you do?"

"I'm still at school," she said. "At the North London School for Girls."

"I hope," I said, "that you weren't too . . . er, upset by what happened last week?"

"Do you mean," she said deliberately, "by my being raped by you?"

"Yes."

"It was an act of God," she said, in an even more deliberate tone.

I would have been quite happy never to have seen that girl again, but by the way she hung around me and came back with me to Blenheim Crescent, without words on the subject being spoken by either side, she imposed herself on me. I dare say that she thought her moving in with me was the will of God—though I would rather say that it was the usual banal phenomenon of a physically mature girl taking her chance to escape from a dull home life. She was at that turbulent age when daughters realize that their fathers are never going to marry them and so start looking for someone else. Or perhaps she was so pure of heart that her ravisher must also be her beloved.

She remained with me for a greater length of time than any other girl—almost four months—and I became increasingly sick of her. For one thing, she interfered with my work; for another it irritated Caspar and Johnny—if not Qazvini—to have her permanently in the house. She was little trouble but she was also little use. She never cleaned up or cooked for any of us but sat on my bed reading books. The only reason I hesitated to turn her out was because I wanted to coax her into the flat in Westbourne Grove. She was an unlikely whore with her skinny figure and bookish face, and her strong belief in the will of God might make it difficult, but it amused me to try the impossible in this way.

My plan of attack was a pincer movement with love on the left and ideals on the right. Love, of course, has been used by pimps throughout the ages, but only in our own age has there been such an abundance of perverse ideals.

I dare say that Rosamund would have sacrificed herself for

me anyway, but I wanted her to believe in prostitution and therefore persuaded her that loving God was an excuse for not loving one's fellowman. With an added pinch of Freud and D. H. Lawrence I convinced her that all love is essentially sexual, and with common sense explained that a man who is willing to pay for sexual affection must be the man who needs it most.

Rosamund was naturally idealistic and, when persuaded that "Victorian" inhibitions or the "nuclear family" were responsible for all the misery in the world, was eager to do something about it—but she disliked the idea of being paid by the hour for her good deeds. I was obliged to return to Freud and point out to her that sex, like psychiatry, is only effective if it is paid for. "Remember," I said, "many of the men who are most inhibited, frustrated and consequently miserable are married men who could, if that was what they needed, have sex for nothing from their wives."

It was a big step, of course, from the intellectual conviction that whores bring happiness to the feel of alien hands on one's body, and until then Rosamund had only slept with me. I could tell, however, that she was fond of making love—indeed, she had reached a state where she required it—and I therefore set about coaxing her to accept it from others in the patient way that Uncle Ernest had brought childless ewes to take orphaned lambs. The way in which I treated her became more detached and mechanical and then, one afternoon, I took her to Westbourne Grove "for a change" and when we were both lying naked in bed I invited Alice to join us.

Rosamund was embarrassed by the situation but all was well prepared, so that when I suggested that she let Alice caress her she could find no argument to support her instinctive reluctance to comply. I played my part too until we reached a stage when Rosamund hardly noticed whose hand or mouth was where or doing what—whereupon I left Alice to finish her off.

[154]

Rosamund remained at Westbourne Grove thereafter and seemed to fit in well to the sorority. Qazvini soon reported that two of our regular customers had especially asked for her.

There was one further incident involving Rosamund. After a year or so at Westbourne Grove she became pregnant. This carelessness was followed by even greater stupidity for she concealed her state from everyone. Alice and Sue guessed after the third or fourth month, but Qazvini and I were not informed until the sixth month.

It was at that time difficult to arrange abortions—it was technically against the law to perform them—and for a pregnancy as far advanced it was almost impossible. The reason why Rosamund had not told us was, she said, because she wanted the baby. Qazvini thought this ridiculous; I thought it vile. He wanted to let her have the child and then kick her out. I was determined that she should not have it but stay where she was as a whore. I was proud of what I had created in Rosamund; even now, with a bulbous body, she was booked by our best customers. She went once a week to the London flat of a government minister and every now and then was hired out for twenty-four hours at a stretch at the full rate. I did not wish to see this investment lost to a bastard child. By her own admission she did not know the father; it could have been one of a hundred men. Her only reasons for wanting the child were expressed to me in a sigh.

Qazvini washed his hands of the business while the other girls ganged up against me. They watched me whenever I came to the flat with doleful eyes—pleading, I dare say, for Rosamund to be allowed to indulge her cow's instinct for a calf. Their looks were to no avail. I was determined that she should not have the child and set about looking for an abortionist. I had no contacts in this world, however, and those I made would not touch a woman who was so far gone.

[155]

The weeks passed. Rosamund waited, listless and unemployed, for her time to come. By her eighth month I had given up searching for an abortionist, but I had also prevented Rosamund from seeing a doctor. I therefore planned to get rid of the child as soon as it was born.

Why did she not run from the flat? Why did those other girls not protect her or denounce me to the police? They were the only others to know of her condition and suspect my plan. The time came when her labor started. It went on for seven hours. We gave her some aspirin but, being thin and nervous, she had a bad time of it. Eventually the head of the child appeared between her legs. I eased it out; in time the body followed. It was held by Alice while I tied the umbilical cord in two places, cut it, then drowned the child in a bucket of water. I must have held it down longer than was necessary. It was certainly dead when I lifted it out. Its screams of life had been short, but they were replaced by the shrieks of its mother. She clutched at the air but was too weak to lift herself from the bed.

I put the body along with the placenta into a plastic sack half full of cement. I added water and later, when it had set, dropped it into the Thames at Hammersmith.

What is so horrible now to write of seemed normal to perform. The women wept and cursed me—but would they not, I thought, have been equally upset if I had wrung the neck of a chicken or drowned a litter of kittens? Had not Sue and Alice both had abortions and had not Carol had two? What difference was there between my two hands and the surgeon's knife?

Things soon returned to normal, but this incident with Rosamund spoiled the atmosphere in the flat in Westbourne Grove. There were fewer cheerful tea parties and I consequently spent less time in the company of the girls. There were also certain tensions at Blenheim Crescent. Johnny complained that he was the only one to pass on his profits to projects for the common good. He was also irritated by

Caspar's shiftiness, Qazvini's self-indulgence and my parsimony. His Presbyterian Midlands morality was reasserting itself. He disapproved of Westbourne Grove, especially of "employing working-class girls," and he was appalled at Caspar's pederasty. Qazvini and I also found this distasteful and in particular I became alarmed that Caspar now took drugs which crumbled the minds of his little friends just as his buggery crumbled their morals.

My anxiety was not ethical but professional. The association with drugs was likely to bring the police to the house in Blenheim Crescent or lead them to pry into details of our lives. It was for this reason that I moved out and bought the freehold of a house in Sheffield Terrace which had a studio at the back. I gave up my studio in Fulham and transferred from it all my canvases and materials. I also furnished the house with some of the finest stuff we had stolen, though each piece had a receipted bill from antique shops that had since gone out of business.

There were other reasons too for my leaving Blenheim Crescent. I was becoming bored with Caspar. His obsession made him a dull companion; he had no conversation that did not center around the puerile anus. I found Johnny's leftist self-righteousness equally annoying. Even Qazvini occasionally exasperated me with his lush self-indulgence. He squandered his profits; he was always without capital.

I cannot pretend that I did not myself contribute to these dissensions. The three others could not understand my care with money: they also thought me "ruthless," largely for my disposal of Rosamund's baby but also because of an incident during a raid on a jeweler's shop in Holborn. I had only agreed to go with them on this job because all three were short of money, but at one point we were surprised by a night watchman. I hit him on the head with a jimmy and on propping him up discovered that the old man was dead. If I had had more experience of violence of any sort, I would not have hit him so hard, but I had never before struck anyone and so made this miscalculation. It was regrettable because it meant abandoning the job at once and lying low for several months.

Having left Blenheim Crescent, however, the strains diminished and I would spend as much time with Qazvini as when I had lived there. I hardly used my house. "You won't let anyone in," Qazvini used to say, "in case they make anything untidy or leave dust on your kelim carpets." Certainly I preferred to meet at Blenheim Crescent—and any girl who came home with me at night would have to leave after breakfast the next morning.

The months passed. I went twice to have lunch with my mother at the Station Hotel in York. On the second occasion she mentioned the Metheralls. She told me that Harriet had married a civil servant and that Mark had left the army and was now working in the City. I was interested to hear news of these childhood friends of mine—not as such, but because the mention of their name still affected me and for a moment drew me out of the growing boredom which was to take hold of me over the next few years.

Part Three

Part Three

9

By the autumn of 1966 I had reached a period of some desperation. I awoke each morning with reluctance, and only with an effort of will could I go through the tedious chores of shaving and dressing. I now had a woman to come in and make my breakfast, and a boiled egg and tea at nine o'clock in the morning were the only things which attracted me to the day at all. I read a newspaper late into the morning and then—well, there was always a chop at lunchtime.

The result of this greed was that I started to grow fat. My only intellectual pastime was adding up the value of my investments. Robbery I now did only for the sake of Qazvini, Johnny and Caspar, who needed the money. I tended to take my share in kind and acquired in this period a German Gothic ivory diptych of four scenes from the life of Christ, four early seventeenth-century Indian miniatures, and quite a collection of Impressionist and modern paintings.

It could be said, of course, that to keep this mass of stolen property was reckless, but I protected myself by keeping only those works which we thought had not been photographed. This did not restrict me in particular. Many of those who found themselves with valuable works of art were either too lazy or too mean to insure them and never thought of having them photographed for any other reason. Without photographs they are difficult to trace, for how many policemen are able to recognize an early Miro or a Schmidt-Rotluff from a mimeographed description? Anyway, police officers never came to my house. No one came to my house except my charlady and a few whores and slags.

On Tuesdays I would paint. It was a chore which I had got used to and found less irksome now than shaving, dressing or robbing homes. I even went hard-edge, which was well received by the critics and set off a spate of buying from the Belgian collectors. This fraudulent success somehow compounded my boredom. I therefore decided to try other genuine arts as a consumer and pursue thereby the traditional pleasures of the cultivated rich. At great expense I would hire Carol, Sue, Alice or Rosamund and take stalls at Covent Garden or the theater. We would dine at a restaurant and then return home to bed—though never together.

In the winter of 1966 I believe I went to every play which was part of the London stage, and I did not enjoy one of them. I always came out feeling great contempt for the audiences, who laughed at any half-baked innuendo or queried with earnest faces the bogus meaning of what they had just watched.

I also went to concerts, which Carol in particular enjoyed. She told me at one of them that she had once studied the cello. I made some coarse remark about her parted thighs and she blushed. It was an extraordinary and embarrassing phenomenon—a genuine blush from an experienced whore—and I could only surmise that she had gone back in her mind to the time when she was a music student and had blushed in that role. For whatever reason it appeared on her cheeks, the blush silenced me for a time and I studied the audience, mostly music students as she had been—young men with thin faces and wiry hair; girls who were pretty, earnest and unself-conscious. They made me think that their underclothes would be without frills or adornment and always slightly soiled.

"I'd like to meet a music student," I said to Carol. Knowing what I meant by that, she did not reply.

I looked at her—the carefully controlled hair and meticulously made-up face, the expensive, colorful clothes and strong smell of scent—and tried to imagine how she had ever been one of those grubby, giggling girls. "I suppose you wish," I said, "that you were still a musician—perhaps that you were married to a musician?"

"I did marry a musician," she said. She spoke quietly and sharply, bit her lip, then turned to me and smiled—a huge, open, genuine smile—the accomplishment of a real professional.

She came back to my house for a drink after the restaurant and stood studying my Miro while I poured champagne into two glasses.

"Did you like the concert?" she asked.

"I'd have preferred it on a gramophone record," I said.

"Oh, no," she said.

"There are so many distractions at a concert."

"Like music students?"

"Yes."

She said nothing while she sat down. "Are you still as bored as ever?" she asked after a while.

"Yes," I said. "It's not your fault or anyone's except my own . . . but I am still very bored."

"There's a man," she said, "one of the customers, who takes Rosie for a whole evening. They go gambling."

I turned and looked at the Miro.

"Why don't you try that?"

"I used to," I said, "but I lost a lot of money so I swore never to gamble again."

"It's great fun," she said.

"I know."

"You needn't do it for a lot of money . . . just twenty or thirty pounds a night. You could afford that."

"Indeed I could," I said, smiling, since it was what I was paying her.

"Well, then, it wouldn't be gambling."

"What do they play?"

"I don't know. Blackjack . . . roulette . . . that sort of thing."

"Do you know any of the places?"

"Oh, yes," she said. "I went to one once. . . . We could go there now if you liked."

It was still only midnight. We drove over Campden Hill and along the south side of Hyde Park toward Knightsbridge and then turned off, at her direction, and went down toward Chelsea.

The club to which she took me was called the Slide Rule. It was small and half empty but there was roulette and several card tables. I bought fifty pounds of chips and gave half of them to Carol. We both went to the roulette table and started to play.

All at once I was excited. I lost a little and felt sick; then I won and felt elated. Four hours later when the club closed I was up thirty pounds. Carol had lost her entire stake.

I returned to the club the next evening—alone—and on the evening after that went to a different club. In all of them I lost a little, but well within the limits of what I could afford for a night out. It was only on the fourth evening when I returned to the Slide Rule that I met its owner— Eric Feber.

He was dressed in a dinner jacket, frayed at the collar, and had an inscrutable expression on his face like Bogart in *Casablanca*, though Eric's face was too plump to carry it off.

For some time after I had recognized him I stood at the roulette table opposite him, watching his face for its moment of recognition. It did not come. It seemed that my appearance had changed since he had seen me last.

Though my initial reaction had been cautious—not to make myself known—I thought in the end that it would be running no risk to do so. I therefore stepped out of the circle of light around the roulette table and went around to stand behind Eric. I tapped him on his shoulder and spoke his name. He turned, blinked, and then spoke mine in the most guarded, uncertain of tones.

[*164*]

"That's right," I said. "Don't you remember me?"

He seemed completely astonished to see me. "Dear boy," he said, "dear boy . . . I . . . what on earth are you doing here?"

I blushed, imagining this to be a reference to my unfortunate behavior in Cambridge nine years before. "Winning some of your money," I said.

He looked down at my pile of chips. "Of course," he said, "of course. . . . Well . . . well, won't you come and have a drink with me?"

He continued to look confused as he led me toward a room at the back of the club. "Are you alone?" he asked.

"Yes."

He closed the door of what appeared to be his office—plush more faded even than in the club itself—and when he had given me a whisky and soda and had taken one for himself, he sat down facing me and said, almost wearily, "I hope you haven't won too much."

"I'm about sixty pounds up."

He nodded, as if that was acceptable. "Where have you been?" he asked. "I used to wonder what had happened to you. . . . I should have got in touch. . . . I did write to your mother once but she didn't seem to know where you were."

"No, she didn't."

"That silly business . . . the poker game. I felt so sorry to have got you into it, dear boy. Was it just because of that that you left?"

"No, not just that."

"You should have told me, you know. I really had enough to pay him off. . . . I did anyway."

"You paid him?"

"Yes, dear boy. It was simpler if I did."

"Four hundred pounds?"

"Was that what it was?"

"Yes."

He sighed. "Well, I was really quite well off at the time.

[165]

I did even better later on, but then . . ." He sighed again.

"What?"

"Oh, dear, Hilary." He sighed yet again, then looked at me. "But you look so prosperous?"

"Yes," I said.

"What . . . what do you do?"

"I'm a painter."

He simply repeated, "A painter. I see."

"And did you," I began, "did you move straight into this" —I gestured at his desk—"after Cambridge?"

"Oh, no, dear boy, no. You can't imagine the ups and downs I've had. I got a terrible degree, of course, but I didn't care about that. No. But I was terribly down when I left Cambridge. In fact, when I'd paid them all off, I was penniless. No capital. For six months I survived on the three-card trick in the lounges of hotels in Bournemouth—you know, rich retired ladies. I lived on that and skimped and saved to get some capital together. . . . Well, I did in the end. I went up again, then down, then up, then down."

"And now you're up again?"

"Alas, dear boy, not for long. Oh, dear." He glanced at the door which led into the club. "I hope someone's losing out there. The croupier hasn't been paid for six weeks."

"You must let me repay the four hundred pounds," I said.

"My dear boy, can you afford it?"

"Yes."

"I must admit, it would be awfully useful."

"And I insist on repaying it with interest." I did a rough calculation in my head. "Would ten percent be acceptable?"

"Ten percent?"

"It would make it easier to calculate."

"Well . . ."

"That would bring it up to . . . it's nine years, isn't it?"

"I've no idea."

"It is. Nine years at ten percent. . . . That's seven hundred and sixty pounds."

"Is it? But my dear boy . . ."

"Of course you could expect a higher return from such a risky investment . . ."

"No, no."

"But then there'll be no income tax to be paid."

"No income tax . . ."

"But then I haven't given you any allowances for capital growth. I tell you what, shall we call it a thousand pounds?"

"A thousand pounds . . . well, that seems an awful lot for you to shell out all of a sudden."

"My dear Eric," I said. "I regard it as the very least I can do." With a flourish I took out my checkbook, and in a minute he held the check in his hand.

Before the evening was out I had made sure that I lost all that I had won. I felt not only pleased to have met Eric again but also immensely grateful that he had settled my debt back at Cambridge. Why had I not gone to him at the time? I could not remember—but all the same, I had made it up to him now. And had I not left Cambridge when I did, I might never have been in a position to do so.

It must be said that a couple of months later I more than made it up to him. I had looked in at the Slide Rule with Rosamund, who said she had learned a system from her client. Eric was standing by the roulette table as we entered. He smiled at me but I could tell that he was unhappy. Later in the evening, when Rosamund had lost all her money, we had a drink with him in his office.

"It's no good," he said. "I can't keep it up. I haven't the capital . . . and anyway, the scale is too small for the overheads."

As he drank more of his own whisky he became more confessional and eventually told me that the night before some poker-playing friends from Cambridge with whom he had kept in touch had doubled on every loss at roulette and had gone away with seventeen hundred pounds. "It was my entire reserve," said Eric. "I've nothing left."

"Who were they?" I asked.

"Well, you know them, of course. Billy Cade, Randall Webster, Mark Metherall. . . ."

"Yes," I said. "I remember them."

He filled up my glass and then his own. "I'm glad I found you again, Hilary. I feel I can talk to you . . . what I mean is, I don't mind telling you things that I'd never tell anyone else."

"Such as what?"

"Well, the humiliation, dear boy, the humiliation."

"I don't see why you should be so humiliated. Isn't it all in a day's work?"

"No, you don't see. Those three—Billy, Mark and Randall—they know I'm short, and whenever I'm up and doing quite well they find me out and come down to fleece me."

"Don't they ever lose?"

"How can they lose? They double if they do. In the end, they're bound to win. My only chance would be that they might run out of money before I did, but I should think they're worth half a million each. Randall lost twenty-three thousand in one night at a private house, but even that didn't really hurt him."

"What would you need," I asked, "to have a chance of breaking them?"

Eric looked into his glass. "A million, dear boy, at least a million."

"And if you had half a million?" I asked. "Would you try it?"

"Oh, one could go a long way on half a million."

We did go a long way and at one point it was on more than half a million, but in the long run I was very satisfied with the investment I made in Eric. On 5 April 1967 I was worth almost half a million myself. I could afford to tie up some capital in a speculative venture.

The club which we opened in Mayfair was called Feber's.

The company which owned it was called Feber's Gaming Company Limited, and Eric owned all the shares. He was also responsible for the overall direction of the venture, but it was understood that the profits should be shared between us. He had sufficient experience in the business to make the correct arrangements with the police, and as the sumptuous club grew up around him—and bearing his name—he lost his pessimistic manner and grew both more cheerful and more authoritative.

When we opened at the end of June 1967 I myself was delighted and amazed at the pleasantness of Feber's and almost forgot the fifty thousand pounds it had cost me to buy the lease and do up the house. After that, the beginnings were slow. We ran at a loss throughout the summer, though the girls from Westbourne Grove did good business with visiting Americans. These customers, however, never left the ground floor of the club, where the minimum stake was ten pounds; the more elegant rooms upstairs, where the minimum stake was one hundred pounds, were rarely used. Our hopes were pinned on the autumn, when Eric's more traditional customers would return from the country, and by the end of September Feber's was not only quite full, on both floors, but quietly pulsing with the click of the ball on the roulette wheel and the sweet sounds of subdued Eton accents.

In early October Eric's old Cambridge friends started to come to the club—including Billy Cade, Mark Metherall and Randall Webster. I recognized the first two at once, though both had changed from when I had last seen them. Billy was fatter around the jowls and in general had become a squat person. Mark was hardly fat, but his face had become pudgy and his eyes were slightly pink. I did not make myself known to either of these old acquaintances of mine but stood in the background wearing tinted spectacles, watching their behavior. I soon noticed, for instance, that they drank a lot. I also noticed that they made fun of Eric, though all three were apparently curious to know where he had found the backing for his new club. It was to Eric's credit that he never told them, and to theirs that they went straight upstairs and played for a minimum stake of one hundred pounds.

On the first three occasions that they came to the club they won. On the fourth I went and stood at the table opposite them. For half an hour they continued to play without recognizing me. I had removed my spectacles—I now wanted to be recognized—and later saw that Mark's attention, distracted because he was losing, came increasingly to settle on me. I affected not to know him but eventually he came around the table to take a closer look—as if to make sure that I was whom he thought I was—and eventually he stood behind me. I put two hundred pounds on black; the wheel spun.

"Aren't you Hilary?" I heard him say from behind me.

I turned, "Yes, indeed," I said. Just then the ball settled in its slot and I turned to see if I had lost or won—a gesture that was surely quite natural. It was black *impair*. I collected the money I had won and returned to Mark.

"How are you these days?" I asked.

He had apparently been uncertain as to whether I recognized him or not.

"Not so bad," he said.

I moved away from the table and he followed me. "It must be ten years," I said, "since we last met."

This reference to our last encounter made him blush; from pink his face went scarlet.

"Yes, or nearly ten," he said.

We walked over to two armchairs and were brought two glasses of whisky.

"I hope," he said, "that you didn't . . . well, sort of hold that business against me?"

"Of course not," I said, smiling. "I've hardly thought of it since. In fact, Cambridge . . . it wasn't really what I wanted to do."

"You've never looked back, have you?"

"How do you mean?"

"Well, you're so bloody famous these days. We're always reading about you. Someone even gave Hattie one of your pictures as a wedding present. She put it in the loo." He laughed. "At least they did put it there until someone who knows about art told them what it was worth. It's in the drawing room now." He laughed again. I was not sure whether he was laughing at me, Harriet, my painting or himself.

"What are you doing these days?" I asked him.

"Oh, nothing much. I'm meant to go to this place in the City . . . a lot of rich men working hard to get richer still."

I examined Mark's face as a marine biologist would study a fish—its puffy eyes and scaly skin, the patches of pink and white, the line of curly blond hair a half inch farther back than it had been before. His eyes looked straight ahead. He still had his shy manner—not the shyness of the unconfident but the halting, casual manner of a man who would rather leave communication to his servants.

"Have you been here before?" he asked me.

"Once or twice."

"Of course . . . you were a friend of Eric's."

I shrugged my shoulders. "I knew him, yes."

Mark laughed again, his Etonian giggle. "He's an awful fool, you know."

"Is he?"

"That's all he ever did at Cambridge: set up games. But he'd always go bust in the end."

"Perhaps he's found some backing."

Mark shrugged and smiled. "We'll see."

"Who's we?"

"Oh, Billy Cade . . . did you ever meet him?"

"Yes."

"And Randall Webster."

"I don't think I know him."

"He's awfully nice. Doesn't gamble much now, though.

[171]

He lost twenty thousand odd. . . ."

There was a pause. I said nothing.

"You aren't married, are you?" Mark asked me.

"No."

"Thought I'd have read about it if you had been."

"Harriet married, though, didn't she?"

"Yes. A few years ago."

"A nice man?"

"Freddy? Awfully nice, yes. You should go round and see them. Hattie's so proud to have that picture of yours. She'd love to see you. They're in quite an arty circle."

"I'd like to."

"Why don't you give me your number?"

I did as he suggested, and he in his turn told me his telephone number and his address. As I was writing it down, Billy Cade and Randall Webster came toward us from the roulette table. "Come on," Billy said to Mark, ignoring my presence.

"What," said Mark. "Are you going?"

"It's not my night," said Billy.

"Do you two know each other?" Mark asked him, gesturing toward me.

"Yes," said Billy, sharply and without moving his eyes from Mark.

Mark stood up. "Well, I'll see you soon," he said to me.

"I hope so," I said.

He hesitated. "It's nice to meet up with you again."

"Yes."

He hesitated further. "I always thought I'd run into you at Lasterby."

"No," I said. "I don't go there much these days."

"No," he said. "Well, we'll just have to see you down here."

After Mark had left with his two old friends, I returned to the roulette table and gambled with the nonchalance of one who, if he loses, loses only to himself. I threw the chips onto red, black, odd, even—the number twenty, the number thirty-three. I played on and on like this—winning, losing, winning —winning overall because I had no need to buy more chips. Rosamund played beside me, silent and empty-headed. I believe she cared as little as I did whether she won or she lost.

I linger over this moment because it was then that I realized that my resolve never to gamble was a dead letter—in my life as on the table. I could not lose except to myself, by which I meant that whatever game I should care to play with Mark, Billy or anyone else, I could never lose what I had not lost already. All the same I played on, for when the ball landed on the number twenty and I raked in three and a half thousand pounds I was reminded of how exciting that would once have been, and when, on the next turn of the wheel, I lost half of it again, I felt a twinge of phony terror like a faint tapping through a thick wall.

10

With professional detachment I broke into Mark's house the next evening. It was an overdecorated terrace house in Chelsea, once the hovel of a Victorian artisan, and it was easily entered. From the evidence of its furnishings it was used largely as a bedroom and as an investment.

My aim was not to rob him—though there was some silver and a Constable drawing from Lasterby—but to inform myself on certain matters, above all to find out that closest secret of an Englishman's heart, what he was worth. His desk told me little, just that he was three thousand pounds overdrawn on his current account at Coutts' Bank. I noted, however, from some correspondence about the purchase of the house, the name of his solicitors and was alarmed to see that the money on completion had been paid by trustees.

When I left the house I removed some candlesticks as cover for my true purpose.

On the next afternoon, it being a Sunday, I entered the

offices of his solicitors in Lincoln's Inn. I went there at about ten in the morning and spent two hours searching for any reference to the Metheralls. Eventually I found a black tin box which had been covered by several others. On it was written, in white painted letters, "Sir Edward Metherall, Bart., and family."

The box was not locked. I opened it and took out all the correspondence and documents relating to the Metherall family over the past fifty years. By four in the afternoon I had been through it all and had noted the following relevant facts: that at the age of twenty-five Mark had been given complete control of his own fortune; that the trust had been dissolved at the same time; that for the avoidance of death duties the estate at Lasterby, the house and all its contents, the farms in Northamptonshire and all the stocks and shares belonging to Sir Edward had been made over to Mark; that Sir Edward had kept for himself the lease on the house in Belgravia and an annuity of ten thousand pounds a year; that thirty thousand pounds had been settled on Harriet and thirty thousand on Martha prior to this settlement; that Lady Clare retained possession of her own money but that it was not a substantial sum.

Attached to one of the letters was a valuation of all that Sir Edward had transferred to his son: added to the money that had accumulated in the trust, it came to three hundred and twenty-three thousand pounds. In my mind I added ten percent of this sun as a rough estimate of the gain that might have been made since this valuation; and on top of that there was the value of Lasterby, its collection of paintings and furniture, the estate and the agricultural land in other parts of England—all of which, I thought, came to at least half a million pounds.

I returned all these papers to the box, having copied down the figures I required, and left the solicitor's office just as I had found it. I escaped unseen and was home by six o'clock in the evening. Rather than rest after this, however, I went to my desk and started to calculate my own riches. I came up with a figure around five hundred and eighty thousand pounds.

It seemed to me an enormous sum, but it was barely enough for my purposes. I could have added to my reserves by robbing the Arnold Collection, for which Qazvini had patiently been collecting buyers in South America and the Middle East. But now that I had another project on my mind, I became cowardly. Already we had had more luck than we deserved in stealing so much over such a long period of time. What luck was left I wanted for private intentions.

Meanwhile there occurred a most romantic reunion with my childhood sweetheart, Harriet. She did not telephone but wrote me a note which began, as in the old days, "My dear Hilary." I sat at breakfast looking at it for almost half an hour. It was no more than an invitation to dinner, but to me, of course, it meant much more. Her writing, for instance, had hardly changed. And she used, as before, blue-black ink. How many times had the sight of that handwriting made my heart beat faster? And did it not . . . yes, even now my heart beat faster—though not, I regret, with love. It was emotion, certainly, which affected me—if not love, then perhaps just excitement at the prospect of seeing what I had once so wanted to see.

She met me at her front door with a real smile and real enthusiasm; none of the girls at Westbourne Grove could have done better. "Goodness, it's nice to see you again," she said in a tone of voice more evocative of my childhood than any tea and madeleine. "I can't think why we haven't been in touch before . . . but we had no way of finding out, had we? I mean, where you lived?"

She blushed slightly and bit her lip, as if she wished she had not said this, and added, quickly, to cover it up, "You haven't met Freddy, have you?"

"No," I said as I climbed the stairs behind her to the drawing room on the first floor. We entered the drawing room and I could tell at once which of the remarkably similar men was her husband. Like the decoration of the room, or the style of the dress she was wearing, he bore all the marks of compromise. He was a civil servant "with a difference," just as my picture above the fireplace was the difference to the otherwise conventional drawing room and the pink bow on her dress was the difference to the otherwise ordinary garment. Freddy's distinction was that his hair was an inch or two longer than was usual for a civil servant, curling over his collar more like that of an officer in the Guards. He also wore a mauve shirt with a soft collar which might have been thought "casual" by his colleagues in the Treasury. And then he liked contemporary art, as he told me as we were introduced. "I'm not much of a collector," he said in the affable Etonian manner I knew so well. "Don't really get time to go around the galleries. We've got a nice Picasso, though, in the bedroom. . . . Come and have a look." He insisted on taking me there and then up a flight of stairs to their bedroom to show me a banal Picasso etching flamboyantly framed. "We only paid fifty pounds for it," he said. "It's worth six times as much now."

"Indeed," I said.

"Your picture's quite valuable too," he said with some skepticism.

I shrugged my shoulders and smiled. "I've been lucky," I said, glancing at the double bed I might once have envied him.

"It must be irritating," he said, "to see people sell your paintings for twice the sum they paid to you."

I looked him straight in the eye and said, "I don't really paint for the money."

He took off his spectacles and rubbed them to cover his confusion. "No, no, of course," he said. "I didn't mean to suggest . . ."

"Though of course," I interrupted, "one's always glad to make a living."

"Yes, yes, of course."

We went downstairs again. Freddy gave me a drink. Harriet came up and took me by the arm—a gesture that might once have given me great joy but now simply informed me that I was off to a good start. "Come and meet Cecily," she said, leading me across to the friend I had met in Paris.

"How do you do," I said.

"Actually," she said, blushing, "we met. I mean, you won't remember, but we met in Paris . . . in your hotel."

"Of course I remember," I said, as if I did not remember at all. "You came with Harriet."

"Yes."

"It's quite a long time ago."

"Yes. About ten years."

"As long as that, is it?"

There was a pause; then Cecily said, "I went to your last exhibition. I do like your work. I mean I know it's frightfully abstract, but I do like it."

"Thank you."

"My husband—he's not here, he's in South Africa—he bought one. He thinks you're by far the best of the younger English painters."

"That's very kind of him," I said.

"He was sorry to have missed you this evening."

At a quarter to nine we went down into the basement of the house and ate a dinner which had evidently been cooked by Harriet. No one seemed to notice or to care whether the food was good or bad—and of course it was bad—but Harriet was quite unaware of her shortcomings and made continuous, deliberate conversation about this and that: how package tours abroad were frightfully common but so much cheaper and you did sometimes meet quite nice people; how her father and mother never came down from Lasterby and had let the house in Belgravia; how Martha hated school; how Martha was spoiled; how Freddy hated working for Labour ministers; how nannies were an awful bore and *au pairs* even worse but having no one to take the children off your hands was worst of all.

I joined in all these conversations with a certain amount of evident effort. I was, after all, unused to these domestic topics and was also absorbed with other things—with Harriet's face, for instance, its slight looseness and its lines; with her body, camouflaged under the dress with pink bows; above all, with her increasingly uncertain glances toward me. I wished to seem enigmatic and did not altogether fail to do so.

At the end of dinner the women left the room and the men hovered around the table as if to show that they were all used to remaining behind to drink port and brandy but were aware that it might not be quite the thing in London.

Freddy, our host, hovered with the rest of us, concealing his indecision under cultivated vagueness. Eventually we sat down again for twenty minutes. The conversation was about politics. Freddy spoke most of the time and made it plain, in a confidential tone of voice, what incompetent asses he thought the Labour ministers were.

When we reappeared in the drawing room, Harriet took my arm again and led me to a corner where we could talk without being overheard.

"Mark wouldn't tell me where he met you," she said.

I laughed and said, "Then it's not for me to give away the secret."

"Father and Mother are rather worried about him. Did you know that he hasn't done anything since he left the army?"

"He's not thirty yet."

"I know. But a lot of people have done an awful lot by then. I mean, look at you or Freddy."

"Yes, but other people don't start up until they're thirty-five or forty."

"The trouble is," said Harriet, "that Mark's no need to do anything. He's much too rich as it is."

"Perhaps he'll lose his money."

She looked at me sharply, her old Metherall look. "Gambling? I suppose that's where you met him. It's that awful Billy Cade. . . ."

"I don't care for him much."

[*178*]

"If you come across them," she said, "do keep an eye on Mark." In her eyes there was an appeal but also the offer of complicity.

I laughed again. "I don't think he'd listen to my advice."

"Oh, I think he would. I mean, you were great friends. I think he's sick of all his Eton, Cambridge and army friends, and he hasn't really got any others except you. And he can't bear to be alone."

"Well," I said. "He's got you and Freddy."

She smiled as if to say, Well, that's not much use. But she said instead, "I hope we see something of you."

"Of course."

"I keep feeling that you'll disappear again."

"No. Not now. In fact it would be very nice to see you . . . well, away from a group."

"Yes," she said, her breath coming a little shorter.

"To talk about the old days."

"Yes."

"Perhaps we could meet for lunch?"

She blushed and then with artificial carelessness said, "I'd love to."

"I'll ring you."

"All right."

She then stood up as if to show that we had talked alone together for long enough.

I left Harriet's house before midnight and went to Eric's to see if Qazvini or any of the girls were there. It appeared, however, that Rosamund and Alice had already taken two customers back to Westbourne Grove and Qazvini had gone back to Blenheim Crescent feeling sick.

"It's his own fault," I said to Carol, who told me this. "He eats too much."

"Yes," she said, turning toward the cards that were being played to her. She went bust. "Where have you been?" she asked.

"Having dinner."

"With whom?"

"A childhood friend."

She looked up at me. "A childhood friend?"

"Yes." I sat at her table.

"I can't see you with a childhood friend."

"Why not?"

"I didn't think you had any friends."

"Of course I have friends. What about Qazvini and Eric?"

She lifted her eyebrows and played another hand of blackjack. As she did so I saw Mark enter the room. "There's another childhood friend of mine," I said and moved away toward him.

"My dear Mark," I said. "I've just been having dinner with your sister."

"I'm so glad," he said. He was already drunk. I took his arm and we went toward the roulette table. "Just wanted to play a bit before going to bed," he said. He held five hundred-pound chips in his hand.

Laughing, I said, "But are you sure you can tell red from black?"

"I'm always lucky when I'm drunk," he said.

Ten minutes later he had proved what he said, having twenty-five hundred-pound chips in his hand.

"Stop now," I said, "while you're ahead. I can see that you're sobering up, so your luck will go."

"Do you think so?" he said.

"Come and spend some of your winnings," I said.

"On what?"

"Well, have a drink anyway. They're free, and it'll give you a second run of luck."

"Do you think so?" he said again, letting me take his arm and lead him over to a sofa.

We were both given a glass of champagne. Mark fidgeted with the black counters which represented what he had won. "The trouble is," he said, "there's nothing to do with these little things except lose them."

"Surely," I said, "you can buy yourself a new suit of clothes or a good dinner."

"Plenty of clothes already," he said, "and I don't really like good food. It's wasted on me."

"Go to the West Indies," I said.

"I'd get bored."

I shrugged my shoulders.

"And lonely," he said.

"Buy yourself a companion," I said.

"Who?" he asked.

"Her?" I pointed at Carol.

"Is she for sale?" he asked, and then laughed.

"Yes." I replied without humor. "They say that you can have her for fifty pounds a night, a hundred pounds for twenty-four hours or five hundred pounds for a week."

He looked at me, then stared at Carol who, that evening, was looking her best.

"I've never had . . . a girl like that," he said.

"She's beautiful, don't you think?" I said.

"Yes," he said; then, "Have you?"

"Had a girl like that?"

"Yes."

"Not her," I said. "But in artistic circles . . ."

He nodded. "I suppose you do, yes."

"When I can afford it."

"I could afford it, but I wouldn't dare."

"It's easy. I'll fix it up, if you like."

"Would you?"

"Of course." I stood up. "For how long?"

"How long?"

"A night or a day or a week?"

He looked confused. "Well, I thought . . . if she'd come with me to the West Indies . . . a week."

"I'll ask her."

I crossed to Carol. "I've found you a customer," I said.

"Your childhood friend?"

"A week in the West Indies."

"Exclusive?"

"Yes."

"All right."

I took hold of her by the shoulder. "It would be nice . . ." I began.

"What?"

"Well, if you could get him . . . involved, as it were."

"I see. Well, I'll try."

"But he mustn't know anything about me."

"No. All right."

Two days later I met Billy Cade in Bond Street. He was about to ignore me when a thought crossed his mind and he stopped me.

"Have you seen Mark?" he asked.

"No," I replied.

"He told Randall that he was going to Jamaica."

I said nothing but made a facial expression of polite interest.

"You don't know anything about it?" he asked.

"Why should I?"

"He told Randall he was taking a girl . . . a friend of yours."

"Really?" I said and began to walk on, but Cade caught me by the sleeve.

"I don't know what you're up to," he said.

I turned and I could see that he had lost control of himself, though like most Englishmen of his sort he went a long way to conceal it. "Don't you?" I said, shaking his hand off my sleeve. He had, it would seem, a suspicious nature and I wanted to get away from him.

"And . . . and I don't trust you," he said. "I never trust a man who doesn't pay his poker debts."

"But it was paid," I said.

"Not by you."

"My debts are always paid," I said, pushing him aside and walking on.

I saw Mark again after his holiday. It was at Feber's, as usual, and Carol was on his arm. He looked healthier and happier than he had a week before. "We had a very good time," he said to me, "or at least I did."

"Oh, so did I," said Carol, smiling at me.

"Have a drink," I said.

He did. So did I. Then he went to play a few hands of blackjack and I talked to Carol.

"He was very shy," she said.

"Did you . . . er, bring him round?"

"Oh, yes." She smiled.

"And he paid up?"

"Of course. And a bracelet."

I saw Billy Cade come in. "Do you know what sort of car Mark's got?"

"A Mercedes."

"Did he bring it here tonight?"

"Yes. Dudley parked it."

"Good." I stood up. "Can you get him drunk?"

"He's drunk already."

"Really drunk."

Carol shrugged her shoulders and smiled. "What's in it for me?"

"We'll waive our percentage on the week in Jamaica."

"All right. I'll see what can be done."

"And could you tell Dudley to have the Mercedes waiting at the front door?"

She looked at me. "What are you going to do?"

"Nothing to him."

She went downstairs to find Dudley, our commissionaire, while I crossed the room to join Mark and Billy Cade at the blackjack table. Cade was not playing and Mark seemed to have lost. I stood on his left. When he was down a thousand pounds and had sent off for more chips, I said to him, "It might be the night to break the bank."

Mark giggled. "Poor old Eric."

"Poor old Eric," I said after him in tones of complicity.

The subject of our pity was beaming at us from the other side of the roulette table.

"Not tonight," said Billy.

Carol came up behind Mark and handed him a champagne cocktail. Mark turned and said, "Oh, thanks," and drank it down. Carol moved off again, saying, "I'll get you another."

"Is that your girl friend?" Billy asked Mark.

"Haven't you met her?" Mark asked him.

"No."

"I'll introduce you." In dribs and drabs he was losing again.

Billy and I watched in silence until Billy said, "You won't break the bank like that."

"I don't want to break the bank," said Mark. "I like this . . . this whole place."

Billy glanced at me and said, "It might be interesting, though."

"Why?" I asked.

"It'd be interesting to see how much it would take."

"Eric must have backers," I said.

"I know," he said. "I intend to pay a visit to Companies House to find out who they are."

I smiled. "I don't suppose that they're on the board of directors."

"I thought," said Billy, "that you might be involved."

"I'm a painter," I said, "not a businessman."

Carol returned with another drink for Mark. His head was beginning to loll and he lost concentration on the game— forgetting, even, to take up his winnings.

"Come on, Mark," said Billy. "I'll take you home."

"Don't bother," said Mark.

"I think I'd better."

"Carol'll look after me, won't you?" Mark turned to Carol, but she had gone to get him yet another drink, disappearing into the smoky darkness of the room.

"She'll look after you," I said.

Billy looked at me again, then said to Mark, "I don't like to leave you with this lot."

[184]

"He doesn't trust me," I said.

"Don't be ridiculous," Mark said. "I've known Hilary a bloody sight longer than I've known you."

Cade turned on his heel, the outraged gentleman. "More fool you," he said over his shoulder. Then he marched out of the room and down the stairs.

"He's taken offense," I said to Mark.

"Let him."

Carol came up with a whisky and soda. She handed it to Mark. He drank it down.

"I don't like to think that you've quarreled with Billy because of me," I said.

"I don't care . . . really, I don't," said Mark.

"What's happened?" asked Carol.

"Come on," I said to Mark. "Let's go after him."

The three of us left the upper room. Mark was supported between Carol and myself. We went down the stairs, passing Qazvini on the way, who raised his eyes in an interrogatory expression. When we got to the door, we found Mark's Mercedes waiting for us with its engine running.

"Come on," I said to Mark, "we'll catch him up."

With Carol I helped him into the driver's seat. Then Carol got into the back and I sat in the front next to Mark.

He set off in first gear and did not change down. It was now very late; the streets were empty except for the figure of a man walking away from the club toward the Park.

"There he is," I said to Mark.

When we were fifty yards from Billy Cade I said to Mark, "Steady on," and took hold of the steering wheel, although his driving, considering his drunken state, was exceptionally steady. My injunction confused him; he flustered at the controls of his powerful car and in the confusion I was able, with my two feet, to remove his feet both from the brake and the accelerator; as we drew up behind Billy Cade, I accelerated and swerved the car. Cade was hit in the hips. The bottom half of his body was crushed against the iron railings which ran along the side of the pavement.

We were not without injuries to ourselves. My face was cut open on the windscreen, Mark was bruised across the chest by the steering wheel and Carol hit her head on the roof of the car. Of course the injuries to Billy Cade were more considerable. None of us thought he would survive; the pain made him unconscious almost at once. With great care, however, he was lifted onto a stretcher when the ambulance arrived and it later emerged that, though his legs and hips were smashed beyond repair, his spine and other vital organs remained miraculously intact.

I was in those days in a remarkably good mood. Each time I was told by Mark or Harriet that Billy Cade would be in hospital for six or eight months, or that he would never walk again, I was as pleased as if I had picked up a hand with four aces—and equally careful to keep a poker face.

I had to get in touch with Harriet over the accident and with her permission arranged for a lawyer to defend Mark. She seemed grateful to me for that, also for the evidence that Carol and I both gave in his defense. She also appreciated, I think, my patient and eventually successful attempts to rouse Mark from a depressed state of mind. He blamed himself, as they say, and would not believe me when I said—to him and in court—that my own attempts to take over the controls had been responsible for the accident. Nor did the magistrate, who fined Mark five hundred pounds and withdrew his license to drive for two years. He would have sent him to prison, he said, had he not thought that the knowledge of what Mark had done to his friend would be punishment enough.

Harriet said to me, as she sat with me at lunch at a restaurant in Knightsbridge, that she knew something like that would happen to Mark. "If people don't take a grip," she said, "and do something positive with their lives, then tragedies always occur."

"I rather agree," I said, glancing at the menu. "Nature

abhors a vacuum." I paused, then asked her if she would like an aperitif.

"Oh, no, thanks," she said. "I can't really take much drink at lunchtime."

"You'll have some wine, won't you?"

"Yes, all right. If you're drinking some."

I could tell from the slight poise in her manner that she approved of the restaurant and the whole style of our lunch together.

"Does it mean," I asked—referring to the theory that disasters happen to the idle—"that you or I, for example, will be saved from these disasters?"

"I'm not sure that I lead such a positive life," she said.

"Surely you do?"

"Not really. I don't think that looking after children amounts to anything special."

"There's your husband . . . his life . . ."

"That's nothing to do with me," she said, with a touch of defiance. "Anyway, I'm not interested in it."

"I thought his job sounded rather important."

"It may be important for ordinary people, but nothing he does would ever affect you or me."

I laughed.

"And it's made him into such a bureaucrat."

"How do you mean?"

She started picking at the bread on her side plate. "He comes home in the evening and treats it like a second office. He likes to have conferences about the overdraft or the Harrods account or the children's schools."

"He sounds very efficient."

"Yes, he is really. I'm not, though. That's the trouble. And I don't really want to be."

"It makes life a little bit too predictable, perhaps."

She shrugged her shoulders and we ordered our food.

"When will you get married?" she asked me, smiling at her own audaciousness.

"I don't know," I said.

"Put it off for as long as you can."

"Why do you say that?"

She blushed. "It's not that I'm not happy. I am. But I wish I hadn't married quite so young."

"I've forgotten how old you were."

"Twenty."

"Some girls marry at eighteen."

"I know. But that's because they can't think of anything else to do. And then, when you're twenty-five or twenty-six you suddenly realize that there are lots of things you would like to have done . . . and now you can't. You're trapped by a husband and children . . . especially the children."

"But you've got someone to look after yours."

"I know. But what can I do now? I've got no A levels."

"You don't need A levels to do . . . well, what do you want to do?"

"I don't know, really. Teaching or social work of some sort."

"Yes. For that, I suppose . . ."

She suddenly looked cross. "I blame Mother, really. All that ridiculous coming out. You're just meant to catch the richest or the smartest man. It's ridiculous, the whole thing. It doesn't equip you for anything."

"Except marriage."

"It doesn't even equip you for that. No one tells you how boring it can be."

As she drank more of the wine, Harriet became more eloquent on the subject of her marriage. She never said anything specifically disloyal about her husband, but she had bitter words on the institution—which comes, of course, to the same thing. I pretended to be concerned, though in reality I was only amused at the banality of what she was saying: the same, the usual, the ordinary intellectualization of frustration and discontent, the age-old refusal to be happy with one's lot.

It was, of course, what I wanted. If her Freddy had been a man of any force or stature, my schemes would have been more difficult to put into effect; but then I knew it was unlikely that Harriet, at twenty, would have married such a man. I also knew that there were few such men around.

"It's a pity," I said, "that someone like you should be limited to a life for which women without the same beauty and intelligence would do just as well."

I could see that at this she looked sharply into my face to see in what spirit I had intended this remark. She was reassured, I think, by the objective and discursive expression on my face—and convinced, I am sure, that I was not laughing at her or trying anything on but merely voicing a straightforward truth. Only then did she let the pleasure she felt at this flattery loose into her body.

"Well," she said modestly, "I can't really speak for myself, but I think a lot of women could make better use of their . . . well, their abilities."

"It's a great waste," I said. "But of course there is a tradition of greatness within the home, as it were. Great wives and mistresses. Madame de Pompadour, for instance, or Josephine de Beauharnais."

"They're French," she said. "And anyway, they were only great because of their husbands or lovers."

"Perhaps that's what you should do."

She snorted. "Freddy will never be great."

"How do you know? He might be the greatest legislator since Napoleon."

"Even if he was," she said, "I wouldn't be involved. His secretary would have more to do with it than me."

I shrugged my shoulders, as if I had given up. "Well then," I said, "perhaps you should take a lover."

At this she directed a second exploratory glance in my direction, and on this occasion my eyes met hers with a purposeful expression. She went red in the face, and to cover her confusion I went on, in a casual tone of voice, "I mean, a lot of women do have lovers, though one must admit that the lovers often aren't much better than the husbands."

She smiled but was still recovering from her great blush. Then she said, very softly, "There aren't always so many opportunities."

"But if you have a nanny," I said.

"No," she said. "I don't mean that. I meant that there weren't . . . well, many candidates for the post."

She did not look at me, and I simply said, in a voice supposedly tightening with emotion, "I can hardly believe that. You just frighten them away."

She looked up. Our eyes met. I was on my way.

The rest of our conversation was more lighthearted, for the emotional intensity of those previous moments, had it been maintained, would have seen us under the table. We returned to the sort of conversation we had had as children: our ages, how we had changed. "It's so unfair," she said. "I mean, I'm quite ancient at twenty-seven, while you're still quite young."

I made some casual remarks about how young she looked, though it was not especially true. Two children, and the intervening years, had loosened her bones and skin and clouded those once fresh eyes with the film of age. Her hair, too, had lost its condition, and her teeth were less solid in her gums. It was not difficult to see why so few would-be lovers were to be found at her feet. It was not that she was even amusing. Indeed, I could not see how anyone who had not my special interest in Harriet could have any interest in her at all.

Our next topics were shared memories of our youth: the Pony Club camps, the gymkhana, the early days with Sam and George and the more recent events like her dance at Lasterby. Did she remember that? Did she remember bursting into tears while dancing with me?

"Oh, that, yes," she said, not even blushing at the memory. "I was gone on Alexander Amotherby, that was all. I can't think why. He's such an oaf."

When we were drinking coffee I returned to the subject of adultery so that she should leave me with the idea of it in her mind. She showed no reluctance to discuss it and indeed seemed fascinated by the subject. She could rattle off two or three case histories—little affairs her friends had had or, more often, had nearly had.

"Do you think," I asked her, "that Freddy has ever had an affair?"

"Freddy?" She looked at me with an expression of amused surprise. "He'd be incapable of it."

"You mean that he'd never risk hurting you?"

"No. He just doesn't think about that sort of thing." Then she added, "It might be more amusing if he did."

"And would he be very hurt," I asked, "if he discovered that you had been unfaithful to him?"

Her expression changed in an instant, from the derisive to the dramatic. "It would finish him," she said. "I don't think he'd ever get over it. But then"—and she gave me a quick half-glance—"if ever I did . . . have an affair, that is . . . I'd make sure he never knew about it."

When we parted out in the street I asked her, with no ambiguity in my expression, whether she would like to meet me again.

She hesitated, then said, "Yes, very much."

"And some time," I said, "you must come and see my studio. I've got some quite nice pictures . . . besides my own."

She did not laugh but with a sultry look for which I would once have given my life said, "Yes, I'd love to do that."

She came the following week after lunch in another restaurant, and she trembled when I laid my hand on her shoulder.

"You must have done well," she said, looking at my German diptych and speaking almost in a whisper, "to have been able to collect all these things."

"I have done well . . . yes," I said, keeping my hand on her shoulder and stroking her neck with my thumb. "But I bought some of them quite cheaply."

She was breathing heavily. I pulled her shoulder around and kissed her. It was dull, naturally, as a kiss—the immobile lips of an awkward and inexperienced woman—but somehow it affected me. My hands, too, began to shake.

"Come on," I said.

Without a word she followed me into the bedroom and with wide-open eyes looked into my face as I took off her clothes. I do not know what she read in my expression for I was, more than anything else, irritated at myself for my shaking hands. She noticed these, for when I had put them onto her uncovered bosom she raised her hands and covered mine. I did not care for this calming caress; I wished to carry through my plan without any sentimentality, yet the sight of her breasts and belly—which once I had so much longed to see—affected me still further. To my horror, I felt tears come into my eyes. I was about to cry.

Biting my lip, I moved my head to hide my tears. I hid it in the folds of her skin and with a pretense of sensuous affection kissed at the rest of her body as I undressed it. But again I was so moved by the sight of her thighs and legs that the tears left my eyes and came down my cheeks, and my body began to shake with involuntary sobbing. Harriet, however, did not notice that I was crying for she was moved, too, and making sounds, so I dared to bring my head back to her breast; and then, not caring any more, to her face. Her eyes were closed; her mouth was open but then covered by mine. I doubt that, with the rest of my body within and around her, she noticed my tears on her cheeks and neck.

For a long time that afternoon we lay clasped together, true lovers reunited. When we moved apart we lay, again in silence, covered by the sheets and blankets of my bed. I turned to her and ran my fingers down her neck, over her shoulder and around her bosom, thinking how none of these features had any distinction but were, all the same, more delightful than any others I had seen.

[*192*]

She suddenly said, "I think I can say the car broke down, can't I?"

"Why?"

"Well, it must be quite late."

"Yes. Say you broke down."

It saddened me to be reminded that she would go. I had assumed that we would remain as we were; in other words, I had forgotten her husband, children and all the intervening years.

"Do you remember Paris?" I began.

She looked blankly at me. "Oh, yes. . . ."

"I had planned to ask you up to my room."

She frowned. "Don't think of the past."

"I always loved you."

"Don't be silly. How could you have done?" Her voice, now, had resumed some of its sharpness.

"Why not?"

"You were a quite different person."

"How?"

"Well, spotty and common and dressed in a ridiculous tweed suit." She laughed, and I pretended to laugh but what she said acted on my mood like salt on a snail.

"And now?" I said.

"Now? You're quite different, I don't really think of you as that Hilary—the rector's son."

As she spoke she seemed to realize that what she was saying annoyed me. "Don't you want to be someone else?" she asked.

"Are you someone else?"

She laughed and sat up. "Can't you see I am? A bored, frustrated wife."

She got out of bed and started to get dressed. I watched her stomach, which was slack and protruded, as she stooped to put on her stockings.

"Have you ever slept with anyone else but Freddy?" I asked her.

"Not since we got married." She turned and smiled at me. "You've started me off."

"And before?"

"Yes. Once or twice."

"Who was the first?"

"You wouldn't know him . . . yes, you would. Do you remember, in Paris, at Madame Vignon's . . . her son-in-law?"

"You slept with him?"

She smiled. "I thought he was smashing at the time."

"You called him greasy."

"I didn't want you to think . . . well, to know."

"And he seduced you?"

"Yes. He tried to seduce Cecily, too. It was part of being a paying guest, I suppose." She laughed and was fully dressed. I got out of bed and put on a dressing gown to see her to the front door.

"We never got as far as your studio," she said.

"That's for next time."

"Yes." She turned and gave me a conspiratorial smile. "But not too often."

"I'll ring you up."

"All right."

"By the way, you took precautions, didn't you?"

She blushed. "Yes."

"Good."

We kissed at the door and she left.

I remained alone in the house that evening, going over in my mind the events of the afternoon. I walked around the empty house, laughing to myself about myself, wondering what would have happened if she had said that she had always loved me at the moment when I had said that I had always loved her. For a moment I was even embarrassed to remember what I had said and was relieved to recall that she had actually reminded me of the truth. What was the truth? I stalked around the drawing room, the stolen paintings shouting at me my ten years of solitary warfare against their whole class. How nearly I had just lost everything through the treachery of my emotions. If I could have whipped whatever faculty within me that was guilty of that weakness, I should have done so; as it was I remembered and relived all the humiliations I had suffered from the Metheralls—from Harriet, from Mark and from the parents. I stirred up the bitterness that had so nearly gone stale.

She had not changed. She had the same arrogance and was using me now as a lover as she had used me then to make up the numbers for a Hunt Ball; but then I had been baffled and helpless whereas now I was powerful and had a purpose far greater than hers. If I was her distraction—a partner in the fashionable pastime of her class—then she was mine; but my game had an end to it, a last show of the hand, a winner and a loser. I had almost lost it all that afternoon, on the first round, but now I knew the weakness of my hand whereas she did not even know what game we were playing. I could now be more sure than ever that I could not lose.

Mark was in a bad state: full of remorse and shame, drinking considerably, leaving his house only to visit Billy Cade. I spent much of my time with him and did my best to improve his spirits, for he was no use to anyone in his present state. I often drove him to Westminster Hospital to see Billy, though I never went in with him. On the first occasion that Mark had been able to speak to Billy, he came out looking particularly shaken.

"How is he?" I asked.

"I talked to him."

I said nothing but drove away, back toward Kensington.

"It's awful," said Mark. "He won't accept it."

"Accept what?"

"That I did it."

"But . . . how else does he think it happened?"

"He thinks you were driving the car."

I hesitated, then said, "Did you tell him?"

"Yes, I told him as soon as I saw him, but he can't accept it. He thinks it was you."

"Poor chap," I said.

"Yes," said Mark. "It must have affected his mind."

Harriet, whom I now saw regularly twice a week, showed less concern for her brother's state than one might have imagined. She had always been selfish and always, too, contemptuous of the weak. In normal circumstances this might have been balanced by her strong sense of family, but she was greatly preoccupied with her love affair and had reached the stage of hinting to Cecily that something was going on.

"Won't she be shocked?" I asked her.

"Oh, no," she said. "I can tell her anything."

"She'll pass it on."

"No, she won't."

I shrugged my shoulders. "About Mark," I said.

She looked at my mouth as I spoke, as if her attention was much more on what it could do than on what it could say. She was in the full flood of her passion, as they say, which put her in no mood for her brother's problems.

"I think," I said, "that you ought to see more of Mark."

"Freddy doesn't like him."

"All the same . . . in a crisis like this."

She broke her gaze from my mouth and stretched her naked legs under the blankets. "I know," she said. "You're quite right. But we couldn't be much help. He gets terribly bored in our house. He thinks Freddy's a bore and Freddy thinks he's a fool."

"Can't you bring them together, having so much in common with both of them?"

She kicked me for what she thought was a joke. "Why don't you?"

"I would if I had the opportunity."

"I don't mind having Mark in the house if you come too."

"Perhaps Freddy'll find me a fool too."

"Oh, no, he liked you. And anyway, he thinks you're the sort of person we should know."

"He might guess . . ."

"What? About us?" She laughed. "No he won't. He hasn't the imagination."

This conversation was the prelude to many visits to Harriet's house in Ebury Street. I would go there on one or two evenings a week with Mark—much against his will—and be told in confidence by Freddy how good it was of me to take care of Mark in this way. "After all," he would say, "his conversation is pretty limited at the best of times."

It was not, I thought, any more limited than his own, but Freddy's complacency made my own pastimes in that household that much more enjoyable. For I started to take risks with Harriet and—in the full flood of passion—she started to take risks with me. Once, for example, when climbing the stairs from the kitchen to the drawing room after dinner, I went last behind Harriet and, halfway up, put my hand up under her skirts and held it there until we had reached the first landing. If Freddy had happened to turn around . . . but then there was the excitement.

On that occasion Harriet stamped on my foot as we entered the drawing room, which would in itself have been a gesture difficult to explain had it been noticed, but it was not.

After that, of course, we graduated to waiting behind in the dining room while Mark and Freddy went upstairs to watch the news on television. Ostensibly it was to load the dishwasher, but the plates and cutlery remained on the table. The discomfort of our surroundings on these occasions gives some indication of the fullness of her awakened passion and the irresistible nature of my resolve.

Harriet would return to her husband and brother with bright pink cheeks and wild, dilated eyes and sit, recovering, in front of the television, her eyes only moving from it to look, sated, into mine.

It was some time before Freddy noticed any of the symptoms of his wife's infidelity. I would touch her up under his eyes—sitting at his dinner table with my foot between her legs, or wiping my fingers on the covers of his armchair—and still he would not change his smug, dreary, self-righteous tone. If Mark noticed anything, he was too drunk to care. I suspect that the first person to smell a rat was Lady Clare, who came down for the day on one occasion and, so Harriet later reported, questioned her closely on why she was looking so well.

As for Harriet herself, I believe that she put the recklessness of what she was doing out of her mind—though every time she would start off with, "Oh, no, we mustn't, no, not here." But by the time we had sullied the sheets of her marriage bed a dozen times and fucked in every room in the house, she must have concluded that Freddy was indeed as big a fool as she had always thought he was; she even began to put her arm through mine and kiss me goodnight as her old, old friend.

I knew, however, that there must come a moment when the stupidest man would realize that his wife was screwing under his nose. My only fear was that Mark would recover his spirits—it was happening gradually—before he did so, and so deprive me of my excuse for such frequent visits to their house. In the end, however, Freddy began to stay behind too, to load the dishwasher, with a badly concealed expression of uneasiness on his face. And then, when Harriet and I came down together from a session on the bathroom floor—her skin glowing, her eyes wide—I saw his look darken and his face contort. At last he had cottoned on.

As I had anticipated, he did nothing about it. What could he do? If he brought it all out in the open, might not Harriet desert him? He knew quite well how little he or their children meant to her. And if he had confronted me directly, as he tried to do obliquely, with conversation about "the family" or "loyalty" or "the institution of marriage," what could he have said? There is no law against adultery, and I

[198]

was both taller and stronger than he was. Above all, my resolve was greater than his.

There was an occasion when Harriet asked me down to their cottage in Sussex. It was a building with exposed beams and thin walls and the children were on top of us all the time. On Saturday night, Mark, who was also staying, went off to bed at ten in a stupor. Thereafter Harriet made it plain that she would like Freddy to go to bed too. We had not had each other for a week and she was determined that we should do so that night. Freddy, however, was slow to fall in with her plans. He dithered and hesitated until well after midnight. We sat making cursory conversation, waiting for him to go.

"Well, I'm for bed," he said at last, finishing his whisky and soda.

Neither of us moved.

"Are you coming, Hattie?" he asked his wife.

"No," she said. "You go. I'll come up later."

He shuffled off with reluctance, and before he had cleaned his teeth we were on the sofa. I had Harriet lie on top of me because I hoped that her husband might return and see her naked rump moving like the big end of a Victorian steam engine. Alas, he stayed upstairs. Nevertheless he can have been in no doubt as to what we were up to and may well have heard the sounds of our rutting through the ancient ceilings.

It was pleasant to have the cottage to visit at weekends. I had hardly seen the English countryside since leaving Lasterby and appreciated the fresh air and quietness. I also appreciated a leisurely enjoyment of Harriet, for increasingly Freddy would stay in London to catch up with his work.

She showed no signs of tiring. "Are you sure Freddy doesn't suspect anything?" I would ask her, walking arm in arm in the garden after the children had gone to bed.

"No, honestly he doesn't. He does have to work, you know. We can't all be painters."

Mark had now recovered from what the Metheralls called

his "breakdown," and when Billy Cade left the hospital and returned to his father's estate in Scotland to convalesce, Mark felt able to take a month to go to Yorkshire. He asked me if I would like to come and stay at Lasterby Hall but I declined the invitation.

"It is odd," said Harriet on one of the last weekends of the summer, "that Freddy never comes down here now."

"It's because of me," I said.

She bit her lip. "I'm sure it isn't."

"He's not a very good loser, is he? At life or at croquet?"

"You cheat, that's all."

"Even so . . ."

She understood quite well. She had settled into her love affair, but if there was now less drama in our meetings, she never missed an opportunity, and when it became too cold and wet to make weekends in the country at all plausible she would turn up quite regularly twice a week at Wilton's or the Berkeley Grill and return with me to my house as of right. I no longer went to her house quite so often because Mark was in Yorkshire. When I did, Freddy avoided my eyes, which were always ready with a mocking expression; indeed, it came to the point where he avoided me, leaving a room when I entered it.

By the beginning of October, everything was going well. Harriet reported that she and Freddy hardly talked to each other now and had not slept together since June.

"He must know about us," I said.

"No," she insisted. "It's not that. Our marriage was a mistake, that's all. We don't suit each other."

"Why not divorce?" I said.

"I don't see the point really. Neither of us wants to marry anyone else." She glanced at me to see how I would take this. I did not react. "Anyway," she added quickly, "there are the children."

It was on this occasion that I "lost" her underclothes and, since she was in a hurry, was forced to let her leave without them. There was nothing wrong with this since it was only the lowest layer of clothes that had been mislaid. When I found them under the bed I put them into a large brown envelope which it was impossible to seal and, happening to run into Freddy outside the Traveller's Club, I asked him to return the package to his wife since he would be seeing her before I did. He took the envelope without a word and was about to leave me when Harriet's underpants and stockings fell out of the envelope onto the pavement. I had unfortunately handed it to him upside down. Cowering he crouched, picked them up, put them into the pocket of his coat and walked away.

I was glad that Mark was in Yorkshire, for it left my evenings free to see Qazvini and the girls at Westbourne Grove —the girls, that is, less Carol, who had, it seemed, been asked to stay at Lasterby.

I was enjoying life at that time but my enjoyment was split, for while the time spent with Harriet fulfilled some purpose it was hardly entertaining. For all her English lechery she was a dull, unamusing girl whose dreary tone of voice and lack of wit made her an excellent match for her equally witless and dreary husband.

Qazvini, Caspar, Alice and Rosamund all made me laugh. I could relax in their company for though—as I have described before—we all had reservations about one another we nevertheless belonged together. I should like to have spent all my time with them, and it hurt me that they should think that now I had money I was trying for some sort of respectability by associating with the Metheralls. It was Carol who told me of this feeling. She, who had been in the car at the accident, knew better, and asked me if she could tell Qazvini and the others that I had some reason for what I was doing beyond a late yearning for an aristocratic milieu. I suspected, however, that she wanted this information for herself as much as for the others and I would not give it to her.

Caspar, to the public good, was increasingly addicted to drugs and would gabble poetically about explosions in his head as once he had glorified explosions up the backsides of his little boys. He lived on the trade in the drugs he loved, while Qazvini, deprived of my supplies of fine art, now specialized in the disposal abroad of property stolen by others. He also enjoyed and succeeded in his legitimate occupation as director of the Persepolis Gallery. Both the gallery and Feber's club continued to do well. Collectors bought my paintings for ever higher prices, and Qazvini was even asked to handle one which had been stolen. Eric was confident that the club would continue on its profitable course.

The sequel to the incident involving Harriet's underclothes went like this. She met me for lunch as usual with a long face and was unusually constrained through the four courses, though she ate quite as much as usual. When we got back to the house, however, and I made the usual opening gestures, she pushed me back and said, "Why did you do that to Freddy?"

I stepped back ten times farther than she had pushed me and looked away from her. "What?"

"Giving him my things like that?"

We were in my bedroom. I looked out of the window and said nothing.

"Why?" she said again.

"What did he say?"

"He didn't say anything. He gave them to me and . . . and then he cried."

I smiled. "And did you comfort him?"

"I tried to."

"And did you promise not to see me again?"

She blushed. "He wouldn't listen to me. He left the house."

"For ever?"

"No. He came back."

I laughed. "Good old Freddy."

We stood in silence.

"Why did you do it?" she asked.

I turned toward her, concentrating for that moment on removing with my tongue a fragment of food that was caught in my teeth. "I see no reason why I should explain any of my actions to you," I said.

She looked startled—and was disappointed, I dare say, that a good dramatic row should be nipped in the bud in this way.

"But if you loved me . . ." she began.

"Love," I said with a snort. "I don't know what the word means."

She sat down on the bed and, like Freddy, began to cry.

"If you don't want to go on seeing me," I said, "you have only to say so. Indeed, you don't even have to say so. Just don't come . . . don't turn up."

When she understood that I was not going to comfort her, she had the sense to stop crying. She sighed, in the way that children do when their tears have at last ceased.

"You're a shit," she said, and looked happier for having said it.

I shrugged my shoulders. "Why don't you get out, then?"

Rather than leave, however, or cry again, Harriet looked up at me and smiled—a particular smile that I had never seen before on her face, a smile of deep complicity. "Come on, then," she said.

"What?"

"Get on and fuck me. It's what we're here for, isn't it?"

On that understanding I was quite prepared to comply with her suggestion—and proceeded to do so.

Mark returned from Lasterby in November. He told me that the week before he had been farther north for a weekend to shoot on Lord Purves' estate in Scotland.

"And how's Billy?" I asked.

"All right, really, considering."

"How do you mean?"

"He's in a wheelchair, of course."

"Does he shoot from a wheelchair?"

"No. He doesn't shoot any more."

"But he gets around?"

"Yes. They've built a lift to take him upstairs."

We were dining together at Prunier's. Mark himself looked quite recovered.

"Will Billy ever walk again?" I asked.

"No, never."

"And how's his mind?"

"He broods."

"Does he still think that I did it?"

"We didn't talk about it."

"Will he ever come back to London?"

"He's coming next week."

"Why?"

Mark looked at me and grinned. "We're going to break Feber."

"Who is? You or Billy?"

"I am. But Billy wants to be there."

"I can see that he would," I said.

"It's become a kind of hobby," said Mark, laughing his old dismissive laugh. "We always used to at Cambridge. Poor old Feber, but it serves him right for being a pushing little Jew."

"Are you sure you can?" I asked.

"Oh, yes, quite sure."

"He must have backers," I said.

"It seems that he hasn't. Billy hired a detective to find out. Feber owns all the shares himself."

"How much do you think it'll take?"

"If I can take him for a couple of hundred thousand, I'm sure it'll break him."

"And what will you play? Chemmy or blackjack or . . ."

"Roulette. It's so simple. If you lose, you just double and you go on doubling until you win."

"Poor old Eric," I said—and I laughed a laugh which imitated his.

The next morning I talked with Eric and also with the manager of my bank. I arranged with the former that Mark should be allowed to place unlimited stakes and be given credit up to a half a million; and with the latter that all my assets should be made liquid at once.

A week later we were all prepared for this special turn of the wheel. Billy Cade came down from Scotland on the night sleeper with a young man from the estate to help him on and off his chair and push it where he was bidden. I was curious as to what was in the mind of this cripple as he heaved about in the first-class compartment and changed the pure air of the Highlands for the sooty filth of King's Cross Station. I had no way of knowing. I assumed that he wished to ruin Eric as some kind of revenge for the accident. Perhaps Eric, as a Jew, was playing the age-old role of the scapegoat. I was content to leave my curiosity unsatisfied since Billy's plans fitted in with mine. My only slight anxiety was that he might add his assets to Mark's and so, in combination, be able to succeed where the one, I knew, could not. This was so likely a possibility that the optimism with which I prepared for the game was quite unreasonable, but it was not that I was gambling again. I had now come to count on luck.

The unfortunate Eric matched my optimism with his own complete pessimism. He was convinced that what had happened to him on a smaller scale two or three times before was certain to happen again. "You can't beat these big boys," he said.

"I can settle as high as Mark," I said.

"But how can you know?"

"I know."

"And what about Billy?"

"He's an unknown factor."

Eric trembled, went white and shook his head, while I continued to feel extraordinarily confident that we would win. It was almost a premonition. It seemed to follow so properly onto what I had achieved with Harriet. It was a belief in poetic justice, but I could not be bothered to explain this to Eric so I just told him to do as I instructed.

They came into the club at around half past eleven on the night of 10 November, 1968. I had been warned by Mark that this would be the night and I was prepared. Billy Cade was in a wheelchair pushed by his pink-faced Scottish servant. He was dressed in a red velvet smoking jacket with satin lapels; Mark was dressed in a similar fashion, like a huntsman, spruce for the kill. All I thought as they entered was that Billy's face was thinner and almost as gray and green as the smoke of the cigar which he blew out of his mouth. Having made this observation to myself, I withdrew into the shadows at the back of the room. Such was my excitement that I could not be sure I could control the expression on my face. Only when the game had started did I come forward to stand at the corner to the right of the croupier.

From this position I was able to watch their eyes. Billy's, which had once been so arrogant, were now deep in their sockets and flitted from baize to wheel in a shifty, manic manner. Mark's retained their pride, their naïve, laughing cruelty. It was his last enjoyment of his ascendancy—the delicious anticipation of humiliating Eric Feber, the Jew, the social worm.

Eric certainly played his part. He was white in the face and pained and spoke with the whine of a condemned man. "What's my credit in this place?" Mark asked him.

"Your credit?" asked Eric, looking around for me but not finding me because I was shielded by the croupier. "Why, any amount, I should say."

Billy Cade leaned forward in his chair. "Let's call it half a million, then."

Mark laughed. "How about it, Eric?"

[206]

"Yes, of course," said Eric, panting with discomfort.

Billy looked at him more intently. "You can meet half a million, can you?"

"There's no limit," said Eric with a last attempt at dignity.

Mark started to play, and for this game no one else's chips were on the table. He put a thousand pounds on red and lost. He put two thousand pounds on red and lost again. He put four thousand pounds on red and won.

There was complete silence around the table. All heard Billy mutter to Mark, "It'll take too long."

"All right," said Mark. He leaned forward and put fifty thousand on black.

"Stick to a color," said Billy.

"From now on it's black," said Mark.

The wheel turned, the ball was thrown in, and it settled finally on red.

Without any sign of distress Mark put a hundred thousand on black. He lost again. He put two hundred thousand on black and lost again. He put four hundred thousand on black and won. There was now a pile of chips representing eight hundred thousand pounds on the cloth, but of this only fifty thousand represented losses to the bank. It was because of this that Billy told Mark to go on, in a whisper which again was heard by all.

Thus Mark left five hundred thousand on black and nodded to the croupier to spin again. He did. The ball landed on black. He had won.

It had all been quick and simple, although there had been great concentration on these turns of the wheel, but when Mark drew the piles of counters toward him which represented a million pounds, there was a roar from the twenty or so people around the table.

It was not surprising that Mark and Billy concluded that they had broken the bank because Eric's face had disintegrated into an expression of panic and despair. This look provoked the opposite in the faces of the gamblers, and Mark beamed as he turned to Billy and said, "I think we'll call it a day."

His friend's expression was more ambiguous, being twisted but not with a smile. He looked up at Eric and said, "Can you pay him?"

"Of course," said Eric in such a dubious tone of voice that no one would have believed him.

"When?"

"Now."

"In cash?"

"Of course."

I realized as I watched this exchange that it might have been a mistake to prepare so much money—every penny of what I had—in ten-pound notes, for I could see that it had made Billy suspicious. But Mark, saying "Let's see it," had followed Eric to his office. Billy remained at the table, surrounded by the other spectators. Suddenly he looked up and stared in my direction. I was almost sure that, since he was under the light and I stood back in the shadow, he could not see me, but the gaze was most specific and recognizable— by me, at any rate—for I too had felt such hatred and bitterness as were expressed in his eyes.

But who was the object of this venomous mood of his? If he still suspected that I was responsible for his broken body, it must be me; or was it Eric, whom he despised with the disdain of centuries? Or was it, since his accident, human nature in general? I concluded, quite cheerfully, that it was this last category, for I was sure that he could not see me, and if it had been Eric he would have looked more pleased that he had just lost more than half a million pounds. Or had he guessed what Mark now returned to tell him, that the bank had paid in full? That it was not broken?

A small crowd gathered around them as they conferred, and I moved from behind the croupier to join that crowd.

"I'll call it a day, don't you think?" said Mark.

Billy did not reply; he twisted his hands together.

"Let's leave it at that," Mark said again. His grin had

gone; he had clearly been disturbed by Eric's ability to pay out such a large sum of money.

"Is it there?" said Billy. "Is the money really there?"

Mark glanced down at his friend. "It's all there," he said.

"But it must be his limit."

"It's pretty well mine," Mark mumbled.

Billy looked at him with exceptionally stern eyes. "You must break him," he said. "You can't stop until he's broken."

Mark looked at him uneasily. "All right," he said. "What shall I put on?"

"All of it," said Billy, nodding at the chips which were still on the table.

"What? The whole lot?"

"Yes," said Billy. "That'll do it."

"It certainly should, but . . . well, what if I lose?"

"Then we'll double."

Mark looked embarrassed. I knew that he was confused but did not wish to seem so. I too was a little confused. Did Billy mean by that that he was in with Mark? That Lord Purves' fortune was added to that of the Metheralls on the green baize of Eric's roulette table? If so, I had lost; indeed, I had probably lost anyway. It was only my irrational conviction that somehow I was destined to succeed that kept me from the same despair that was so evident in Eric.

"All right," said Mark, looking down at the chips in front of him. He nodded to the croupier. "All this on black," he said.

We were all silent now. The wheel turned, the ball was thrown in. It landed on number seventeen red.

There was another gasp from the small crowd.

"Damn," said Mark.

"Double it, double it, for God's sake double it," said Billy.

"I can't," said Mark, who had only three hundred thousand left before him.

Billy turned to Eric, who was standing across the table from him. "Won't you extend his credit?" he asked.

Eric, who seemed as unhappy to have won as he was to

lose, looked blank. "I'm not sure," he said, "that we ought not to close . . ."

There was some protest at this, whereupon Eric began to look for someone—and fearing that it was me he was seeking, and that he might give me away, I shouted in the tone of voice of a spectator, "Go on, Eric, give him another million."

He heard me and said to Mark, "All right, another million."

I think that no one at this stage took the game seriously. The sums that were being won and lost were far beyond the records set by the larger, grander clubs in London. The spectators thought that Eric and Mark were friends—or at least acquaintances—and that for that evening the serious gambling had degenerated into a children's game. It was only the four principals—Eric, who shoved the stack of chips to Mark; Mark, who shoved them back onto black; Billy, who twitched and twisted his hands; and myself—who knew that the checks and chips and shouted sums of money represented not only legal currency but the fate and fortunes of a family.

As the croupier turned the wheel, Eric came up behind me and whispered, "What if he wins?"

I turned and led him a few feet from the table. "If he wins," I said, "we're bankrupt. If he loses, he is, so call him in. Whatever happens, this is the last throw."

The wheel was turning; the ball was thrown in. We all watched it roll around and around in decreasing circles and then knock against the silver studs and bounce off one number near to the zero and finally settle in number three red.

At once I had to turn away from the table, for I was in one of those uncontrollable states, half laughter, half tears. A waiter was passing with glasses of whisky on a tray. I snatched a glass and drank it down and then turned back to the table. There I saw that Mark was sitting alone. I looked toward the door and saw Billy Cade being wheeled in his chair toward the stairs.

Eric looked as wretched as if he had lost nearly a million

instead of having won it. He stood beside Mark with his mouth open. I came up behind him; he sensed my presence and turned around. I nodded toward Mark. He understood, stooped and said quietly to Mark, "Would you like to come to my office?"

Mark sat up straight, a resolute gesture. "Yes," he said. He stood and turned and saw me. "Hello, Hilary," he said. "Did you follow all that?"

"Yes," I said. "Can't you go on?"

He tried to laugh, but I could see that he was nearly in tears. "I seem to have lost my reserves," he said, nodding toward the door through which his crippled friend had now departed with his gillie.

I went with Mark and Eric to Eric's office, wondering if Mark would have the sense to do what I had done and ditch the debt. The law courts would not help Eric to recover it, and he certainly had no other means. Nor, I imagined, would his friends in the Pitt Club, or Boodles or White's or wherever he belonged, think it dishonorable to welsh on a debt to a Jew. I counted, however, on his sense of probity—his class sense of probity—and certainly, as we discussed the matter in Eric's office, where I acted as a kind of mediator, he made no suggestion that he might not pay every penny of what he owed to the club. All he asked, he said, was that he might have some time to assemble the nine hundred and fifty thousand pounds. I suggested to Eric that he might be satisfied with half by the end of the year, and the second half six months after that. Eric, of course, was content to agree; indeed, if I had not been there he might well have fallen to his knees and wept on Mark's shoulder and let him off the debt because he was warmhearted and could not feel malice even for those who deserved it.

When this was settled, I walked with Mark back to his house. "It seems an awful lot of money to have lost," I said.

"It is, rather, isn't it?" he said.

"Have you got it?"

"I don't know."

"Why not," I said, "why not just . . . not pay?"

He looked up at the street lamps as we walked under them and I could see, from the wetness of his eyes and the wobbling of his throat, that he was doing his best not to cry. "Oh, no," he said, "one must pay. I mean, it was all fair enough."

"I suppose it was," I said.

We took a taxi, after walking for about a quarter of an hour, and I dropped Mark off at his house. He asked me in for a drink but I said that I had better get back.

"Did you see Billy?" he asked, standing on the pavement while I sat in the taxi with the door open.

"No. What happened to him?"

"After that last spin . . . he just went off."

"What did he say?"

"Nothing."

"I thought," I said, "I thought he might have put some of his money behind you."

"Yes," said Mark, "so did I. He was the one who was so bloody keen to break the bank."

I returned home that night pleased enough with the way things had gone. I will not say that I could not believe my luck—the luck that had led Billy to persuade Mark to risk his fortune, the luck that had seen the ball fall twice on a red number. On the contrary, I took it for granted. The only element in the whole affair which continued to puzzle me was the motive of Billy Cade, first for inciting Mark and then for deserting him. Certainly, if he had not done first the one thing and then the other, I should never have succeeded in ruining Mark; thus the man I had crippled was my prime accomplice.

I turned this matter over in my own mind but I did not discuss it with Mark, who was preoccupied, in the following weeks, with raising the large sum of money that had to be found by December 31. He managed it only by selling all the stocks and shares he possessed and both of the farms in Northamptonshire. He did all this without letting his parents or family know—and I said nothing to Harriet. Mark went back to Lasterby for Christmas, having already started negotiations to raise a mortgage on the place.

Christmas is a most oppressing time of year and I had nowhere to go, being still disinclined to set foot in my parents' home. Eric and Caspar both returned to their families, and so on Christmas Day itself I sat and ate turkey in a hotel with Qazvini, Carol and Rosamund. It was dismal—we all felt it —and I cursed Christ for imposing this insufferable day on humanity.

Then, on the day after Boxing Day, Mark returned from Yorkshire. He asked me around for a drink and showed me the Christmas card he had received from Billy Cade. It was of the cheapest sort, with a robin and a sprig of holly depicted on the front and "Season's Greetings" printed on the inside. Beneath this Billy had signed his name, but on the back he had written a note. "It was trial by ordeal," it read. "It was red because of your sin. I did not believe it could have been you but now I do. Have you lost everything? I hope so. You are still better off than I am." He had not signed his name again, but the handwriting was clearly his.

"He's off his head," I said to Mark.

"Poor Billy," said Mark rather vaguely.

When I next met Harriet, she asked me if Mark confided in me.

"Why?" I asked.

"Well, it seems that he's sold the farms in Northampton-shire without telling Father."

I ate my food. I drank my wine.

"What's more," Harriet went on, "Father was told by Mark's stockbroker that Mark's been selling his shares."

"Why?"

"No one knows."

"Has he sold them all?"

Harriet shrugged her shoulders and ate her food with an appetite undiminished by her brother's behavior. "Father's afraid he may have lost a lot of money," she said.

"How?"

"Gambling."

"Does he gamble?"

"You know he does. Don't you go with him?"

"Sometimes."

She looked straight into my eyes. "Has he lost anything? I mean, a lot of money?"

"Not while I've been with him."

She finished what was on her plate and turned to look down the restaurant at the trolley loaded with chocolate éclairs and oranges in kirsch. I called the waiter. She ordered some sort of blancmange and sat staring at it. "It looks awfully good," she said.

I watched her as she ate it. "Perhaps," I said, "he's planning to run away to South America."

"Has he said he is?"

"No. It was just a guess."

She licked the cream off her lips and then smiled at me. "It's not very likely."

"Why not?"

"Well, why should he?"

Now I shrugged my shoulders. "He's not very happy."

"If only he'd get married," said Harriet.

"Would that make him happy?" I asked.

"I doubt it," she said quickly, "but at least it would anchor him."

"Are you afraid he'll drift away?"

She frowned slightly at this extension of her metaphor. "Not to South America."

"Where, then?"

"I don't know."

She meant, I believe, that she did not want to think about it. We drank coffee and I smoked a cigar. For a time we did not talk. Harriet eyed her next course, which was to be me. I became interested to know whether anything would quench her lechery so I said, in an offhand manner, "Well, as a matter of fact you might as well know. I had promised not to tell you but . . ."

"What?"

"He did lose some money."

"Oh, dear." She did not look especially upset. "Was it a lot?"

"Yes."

"Really a lot? I mean . . ."

"Everything."

The nature of this information seemed to penetrate her egoism. She looked perturbed.

"He's lost everything?" she asked again.

"At roulette."

"But . . . I mean, how do you know it's everything?"

I shrugged my shoulders.

"But . . . but does he have to pay?"

"I think he wants to pay."

"Why?"

"A debt of honor."

"But that's ridiculous. I mean . . . I mean he can't ruin himself just because . . . because of a game."

I shrugged my shoulders again. "It's nothing to do with me," I said.

"Were you with him?"

"I was there but I wasn't with him. He was with Billy Cade."

"I thought he was in Scotland."

"He came down—just for twenty-four hours."

She sighed, an angry sigh. "My God, he's so stupid. Why on earth he has to . . . oh, he's always been spoiled. Why on earth did Father make it all over so soon?"

"To avoid death duties."

"I know. But it was stupid. I mean to say, Lasterby is in Mark's name."

"I know."

She went pale. "But he can't . . . he won't sell Lasterby, will he?"

"He may have to."

"Oh, God." She was quite silent, but it was not difficult to guess what she was thinking. She was pitying her parents.

"Don't they know?" I asked.

She shook her head.

"It won't be very pleasant for them."

"Does it mean that they may have to . . . to leave?"

"I don't know. I suppose . . . if he sells it . . ."

Harriet shook her head violently as if that might prevent the eventuality.

"Of course he might get by with a mortgage."

She looked at me gratefully. "It would be . . . the end . . . if we had to sell Lasterby."

We left the restaurant. "It's so awful, all this happening just when I'm getting on so badly with Freddy," Harriet said.

"Do your parents know about that?" I asked.

"I think they've guessed that something's not quite right."

"Then perhaps you'd better try and improve matters."

She turned to me sharply to see what I meant. Then she said, bitterly, "Rats deserting the sinking ship?"

"Not at all," I said, pretending to be injured by that. "After all, I've stood by Mark."

[216]

She took my hand, as we walked along the street, and a lock of hair fell over her face. "Well, please stand by me," she said.

"Of course," I said, calling a taxi.

We stayed only a short time in my house because Harriet had to be back in Ebury Street for tea. "Martha's coming up," she said.

"Coming up?"

"From school. Just for the afternoon. Evidently she's hating it—another problem for the Metherall family."

"How old is she now?"

"Fourteen or fifteen. I don't know. She's a bloody nuisance, anyway. But Mother and Father worry about her, and they can't come down from Yorkshire every time she writes an unhappy letter home, so I have to take her on."

Harriet was getting dressed. I watched her and said, "I'd like to meet her."

"Come back, then. Freddy won't be there."

"Wouldn't you mind?"

"Of course not."

I got off the bed and got dressed myself. "What's she like?" I asked.

"Oh, she's all right. I don't know her very well—she's so much younger than I am. Quite pretty, anyway, and spoiled, of course."

There was nothing in Martha's appearance to lead me to doubt her sister's assessment of her character. She was like numberless other girls of that age: shy, arrogant, pretty and pretentious. We found her waiting in Harriet's kitchen with the nanny and the children. She looked up as we came in, said hello and then returned to talk to the children as if we were not there.

To describe her from top to toe: she was wearing her school uniform, a dark green skirt and blazer with a white blouse. She wore brown, old-fashioned shoes and thick brown stockings on long thin legs. She had, so far as I could see, no bosom, but a long neck. In many ways she was like a Degas ballet dancer, except that her head was covered with thick black hair which came down to her shoulders in curls and ringlets. This hair, parted in the middle, together with her eyebrows, made more of an impression of a 1930s film star—say, Merle Oberon in *The Divorce of Lady X.* She had also the lips and nose of that period, simple and straightforward. Her eyes were blue but I hardly saw into them for she affected not to notice my presence. Her short-comings were the scragginess of a girl who had grown quickly in the past few months and a complexion which she had not attempted to disguise or prepare in any way. There was nothing wrong with it beyond a slight greasiness natural to dark-haired women, but I was used to faces on which color, texture and expression were studied and manufactured.

Setting eyes on Martha, I felt not the slightest physical attraction toward her, but I wanted to find out something about her all the same. Was she not a Metherall? And were the Metheralls not my special subject?

At six the children were taken up to be bathed and put to bed. Harriet and I also moved upstairs to the drawing room. Martha, it appeared, would have gone with the nanny and children, but at my request she came into the drawing room. She refused a drink.

"What time do you have to get back?" Harriet asked her.

"There's a train at half past seven," said Martha.

"From Victoria?" I asked.

"Yes."

"Where is your school?"

"Ascot."

"And what's it like?"

Martha looked uncomfortably toward Harriet.

"You don't like it, do you?" said Harriet in a bored tone of voice.

"Not much," said Martha, looking at her fingernails.

"Why not?" I asked.

"Oh, it's all so stupid." Her voice, even when talking reluctantly like this, was exceptionally pleasant in accent and tone.

"In what way?"

"Well, having to wear uniforms . . ." She fingered at her blazer. "And playing stupid games."

"Hockey?"

She looked up and smiled. "Lacrosse."

I nodded and smiled back at her.

"It's not just that, though," she said. "It's the whole idea."

"Of a girls' boarding school?"

"Yes."

"Dormitories and prefects . . ."

"Yes."

"It's much worse for boys."

She shrugged her shoulders.

"At least they don't beat you," I said.

She blushed. "No," she said.

"Well, then, things could be worse."

Martha looked at Harriet, who was helping herself to a second drink.

"Don't you want a drink?" Harriet asked her sister.

"No, thanks."

"Why not have one?" I said.

"No, honestly. Oh, perhaps just some bitter lemon."

I rose to replace Harriet at the trolley on which Freddy's drinks were laid out. "With a little gin in it?"

"No, thanks."

"Some vodka, then?"

I turned to look at her. She did not smile but said, "All right, a little, then."

I poured in a lot but was quite aware that I might quickly become—in Martha's eyes—someone intolerably smooth. I thus gave her the drink and then paid no attention to her. I talked to Harriet about a charity for which she planned to work part time. I remarked that, in her case, charity might have to start at home.

She raised her hand to her forehead. "Don't remind me," she said. She glanced at Martha, then at me. "If you're seeing Mark," she said, almost in a whisper, "ask him to go up to Lasterby and talk to Father."

Martha must have heard this but she said nothing.

"I'll ask him," I said. "It'll mean telling him that I've told you, but that might be for the best in the long run. I just hope that it won't mean that he no longer trusts me."

"Yes," said Harriet. "He must go on trusting you." She was by now a little drunk. I wondered if she prepared herself for Freddy every evening in this way. She was, I thought, so completely pitiable that there was little more I could do to degrade her. Only two more developments were necessary for my satisfaction, and they would come without me: the one was time, which would age her badly; the other was her own realization of the muddle and futility of her life. I would not wait around for the former—it needed a few more years—but hoped to be a witness to the latter—indeed, to precipitate it. The drinking showed what was going on inside.

At ten to seven I stood up, looked at my watch and said that I must be going. Then, as if it had suddenly occurred to me, I asked Martha if she would like a lift to Victoria.

She hesitated, looked at Harriet, blushed, then said, "Oh, no, I'm sure . . . I mean, I can easily walk."

I fixed my eyes on her. "Why not come with me? Wouldn't you prefer a lift?"

"Well, of course, yes, if you're sure . . . I mean, that it won't take you out of your way."

"Absolutely sure," I said.

I turned to say good-by to Harriet.

"It's not really on your way," she said.

I shrugged my shoulders and then kissed her on the cheek. "It's not far out of my way, either."

In the car Martha sat in silence and I did not speak for a few moments. Then I looked down at her knees and said, "What time will you get back to school?"

"About nine."

"Will they keep supper for you?"

"Yes, I should think so."

"I'm afraid that you didn't have much chance to talk to Harriet."

"That didn't matter."

"It was my fault, I'm afraid."

"No. I didn't want . . . I mean, I hadn't anything particular to say."

"Didn't you want to talk about school?"

"Not really."

"Don't you want to leave?"

"Yes."

"And do what?"

"Come and do my A levels in London."

"What . . . at a tutor's?"

"Yes."

"I'm sure it would make more sense than staying at school."

For the first time she looked at me with some feeling. "Do you think so?"

"Yes."

"I wish you'd tell Mummy that."

"I will if you like."

"Oh, do."

"Why do you call her Mummy," I asked, "when Harriet calls her Mother?"

She shrugged her shoulders. "I don't know. I always have."

"And do you call your father Daddy?"

"Yes."

"And will he let you leave?"

"He says I can, yes, at the end of the summer."

"How old will you be by then?"

"Sixteen."

"Well, that's something, isn't it?"

"What?"

"To have that promise."

"Yes."

"But it must seem a long way away."

"Yes."

We had reached the station. I stopped the car. "Are you ever allowed out of school?" I asked. "I mean . . . to lunch or something like that?"

"Well, sometimes," she said, uncertainly.

"I'm down in your area every so often on business," I said. "I thought you might like to come out to lunch."

"Well, I would. I'd love to, but they only let us go out with our family."

"What a pity."

"Of course . . . of course, I could say that you were my brother." She spoke in an uncertain but excited voice.

"Yes," I said, laughing.

"They don't know Mark."

"Why don't you do that, then?"

"All right. I'd love to. It would be something to look forward to."

We got out of the car and went into the station. I saw her onto her train, and before it drew away from the platform we had arranged that I should call to take her out to lunch a week that Saturday.

It was to be expected, I think, that I should continue my blood feud against the Metherall family in the younger daughter. I had nothing against her as such—she had been only four or five when I had last gone to Lasterby—but she was very much one of them. Her face contained both the Norman knight of Lady Clare and the squire's physiognomy of Sir

Edward. What is more, she was part of their property, their last chattel, her father's darling. What more exquisite revenge could one have on a whole family than in harming this innocent abstract of their condescension?

I did not foresee the need of luck in making off with her. What had been so useful—indeed, necessary—in parting Mark from his money would here be superfluous. I had no need to spin a wheel or draw a hand of cards. All I required was a modest knowledge of the behavior of women, which I felt I already possessed, for the power to do enough damage for my satisfaction. Six months, I thought, would be enough to leave a depraved and disillusioned child, a girl privately despairing and publicly debauched.

It did occur to me that I was taking things too far and that I should rest on my laurels and be content in the part I had already played in spoiling the marriage of one Metherall and losing the fortune of another. I argued to myself that I should return to a more general assault on the rich—to robbing, swindling or perhaps the kind of political agitation at which Johnny spent his time. What difference would it make to the sum of things if one more adolescent girl was prematurely seduced? Alas, the indulgence of a general emotion is most powerful in a particular application; a man will do more for the sake of a single woman than he will for all humanity. So too with hate. The idea of robbing the rich, as such, no longer appealed to me. I only cared for the Metheralls. They had become my only interest in life, a private and mature obsession with roots reaching deep into my personality.

The only one of my former enterprises which retained my interest was the flat in Westbourne Grove, for a novel of Simenon's, *The Stain on the Snow*, had given me the idea of the particular circumstances in which little Martha might be recruited to serve in it. Indeed I marked that day as Victory Day when, in a dark room, she would lie virgin and naked waiting for me but be visited instead by another, and in my cellar I put aside a dozen bottles of Krug champagne to celebrate the occasion.

Women, being like other higher mammals, are susceptible to generalization; indeed, they are easier to study because their language can be understood. I based my plans for the seduction of Martha on the following observations: that like all women, she would turn out to be vain in a sexual context and therefore susceptible to flattery, especially that of an older man. I could assume, I thought, that she had reached the age of puberty—however scraggy—and that her asexual gaucheness was defensive. It was probable, I thought, given the evidence of her restlessness at school, that she was remote from her parents yet not close to anyone else, thus possessing a vacuum in her affections. I also knew that she would be romantic and idealistic—most susceptible to and influenced by hot breath down her neck and talk of love.

All the same, I worked cautiously and slowly. My love for her was supposed to be love at first sight, but I did not blurt it out until the third or fourth occasion on which I sneaked her out from school. By then I had no alternative but to open the subject of love, having exhausted my knowledge of O-level geography and biology and paid all the oblique, matter-of-fact compliments that would not have been palpably ridiculous.

My attentions were not without effect from the very beginning. I was like a politician talking to a constituent—bored in one sense yet interested in another, with the boredom concealed and the interest most successfully exaggerated. From the moment she first got into my car—blushing terribly—I was curious about her life at school, and my questions about her everyday habits—about what she had had for breakfast, for example—enabled her to get over her shyness.

"Awful muck," she said (in answer to the question about breakfast). "Porridge and thick, wet, flabby bacon."

"And do they force you to eat it?"

"Not really."

We drove toward Windsor, where I had booked a table for lunch.

"Did they believe you . . . about my being your brother?"

"Oh, yes. I mean, most girls go out sometime or other during the weekend."

"With their parents?"

"Or cousins or something like that."

"And do they sometimes . . . pretend?"

"I don't know."

"Some of the girls must have boy friends."

"Oh, yes, they do. In your last year you're allowed to go into Windsor and meet boys from Eton."

"It has to be boys from Eton?"

"They're terribly snobbish."

"It won't be so long, then, before you're allowed to do that."

"A year at least."

"It's something to look forward to."

"I hope I'll have left by then."

"Yes, of course."

"Anyway . . ."

"What?"

"It's not so wonderful . . . having tea with boys from Eton."

"Don't you like them?"

"They're pretty stupid."

"Stupid?"

"I mean . . . well, full of themselves."

"Not all of them, surely?"

"All the ones I've met. They think they're so wonderful, just being Etonians."

I smiled. "It doesn't help them much afterward."

"I'm sure it doesn't."

"I've met so many of them," I said, "with so much charm

and ease and confidence that there's no room in them for anything else."

"Exactly," she said. "I mean, look at Mark. He hasn't done anything since he left the army."

I smiled again. "You're both very strict about Mark. Harriet thinks he's spoiled."

"He is."

"She thinks you're spoiled too."

I glanced at Martha to watch her reaction to this. She lowered her head, blushed slightly and said, "I probably am."

"Well, in my opinion," I said, "so is she."

She laughed. "Most people are."

"And I think it improves them," I said. "Unselfish people are dull."

She laughed again.

At lunch she ate quite ordinarily but would not drink wine. We continued to talk about her school and family, though I admit that from time to time I found myself making certain observations about human nature such as those I have already described. It must have been her youth which inspired these homilies—and her innocence.

I have no idea what the other people in the restaurant thought of us. I should say that as a couple we were a convincing brother and sister, for while we were not particularly alike, there were quite obviously no outward signs of a relationship of flesh rather than blood. There may be those who are attracted to schoolgirls in their uniforms—indeed, I knew there were, for I had watched Rosamund and Alice change into such costumes at the request of customers—but I was not one of them. I found the thought of sleeping with her unpleasant. My pleasure nowadays was in the frustration of nature in one form or another; with her I would be bringing it on. Moreover she was thin, and thin women always remind me either of insects or of photographs of the inmates of Belsen. But my will was not weak. There was no question but that I would pursue the plan I had arrived at.

[226]

When I returned her to her school, I said, "I dare say you've been bored."

"Oh, no."

"But it's been nice for me."

"I . . . I liked it too."

"I realize I'm rather too old to be asking out a girl of your age"—I hesitated, but she did not interrupt to dispute either my statement or its implications—"but I should be glad if you'd have lunch with me again some time."

"I'd love to, but . . ."

"What?"

"They might get suspicious."

"At your brother's sudden interest in his sister?"

"Yes."

"Then say I'm Harriet."

"All right."

"Or an Etonian."

She smiled.

"I'll write to you," I said, as she got out of the car, "to say when I'm coming down again."

"All right," she said, "and thank you very much."

She walked back into the school and turned and waved just before she disappeared from my view.

There were two more meetings of this sort before I declared myself; even then I did so obliquely, in a most matter-of-fact voice, between a mouthful of meat and a mouthful of cabbage. "I hope you don't mind if I tell you something," I said.

"No. What?"

"It's rather personal . . . and pointed."

She was quite relaxed with me now. "Go on," she said. "Is it about Harriet?"

"No. It's about you."

I could not tell from her inquisitive eyes—the inquisitive eyes of a child—whether she had any idea of what I was going to say.

[227]

"About me?" she asked, rather as if there could be nothing to be said about her, at any rate nothing personal and pointed.

"Yes." I put my fork carrying food into my mouth and continued to speak with my mouth full. "It's rather self-indulgent of me to say this, but I've really rather taken a fancy to you."

She did not blush; she looked me straight in the eye. Perhaps she expected me to bring out a bag of sweets—or was she deliberately making my declaration more difficult for me?

"A fancy to you. . . . Yes, I really have," I said in conclusion.

"Well, I'm awfully grateful to you for taking me out like this," she said quickly. "I'm always glad to get away from school."

"I don't think you understand," I said. "What I mean is . . ."—here I pretended to be confused—"what I mean is that . . . well, I know I'm much too old and that you're really rather young, but I have . . . well, fallen for you . . . as a woman."

The only reaction she could have made which would have been disastrous for my purposes would have been to laugh, but she did not. Nor did she giggle. Nor did she blush. She merely looked down into her lap and said, in a tone of voice far from a childish one, "I thought there might have been something."

"Why? Do I look smitten with love?" I asked, in a slightly cynical tone of voice for someone who was supposed to be just that.

"No," she said, "but you said you had come down here on business and . . . well, you never seem to do any business and no one does business on a Saturday."

"How do you know," I said, "that I'm not painting someone's portrait, one of those rich racing women in Ascot?"

"You don't paint portraits, do you?"

"No. That's true. But I could just be visiting a prospective buyer . . . a collector . . . or painting a mural."

"Are you?"

"No."

"So you don't have any business down here?"

"No. You're quite right. It was an invention, a lie forced on me by necessity—the necessity being that from the first time I set eyes on you in Harriet's kitchen I . . . well, I loved you."

It was not surprising, since my tone of voice was caustic, my words pompous and my mouth intermittently full of food, that Martha should look up to see if my face could be evidence of my sincerity—and when my eyes met hers, I believe it was. I looked into her eyes and, with tears practically in them, added in a quieter tone of voice, "It's true. I swear it."

She said nothing, so I asked her if she minded my saying what I had said.

She shook her head. "No, of course not."

"I know it's hopeless," I said. "I'm much too old and all that . . . but it's rather nasty to have to keep something like that to oneself."

She opened her mouth to say something. I could see that it was difficult for her. "It's . . . it's terribly flattering," she said at last.

"For God's sake, don't be flattered," I said. "In fact you've no need to react at all. It's all a little embarrassing, and I'm old enough to know better. It's just that . . . well, it has made me a little happier to know that you know."

After this I changed the subject and did not refer to it again. Back at the school, I took my leave of her in the usual manner.

I now left her alone for a month or more, so that the idea which I had put into her mind could incubate. I felt sure that it would be more likely to take root in my absence, for she was bored and enclosed and would be better persuaded by her own imagination that some sort of love existed between us than she would be by my rather poor protestations over lunch in Windsor. I also wanted her to miss me—to feel the lack of the attention and interest and flattery she had been getting each weekend.

There was plenty to keep me amused in London. Mark had at last told his parents that he had lost every penny he possessed and might have to sell Lasterby. He had gone up to Yorkshire to give them the news, and so far as I could tell it had passed just as one might have expected—phlegmatically. There had been no screaming despair or poisonous recriminations, just a matter-of-fact statement followed by a slight blanching, a few further questions, a sigh, and much busying oneself with gardening and other small matters.

It appeared, however, that Lasterby was not to be sold immediately because a loan could be raised on it and Sir Edward could pay the interest out of his annuity. Lady Clare must have had some money too. The truth remained, all the same, that the family, previously so rich, would now be left in a state of genteel poverty.

"It's fate, really," Mark said to me, sitting back, drinking, in the drawing room of his house which he was soon to sell. "All going like that." He puffed at the palm of his hand.

It was just as well that he had fate to blame, for it saved him from facing up to the enormity of what he had done to his family; indeed, he seemed surprisingly happy for a man who had squandered his heritage. "You know," he said to me, "it might turn out to be for the best."

"How do you mean?" I asked.

"Well, with all that money I would never have done anything. Now I'll have to do something—to get it all back or just to make a living. I'll have to work, and I might make something of my life."

I would pretend to agree with him but reflect to myself

that with one hand holding a glass of whisky and the other stroking the neck of a whore he was unlikely to conquer the world.

That reflection led to other reflections. How was it that Carol still spent so much time with him? At fifty pounds a night, how could he possibly afford it? I put the question to Qazvini, who was evasive; then to Alice and Rosamund, who were also shifty in the answers they gave. Finally I put it to Carol herself on an afternoon when I found her in her room in the flat in Westbourne Grove.

She had been resting. I had woken her up. Her long beauty was warm and disheveled, and in that state she could not prevaricate but said at once that Mark no longer paid her.

"How do you mean?" I said.

"He hasn't any money now," she said. "We said good-by, but then I went back to him . . . on my own."

"My dear Carol," I said, doing my best to be calm but feeling all the same a hard fury rising within me, "it's not in the nature of your contract with us that you take up charity work of this sort."

She looked cross. "It's not charity work," she said. "I like him."

"The golden-hearted whore," I said, scoffing at her.

"Fuck off," she said.

I hit her, which showed, as may be imagined, the anger I felt toward her, for I detested violence, above all in myself. I did hit her, however, in the face, just as she was rising from the bed, and I hit her hard enough to send her back off her feet again.

"Look," I said, "you don't. If he can't pay, you leave him."

"I'll do as I like," she said, without any confidence.

"If you do as you like," I said, "I'll do as I like."

"Qazvini said . . ."

"It's nothing to do with him. I sent you to Mark Metherall and I'll take him back from you."

"I'll do as I like," she said again.

I hit her again and said again, "Then i'll do as I like. I'll split your nose and cut off your nipples. Then see if he wants your charitable fucking."

"If he knew . . ." she began.

But she did not finish, for I took her by the neck and said, "If he knows anything from you, you'll lose more than your nose and your tits." I threw her down. "Just remember what happened to Billy Cade."

She looked at me. "What is it?" she said. "What's he ever done to you?"

"Never mind," I said. "Just take it from me, he's done something."

"It doesn't make sense," she said. "How can someone as harmless as that have made you so nasty?"

"Leave him," I said. "I don't want to see you with him again."

All this time I was seeing Harriet almost every week, but I had lost all interest in her and she knew it. She once said, rather timidly, "I bore you, don't I?"

I looked at her and laughed. "Bore me? Why should you bore me? Just because you've no mind, no wit, and no experience of life . . ."

"Then why do you keep on seeing me?"

"For old times' sake."

"What old times?"

"You don't understand," I said in a silken voice, "how grateful I am to your whole family for the light and civilization they brought into my life. I fuck the daughter as a small token of thanks."

This all took place just after we had made love.

"You're not so bloody good at it," she said. "I don't know why I . . ."

"Nor do I."

"I could find someone else."

"Why don't you?"

"I will."

Then she burst into tears. It appeared that she had discovered a woman's hair on one of Freddy's suits and on this evidence had accused him of flagrant adultery. He had admitted it. Harriet sniveled as she told me this. "Not even a secretary," she said. "Some other bloody woman civil servant. She's getting a divorce. He wants one too."

"Well," I said to Harriet, "at least you can have a little experience of life on your own."

"I don't want it," she said. Then she gritted her teeth and said, "How dare he!"

"This whole business doesn't make you more interesting," I said to her. "It's a banal situation and I don't want to talk about it."

"How dare he!" she repeated, though under her breath and to herself.

"I should have thought you'd be delighted," I said. "You'll be free to find someone else. You must do the rounds— see who's on the market. There must be other marriages on the rocks, some other husband who won't mind your sagging bosom and belly and ceaseless, neurotic lechery. You can pass it off for passion. Or find yourself a black. Any white woman's beautiful to them, and if myths are to be believed they can keep it up forever."

"Oh, fuck off," she said. "Just go to hell and fuck off!"

She screamed. I laughed. This was the last time we ever slept together.

While waiting for Martha to ripen, I drew up a list of what I had in mind for her "season." I wished to establish a state of sexual thrall without depriving her of her virginity. All the pleasures to which she would become addicted had to be perverse. Her first love, I hoped, would be some senile businessman who would pay a thousand pounds to deflower the virgin daughter of an English baronet. Before that, however, I would take her on a grand tour of fetishes—rubber, shit

[233]

or milk bottles, it did not matter which or what or whether either of us would be moved by them.

I might start by having her "model" (I knew of several "classes" for amateur photographers), for a besotted child might easily be persuaded that there was nothing wrong with that; or we might run "anatomy classes." Her scragginess, of course, would exclude her from the normal markets of voyeurs who liked women's features, especially their breasts, to be exaggerated, but there was a specialist audience for adolescent girls.

Photographs of Martha in lewd poses could be sent, I thought, to Sir Edward and Lady Clare; perhaps also to a few of their neighbors. It was also my ambition that Martha should somehow contract crabs or gonorrhea and pass it on to the household at Lasterby Hall. By then, I thought, I would not care whether or not I was identified as her tutor in these tricks. She was, after all, my swan song. Indeed, I became increasingly sure that I would ultimately want them all to know what I had done, for how else should they feel remorse and regret?

It was a criminal offense to sleep with a girl under sixteen, but then that was not something that I intended to do. And even if I did, I knew quite well that it was rare for a jury to find a man of my age guilty of the crime. As for corruption —well, it was a risk, but I was so drunk with these ideas in my mind that I thought the danger a fair exchange and would be happy to barter a year or two in prison for the certain knowledge that Sir Edward and Lady Clare had found a lewd photograph of their little daughter in the morning post.

I was about to write to Martha to put these plans into effect when she wrote to me. There was, she said, a school holiday on the following Wednesday. Her parents could not come down from Yorkshire—there was some crisis—and she wondered whether I had any "business" in Ascot that day.

I sent back a telegram saying something like this: "My dear Martha, how nice it is to think that you have the whole day off on Wednesday stop will it be all right if I fetch you at ten stop we can then decide what to do stop with love from your brother Mark." The telegram was long, for girls, I knew, are impressed by petty extravagances. Only major and necessary expenses leave them cold.

The night before I went down to Ascot I saw Harriet at her home. She was in what is called a bad way. Freddy had actually left—had gone to live with his female colleague—and she felt humiliated. I suspected that she was less humiliated than lonely and expressed the view. She told me not to be ridiculous.

The scene took place in the drawing room. Like Mark, she had taken to drinking whisky. I told her that it would not do her figure any good. "Women who drink get beer bellies," I said, "and look as if they're pregnant."

"I don't drink as much as that," she said.

"It's funny," I said. "Neither your mother nor your father drink, yet you and Mark are both becoming soaks."

"I don't drink as much as Mark," she said.

"Very nearly."

"Have you seen him lately? He's really gone to pieces. That slut left him."

"Why did she leave him?"

"Because he's lost his money, I suppose."

"Is that what he told you?"

"No. He didn't say."

"I must ring him up."

"Why? Why ring *him?* You never ring me. At least I'm your mistress."

"No longer."

"Well, I was."

"You're my ex-mistress, then."

"Don't people ring up their ex-mistresses?"

"Sometimes . . . sometimes not. Not when they're drunk and tedious."

She sat down. "Oh, God, Hilary, I'm so unhappy."

"It's all your own fault. You treated Freddy like shit."

"I know . . . I know."

"He was very fond of you."

"I know."

"And I dare say you were very fond of him."

"I was, really I was."

"Then why did you kick him about like that?"

"I don't know. He was so . . . so dull."

"But so are you."

"Shut up, please shut up."

"You were really well suited."

"I know. We were, really. Should I ask him to come back?"

"I would if I were you."

"I think I will . . . but it's so humiliating. I mean she'll probably answer the phone. They work in the same office."

"Do you think he fucks her up against the filing cabinet?"

"Don't. I hate thinking about it."

"Are you jealous?"

"I'm humiliated."

"You've said that already."

"I'm sorry."

I stood up to go. "I should try and get him back," I said. "It's very unlikely that you'll find anyone so well suited to you . . . and without a husband you'll become an old tart. You'll probably become an old tart anyway, but it's more dignified with a husband."

"Don't go," she said.

"If you're discreet, the husband won't mind." I put down my glass. "If only you'd been discreet, he'd still be here." I moved toward the door.

"Can't you stay and have some dinner?"

"I'm afraid not."

"I'll cook you something."

"I don't like your cooking . . . and anyway, I've an appointment."

[236]

She stood up with a quick, nervous movement of her limbs. "Have you got someone else? Have you?"

I smiled. "Just nicely coming to the boil."

"Who is she? Do I know her?"

"No."

I went downstairs toward the front door.

"Are you going to see her now?" Harriet asked.

"No."

"Do stay, then. One can't cook dinner for oneself."

"Where's the nanny? Why don't you have dinner with her?"

"Oh, shut up."

I put on my coat.

"You will come and see me sometimes, won't you?" she said.

"When I can."

"Ring up."

"Yes."

I closed the door and left Harriet alone in the house with her children and the nanny.

Part Four

13

Martha was waiting for me outside her school in the usual way. It was a wet day and she wore a brown mackintosh over her uniform. She got into the car and I could tell at once from her color, and from the breathless way in which she said hello, that my formula (idea plus solitude plus imagination equals love) had not been wrong. And as we drove off she looked at me with the shy, nervous, blushing glance that is the usual symptom of an early stage in the disease.

Realizing that I had succeeded in the most difficult part of my plan, I was put into a good mood which I directed upon Martha. I felt grateful to her that she had responded so well. "Have you got the whole day?" I asked.

"Yes," she said. "I don't have to get back until seven."

"What would you like to do?"

"I don't mind, really."

"What about going up to London?"

"Well . . ."

"It would save us sitting around restaurants in Windsor."

"Yes."

"We could have lunch and then go to a film or to the National Gallery or something like that."

"Yes," she said. "And I can take a train back."

"No," I said, "I'll drive you."

"It's an awful bore for you."

"No. I like driving."

We were silent for a time; then I said, "You haven't ever seen my house."

"No," she said hesitantly.

"Wouldn't you like to?"

"Yes." Her voice was still uncertain.

"You can't really tell what a person's like until you see them in their homes," I said, "surrounded by their objects and possessions."

"That's true."

"I have the advantage," I said, "of having seen Lasterby."

"But not for a long time."

"No."

I did not drive fast, using the power of my car as cautiously as I was using my own. "I'm very glad," I said, "that you wrote me that note."

"I nearly didn't."

"Why not?"

"I didn't want . . . well, to bother you."

I smiled. "I very much wanted to be bothered. I was bothered anyway."

"By me?"

"Yes."

"I'm sorry."

"It's my own fault."

She looked, nervously, at her hands and said, "I'm sure you have so much else in London . . . to think about."

"There were plenty of things I might have thought about, if I could have got you out of my mind."

She did not reply; I believe she was made breathless by what I was saying, but the noise of the road and the car made it impossible to tell.

"The reason why I didn't write to you," I said, in a halting, awkward manner, suited to an embarrassed lover, "was . . . well, that I really wanted to try and get over you."

Again, she did not reply. I glanced to my left but she still looked into her lap and so her face was hidden by her thick hair.

"It's so hopeless," I said, "a man of thirty being in love with a girl half his age."

I waited, and eventually she said, in a quiet, firm voice, "It needn't be hopeless."

"But I can't imagine," I said, "that you could ever feel ... I mean, that you could ever love me."

She looked up but at the road, not at me. "I could," she said. "In fact, I . . . I think I do."

It was my turn to say nothing.

"I missed you," she said. "I missed you very much."

"Does that mean that you love me?"

"I think so, yes."

"But you miss your parents too, don't you?"

"Not especially."

"And Mark and Harriet?"

"No."

With my left hand I took hold of her right hand. She let it lie limply in mine. "You see," I said to her, "the love I feel for you is a real, mature love, a man's love for a woman."

"I know."

"It's affection, great affection, but it's also . . . well, physical love."

"I know."

I made free with her fingers and fingernails as if to illustrate what I meant.

"But can you . . . I mean, are you old enough to be able to feel that kind of love for me?"

"Yes," she said. Then she added, "Of course I am."

"You can't imagine," I said, "how happy it makes me to hear you say that."

"I'm happy too," she said awkwardly.

I took her to lunch at the Ritz. She did not seem to be impressed or unimpressed by her surroundings; nor were we especially incongruous as a couple, for among the businessmen there were one or two other family groups.

"It's so long," I said, "since I was your age that I can't remember what it was like."

"It isn't so different."

"But there must be a moment when one stops thinking and behaving as a child."

"I suppose so."

"When is it, then?"

"I don't know."

"But it must be quite recent for you?"

She thought about this question and then said, "Why must it be?"

"Didn't St. Paul say that when we are children, we think and act as children; and when . . ."

"Yes," she said, "I know he said that. But it happens gradually."

I smiled and said, "Perhaps you don't think you've changed because you haven't changed."

She saw my glance at her meager bosom and blushed. "I thought we were talking about changes in . . . well, sort of . . . thinking and attitudes," she said.

"Certainly," I said. "And you sound very grown up. But then so do some children."

She looked almost irritated, which was what I had intended.

"Maturity," I went on, "is less of the mind and more of the body, whatever anyone may say to the contrary. After all, you get children who can play chess as well as a grand master—and infant prodigies like Menuhin or Mozart."

"I suppose it is mainly . . . well, physical," she said.

"Look at the etymology of the word maturity," I said. "It's from the Latin *maturus*, isn't it? Which means seasonable or ripe? And what does ripe mean?"

I had intended the question to be rhetorical but then changed my mind and waited for an answer like a tutor with a student.

"What does ripe mean?" she repeated.

"Yes."

"Well, ready to be eaten."

[*244*]

I smiled. "Well, yes, that's from our point of view. But from the fruit's point of view, it means . . . well, that the seeds are fully formed, that it is ready to reproduce itself."

"Yes," she said. "I suppose it does mean that."

"With human beings, it's the same thing. The male and female hormones are secreted into the blood; they bring about the necessary physical changes and there we are—mature—ready to reproduce ourselves."

"Yes," she said.

I started to eat the oysters in front of me. "I can't remember," I said, "how we got onto the subject."

"You asked about being a child—and then grown up."

"Yes. And you said that you were grown up."

"Yes," she said, almost with defiance.

"I believe it," I said. "I mean, I dare say that under the definition we were just discussing, the seed being ripe and all that . . ."

She went red in the face.

". . . you come under the category of mature."

"Yes," she whispered.

"Well, my belief is that if you're physically mature, you're almost certainly emotionally mature—so that if you do love me, it's the real thing, not just a redirected love of your father or anything like that."

"Yes."

"But, you see, the law of the land, for instance, would not accept that."

"How do you mean?"

"Well, the expression of mature love is . . . well, what we were talking about."

"What?"

"Reproduction."

"Oh, yes."

"Of course it's quite possible for human beings to control their fertility . . ."

"Yes, you mean . . ."

"Contraception."

"Yes."

"But the expression of mature love between men and women remains what it has always been."

"Yes."

"Yet the law forbids it between you and me."

"Why, because I'm . . ."

"Because you're not yet sixteen."

"I didn't know."

"Yet where else in nature is a mature girl restricted like that by conventions from expressing her mature emotions?"

"I . . ."

"Nowhere. In all other species, as soon as the female is able to, she does."

"What?"

"Well . . ."

"Oh, I see."

"Don't you think?"

"Yes."

"You should know, with your O-level biology."

"Yes. I'm sure you're right."

"Now the age of puberty is, on average, around twelve or thirteen these days, yet the law still says that a girl of fifteen may not make love with a man—well, with a man of any age."

"It's ridiculous."

"Don't you think it is?"

"Yes."

We gestured to the waiter to bring in our next course and to change the wine from German white to French red. I was pleased to see that Martha was drinking what was poured into her glass. Indeed, the wine did its work excellently, for as we ate our way through the next course a flush came into her cheeks, nor was it a flush that was put there by anything I said, for our conversation by then had become almost chaste. I was describing the life of a painter. The flush appeared, then disappeared, then came to stay, like a distant light in darkness, and as it did so Martha's gestures too became less inhibited and her glances less shy. She looked at me and smiled at me and wet her lips with her tongue as if preparing them for a kiss.

At the end of lunch she was just *à point*—not only ripe but perfectly cooked—and I was eager to get her back to my house before the effect of the alcohol and salacious conversation had worn off.

"Now," I said lighting a cigar and paying the bill—the one after the other—"would you like a film or a museum or a tour around my house?"

Can anyone say that I ever forced her? Was she not given a choice? "I would . . . well, it would be quite interesting to see your house," she said; then she grinned a girlish grin and added, "after what you said about judging people by their houses."

"All right," I said.

We went out into Piccadilly, walked to my car and then drove along the south side of Hyde Park and Kensington Gardens. It was a nice afternoon. We did not say much. The situation was beyond words.

I have acclaimed the effect of the wine on Martha; I might also commend it for its effect on me. For as I have said, I did not find the chit beside me in her knee socks and school uniform in the least attractive—that is, when I was sober. Being now a little drunk, I could think of my imminent obligation with less distaste, indeed, almost with pleasure. She was, after all, a woman—or so she said—and if she was too bony, I could always pad her out with pillows. In any case, it was part of my plan that we should not go "all the way"—or, rather, that we should not go all the way in the ordinary way but content ourselves with irregular gestures and behavior. I wanted her debauched but intact, for certainly she loved me, and how can it harm a girl to lose her virginity to a man she loves?

It so happened, however, that in this scheme I was frustrated. It all went well up to a point but went wrong thereafter. I showed her around my house, paintings and objets d'art, and she seemed to like them. We went upstairs and, by the Renoir in the bedroom, kissed and kissed again. She had the drowsy look in her eyes of a woman in heat and I assumed that like all the others she would "let it happen." I murmured lovingly, "And how do you like my house?"

"It's very nice," she whispered.

"And what sort of character does it give me?"

She was silent; then she kissed me and said, "None."

This remark was a jolt. I drew back from her. "How do you mean?" I asked, in a sharper, less romantic tone of voice.

"Don't be cross."

"I'm not cross."

"We must tell each other the truth."

"Of course."

She smiled at me with an almost impudent expression. "Well, this house, it's like a museum. It's not lived in. There's no sign of any character."

I was irritated by this, but we still had our arms around one another and the wine was still in our blood so we kissed again and I started to take off the school uniform and the knee socks, implanting the odd kiss on the goose-pimpled skin that I uncovered in the course of my labors. Eventually she was naked and so was I, and though thin she was quite pretty. There was more of a bosom than I had expected; her stomach was pleasant and her legs were slender, straight and thin at the ankle. What was unusual was her behavior, for instead of lying back and waiting for me to do with her what I would, she put her arms around my neck and drew me to her. Had she read a manual of sexual instruction that enjoined this? For whatever reason, her arms were strong and her legs parted without wasting any time. I tried to extricate myself from this classic position, in case it led to classic behavior, but she mistook my motives for doing so and said, "What's wrong?"

"It's nothing. I just think . . ."

"I'm *not* too young," she said.

"No," I said, "I just thought we'd . . . well, lead up to it."

"I want it done," she said. "Come on."

In this position, and in the face of such determination, there was nothing I could do but comply.

She had a plan whereby "we could spend several days together" which she described to me, sitting back on my bed, covered by a blanket, while I looked morosely at the sheets.

"Mummy and Daddy don't really know when term ends," she said, "so I'll just say it's a week later than it really is."

"Yes," I said. Then, "Have you ever slept with anyone before?"

She blushed. "Of course not."

"Are you sure? A teacher at school, perhaps."

"Don't be silly."

"Usually," I said, "when you're a virgin . . ."

"It's riding," she said, quite firmly.

I looked at her, trying to tell if she was inventing a story or telling the truth. When one has made a false assessment of a person, it is difficult to recover and make a true one.

"Would you like that?" she asked.

"What?"

"For me to come and stay here for a few days?"

"Yes, of course," I said.

"I wasn't sure."

"Why not, since I love you?"

"I wasn't sure about that either." She smiled. "It has been known for men to say they love girls just to seduce them."

"It has been known, yes."

"And you're a pretty likely candidate for that sort of role."

"Why?"

"Well, you're obviously not queer. You seem to fall in love quite easily, and yet you've never married." She laughed. "Looks suspicious."

I smiled uneasily. "I was waiting for you," I said.

"And you're so ironic about everything."

"I . . ."

"I don't mind. I like it. It makes you interesting."

At that moment, I loathed her for her adolescent conceit and precocity. "I'll always be interesting," I said. "I can promise you that."

"I'll hold you to it." She got up onto her knees and said, "Can I make some tea?"

"If you like."

"I feel like some . . . after all that wine."

She got up, wrapped in a sheet, and went toward the door. "I hope you've got some tea in this museum?"

"Yes," I said. "There should be some."

I got up too and put on my dressing gown and slippers. I followed her down to the basement.

"I hope Harriet won't drop round," I said, to try and rattle Martha's irritating calm.

"Does she?"

"What?"

"Just come round?"

"Sometimes."

Martha looked at me, as if wondering if she could risk a remark, then said, "Well, if she does, it'll give her something to write home about."

I laughed, but inwardly I was full of rage at her good humor. She was not behaving as she should. Her conceited manner made me feel that I was the one who had been tricked and seduced.

She made tea not at all in the way that Pamela had made tea. There were no mats or sugar tongs. The cups were put on the kitchen table without saucers and the milk was poured out of the bottle. Still swathed in a sheet, Martha sat down on a stool and drank her tea. "Why don't you ever go to Yorkshire?" she asked me.

"I don't get on with my parents . . . at least, not with my father."

"I hardly know him; we just see him on Sundays. He looks quite harmless to me."

I did not say anything.

"What about your mother?"

"I meet her in York sometimes."

"Did your father . . . did he do anything against you?"

"Nothing in particular, no. I just don't like him."

"I feel sorry for him."

"Why?"

"In the pulpit . . . he looks so tired and sad and ill."

"Does he go to dinner with your parents every Sunday?"

"Yes."

"And does your Father go for a drink with him on Wednesdays?"

"Yes. Did he always?"

"Yes."

"I don't remember you at all."

"I used to come to your house almost every day."

"Why didn't you . . . I mean, if Mark and Harriet were such friends, why didn't you keep in touch with them?"

"I don't know," I said. "I came to London and . . . well, we just moved into different worlds."

"It's not surprising, really. They're not your sort."

I looked away. I took this remark to mean . . . Then she said, "I'm more your sort," and she smiled.

"How do you mean?"

"Wait and see," she said.

In the evening I drove her back to Ascot. She was not so conceited that she did not offer, again, to take the train, but I had nothing else to do so I drove her. By then we had arranged that in ten days' time, when her term came to an end, she would come and spend four or five days with me in London, before going up to Yorkshire. I went along with this plan, hoping that I would be able to succeed then in what I had that day so clearly failed to do. In thinking about this fiasco, I made myself angry—so angry, in fact that I did not kiss her good-bye. She looked puzzled by this but not hurt. After all, it was the only matter in which she had not had her own way.

It was late when I got back to London, but rather than return to the house I went to the club. There were few people there, and Eric told me that things were not going as well as usual. "Can't you arrange for someone else to lose half a million pounds?" he asked.

Rosamund was hanging around the tables looking for customers. "Where have you been?" she said. "You never come round these days, and Qazvini says you don't go to his place, either."

"I've been busy," I said, "but it'll be over soon."

I played the five chips I had bought and lost them. Rosamund watched and said, "Bad luck."

"You don't seem to have done much better."

"I never win at that," she said, nodding at the roulette table, "but I'm usually luckier in love."

"What about the others?"

"The same. Carol's off the game, anyway."

"Off it?"

"She's still at the flat, but she's not working. She must be ill. She's taken against you. What did you do to her?"

"She was giving too much credit."

"It isn't like you to mind about that sort of thing."

"She was giving it to the wrong person."

Rosamund said nothing, and not wanting to discuss my quarrel with Carol I moved away from the tables and then left the club. By half past two I was back in my house and preparing to sleep, reluctantly, on the messed-up bed.

The next morning I felt the sort of restlessness from which it is so difficult to escape in a city. All around me there was life and movement—a loud and healthy pulse in the midst of which there could be no calm—yet how could I be part of the general vitality when I had nothing to do? I went

[252]

into the studio to cover my quota of canvases and then, with paint on the palette, found that I could not.

I went back into the house and telephoned Harriet to ask her to have lunch with me. She said that she could not come out since it was the day off for the nanny, and she suggested instead that I go to her. Knowing quite well that I did not want to see her, I agreed and went straight out to find a taxi.

The door to the house was opened by one of her characterless sons. "She's in the kitchen," the boy said.

I went downstairs and found her by the stove stirring a sauce of some sort. She smiled at me and for a moment looked like her old self—healthy and haughty—but then she looked back at her sauce with a kind of tired concern.

"How are you?" she said.

"I'm all right. How are you?"

"Coping."

"Won't he come back?"

She glanced at the door to see if either of the children were within earshot and, seeing that they were not, said, "No, he won't. We're getting divorced."

"I'm sorry," I said.

She shrugged her shoulders. "It might turn out for the best. He was an awful bore, really."

"He was company."

"Mark's coming to stay here for a bit. He'll be company too."

"Has he sold his house?"

"Yes." She stirred the sauce and asked, "Do you like custard?"

"No."

"Nor do I. The children love it, though."

I leaned across the kitchen table. "What's Mark going to do?"

She laughed. "Believe it or not, he's a trainee bank manager."

"What?"

"He's going to be a bank manager."

"He already is a banker of some sort, isn't he?"

"No. He had to leave all that when he lost his own money. After all, who'd lend their money to someone with such a bad record?"

"Then why should they make him a manager?"

"It's a different firm, and anyway he's only a trainee. But as he says, he's got to earn his living."

"Won't he have to live in Croydon or Southend or somewhere like that?"

"I suppose so, yes. I'll have to find someone else, then, won't I? Another lodger." She gave me a suggestive smile. "You may have grown tired of me, but there are better fish in the sea than ever came out of it."

"Yes," I said. "I'm sure there are."

Her smile faded, as if she did not believe what she had just said. "Anyway," she said, "if Martha comes to London to a tutor's, she'll probably live here."

"What will that be like?"

She shrugged her shoulders. "Pretty awful."

"Why?"

"She's so spoiled and . . . well, I don't know. She really makes me quite nervous sometimes. She's so intolerant."

"She seemed quite grown up for her age."

"In some ways she's already middle-aged. She likes everything to go her own way."

"She'll lead a life of her own. You probably won't see much of her," I said.

"God help any young man who falls in love with her."

I smiled to myself, but Harriet noticed my smile and said, "Why are you so interested in her?"

"For no particular reason."

"You never do anything for no particular reason. I dare say you . . ." An idea entered her mind. "You haven't been seeing her, have you?"

"Of course not. How could I?"

[254]

"She's only fifteen, you know."

I smiled. "But she's already middle-aged."

She looked at me most suspiciously, and since it was not my intention to give anything away I leaned forward and said, "My interest in her is only as *your* sister. It's you I'm interested in."

Whether she believed this or not, Harriet was clearly relieved to return to conversation about herself and her problems. She began to say what a terrible mistake it had been to drive Freddy out of the house.

"It was partly my fault," I said.

"No, no," she said, too egotistical to admit my role. She went on and on until lunch was ready—about how a husband and wife should live together like a brother and sister if they no longer found one another attractive. "I mean, you can't divorce your brother, can you? Look at Mark. You love them even if you don't fancy them. Divorce is so middle-class."

The children were called to table. They fought with each other at lunch and the food was disgusting. I left as soon as I could afterward, but once in the streets I felt no less at a loose end. It seemed especially annoying that the thousands of others in the street seemed to have such definite purposes to their daily lives. I thought of going to a film, but in doing so I would only be filling an empty space in my mind. I walked to Hyde Park, but the sight of the children with their mothers and nannies only depressed me more. I thus went back through Notting Hill to Blenheim Crescent, hoping to find Qazvini. I went into the hall of his house and knocked on his door. There was no answer. Either he was out or did not want to be disturbed. I went up to the top of the house but there was no one there either. I then went down to the basement. There were sounds of talking but the stench was strong and the likelihood of seeing Caspar either drugged or groping at some other man revolted me, so I was about to go upstairs again when the door opened and Caspar came out.

It seemed as if he was not drugged, but he looked as vacant and filthy as ever. "Hilary," he said. "Well, come in . . . it's been a long time."

I went into his room. Another man with equally dirty clothes and the same long, unwashed hair sat on the mattress on the floor.

"I was looking for Qazvini," I said.

"He went out, I think," said Caspar.

I sat down on a chair and Caspar sat down next to his friend on the mattress. "What have you been doing?" he asked.

"Nothing in particular," I said.

He gave a most unpleasant, knowing laugh. "We have eyes, we have ears," he said.

"What do you mean?"

"My dear Hilary, I wouldn't want to embarrass you."

"What do you mean?" I was put in a worse mood than ever by Caspar's innuendo and felt like throttling out of him what he meant. "Nothing would embarrass me," I said, "but I hate vagueness."

"All right," said Caspar. "Cool down." His shifty eyes lit for a moment with junkie's panic as if he sensed how near I was to violence. "It's just that I saw you yesterday with that schoolgirl."

"Oh, her . . . yes."

"I think it's fantastic. I mean, welcome to the club."

"What club?"

His friend now looked at me mockingly. "Or was she your sister?"

"I haven't got a sister," I said.

"Of course you haven't," said Caspar. "I mean you just . . . I mean, *I* don't mind. I didn't know you liked schoolgirls, that's all."

"I don't.

He ignored my denial. "Schoolgirls are like schoolboys. It's the beauty of being the first one . . . the first little excitement, the shyness, the shame, the joy—then, boom, the first little explosion of ecstasy."

I said nothing. I could think of nothing to say that would not sound pompous and unnecessarily untrue.

Caspar leaned forward. "But what's it like? Is it as tight for you as it is for me? Or do you just wrap her little legs around your neck?"

I stood up. "Did Qazvini say where he'd gone?"

"Don't go," said Caspar. "I want to know what it's like, a little girl like that. Did she cry? I mean, did it hurt her?" His eyes were wide and bright. "Was she surprised? They never expect it to be as big as that, do they?"

I turned to go.

"Leave him, man," said the friend. "He doesn't like to talk about it."

"What's wrong?" said Caspar in a kind of whine. "A little cunt's the same as a little cock, isn't it?"

"You disgust me," I said. "You've always disgusted me."

"Come on," said Caspar, following me out of his room. "Come on, Hilary, don't be like that."

I did not believe that human behavior could affect the stomach, so I decided that it was the smell in Caspar's basement which made me feel sick when I came out of it. All the same, I was ringing with the revulsion I felt toward those two lecherous pederasts and felt sullied by their suggestion that I was one of their kind. It was especially grotesque that their instincts were right—that I had been with the schoolgirl to seduce her—but then why was I so angry that they had guessed as much? Was it so important that my motives were not as they seemed? That it was hate, not lechery, which led me to debauch the little girl as they did little boys?

For some reason I was unable to answer these questions which I posed to myself and yet was kept in the grip of my revulsion. The realization that it was unreasonable, since I rejected any notion of good or evil, only made me more

[257]

nervous, and in this state it became all the more important that I find Qazvini, for he alone could be counted on to calm me; he alone with his laziness and common sense could dispel my panic and neurosis.

I went to Westbourne Grove, first to the flat, then to one of the antique shops that he used as a front. He was at neither of them. I then tried another of his shops—the one where I had first met him after leaving school—and was told that he was expected there at any time. I therefore waited, and after twenty minutes he waddled in. Just the sight of his figure at the door did much to make me feel better.

Though we had seen little of one another in the past six months, he met me with the usual grin and slap on the back. "How are you?" he said. "Come and have some coffee."

We went into the same back room where the same coffee pot was ready with the materials for making Turkish coffee. We sat down and he lit the gas ring. "How are you?" he asked again.

"Not so well."

"What's wrong?"

"I don't know. I'm bored, really."

He laughed. "You're too rich and successful. Give your money to me and go back into the business."

"No," I said. "I'm past it."

He shrugged his shoulders. "Life is a struggle," he said. "You have at least to be improvident, extravagant or greedy and you're none of these things."

"I know."

We sat in silence for a while.

"Anyway," said Qazvini, "you have secret areas of your life that you never describe to me or to anyone else."

I nodded. "Yes."

"You do nothing for the obvious reason. You are pursuing something ... or perhaps you are pursued."

"I've almost tracked it down."

"Or has it almost tracked you down?"

"It comes to the same thing."

"What is it, then?"

"I don't know."

He studied my face. "You are a mystery to me," he said. "I have never once seen you look happy. You're energetic and capable, a real North European, and yet nothing you've done has made you any happier."

"Soon I'll be happy," I said.

"How?"

I smiled. "I shall make mine enemies a footstool under my feet."

Qazvini shrugged his shoulders. "I hope you're right. I hope it does make you happy."

"Well," I began. I was going to ask him what he meant by happiness but then was afraid to admit that I did not know. "You always seem so calm," I said.

He laughed and said with self-deprecating irony, "It's the inner contentment of the Orient."

"I envy you."

"My dear Hilary, there's nothing to envy. I take life very easily, but then there's no reason why I should not. I could never be a great man. Soon I'll go back to Iran where my father will get me a post in the civil service from which I shall continue to make a dishonest living."

"Can I visit you out there?"

"Could I trust you with my wife?"

"Will you have a wife?"

"Of course."

I smiled. "No woman is worth the sacrifice of a friend."

Qazvini lit a Turkish cigarette and we went on talking, first in the shop, then at an Indian restaurant where he ate five different curries and two bowls of rice. Toward the end I started to tell him about the Metheralls—to illuminate for him the dark areas of my life—but either he was not interested in what I said or he was unable to understand the strength of my feelings. All he said at the end was, "You English are all snobs of one sort or another."

For all this incomprehension, his company succeeded in calming me. I slept well that night and next morning felt fresh enthusiasm for the corruption of Martha Metherall.

She wrote me a short letter in a solid, childish hand, explaining that it would be better if I did not fetch her from school because she normally took the train to London at the end of term and any departure from this might cause suspicion. For the same reason—since there would be several companions on the train—she thought it best that I did not meet her at the station. She had my address and could take a taxi. She hoped I would not mind if she brought rather a lot of luggage, but she would have to bring everything that she would be taking up to Yorkshire.

She started the letter with "Darling Hilary" and ended it "With all my love." I used the same expressions of endearment in my reply, which merely confirmed that her arrangements were suitable.

Thereafter I waited. I saw a little of Qazvini and of Harriet and something of Mark, who now lived with her. He went off every day, however, to his course as a bank manager and got very drunk at night. He was still depressed about Carol—or so he told me one night—but agreed with me, morosely, that a whore is always a whore.

The only other thing I remember doing in those two or three weeks was trying to make my house look more lived in. I was unsure of quite how to do this, but I threw some magazines on the sofa and put the television on the floor. Unfortunately the woman who came in to clean the house put the television back on its stand the next morning and picked up all the magazines. After this I thought the best method to obtain a lived-in effect was to stay in the house as much as I could, cooking my own meals and eating them in front of the television, which was back on the floor. But every morning the kitchen was cleaned and tidied and the television placed once more on its stand. I felt unable to tell the woman that I wanted it left on the floor.

I gave up. I just waited for Martha and planned her degradation. It was difficult to summon up the spirit to do this, for much of the cold fervor with which I had ruined Mark and corrupted Harriet had been dissipated by the success of these endeavors. Moreover Martha was my enemy at second hand, rather like a Romanian or a Finn in the Second World War. Against her as an individual I had nothing—indeed, I had to admit that she had little of the conceit of her class. My only interest in her was her worth to her mother and father, and it was the memory of their arrogance and condescension which kept me going. Even that, of course, was a long time ago. In retrospect, they seemed to have lost much of their cruel glitter; they were as ludicrous and pathetic as any other pair of country buffoons, coming up to London in their tweeds and mackintoshes as if paying a visit from the last century.

It was essential, as I sat in my house waiting for Martha, that I refresh my memories of my intolerable childhood and gloat in my imagination over the assault I would make on the parental sensibilities of those two old fools. If only Martha had bled in losing her virginity, I might have sent them the sheets.

I dwelt on that, on the fact that there had been no bleeding. Her explanation—the horses—how likely was that? More likely the groom. With sudden terror it occurred to me that I had not been the one to deflower her, that some local boy had been there before I had had the chance. The idea was humiliating, but the newspapers of the time were full of stories of adolescent immorality. But then could she have lied to me so easily? Do not women in love tell the truth?

Of course I knew that they did not. Quite the contrary. Love inspires the lie and makes them more convinced of it than they are of the truth. I remembered Harriet in Paris, her gay assertion that Madame Vignon's son-in-law was greasy. I even remembered the way she had wrinkled up her nose with revulsion. What liars, what liars!

I became quite incensed as I thought of Martha's deceit, for I had convinced myself that she had been sullied before I had touched her. Was that not the reason why she had made me behave in a normal manner? If she had not done it before, how could she have been so definite and confident in her gestures?

I almost stamped with rage but also, I dare say, with a kind of fear, for never before had I been so taken in. What is more, to have been deceived in this, a sexual matter, left me somehow without resources, for my only weapons had ever been my skill at burglary, my convincing hypocrisy and my sexuality. If she had no property that I could steal, if she could successfully pretend to be what she was not, and if she was already debauched, then she was, as it were, impregnable.

I was put in a bad temper. I only came out of it by convincing myself that, while all this might be possible, it did not mean that all was lost. Even if she had had a tumble in a haystack with a farmer's son, she was still more or less innocent. Did she not love me? Did not that make her vulnerable? Was there not that to destroy?

She arrived just as she had said she would, in a taxi, and brought with her a suitcase and a trunk. I came out and with the taxi driver carried this luggage into the house. Martha was still wearing her school uniform and out of a pocket took a pound note with which she paid for the fare. I offered to pay but she refused to let me.

The taxi departed. We went into the house and found ourselves standing alone in the hall. Martha looked shy and I suddenly felt embarrassed, but only because I was confused by her shyness.

It was four in the afternoon, so I suggested that we have

tea. She agreed and we went down to the kitchen, where I filled and then switched on the electric kettle.

"How was school?" I asked her.

"Pretty ghastly," she said.

She seemed almost too shy to look me in the eyes—more shy, certainly, than she had been on the last occasion we had met. I too continued to be confused because I had convinced myself that she was confident and deceitful, yet here she was with blushes which, if they were simulated, would do credit to the best drama school in the country.

The tea was made; I sat on a stool drinking mine while Martha lifted her light body onto the kitchen table and sat there, dangling her legs, facing me.

"Did you miss me?" I asked her, for something to say.

"Yes." she said. "Did you?"

"Yes."

We sipped the hot liquid in silence. Then I said, "Did anyone suspect anything?"

"No. I don't think so. I just hope we don't run into Harriet."

"Is she expecting you to stay with her?"

Martha smiled. "I'm having lunch with her on my way through. On Wednesday."

"Good."

While saying this, Martha looked at me, and when the remark was finished and the smile had gone from her lips she did not stop looking at me. For a while I met this oppressive stare but then, as if directed by it, let my own eyes travel down her body, past her slouched shoulders and school shirt to her dangling legs. With no visible movement of any muscles, they moved backwards and forwards from the knee, and at the knee they were slightly parted, the brown stockings disappearing into darkness under the green skirt.

I was hypnotized by the dangling legs. I must have watched them in silence for five minutes, and all the time her eyes were on me and did not move. Eventually I looked

[263]

up and met her gaze again. Its meaning was unmistakable, and almost involuntarily I stood up and went to her. Her eyes half closed, she leaned forward on the table. I held her shoulder and kissed her lips and then carried her upstairs to my bedroom. All the time she lay in my arms as if in a kind of coma and all the time I acted as if I only half controlled my movements. I placed her on my bed and began to undress her but with unusual care and gentleness, treating her skirt, her blouse, her stockings as if they were rare and fragile garments; the stockings, even, I held to my lips as if they were the relics of some saint.

Through all these sentimental movements she remained passive, her eyes half closed, opening occasionally to stare at me with the same expression as if reinforcing the spell she had cast over me. It was only when I was as naked as she was that her body came alive and clung to mine with all its warmth and strength. I felt a longing to the tips of my fingers and toes. Never had I felt my whole body take on a will of its own; never had the body of a woman demanded with such imperiousness that I feel and behave in a certain way; nor, since, has there been an occasion when my mind so happily abandoned its prerogatives to the dictates of my body.

I recovered from the sentimentality of that afternoon and made repeated attempts in subsequent sexual encounters to interest Martha in various perversions, but while willing to try anything she always concluded that she "preferred the ordinary way." Some practices she thought "unhygienic," others "painful," and she thought "wearing rubber macs and things" was ridiculous.

She never got tired of ordinary humping and in time began to exhaust me. Much of her visit to my house was spent in bed, making love or recovering from it. "We'd better not go out," she would say. "We might run into Mark or Harriet"; and then, "Since we're staying in, we might as well . . ."

The worst fiasco in her education in perversity was the lesson in masochism, for when, in the course of making love, I proceeded to bite and scratch her, she stopped, opened her eyes and said, "You're hurting me."

"Don't you like it?" I said.

"Like it? Why should I like being hurt?"

"Some people do."

"Don't be stupid."

We started up again and I kept my claws drawn in and my mouth shut.

While showing me in this way her own indestructible normality, Martha also gave me a lesson in making a house look lived in. She left her clothes lying all over my bedroom and hung her navy-blue bloomers to dry over the bath. The kitchen was a mess, and because of her presence I had had to tell my cleaning woman not to come in. In the sitting room, the television remained on its table but magazines and cushions were strewn around with a genius that left no corner tidy. My statuettes and bric-a-brac were moved to make way for a glass of wine or her transistor radio, which she never switched on but carried around like a trophy. It had been her last birthday present.

Her trunk, which she opened in my bedroom, was filled with hockey boots and exercise books. The only clothes she possessed besides the various sets of uniforms were a brown tweed skirt and a matching jersey. I therefore offered to take her out and buy her some clothes at the boutiques, an offer which she accepted with evident joy. It appeared that Lady Clare would never let her wear the clothes she wanted, thinking them unsuitable for Yorkshire. What she wanted, it turned out, were the kind of skirts, slacks and dresses that every other girl of her age wanted. They were easy to find and to buy. She was worried at first that I was spending too much money on her but then decided that it was "rather fun being a kept woman."

[265]

"Of course," she said when we got home, "I shall have to leave them here. I could never explain to Mummy where I'd got them."

"Of course," I said.

"You won't mind, will you?"

"No. Why should I?"

"It might be rather embarrassing if some other woman paid you a visit like this."

"But no other women do."

"Really not?"

"Don't you believe that I love you?"

"Of course I do. But it is possible, isn't it, that you might love someone else as well?"

"Can a man love two women at the same time?"

"I don't know. How should I know? I'm only fifteen." She smiled at me and revived all my doubts about her constancy.

"Could you?" I asked.

"Oh, no," she said, most seriously.

"Have you ever loved anyone else?"

"Never."

"Have you ever been kissed by anyone else?"

"Yes, at Pony Club dances."

"Did you like it?"

She shrugged her shoulders. "It was quite exciting."

"And did you do a little bit more than kiss?"

"No."

"Such as getting fucked."

She frowned. "Don't talk like that."

"Like what?"

"Using that word. It's very ... unattractive."

"Lying is unattractive too."

"Who's lying?"

"You are."

"What about?"

"About ... about never having slept with anyone before."

[266]

"Of course I'm not. Who could I have slept with?"

"The boys at the Pony Club dances."

"Ugh."

"I don't mind if you did. I just want you to tell me the truth."

"I didn't. Anyway, how could I have done? Upstairs? Things have obviously changed since your day, if you think one can just go upstairs at a Pony Club dance and . . . well, what you said." She smiled.

It infuriated me that she could laugh at me when I was so plainly upset. I was also no nearer to the truth. She could be lying or not. There was no way of telling. I therefore let the matter drop, but she continued to seem to laugh at me. At one moment we were talking about Harriet. "Does she have lovers?" I asked, hoping to shock her by the suggestion.

"I wouldn't be surprised," she said.

"Doesn't that shock you?"

"*I* can't talk."

"You're not married."

"No." She smiled again. "And Hattie's not still at school."

On her last evening we risked recognition and went to *Fidelio* at Covent Garden. I poured myself a drink and sat reading the paper when waiting for her to change into one of the dresses we had bought the day before, and when she appeared before me I was struck—almost shocked—by her prettiness and elegance. She had style, I thought, more style than one would expect from a girl from the counties.

I felt almost proud to be seen with her at the opera. The only flaw in the evening was a remark she made in the interval about the prisoners' chorus. "It makes one think," she said, "of what it must be like for all the political prisoners in Russia."

"What do you know about that?" I said sharply.

She blushed and said, in a much less certain tone of voice, "Only what I've read, I suppose."

"Well, it's mostly lies," I said. "What do you know about

darkness of any sort anyway? What have you ever had but light?"

"Please don't get angry," she said. "I didn't mean to upset you, and if you go on you'll make me cry."

I was pleased by this. It showed that I could upset her if I chose, that I had some power over her happiness.

We had dinner after the opera at a restaurant nearby and I sat back and let her talk, which she did almost nervously, as if my outburst in the theater had taught her to take more care. She said nothing in particular but I could see that she was trying to entertain and amuse me and to some extent she succeeded.

After a while, however, she suddenly said, "Why don't you talk to me, now?"

"What about?" I asked.

"About . . . well, your life."

I shrugged my shoulders. "There's nothing much to say about it."

"One would have thought," she said, "that a painter's life would be very full and . . . interesting."

"It's not."

"Do you have friends who are painters?"

"No."

"Who are your friends?"

"Mark," I said.

"Who else?"

"I have one or two others. You wouldn't know them."

"Can't I meet them some time?"

"Why?"

"Well, you can judge someone as much by his friends as by his house, don't you think?"

"You might find that they revealed as little as my house."

"If they aren't artists, who are they? What do they do?"

"One of them," I said, "is an art dealer . . . my dealer."

"Yes."

"Another is a sort of . . . teacher." I was thinking of Caspar.

"Anyone else?"

"A third makes his living in . . . well, radical politics."

"They sound quite interesting."

"They're not especially interesting."

"At least they're not bankers and stockbrokers or land-owners."

"Are they boring?"

"I think so."

I said nothing.

"Don't you?"

"I don't know," I said. "I don't see why landowners should be more boring than their daughters."

She blushed and bit her lower lip. But then, instead of threatening to cry, she frowned and said, "If you find me boring, you've no need to see me."

I blushed in my turn. It did not serve my purpose to distance her by my rudeness. "Not at all," I said. "I don't find you boring."

"Then why did you imply it?"

"I don't find your father boring, either."

I thought that that would somehow catch her but it did not. "You haven't spoken to him for years," she said.

"No," I said, "but I remember him."

"Then he must have changed," she said, "because he is rather boring now. Anyone is boring who shuts themselves up in the country for all their life."

"Perhaps," I said.

She paused; she simmered down. "You can't remember much about Yorkshire," she said, "but the social life up there is . . . well, limited."

"I don't remember," I said.

"And what there is is quite unrealistic. They're all acting."

"Acting what?"

"I don't know . . . a kind of historical charade. They drive cars instead of coaches, but otherwise they could be living a hundred years ago."

"Don't you like that?"

"No."

"Why not?"

"I don't know. I want to live the life of the age I live in."

"I'm glad if you think you can pin it down."

"I can't . . . just like that. But you know what I mean."

I shrugged my shoulders.

"You paint abstract paintings, don't you? Whereas Lasterby is filled with old pictures, and the best the neighbors can show on their walls are hunting prints."

I looked into her face, into her bright, fierce eyes. "I don't disagree with you," I said. "I used to feel something like that."

She paid no attention to what I had said but went on, "And the schools they send us to are just as bad. I don't see why everybody can't go to the same sort of school."

She looked at me as if I might disagree but I did not.

"Look at Mark," she said. "What use was Eton to him? It got him a job in the City, but at the same time it made him hopeless and useless, when it comes to the modern world."

"Quite," I said.

"Whereas you . . . you didn't go to Eton, did you?"

"No."

"I thought not, because an Etonian painter . . . well, just the idea is absurd."

"They're meant to be prime ministers."

"Even that; they can't do that any more. Look at stupid old Sir Alec."

"So you wouldn't send a son of yours to Eton?"

"Most certainly not."

"Where would you send him?"

"To the ordinary local grammar school."

I nodded.

"Wouldn't you?"

I shrugged my shoulders. "The thought of having a son had never entered my head," I said.

As it entered hers it suddenly made her think of something, and her tone changed from the strident to the bashful. "I don't need to worry, do I? About that?"

"What?"

"I mean . . . about getting pregnant. I've rather assumed that you've been taking precautions."

"Oh, yes," I said vaguely. "Anyway, it's easy to get an abortion if you've got the money."

"Yes," she said, "but I'd never have an abortion."

How could she have thought that I was "taking precautions" when it was patently obvious that I was not? Or was she really so innocent that she did not know what taking precautions meant? I did not think of it again. After all, why should I care if she became pregnant? Indeed, it would suit me quite well if she did.

We went to bed that night quite like a married couple after a night out on the town. The next morning I helped her pack her trunk.

"Are you sure you don't mind me leaving these clothes behind?" she asked, looking at the entire wardrobe she had requisitioned.

"Not at all."

"I'll wear them when I come back . . . that is, if you ever ask me back."

"When can you come?"

"At the beginning of term? I'll do the same thing. I'll say it starts earlier than it does."

"Very well."

"Are you sure you want me?"

"Of course."

"I thought you might have had enough of me."

"Never."

She came across and hugged me. "Well, I must say, I don't know how I'm going to last that long."

Later, just as she was about to leave, she said, "Will you write to me?"

"All right," I said.

"But don't say anything specific—I mean, rude—because Mummy might read them. She snoops when I'm out riding."

"Very well."

I rang for a taxi and she set out for Harriet's house, where she was to arrive as if from Victoria.

Soon after that I received a letter from my mother to say that my father was ill and I should come home to see him. I wrote a short note to say that at present it was impossible. A week later she wrote again to say that, though the doctors had not said so, she thought he was dying. Apparently he had cancer. I wrote again to say that I was sorry to hear that he was ill; that he must be an intolerable patient; that he would be better off in a home or a hospital; and that I was working hard for an exhibition and so could not come north in the foreseeable future. "If he is dying," I added, "my presence would only spoil his last hours. Has he asked for me? I doubt it. If I was sure that you needed me, I would come —but I am confident that your plight has been pounced upon by the idle, well-meaning neighbors."

It occurred to me that this reply was a little cruel, but my mother, like all mothers, liked to create sentimental situations where it were better there were none.

I had not counted on my mother's closeness to Lady Clare, and Lady Clare's closeness to her daughter, for three days after this I received a letter from Martha. I knew it was from her from the writing on the envelope. "Darling H.," it read. "How can you be so heartless? Daddy says your father's going fast and your mother is miserable that you won't come. And anyway, don't you see? It would be an opportunity for us to see each other, so you must come. With love and many passionate hugs () () () and kisses x x x Martha. P.S. Don't bring this letter with you since your mother might find it."

I put this letter back in its envelope and for an hour wandered around the house—the floorboards creaking under the carpet, the brown backs of the houses overlooking my garden staring in like dead beasts. From the top floor I looked out at the skyline of roofs, chimneypots and odd, characterless modern constructions. I imagined what it would be like going back to Lasterby: to the granite rectory, the lanes, the village and the hall. I felt a kind of horror at the prospect, also a fear that Martha, in her father's house, would change from the cheerful, lively schoolgirl to the same haughty, horselike girl that Harriet had been. But then why should I care if she did? It would make it easier.

I found myself in my bedroom looking once again, as I had so often done in the past fortnight, at the clothes she had bought and worn and left like the end of a string which would lead me to Lasterby, and from curiosity, more than anything else, I followed the string. I packed a suitcase and drove out of London to the north, telling myself as I did so that at any time I could turn back. I stopped for petrol but drove on, past the singed, dusty grass of the countryside around London and around the eastern cities of Stamford, Grantham and Newark until I reached York. It was three in the afternoon. I stopped the car in front of Monk Bar and thought again about what I was doing; but ten minutes later, with no clearer idea of what I was about, I drove into the city and then out again to the north, and though I had not been on that road for more than ten years I had no need to ask the way for I remembered every corner and gradient and recognized every brick-built farmhouse on the way.

Then, after ten miles or so, the barns and farmhouses ceased to be built of brick and became built of stone, the gentle, crumbling limestone of my childhood. I had forgotten the beauty of these buildings, the last band of gracious everyday architecture to the north. I had forgotten, too, the calming presence of the trees by the side of the road. They were now half in leaf and stood over my car as I drove, or were to be seen far away in a vista through the Howardian Hills. On the last ridge of those hills I saw, in the rare clarity of that spring day, the dark mauve line of the Yorkshire moors and there below me the secret kingdom of Ryedale.

The effect of my drive through this countryside was such that, when I reached the rectory at Lasterby, far from feeling dread I felt elated. I parked the car and forgave the house its somber walls and dark windows as if this one sick cell was smothered in the health and beauty surrounding it.

I walked into the house and smelled at once the illness of my father. I went into the kitchen and saw my mother at the stove. She turned and said, "Oh, Hilary!" and burst into tears. Having always been fond of my mother—and being in this mood of elation—I went to her and hugged her. She kissed me and then went back to the stove, where she was mixing some kind of gruel.

"Is that what he eats?" I asked.

"He tries," she said, "but he can't really eat anything— nor even drink."

"Is he asleep?" I asked.

"I don't know," she said. "I don't think so."

"I'll go and see him," I said.

I said all this without thinking, but even if I had reflected I would not have acted otherwise, for I could not have imagined my father's appearance or the effect it would have on me. Had I done so I would certainly have left the house and returned to London.

I entered his room. It was dark because the curtains were drawn shut. I went toward his bed and looked for some moments to make out his face, for it was hard to recognize— partly because it was now covered by a beard, partly because

[274]

his hair, once so short, was now long, which made his face seem thinner still.

When, at last, I did see—increasingly clearly in the half-light —his emaciated form, I found myself trembling. His eyes were closed so he could not see me, and I tried hard to regain control of myself before making my presence known. What shocked me was how near the living man already was to a corpse—indeed, to a skeleton. His skin, which was yellow, was stretched over the bones so that the hand which lay on the sheets seemed to have no flesh on it at all. His beard, too, was appalling; but most shocking of all were his eyes, which he now opened, for they were large and frightened and they moved slowly as if stiff, or afraid of what they might see.

If he had been expecting to see the Devil, he would not have behaved much differently than he did on seeing me, for when his eyes met mine he shrank away and grunted. I could think of nothing to say but from a kind of perversity moved nearer to him and said, "I'm sorry I couldn't come sooner."

He seemed to understand and relax at my conciliatory tone. I intended to say nothing more but again was impelled to say, "I'm sorry to see you so sick."

He made a movement of his body as if shrugging his shoulders; then he made a series of sounds which were clearly meant to be words but were indecipherable as such. I leaned forward but he waved me aside. With great effort he leaned over and took a pencil and pad from his bedside table and wrote, in the most wavering handwriting, "I had cancer a year ago."

"I didn't know," I said.

He nodded and closed his eyes again.

"What do the doctors say?" I asked.

He gave an exasperated shrug to his shoulders.

"They always prevaricate," I said.

He nodded.

"Is there anything you want?" I asked.

He shook his head so I left the room.

Later I went in again with my mother, and together we tried to help him to drink the gruel from an invalid cup. It appeared, however, that he could not swallow and after some minutes he gestured to us to stop trying.

At seven the doctor—new since my time—came to call on his patient. He went in to see my father and I heard him say, in a blustering voice, "How are we today?" My father made no reply.

Afterward I asked the doctor to describe the situation. He was thin, middle-aged and wriggled in his tweed suit. "We're not positive," he said. "Your father had cancer in his throat a year ago but the operation was successful. Now . . . well, there doesn't seem anything wrong with his throat but there's a swelling in his ribs. We've X-rayed it."

"Is it cancer?"

"Well, it could be," he said. "The specialist thinks it may just be a cracked rib."

"A cracked rib?"

"They crack easily at his age."

"And what do you think?"

"Well," he said. "It could also be senile arthritis. We can't be sure."

"Shouldn't he be in hospital?" I asked.

"Oh, no, I don't think so. I mean, your mother looks after him so excellently here. It might just alarm him to be taken into hospital."

"It would seem to me," I said, "that he hasn't long to live."

The doctor sucked his gums and said, "It may seem like that to you, Mr. Fletcher, but you've only come up today, haven't you?"

My mother came in with a tray on which were three glasses of sherry. The doctor turned to her and said, "We've seem him looking quite perky on some days, haven't we, Mrs. Fletcher?"

"Oh, yes," she said. "On some days he's definitely better."

Being tired after my drive, I went to bed early that night but I was awakened at two or three in the morning by my mother. "He's ringing his bell," she said—and indeed I could hear the bell which had once been used to bring me into lunch from the garden.

"What does he want?" I asked.

"I don't know, but come in with me, Hilary."

I got up, put on my dressing gown and went into my father's bedroom ahead of her. There was a lamp in the corner of the room, covered by a rug to subdue its light. I went to his bed; he lay in a position of apparent discomfort and this may have been why he called us. I leaned over to set him on his back, but my touching him must have caused him great pain for he cried out with a croak. I let him go and then, more gently, took hold of him again and helped him to lie in a more comfortable position.

"Are you all right now?" I asked him.

He turned his huge, gloomy eyes onto me and said something. I could not make out what it was so I gave him his pencil and pad.

"Stay," he wrote.

"All right," I said. I turned to my mother, who was standing behind me, and told her to go back to her room; then I sat on the end of my father's bed and waited, watching. His eyes were closed again and his breathing was difficult.

"Are you in great pain?" I asked him.

He shook his head.

I sat in silence for a time. It looked as if he might have fallen asleep, but then he suddenly opened his eyes, which darted to and fro with an expression of uncontrolled terror. He must have forgotten I was there, and in the face of his fear I felt helpless; indeed, his panic was so acute that in this foul dark and silence I too became afraid and would have left him but instead leaned forward and took hold of his hand. It was cool and it gripped me with morbid strength. His eyes

[277]

met mine and fixed on me the full expression of a hysterical, irrational fear of death.

I kept his hand in mine until dawn. In time his eyes closed and he slept again, and as he slept I pitied him and prayed that he would never wake again to realize that he was dying.

At seven my mother made breakfast and I went down to the kitchen to eat it. She looked so much older, and from plump she had become fat, yet in her docile eyes there was none of the fear that during the night had spread from my father to me. With none of the sense of horror and disgust which I felt for this dying man she bathed my father's ghastly body and changed his soiled sheets. I helped her and then, at my own instigation, clipped his fingernails, which had grown long. He was conscious while we did this but said nothing. His eyes when they were open were peaceful, as if all the terror and panic had left him.

I sat with him that day. The doctor came and went with his bluster and evasion; my mother gave him a glass of sherry downstairs. Into the night I waited, sitting on a chair by my father's bed. I held in mine his cold and bony hand, and when they were open I watched his calm but emptying eyes. His breathing became slower, heavier, intolerably difficult. I waited like a mechanic for the end to come, for his heart would not long stand the strain. At eleven my mother came in. I sent her out again to call the doctor. As she left the room I watched my father. I longed for his eyes to open and show hope. They did open, just as his breathing stopped—but only to show me that the gaze was finished and roll around into his skull.

When my mother returned, having rung the doctor, I told her that it was too late, that her husband was dead. She stood by the door and came no nearer his body. Then she sighed and said, "Oh, dear, then we needn't have bothered Dr. Brown."

My father lay in his coffin in the sitting room for a day. There were no relatives to be called to his funeral, and he had had few friends who might want to take a look at him before he went into the earth. I myself spent some time looking at his face, just the eyes and nose showing out of the shroud. These features were not expressionless, but the expression did not seem to belong to the man who had been living. It seemed too feminine—or perhaps it was the shroud which made it seem so.

My mother looked in once or twice, and in the middle of the morning the Reverend Mr. Brawley from the next parish came to make arrangements for the funeral. Also one or two members of the Parish Council made short visits "to pay their last respects." The last of these was Sir Edward Metherall.

I noticed at once how much older he seemed to be than the man I remembered. Nearly twelve years had passed since then, in which time he had suffered certain family disasters; all the same it astonished me that he looked like an old man and moved like one, shuffling into the house as if he was wearing slippers. He kissed my mother—which he never used to do— and she cried. Quite firmly, then, he patted her on the shoulder and asked to see the corpse of my father. I showed him into the sitting room.

"I'm glad you got back in time," he said to me as we entered.

I did not reply but took him across to the coffin. There he stood in silence, watching my father; as he did so I glanced at his face to see if fear of his own death would show on his features. The expression, however, was placid, almost benign. He looked sorry, not angry or afraid.

"He suffered a lot of pain," he said to me.

"He must have done."

"It lasted too long," he said.

I said nothing, for I felt that the remark was not addressed to me but rather to the corpse or to fate or to God. Sir Edward behaved for a time as if I was not there. He walked across the room to the window and looked out onto the lawn. Then, suddenly, he turned and faced me. "Did you talk to your father before he died?" he asked.

"He couldn't really talk," I said. I walked a few steps

[279]

toward the door, fearing that Sir Edward was about to begin an awkward conversation. He was puffing up as if duty was impelling him to an unsavory task.

"He talked to me about you," he said. "It was a pity that you didn't understand him."

"We didn't get on very well," I said.

"He was afraid of you," Sir Edward said, sitting down on the sofa.

After that, in the presence of my father's body, I was all the more eager to leave the room, but somehow in this room with this man all the constrictions of my upbringing returned to me and from politeness I stayed.

"You see," Sir Edward said, "your father was always a little . . . fainthearted."

"You mean a coward."

A look of irritation passed over his face. "A coward, yes, if you like."

"He was terrified of dying," I said.

"I know."

"Is that why you liked him?" I asked, unable to disguise a tone of mockery in my voice.

"He had a strong and . . . pessimistic imagination."

"But you were brave."

"I've no imagination."

I shrugged my shoulders.

"It's something you have or don't have," he said. "When you were a child, for instance, you were terrified of the dark. Mark and Hattie didn't mind it at all."

"Is that all it is?"

"I think so."

Still in a scoffing tone of voice, I said, "It's a pity that my father made so little of his great imagination."

"He was afraid of it," said Sir Edward. "He was terrified of sin. He did not want to test himself. He'd have made a better monk than a rector."

I gave a short laugh, almost a snort. "He'd have made an

[*280*]

excellent monk, except that he seems to have possessed neither faith, hope nor charity."

Sir Edward stood up. "He certainly had faith," he said. "More in the Devil, perhaps, than in God. He reached out for God but never seemed to touch him—and the Devil was always close behind."

"He should have seen a psychiatrist," I said, at which Sir Edward gave me such a sharp look of pity that I blushed and regretted what I had said.

Sir Edward went to the coffin again and looked for a last time at my father's face.

"Why did you like him?" I said.

For some time he did not reply; then he said, "I don't know," and added, "but I shall miss him."

When we reached the kitchen Lady Clare was there with her arms around my weeping mother. There were a few minutes more of commiseration and an invitation to have lunch at the hall after the funeral. Then they left.

They reappeared at the graveside the next day, and Martha was with them. She was dressed in somber colors but did not wear a veil like her mother. In church she behaved with decorum; not a glance was directed in my direction, though I was just across the aisle in the front pew on the left-hand side. It was only when we were standing around the grave that our eyes met. Mine must have been blank; hers were decidedly expressive but I cannot say of what. I did not look into them for long but moved my attention onto the rows of tombstones—some granite, some marble, some sandstone—and the line of evergreen trees. It was a day so typical of the countryside—damp and white—with the earth and grass callously continuing their life.

I looked down at the coffin as it was lowered into its pit and for the first time felt that my father was leaving me. Inexplicably I wanted to clutch at the straps and draw him up again. It seemed senseless to cover him with earth, to leave him to the damp clay. I was suddenly sorry that he was dead and felt about to choke and cry. From embarrassment at this state, I half turned away from the grave as shovels began to refill the hole in the ground, and when the group broke up I clutched my mother's arm and walked away quickly so that no one should see the tears on my cheeks.

In the car I regained my self-control. Though the sorrow I had felt at parting with his body lingered within me, a stern inner voice dismissed all regret and remorse, insisting that my sadness was just the last twitch of weaning. I turned dutifully to my mother who was sitting beside me, preparing to comfort her, but she too had regained her composure and was straightening her hat. I then remembered that we were to have lunch at Lasterby Hall.

Because we had led the procession away from the church, we reached the hall before the Metheralls and had to wait for a few minutes until they arrived. When they did so we got out of the car and met them on the gravel at the foot of the Palladian steps.

"Do you remember Martha?" Lady Clare said to me.

I turned to the daughter. "Yes," I said. "We met at Harriet's." I shook hands with her. She smiled but said nothing, nor did her hand linger in mine but returned to her side as if this was the first time we had touched.

They went into the house. I returned to tell our driver that he need not wait for us. I watched the large black car turn on the gravel and then followed my mother and the Metheralls into the house. In the hall I waited for a moment, dizzy with the recollections that its sound and smell and light provoked in my mind. My senses were smothered by these memories, so I did not notice at first that Martha had left her parents and had returned down the wide stairs to meet me.

"Hello," she said quietly when she reached my side.

Still half in the past I looked at her in surprise, imagining her to be the ghost of Harriet, but her eyes were so confident and excited that they brought me out of my dream.

"How are you?" I asked her.

[*282*]

"All right."

We started to go up the stairs.

"I'm awfully sorry about your father," she said.

I shrugged my shoulders.

"Are you glad you came?"

Thinking of my father, I said that I was, but then glancing at her I realized that she was referring to the other reasons. Unfortunately I was unable to summon up my usual duplicity and at the thought of her expectations became increasingly confused; not only was she a stranger to the nostalgia provoked by Lasterby, she was equally foreign to my conscious mood. Indeed, it was a sign of my muddled mind that I could not quite remember the connection between us. I knew, of course, what had happened but I could not remember why. The look in her eyes was a sign of some involvement, but what had been the source of it?

We went into the small drawing room for a drink before lunch. I asked for a glass of sherry, and as I drank it I noticed that Lady Clare's eyes were upon me rather like those of a startled pheasant. It occurred to me that Harriet might have told her something—about my relationship with her, or my interest in Martha—but if she was looking for some evidence in my face and in my behavior toward Martha she must surely have been convinced that we were more or less strangers.

Unfortunately I saw that the mother was also studying the daughter—and though Martha's performance was not so bad it was not good enough to deceive a mother whose intuitive suspicions had been tipped off from an outside source. Of course, nothing was said. The conversation at lunch was general and sympathetic. I was silent, almost morose. My mother was enjoying her extra lunch at the hall. Martha was behaving a little too graciously and frowning whenever her mother said or did anything which implied that she was a child, such as telling her to clear the plates away or fetch sugar for the coffee.

Over the coffee we talked about my mother's future. "Have you any idea of what you want to do?" Lady Clare asked her.

"Not really, no," she replied. "I could always . . . I don't know. I don't think I want to leave Yorkshire." Her fear, I knew, was that she might have to live with her brother Ernest and never again have dinner at eight.

"I'll buy you a house wherever you want to live," I said.

"There won't be any need for that," said Sir Edward. "Carr's farm has just been merged with Baxter's so the farmhouse is empty. If you'd be interested in that, Susan, we could do it up quite nicely."

My mother looked embarrassed but was obviously delighted that she might be able to stay so close to her "only friends." Not knowing the state of bankruptcy that had descended on the Metherall family, she was in no position to understand the extent of Sir Edward's generosity.

I, who appreciated it, felt only irritation at the old man's quixotic gesture. I also felt that he had no business to give away the tenancies of an estate that would soon be mortgaged.

"Why don't you let me buy it from you?" I said.

"No," he said. "It's your mother's for life if she wants it."

I shrugged my shoulders and looked out onto the lawn through the large windows which faced me. My mother thanked Sir Edward with deferential exaggeration and, so far as I could make out, accepted his offer. Indeed, she seemed to be so well cared for by the Metheralls that I thought to myself that I could return to London the next morning.

The only constriction I felt in planning this escape was Martha's glances across the table in my direction. She also managed to get in the car next to me when Sir Edward drove us back to the rectory. I suppose that my hand was meant to reach for hers or my knee rub against her knee. As it was I neither moved my limbs nor took my eyes off the hedgerow as we drove to the village.

When we reached the rectory, however, she was clever enough to say to my mother, "I wonder if I could have a last look in your house? I'm sure we won't be nearly such good friends with the next rector."

Upon which my mother replied, "Well, of course. Hilary will show you around."

Bored and embarrassed by this improbable request, I started on a tour of our dingy house as if it were Versailles. As soon as we were out of earshot, however, Martha said, quite brightly, "I'd like to see your room."

"It's not interesting," I said.

"I'd like to see it, all the same," she said.

We went upstairs and when we were in my bedroom, which was just as it had always been, she sat down on the edge of the bed. "A little boy's room," she said.

"I haven't lived here for a dozen years," I said.

There were still pictures of airplanes on the walls and boys' adventure stories on the shelves.

"Does it bring back happy memories?" she asked.

"Unhappy ones."

"Were you unhappy?"

I shrugged my shoulders and shuffled toward the door.

"Are you off me?" Martha asked sharply.

I turned to look at her; she had blushed in saying this. "No," I said. "Not really. I just . . . well, my father's death has upset me."

"Yes, of course. I'm sorry."

"It's made me think that perhaps . . . after all, you're so young . . ."

It was the wrong thing to have said and I said it without thinking of the consequences, but I had no clear idea of what to do or to say.

"I was old enough in London," she said.

"Yes, of course," I said. "I didn't mean that. What I meant was that up here it all seems so difficult . . . especially just now. . . . The funeral . . ."

"Yes," she said. "I'm sorry. I understand. It's just that I've missed you so much."

"And I've missed you," I said automatically.

"Have you?" she asked intensely, looking fully and bravely into my shifty eyes.

[285]

"Yes, I have," I said, "but I've also thought a lot. It's all so complicated. I feel, perhaps . . . I don't know."

She stopped looking at me and glanced at the door.

"We'd better go down," I said.

"Yes." She turned to me again and said, "We can meet in London, can't we? Just as we arranged."

"Yes," I said.

"I think you're right," she added, going toward the door. "It's different up here . . . especially with your father . . . and all that."

I watched her shoulders and back as she went down the stairs, so steady and poised, but at that moment without any power to sweeten her personality so far as I was concerned. When I saw her drive off with her father, I thought to myself that it would be better if it was the last I was to see of her.

That evening alone with my mother was awkward for both of us. As regards my father, I believe she was more relieved than sorry that he was dead but was afraid to show this to me. What she wanted now was to enjoy her role as the rector's widow. Since I did not conceal my contempt for the provincial stage on which she was to act this part, she could not prepare her lines while I was there. She could not even think about it and yet had nothing else to put into her mind. I too had nothing that I could discuss with her but could only attempt to order my thoughts in silence. This brooding upset her so she chattered nervously to fill the silence, which irritated me further.

She was not sorry, therefore, when I left the next morning. She kissed me as I left the house, saying that she would come and see me in London quite soon.

My mother did not come to London but she wrote letters. The first came a week after I had left Yorkshire, saying that Lady Clare—or Clare, as she now called her—had asked her to stay at the hall until Carr's farm was made ready for her. I could tell from her account of this invitation that she was excited by the idea. She accepted, she said, "to give the new rector plenty of time to move in. I feel that Edward might delay the appointment if I stayed in the house, and the parish is in need of a new rector since your father did not get around much in his last years."

Her next letter was written on the thick, headed paper of Lasterby Hall. It contained a detailed account of the daily life there, as if my mother was recording it for posterity. "I keep out of the way as much as I can," she wrote, "and try to make myself useful. Clare does most of the cooking herself now (I never knew!) and is very glad if I do the shopping in Malton. It is a little awkward because I feel I ought to pay for something but she won't hear of it. All I can do is buy chocolates now and then for the household. Martha is most useful because she knows which ones her parents like. She came with me to Malton on Thursday and talked about you. Edward and Clare are most interested in you, too. I never realized that you were such a successful painter. They tell me that you have had an exhibition in Brussels! Why didn't you tell me?"

It was evidently the Metheralls' interest in me that made my mother keep writing. The third letter was about Martha's health. "She has discovered a lump in her tummy which is very worrying as everyone thinks of cancer, especially with your father's death so fresh in the mind. Clare has taken her into York this morning. I do hope it is nothing serious."

My mother completed this letter later in the day. "Thank God," she wrote, "it's nothing serious. Clare is a little vague about what it is, and looked queerly at me as if it might be the rhubarb crumble I made yesterday that is responsible. Martha looked very cross. She can be so rude to her mother."

A week later came a fourth letter from my mother. "There is a great quarrel going on between Clare and Martha. She should have gone back to school yesterday, and I don't understand why she has not. Clare told me that Martha might have to have an operation.

" 'It is a growth, then,' I said.

" 'Of a sort,' she said.

" 'But surely not malignant.'

" 'No.'

"I met Dr. Brown in the shop yesterday and asked him if the growth shouldn't be operated on at once. 'It depends on your point of view,' he said, and then looked quite cross also.

" 'What a relief that it wasn't cancer,' I said.

" 'I made a fool of myself,' he said, 'and no doctor likes to do that.'

" 'It's always better to have a second opinion,' I said.

" 'I'd not have needed a second opinion,' he said, 'if I'd known what the girl had been up to.' "

At this point in my mother's letter I began to have suspicions which had apparently not entered her mind.

My reaction to these suspicions was as flat as all my other thoughts since returning to London. I had seen no one and done nothing except read newspapers and watch television. I also drank and went to sleep each night in a stupor. At breakfast I would mix vodka in my orange juice, all of which was to keep my thoughts flat—to stop them rising, filling out, taking shape. I was filled with dread as to what they might be.

Equally, however, I was unable to escape them. I was incarcerated in my own mind, quite unable to think of anyone but myself. There were ten million people around me but I might as well have been in solitary confinement. I did not even think of Martha; Mark, Harriet, Caspar, Johnny and Qazvini were all quite forgotten. The only other to visit my stifling, claustrophobic cell was my father with his emaciated, bearded face, his croaking voice and wide, scared eyes fixed in terror at the dark pit of death, and forcing me to look the same way.

What tortured me now was the certitude of death. From

what I had experienced I was forced to acknowledge that however I might spend the next thirty or forty years, it would all end in helpless squalor and pain, mumbling for gruel that could not feed me, and praying for solace that would not come. I knew that just as I had inherited from my father a certain shape to my nose and sound to my voice, so I had inherited his mortality and his cowardice in the face of it. His irrational fear, which at first had surprised me, had now taken hold of me like an infectious fever. I sat alone, half drunk, imagining that every pain was the start of a malignant growth, the beginning of a protracted, ghastly death. Such was my panic that I wondered if it would not be best to get it over and done with now—a gun or drugs—rather than live another forty years in such unmanly fear.

I was brought out of this suicidal mood by the arrival at my front door at nine o'clock one morning of two men who introduced themselves as Detective-Sergeant Graham and Detective-Constable Burton. I had no reason to doubt their identity for, like all policemen, they bore the marks of the lower middle classes. The Detective-Sergeant asked if he could have a few words with me—a question which had the most exhilarating effect on my spirits, like the sound of rifle fire to a soldier or the huntsman's horn to the hounds.

I asked them in, wondering politely if they would not mind coming down to the kitchen so that I could continue my breakfast while they asked their questions. They accepted my invitation and came with me through the hall and down the stairs, past half a dozen stolen works of art. The detective-sergeant glanced at the pictures but said nothing, while I, in my mind, searched my files for the forged receipts and certificates of provenance.

The policemen stood uneasily in the kitchen while I poured my vodka and orange juice down the sink. I then invited them to sit down and they did so. I sat down myself, took a sip of my coffee, and asked them what I could do for them.

The detective-sergeant looked confused and then, to cover

his confusion, told me in an aggressive tone that they were making certain inquiries at the request of the Yorkshire Constabulary.

Like a computer, my mind went over my collection for anything that might have come from Yorkshire. I knew at once that I had nothing from outside the London area and so breathed more easily.

His next question showed that I was on the wrong tack. "Can you tell me, sir," he said, glancing at his notebook, "if you are acquainted with a Miss Martha Metherall?"

"Yes," I said, without thinking; then, more cautiously, I added, "I've met her."

"Could you tell me the circumstances of your meeting?"

"It was after my father's funeral," I said. "In Yorkshire. I was invited to her parents' house for lunch with my mother. Martha was there, and she came in the car with her father, who drove us home."

Detective-Sergeant Graham wrote what I had said in his notebook. Detective-Constable Burton looked on with sullen eyes.

"Have you met her on any other occasion?" the detective-sergeant asked.

"I believe," I said, "that I must have seen something of her twelve years ago when I lived in Yorkshire."

"But not recently?"

"Yes. On one other occasion. I met her in her sister's house here in London."

"When was that?"

"Two or three, or perhaps even four months ago."

"Were you alone with her at that time?"

"I drove her to Victoria Station from her sister's house in Ebury Street."

"Have you seen her at any time subsequently?"

"Only at lunch in Yorkshire."

"On no other occasion?"

"No."

"It is alleged," said the detective-sergeant, "that you have had unlawful intercourse with her."

"That's nonsense," I said. "Why, I can't have spoken more than half a dozen words to her."

The policeman sighed, finished his scribbling and then said, "It is my duty to inform you that following certain allegations made against you by Lady Clare Metherall concerning Miss Martha Metherall, who is under the age of consent, you are to be charged under Section Six of the Sexual Offenses Act, 1956, and I should warn you that anything you may say will be taken down and may be used in evidence against you."

I smiled and said nothing. I had so often rehearsed this moment that I was almost pleased to be acting it, especially over such a trivial matter. I raised no objections when they asked to look around the house. I quickly finished my breakfast while they did so and was then permitted to get dressed before accompanying them to their police station in Kensington.

There I was asked the same questions as before and gave the same answers. I was then charged by the station inspector and asked to make a statement. I did so, putting into prose what I had stated in my answers: that in the past ten years I had only met Martha Metherall twice, once at her sister's house in London, once at her parents' house in Yorkshire, and that at no time had sexual intercourse or any other acts of a sexual nature taken place. This was typed out and I signed it. I was then released on bail of my own recognizance of one hundred pounds.

I went home in an excellent mood and telephoned a solicitor, Craxton, whom we had used a great deal in various enterprises. We met for lunch and he listened to what I said with an expression as colorless as the skin on his face. I told him what I had told the police for, like all lawyers, he was not interested in the truth of the matter; and like all lawyers, he emitted puffs of stale confidence about my case. "If it's really true," he said, "that you were only ever alone with the girl when driving her to Victoria Station or showing her around your home in Yorkshire with your mother and her father downstairs, then they haven't got a case. They can hardly suggest that the offense took place on the back seat of your car on Buckingham Palace Road."

"I should have thought not."

"And presumably the school can testify that she returned home at a time consistent with that at which you both left her sister's house?"

"I imagine so."

He looked away from me and said, "And there's no question of witnesses to any other meeting?"

"No question, no."

"Though she may have been meeting someone?"

I nodded. "Oh, yes, I dare say it'll come out that she's been meeting someone."

"Some schoolboy, I suppose."

I shrugged my shoulders.

"We'd better get a good counsel for you, all the same. The girl must have made up some yarn, and it could come down to your word against hers."

"I'm sure it will come to that."

"At your age, intercourse with a minor is an absolute offense. Your only defense is that you didn't do it, and the only line for the prosecution is that you did, with her evidence to prove it. A good barrister, however, should persuade the jury that she's imagined it . . . or that she's trying to protect someone else."

"I think she may be pregnant."

"Hmm. So there's certainly someone else."

"Yes."

Craxton appeared with me the next day at Marylebone Street Magistrate's Court for remand. There was no police objection to bail, but it was made a condition of bail that I would in no way attempt to contact Martha—a condition with which

I was pleased to comply, since I had no wish to see the treacherous wretch. So much for her love, I thought to myself. So much for all love. It would give me great pleasure to see her in the witness box—a public sinner humiliated in cross-examination, perhaps fat with the child. This prosecution had revitalized my old hatred for the Metheralls and, at the same time, provided a vehicle for its satisfaction. I could not myself have contrived a better end to that venture; once again I had had the Devil's own luck.

With my trial, a sense of purpose returned to my life. I prepared in detail the degrading questions I would suggest to my counsel for Martha, and in between these sessions on strategy I visited my old friends—Eric, Qazvini, Rosamund and Alice—and was, I believe, conspicuously better company than I had been for eighteen months. I told them about the case and they laughed at me for getting caught at last. Rosamund and Alice, who guessed that I had planned to recruit Martha into their company, mocked me for losing my touch. "You're getting old," they said.

I did some more painting and decided with Qazvini to have an exhibition during my trial, for I wanted as much publicity as possible for my so-called crime and even arranged for a story of the charge to appear in the society column of the *Daily Express*.

The one matter which upset me—and that only a little— was my mother's involvement in the whole affair, for after a week of silence she wrote to me again, a pitiful letter, "not knowing what to believe." "I cannot think that you would do such a thing, Hilary, even though you now live among artists, yet Clare insists that it is you and says that Martha has admitted it. Of course it would never have been discovered if it wasn't for the baby, and even now they find it difficult to discover from Martha where it all took place . . . but the police say they must know and have come every day to question her.

"Oh, Hilary—the police! Edward says there may even be a court case but says he hopes there won't be. It is Clare who

[293]

is so angry, and she even looks coldly at me though I've had no control over you for twelve years now; and Mrs. Bosomworth says that anyway it's the lass that wants to watch herself, not the lad, but then that's just the way of thinking of the village and doesn't make my position any easier."

On receiving this letter, I wrote at once to my mother a letter of some skill, asking her to trust me and believe that it was all untrue. "I don't know why Martha should pick me to blame for her state: doubtless to protect the young man who is really responsible. I must say, though, I wish she had chosen someone else. This whole business is extremely awkward and embarrassing, especially for you. If you feel your presence at Lasterby is impossible, do not hesitate to come to London, where I have a room always ready for you."

My mother wrote back that she believed me but would rather keep her convictions to herself for the time being, since the subject made Clare go black with rage and Edward look so unhappy. "And anyway, it might be useful for you to have me here."

In another letter she told me how she had met Martha in the orchard and "we had a long talk. Martha said that she hated what her parents were doing, and what they were making her do, but her mother had said that if she did not tell everything to them, and to the police, she would have to have an operation to remove the baby. Poor little Martha, she cried when she told me this because she wants to keep the baby. I said I was sure that her parents wouldn't force her but she was afraid they would if she didn't give evidence.

"I told her that you denied it was you and she stopped crying and said she was glad and that it was the best thing for you to do because she didn't want you to go to prison or pay a fine, and that she would try to be bad in the witness box so that they would believe you and not her.

"I put my arm around her, and since it had started to rain a little we walked back toward the house. She told me she loved you very much and that she hoped one day you might be married.

"Oh, Hilary, it really is so difficult not to believe her, but then I must believe you because you are my son and have no one else, but Martha and I are great allies now. I don't believe Clare is pleased about it but there is nothing she can say. Edward came up to me again after dinner and said that the whole trial was a mistake but that Clare was set on it and that now they had told the police they couldn't call it off anyway."

Though it was unnecessary, I attended the committal proceedings at the Magistrate's Court. The police produced a copy of Martha's birth certificate, proving her age, and both her statement and my own were read out in court. No one went into the evidence; my defense was reserved.

There now followed two more months before the trial itself—happy months for me for, rather than hang over me, the trial led me on. It gave my life a purpose. All that made me anxious was the lack of anything beyond it.

It was now summer. The leaves on the chestnut trees already made London seem green, and the blossom in the side streets of Campden Hill was almost over. In early July I went for a week with Qazvini, Alice and Rosamund to the West Country. It was in the nature of a farewell party because Qazvini had at last decided to return to Iran and was to leave when we got back to London. Partly because of this—but also because business had dropped off—the flat in Westbourne Grove was to be closed down. Some time prior to this I had given my share in the enterprise to the "workers" and so had no real part in the decision, but Alice and Rosamund both had "blokes" whom they thought they could live with or, as Rosamund said, "If the worst comes to the worst, we can always go free lance."

"What about the others?" I asked.

"There's only Carol," said Qazvini, "and she's staying with her mother."

"Her mother?"

"Yes," said Alice. "She's ill."

It was because of this atmosphere of parting that there was

something melancholy about our holiday together. Many of the evenings were spent in nostalgic recollections of the early days and then, as if to show just what had gone out of our lives, we would retire separately to single beds in single bedrooms; or Qazvini and I would smoke a last cigar together and complain to one another about the standard of cooking in English provincial hotels.

"I shall miss you," I said once to Qazvini.

"And I shall miss you."

"I can visit you, perhaps."

"Of course. Once a year."

We both knew, as we spoke, that I would never visit him; and I became increasingly dejected at losing my only friend.

Back in London there was another letter from my mother. She had now moved to Carr's farm but seemed to go to the hall every day. There had been a scene the day before because Lady Clare had told Martha of the arrangements she had made to have her child adopted, upon which Martha had gone into a rage and run up to Carr's farm and my mother. "I didn't know what to tell her," my mother wrote. "The poor child still believes that in the end you'll marry her, and I can't bring myself to say that I think it's unlikely, and even if you would, Clare would never let her."

Bagatelle. I was now impatient for the trial. It was scheduled for the end of August, and by the time the date arrived I had had several discussions with Craxton and Thompson, my counsel. I had made it clear what I wanted of them. The barrister was tall, thin, pompous, angular and prepared to argue his mother's soul into hell for three hundred guineas; it was what I expected and I was satisfied.

The moment came. I appeared at the appointed hour with Craxton at the Middlesex Quarter Sessions in Parliament Square. There we were met by Thompson and together we proceeded into the court, they to their respective benches, I to the dock.

The court filled up. I could see Eric and Johnny in the

public gallery and two journalists on the Press Bench. The jury then took their seats—ten blank men and two blank women. The Deputy Chairman entered and took his judge's seat and the charges were read—that contrary to Section Six of the Sexual Offenses Act . . . etc.

The prosecution opened their case. They would, they said, prove that Martha Metherall, a minor, had on several occasions gone out from school, purportedly with her brother but in fact with the accused. The jury would hear in evidence that on one of these occasions the accused drove the girl to his house in London and seduced her. They would also hear that there were five days between the girl's leaving school at the end of the spring term and arriving home for her Easter holidays which were spent in the accused's house in London and that in the course of these five days, sexual intercourse had taken place "several times."

Witnesses were then called: first the headmistress of the school, then Mark. He was shifty and apologetic and his eyes never met mine. In monosyllables he agreed with the prosecuting attorney that he had never taken his younger sister out from her school. My counsel had few questions for either of these two witnesses; he only asked them both to admit that they had never seen me with Martha, which they did.

Next came Lady Clare. She agreed with the Crown that the birth certificate (Exhibit A) proved that her daughter was well under sixteen when the alleged offense had taken place. She also gave evidence about her daughter's late return from school and admitted that she had had no suspicions at the time but had only realized that some offense must have taken place when her daughter was found to be pregnant.

"And did your daughter readily volunteer the name of the father of her child?"

"No. She was reluctant to tell me."

"And did you have any idea yourself as to who it might be?"

Lady Clare glared at me, with more a look of fear in her eyes than a look of loathing. "I had some idea, yes."

"Can you tell us what it was?"

"I thought it might be Hilary Fletcher."

"Can you tell us why?"

"I had been warned by Harriet, my elder daughter, that he had asked after Martha."

"Was there any other reason?"

"When he came to lunch with us just after his father's funeral, it seemed to me . . ."

"Go on."

"Well, from the way Martha looked at him, I thought that she might have formed some . . . well, some silly attachment to him."

"The accused maintains that he had only met her once before, discounting the period when she was a child."

"I know."

"Was their behavior inconsistent with this hypothesis?"

"I could tell that she was trying to hide something."

"Of course," said Mr. Ferguson, the Crown counsel, "of course any mother can tell that sort of thing, don't you think?"

"Yes," said Lady Clare.

Ferguson sat down. My counsel stood up. "Would you agree with me," he asked Lady Clare, "that your daughter Martha is a very deceitful girl?"

"I . . . no, not in particular."

"She is still only fifteen, isn't she?"

"She has just turned sixteen."

"Yet at this tender age she has most successfully lied to her headmistress and lied to you."

"I suppose so."

"Most successfully?"

"Yes."

"Her headmistress has told us that she had no suspicions at all that your daughter was not going out with her brother."

"Yes."

"And you had no suspicions at all that when your daughter

told you that her term ended on March twelfth, it in fact ended on March seventh?"

"No."

"Wouldn't you call that deceit on her part?"

"Yes."

"Very successful deceit?"

"Well, yes."

"If it hadn't been for this pregnancy, you would never have known that your daughter had a lover?"

"No, probably not."

"Has it occurred to you that your daughter, having deceived you so far, may be deceiving you a little further?"

"No, I'm sure she isn't."

"But on your own evidence, it was you who first put the idea of Mr. Fletcher as the father of the child into her head."

"I thought it was him, and later she admitted it."

"Later?"

"Later, yes. She was trying to protect him."

"She was trying to protect him, was she?"

"I imagine so."

"And is she trying to protect him now?"

"No. She's decided to be more sensible."

"More sensible. I see. You don't think she might have decided to take up your offer to make a scapegoat of someone whom she hardly knows and does not care about?"

"No."

Thompson paused and looked at his notes. He spoke slowly anyway, so that the shorthand writer could keep up with him.

"Let me go back to the lunch, Lady Clare," he said at last.

"Which lunch?"

"The lunch after the funeral."

"Yes."

"You say that your maternal instincts informed you that there was something between Mr. Fletcher and your daughter?"

"Yes."

"But the suspicion had been put into your mind by your elder daughter?"

"Yes."

Thompson sighed. "You must forgive me if I make this suggestion, Lady Clare, but the jury may be wary of a mother's instincts which cannot tell when her daughter has lied about the end of her term but can suddenly divine a relationship from a few glances over a luncheon table."

"No, well, it wasn't just that. It was her pregnancy."

"Of course. When you discovered that she was pregnant, it all suddenly made sense."

"Yes."

"But I think, Lady Clare, that you might be prepared to admit to us that it doesn't fit together quite so easily and that it was your suspicions over the luncheon table which, some weeks later, enabled your daughter to protect the true father of her child by laying the responsibility onto my client."

It was at this point that there was an adjournment for lunch. The law is very slow: it starts late and ends early, but since barristers are paid by the day, why should they hurry? I did not complain. I was enjoying myself and could not claim that the money with which I paid Thompson was more honestly gained than his fee.

After lunch, Harriet was called to the stand. She looked at me with a well-prepared expression of "bitter triumph" but it soon changed to one of bafflement and irritation when all her evidence was excluded as conjecture except the facts relating to the day I had taken Martha to Victoria Station.

Thompson returned to that in cross-examination. "Are you suggesting," he said, "that anything improper took place in this short journey from your house to the station?"

"I wouldn't put it past him," said Harriet.

"You wouldn't put it past him? I see." Thompson shuffled his papers. "You are, it would seem, almost an expert on what my client would or would not do, aren't you, Mrs. Hanbury?"

"I know him quite well."

"How well?"

"Well enough to know what he's capable of." Harriet laughed but no one in the court laughed with her.

"It might help the jury," said Thompson, "to know more about this relationship."

Harriet blushed. "We grew up in the same village."

"Of course, but you are not surely suggesting that these . . . infantile frolics are the basis of your assessment of my client's character?"

At this the Crown intervened. Was it necessary to go into Mrs. Hanbury's relationship with the accused? The Deputy Chairman asked my counsel for his comments on this objection and was successfully convinced by him that, since Mrs. Hanbury's suggestion to Lady Clare might have been responsible for my involvement in the whole affair, it was only proper that this suggestion should be investigated.

"Very well," said the Deputy Chairman, "you may continue."

"Let me repeat the question," Thompson said to Harriet. "You said that you were well enough acquainted with my client to know what he was capable of?"

"Yes," said Harriet.

"To know that in taking your sister to Victoria Station he was starting an illicit relationship with her?"

"Yes."

"What made you think that?"

"Because I know him."

"We know that you know him, Mrs. Hanbury; but what do you know about him that makes you so sure of this particular fact?"

"He's . . . he's immoral."

Thompson sniffed. "He's immoral, is he?"

"Yes."

"What makes you think that?"

"I . . . I just know."

Thompson sighed. "Mrs. Hanbury, I think you're wasting

your own time as well as this Court's by prevarication like this. Let me ask you as simply as I can: What had my client done which made you think him so immoral that his giving your sister a lift to the station, and mentioning her in conversation a month or two later, is evidence of an illicit relationship?"

Harriet did not reply.

"Am I right in saying," Thompson asked, "that it was in fact you who had been having the illicit relationship with my client?"

Harriet did not reply. Thompson waited.

"Please answer the question," said the Deputy Chairman.

Harriet, red in the face and looking down at her twisted hands, mumbled her answer so that it was inaudible.

"Please, Mrs. Hanbury," said the Deputy Chairman, in an irritated tone of voice, "please be so kind as to answer so that the jury and I may hear you."

"Yes," said Harriet.

"You were having an affair with my client?" Thompson said.

"Yes."

"And this led you to suppose that he would go on to seduce your sister?"

"Yes."

"Go *on* to her because . . . how shall I put it . . . he was going *off* you?"

"Not because of that."

"But he was going off you, wasn't he?"

"It was coming to an end."

"Your husband had left you, hadn't he?"

"Yes."

"What I suggest, Mrs. Hanbury, is that you had hoped that Mr. Fletcher would marry you, and that, upon realizing that he was in fact tired of you, you invented this slander about your sister for a little revenge."

"No."

"Isn't that the truth?"

[302]

"No."

"No further questions."

Thompson sat down. He was worth his money. Harriet remained standing in the witness box as if she believed it was the dock. When the Deputy Chairman told her that she could go, she looked up—not at him, but at me—with defiant eyes and blotchy, tear-stained cheeks. She then left the stand. I watched her as she crossed the court and went to sit next to her parents. Her mother refused to look at her but stared straight ahead like a sentry; Sir Edward, however, smiled at her and took hold of her hand.

I looked back at Lady Clare with her stupid, stoical expression. It was a moment to feel triumph, but for some reason I did not do so—indeed I felt a quite different emotion—and as I glanced back at the father and daughter I felt even more strongly what can only be described as pity, not derisive, mocking pity but genuine sorrow for their state.

Detective-Sergeant Graham was in the witness box, going over my statement and the details of my arrest. He was then asked about his inspection of my house and told the court of how he had found a wardrobe full of women's clothes.

"Could they have belonged to Martha Metherall?"

"In size and type, yes."

Thompson stood up to cross-examine. "Detective-Sergeant," he began, "can you tell me if those clothes did belong to Miss Metherall?"

"No, sir."

"Were there any name tapes or other identifying marks?"

"No, sir. They were all new and unmarked."

"They could have belonged to anyone of a similar build?"

"Yes, sir."

"Were there any other signs in the house that Martha Metherall had stayed there?"

"None, sir."

"Thank you, Detective-Sergeant."

The court now adjourned until the next day. Craxton and

Thompson were both optimistic about the outcome. "Of course," said Thompson, "they're calling your cleaning woman, and there's the girl's evidence, but there's no corroborative evidence at all."

"And we've given a motive for the misunderstanding," said Craxton. "That was excellent work on Mrs. Hanbury."

My own mood was not as good as theirs. It was not that I was pessimistic, but I was not enjoying my success as much as I should have done. I had looked forward to it so much for so long, and yet now that it was all working out as I had planned, I felt no elation but only the kind of gloom that had gripped me before my arrest. The images in my mind were of Sir Edward's hand reaching out to Harriet and Lady Clare's stony suffering, and they irritated me because I found I could not gloat. I seemed to have lost the thread of things and in groping for the joy of a just revenge had only found pathos. What poor buffoons they had been to let the police prosecute me, and have the sheets stripped back from their daughters' beds before the public gaze. Who of their class would marry Martha now, debauched as well as penniless? Who would ever think of Harriet as anything other than an easy divorcée? They were all fools, and what joy could there be for me in outwitting such simpletons?

The first witness the next morning was my cleaning woman, Mrs. Partridge, who admitted that I had asked her not to come in as usual for those days between the end of Martha's term and her arrival in Yorkshire.

"And on your return?" she was asked by the Crown, "did you notice anything different about the house?"

"It was in a terrible mess."

"Consistent, shall we say, with a guest?"

"I should say there was someone else, yes, because Mr. Fletcher's so tidy."

"Were there any objects or belongings in the house which had not been there before?"

"Only the clothes."

"The clothes in the wardrobe?"

"Yes."

Thompson cross-examined. "Could you positively say, Mrs. Partridge, that the clothes were not there before?"

"Oh, no. . . ."

"You couldn't say?"

"They might have been."

"You don't look into my client's wardrobe every day."

"No."

"So far as you know, they could have been there before?"

"Yes."

"Now tell me, Mrs. Partridge, had Mr. Fletcher ever asked you not to come in before?"

"Oh, yes."

"Quite often?"

"Not recently, but he used to."

"Did you ever wonder why?"

"Well, I thought it was because of ladies."

"A gentleman should be discreet, don't you think, Mrs. Partridge?"

"Oh, yes."

"Perhaps he wished to save you embarrassment?"

"Yes, I'm sure."

"You have never been embarrassed by finding Mr. Fletcher with . . . er . . . ladies in his house?"

"Oh, no, sir."

"And you never saw him with a lady, or even a schoolgirl, around the dates we have mentioned?"

"No, sir. No, I didn't."

"Thank you, Mrs. Partridge."

The dejection I had felt the day before was still with me. I was therefore in no way excited to see Martha—the Crown's principal and final witness—come onto the stand. She looked pale and, though tall for a girl of her age, she could not conceal all the signs of her pregnancy. She wore a dark dress as if in mourning for her lost virginity; with her black hair and her pallor it made an effective spectacle. Unfortunately for my case, she looked a good year younger than she was. If the twelve good men and true of the jury had expressed anything in their faces but their own honest stupidity, it would surely have been consciousness of a crime. A child with child is an emotive sight. At the instruction of the Deputy Chairman, a seat was found for Martha but she declined to use it.

The prosecuting counsel opened his examination patiently and kindly. In quiet, firm, girlish words Martha told the court how she had first met me; how, in being driven to Victoria Station, I had suggested taking her out from school; how she had welcomed the suggestion; how she had told the headmistress that she was going out with her brother; how the first outing had been followed by a second; how on the second or third occasion we had driven up to London.

"And that, is it not," asked the Crown, "is when sexual intercourse first took place?"

"Yes."

"And did it take place on any subsequent occasion?"

"Yes."

"Could you tell us when?"

"At the end of term I went to stay with Hilary. . . ."

"In his house in London?"

"Yes."

"For how long?"

"Five days."

"You told your parents that your term ended on a later date, is that not right?"

"Yes."

"Now, when Mr. Fletcher suggested this plan . . ."

"He didn't suggest it. It was my idea."

The Crown counsel looked down at his notes; the Deputy Chairman looked up from his. "You should understand, Miss Metherall," he said, "that the charge against the defendant is, in legal terms, an absolute offense. It is immaterial that you may have cooperated in the offense—just as it is immaterial that he may have thought you over the age of sixteen."

Martha nodded.

[*306*]

The examination continued. "Whosever idea it was, Miss Metherall, you did spend those five days in his house in London?"

"Yes."

"And sexual intercourse took place?"

Her reply was inaudible; the Deputy Chairman asked her to speak up. "Yes," she said.

"Several times?"

"Yes."

"Did you sleep in the same bed?"

"Yes."

"Can you tell us anything about the clothes in the wardrobe? Were they yours?"

"I only had my school clothes. Hilary bought me some new ones."

"Which you left in the house?"

"Yes."

"Intending to return?"

"Yes."

"Did you arrange this when you saw the accused in Yorkshire?"

"Not really."

"How do you mean, not really?"

"He was upset about his father."

"Yes?"

"And was . . . well, I wasn't sure if he wanted to see me again."

"Did you write to him?"

"No."

"Did he write to you?"

"No."

"I assume, Miss Metherall, that you felt you loved the accused?"

"Yes."

"You would never have allowed relations of the sort that took place between you if you had not felt you loved him?"

"No."

"Did you allow these relations?"

"Yes."

"Do you still love him?"

"Yes."

"You don't feel that he has let you down?"

Martha did not reply. Thompson looked at the Deputy Chairman as if inquiring of the relevance of that question.

"I ask that," said the prosecutor, "simply to establish whether there is any feeling of vindictiveness behind the evidence."

The Deputy Chairman waved him on.

"I repeat, do you feel that he has let you down?"

"No," said Martha.

"You could quite legitimately feel that he has let you down."

"No," she said, "but I feel . . . I feel that I've let him down."

This closed the case for the Crown. It was now the turn of Thompson, my counsel, to cross-examine this star witness.

He began as gently as the Crown had begun. "Please don't think, Miss Metherall, that the defense—including, I may say, my client himself—do not appreciate the delicacy of this matter, but you must understand that he totally rejects your evidence . . ."

Martha said nothing.

". . . and it is my duty to show to the jury that, while you may have convinced yourself of its truth, your evidence is in reality a tissue of lies."

Martha still said nothing. I watched her; she glanced at me. Involuntarily, we both smiled. Thompson noticed this and snatched at it. "It may be amusing to you, Miss Metherall, but it will not be amusing for my client if he is found guilty."

"No," said Martha, her face serious again. "I know."

"He will almost certainly be sent to prison."

She said nothing.

"Therefore," said Thompson, "let me go over some of the

things you have said in evidence. You have had a lover; that fact is uncontested. It is his identity which is the subject of our inquiries. Now leaving aside the years of your infancy, you say you met my client for the first time at tea with your sister?"

"Yes."

"Did you talk to him there?"

"No."

"But he offered to take you to the station when the time came for you to leave?"

"Yes."

"And in the car he suggested taking you out from school?"

"Yes."

"And you accepted his suggestion?"

"Yes."

"Even though you knew you would have to pretend that he was your brother?"

"Yes."

"It seems a quick and easy descent into deceit, Miss Metherall."

Martha did not reply.

"You see," said Thompson, "my client denies that he ever made such a suggestion and he denies, part and parcel, all your other allegations."

"I know."

"Can we agree, Miss Metherall, that you loved the father of your child?"

"Yes."

"That if it had not been for the child, you would have concealed this lover's identity?"

"Yes."

"You knew that there would be trouble if you were discovered?"

"Yes."

"Especially for him."

"Yes."

"And you have said in evidence that you still love this man."

"Yes."

"Now, I accept that, Miss Metherall. And I accept that it is natural for you to wish to protect the man you love; and I suggest that that is just what you are doing now, by making these allegations against my client."

"No."

"I suggest, Miss Metherall, that deceit and invention come most naturally to you."

Martha said nothing.

"And that just as you lied to your headmistress about your brother, and to your mother about the end of the term, so you are lying to us now about the true identity of your lover."

"No," she said.

"I suggest that at the moment your pregnancy was discovered, you were hard pressed to find a scapegoat—but that your mother's suspicions, inspired by your sister's chagrin, provided you with the answer, and that you blamed a man you hardly knew to save the real father of your child."

"No. No, I didn't. I told them . . . I told them because they said that . . . that if I didn't I would have to have an abortion."

"But surely," said Thompson, with a sneer, "but surely you know that your parents could not force you to have a termination of pregnancy against your will?"

Martha looked startled. "I thought . . . I thought that if I was under twenty-one . . ."

"Under twenty-one?" asked Thompson.

"Or under sixteen . . ."

"Under sixteen?"

"I don't know. But I thought that they could."

"Will you accept from me that they can't?"

Martha glanced at her mother, but her view was obstructed. "Yes," she said.

[310]

"For the sake of the continuance of this cross-examination, I will accept from you that you believed that your parents could force you to have a termination, so you traded the life of your baby for the identity of your lover. Is that it?"

"Yes."

"And that is why you are giving evidence now?"

"Yes."

"Now that you know that your parents can't force you to have a termination, would you like to change your evidence at all?"

Martha was now quite evidently confused. She looked around for some advice and her eyes came to rest on me. If I had been prepared for this, I might have avoided her glance or met it with no expression, but taken by surprise I smiled again and slightly shrugged my shoulders. The jury may not have noticed this but the Deputy Chairman did. He looked at Martha. "Do you wish to change your evidence?" he asked.

"No," she said. "It's too late."

"I think it is too late," said Thompson, "to convince the jury that you have any respect whatsoever for the objective truth."

She said nothing; she was almost in tears. Thompson sat down, quite evidently satisfied. Crown counsel stood up to reexamine.

"I have only one further question, Miss Metherall, and before answering it, I would like you to ponder on the oath you have taken to tell the truth, the whole truth and nothing but the truth."

Martha nodded.

"Now my question is this. Is it true, or is it not true, that the defendant, Mr. Hilary Fletcher, has had sexual intercourse with you?"

"It is true."

"And is he the only man who has ever had sexual intercourse with you?"

"Yes."

"And is he the only possible father of your child?"

"Yes."

After lunch the defense called its sole witness, myself. When I crossed the dock to the witness box I felt that opinion was in my favor. Unfortunately this knowledge depressed me more than it pleased me. I was almost irritated that Martha, who was so truthful in her fashion, should be thought a liar. It irritated me that some young Etonian or music teacher should be thought the father of her child. I was also particularly indifferent to the verdict of the jury on the actual charge. I might almost have changed my plea to guilty, there and then, but felt that to do so would be like upsetting a chess board when the game was at its most interesting stage.

All the same my evidence was appalling. I could not concentrate on the questions. I forgot my alibi, which had no corroboration anyway. I was evasive about the clothes in the wardrobe. My explanation for asking Mrs. Partridge to take a week off was that I must have entertained a girl—or several girls—but could not remember who they were.

Of course the jury might have accepted this as part of my famous "discretion," but it hardly made me seem a moral character, a man incapable of the charge on the sheet. All the same, they might have acquitted me had it not been for the Deputy Chairman's summing up. In this all the points were in favor of the Crown, except one, placed at the beginning and never repeated—that they should beware of convicting on uncorroborated evidence.

By the end of the summing up, however, and a detailed repetition of all the circumstantial evidence such as the clothes in the wardrobe and the coincidence in Martha's dates and those of Mrs. Partridge, this initial warning was forgotten. The stuttering child was believed over the immoralist—doubtless because the jury wanted to believe her. I was found guilty and sentenced to three months' imprisonment.

Part Five

16

I served my sentence in an outdated prison in the wasteland of South London. It had been built one hundred and fifty years ago for seven hundred prisoners; consigned to it now were more than double that number of men, all sentenced for five years or less for crimes from robbery with violence to loitering with intent. Because of this overcrowding, I was put in a cell with two other men, one a Londoner, the other an Irishman, both convicted of theft. I saw a lot of these two men—Selden and MacSweeney—for we were shut in our cell, measuring thirteen feet by nine by seven, for fourteen hours of the day. "Bang up" was at ten past five in the afternoon. Two hours later there was a brief opportunity to slop out, and supper was brought to our cells; but then the doors were locked again until seven the next morning.

By that time all the cells stank of the urine and feces which had been evacuated into our chamber pots during the night, and indeed the smell never left us, for the pots and buckets were emptied at a recess on each landing; it hovered in the air and was there when we ate our food. It was no wonder that we had to return our razorblades after shaving, and that there were nets slung from railing to railing in the well of our prison wing. Many a poor devil must have been inclined to kill himself rather than spend five years of his life in such conditions.

My own term was bearable because it was short. I knew that with remission for good behavior I would be out in two months' time and was grateful to fate that after ten years of crime I should only have to serve that long. What is more, I had had experience of a much longer sentence at a similar institution—by which I mean my five years at Newton College. At school, certainly, the boys did not excrete within a foot or two of one's sleeping face, but the masters were called "sir" like the prison warders, and there was the same system of organized and tolerated bullying among the boys as there was among the prisoners. The food was much the same as it had been at Newton—porridge, baked beans or powdered eggs for breakfast, for example. I made no friends in prison as I had done at school—but then, as I have said, my sentence was short whereas at Newton, to my child's mind, the sentence had been for life.

The time that we did not spend in our cells was spent in the prison workshops. Some would launder, weave, tailor or put string through plastic bags. My own job was painting toy soldiers, an occupation which I came to enjoy. Between half past ten and half past eleven we exercised in the prison yard. Watched closely by the guards, we trudged around in circles, our eyes on the ground.

The worst of it all was the smell of excreta, but Selden and MacSweeney, my cell mates, were not to blame for the imposition of their bodily functions upon me, and they had to suffer mine. It was hard to be irritated, too, for the nicer man—MacSweeney—smelled worse, while the nastier of the two—Selden—was the more discreet and fastidious. They were alike only in that both were convicted for the same crime and both, like me, were star prisoners. The difference in character, however, was great and I soon started to think of them as the good and the bad thieves.

The good thief was the Irishman, Mick MacSweeney, for though he was dirty, clumsy and untidy—qualities which can cost you your life in a prison cell—he had a good nature and simplicity which were endearing and a solid philosophy of life based on his Catholic religion. He was large and heavy: half muscle, half fat. I imagine that out of prison he drank a lot, for he had the bleary eyes of a semialcoholic and suffered from the absence of liquor in prison. He must have been drunk when he was arrested—one of a thousand points in his account of his crime which showed him up as an amateur—for he was only at the petty cash of a flooring company in Fulham but made the mistake of punching a policeman and was therefore convicted of robbery with violence and resisting arrest.

MacSweeney was around my age whereas the bad thief, Selden, was ten years older. He was English, the kind of Englishman I would rather not recognize as such—greasy, shifty, assertive, self-righteous and idle. He had a garage somewhere out by London airport and had been unable to explain the presence of a stolen Jaguar among the second-hand cars he was offering for sale. He was married, like Mac-Sweeney, and I pitied both their wives, but I pitied Selden's more for she sounded as dull and ugly as he made her out to be. He apologized for her and insisted that he never now went near her but had other women in the back seats of his stolen and secondhand cars. It was in this context that he used the words "fuck" and "cunt," with a greater degree of accuracy though no more frequently than MacSweeney, to whom they were neutral sounds like "um" and "er." "It must be a fucking lovely day today," MacSweeney would say. "Some lucky cunt'll be off to the bloody races." Or, "Could you hand me over the fucking mirror, squire?" He called me "squire" because of my accent and Selden picked up the name too.

Selden's reminiscences about his sexual exploits with the women of Isleworth and Hounslow had the unfortunate effect of arousing his sexual desire and leaving him in a state quite opposite to that in which he would have us believe he left the women. To relieve himself of this unsatisfied desire he would resort to masturbation, the sounds and movements of which he did not bother to conceal from his cell mates.

MacSweeney too was tormented by lascivious thoughts and so was I, though both of us, I think, dreamed as much of whiskey as we did of women, and between the pin-ups on the walls by his bed MacSweeney had a crucifix before which he prayed each night and each morning, on his knees, on the concrete floor. He did not pray aloud, but I soon learned that a certain periodic inhalation meant the start of another Hail Mary, for just as he drew in his breath his thumb pulled along another bead of his rosary.

This praying did not irritate me as it might once have done, but it annoyed Selden. It did more than annoy him; it seemed to anger him. "Get off your knees, you bog rat," he would say.

"Now shut up," MacSweeney would reply, "and leave me alone."

"What the fuck do you want to pray for?" Selden said on one occasion in his London whine. "Pray for a cunt to come down from heaven—see if he'll send you that, a piece right here in the fucking cell."

"Now be quiet," said MacSweeney.

Since the Irishman was heavy and muscular and the car salesman was bony and gray in the face, the latter always made sure that he did not provoke the former too far. He would continue, all the same, "Didn't your mother tell you there's nothing up there . . . now is there, squire? You tell him."

"I don't know why it worries you so much," I said.

"But you don't believe that shit, do you?" Selden asked. I did not reply.

"You see, Mick? The squire here doesn't believe that God shit, so why not pack it in?"

Mick crossed himself and stood up. "I will not pack it in," he said. "I'll not be abandoning the Son of God for a couple of English atheists."

"Ha, ha," said Selden. "We're sent by the Devil to torment you."

"Or by God to test you," I said.

"We all work for the Devil, squire," said Selden. "You do, anyway, sticking your fingers up the cunts of little girls . . .

[318]

and so do you, Mick. We're all in for evil, lad. Your praying won't help you."

"I've confessed my sins, now, haven't I?" said the Irishman.

"But you'll do it again, boy, you'll do it again. And you'll do all the other dirty things you do and have all those filthy thoughts."

MacSweeney blushed and lay back on his bunk. "Perhaps I will," he said, "and perhaps I won't. But if Christ is merciful, I'll be sorry afterward, and when you're sorry, you're forgiven."

For the most part I remained aloof from these arguments, for though in the first week I thought I agreed with Selden that the Irishman's faith was the silly superstition of a stupid man, I found his mutterings to God more bearable in the confines of the cell than the coarse objections of my fellow atheist. Indeed, Selden's behavior during MacSweeney's prayers became increasingly curious. It was as if the sight of a man kneeling before his crucifix sent a virus into Selden's blood, for he changed color and became restless and seemed quite incapable of restraining his interruptions. Atheism, I had always thought, was reasonable and should therefore be reasonably propagated, but Selden's convictions took increasingly the form of irrational loathing, and when it had become plain that argument would not stop MacSweeney from telling his beads Selden went almost insane and began to recite a counter-litany of blasphemy. MacSweeney would shut his eyes and block his ears, which left me as the only audience— an observation I communicated to Selden with no effect at all. Indeed his only reaction was to embroider his chant of profanities by the airing of his swollen penis, which he stroked with his fingers and waved in the air like the standard of Godlessness.

I present this unpleasant tableau of life in a prison cell because it was the backcloth to my own moral reflections.

Life was dull but regular. I kept to myself and refused the

opportunity of association with other prisoners when it was offered to me. I was left to my own thoughts, which became increasingly introspective; and I was now unable to muddle them by adding vodka to my orange juice at breakfast. As I painted the toy soldiers—putting a dab of red on their tunics, a dab of brown on their shakos, a dab of silver on their bayonets—I let my mind range over its memories. I prodded the various incidents as I remembered them to see what life was left in these fragments of past experience, and many were alive enough to shrink from the spike of my recollection. There were some episodes I was happy to remember, that brought calm to my mind and an inner smile; more often, however, my mind shied away from my recollections and, when forced to remember, provoked an emotion that I can only call regret.

I could not now understand how I had felt such passion about a dinner jacket or a white tie and tails. I could not reanimate my feelings for the Metheralls—neither the early love nor the subsequent hate—yet without those feelings much of my life became incomprehensible, not just the ruin of Mark and the destruction of Harriet but the robbery, the swindling and the cheat of my paintings.

When I thought of Billy Cade, a flicker of my old loathing for him and his class returned to me, but then the pathos of his arrogance grew larger than the arrogance itself and I pitied him. I pitied him as I had known him first—I pitied the sneering, walking man—and felt all the more remorseful that through me he was now a cripple.

After that I thought of my more absolute actions, the deaths I had caused: the old man in the jeweler's shop whom I had hit too hard and the baby whose head I had stuck in a bucket. Clear images of my actions started to wrap me like a lunatic's straitjacket. I could see the man's grizzled chin on the concrete floor, his wrinkled lids half opened; I could hear the spasmodic exhalations of his dead lungs. And then again I could feel the baby's legs in my left hand and its little neck between the two fingers of my right hand; I could feel its wriggling movements as if electric shocks were passing into me and reliving that ghastly moment. I felt more and more intolerably what I must call remorse. I wished, I wished even to God, that I had not done these things.

I tried to escape this mood of regret. I argued with myself in my own mind, pleading like a barrister the case of my amorality. What was this remorse but a weak offshoot of fear? I had been shocked, I told myself, by my father's death; it had stirred up my settled opinions and let loose the old superstition about justice and retribution that I had been taught as a child.

This defense, however, did not convince me. There was good reason to be shocked by death and to fear its implications, for what if I had a soul and that soul was immortal and the quality of its immortality decided by my behavior while alive? This Christian hypothesis, which had seemed so absurd when I was young, seemed less unlikely now that I had looked into the eyes of a dying man, for no one who had half a chance of oblivion would have looked so scared. We do not lie in terror every night before going to sleep, nor would we even if we knew that the sleep would last forever. We are only afraid if that slumber might contain dreadful, tormenting dreams with no end.

I trudged around the prison yard. I sopped up gravy off my metal plate with coarse bread. All the time I thought of what I had done, and each night the Irishman knelt down to pray while Selden swore and cursed with his unreasonable hatred of MacSweeney's prayers.

There was a mirror in the cell which was shared by the three of us, and there were moments after I had shaved when I would study my physiognomy, for it seemed to betray my most secret sins. The skin was flaked with excess; the lines between my cheeks and nose gave a permanent scoff to my expression, a mask of cynicism, a sneer at simplicity and goodness. My lips had become fat and flabby—sensual lips, one might say, lips which proclaimed that truth lay less in the words they might enunciate than in their own sensations.

I was disgusted at what I saw and I became disgusted at everything about me: my eyes, my arms, my genitals, my grotesque torso and clumsy hands. I was afraid that something within this mass would counterattack and destroy the state of contrition I felt rising within me, for I knew from my experience that men rarely change course in their lives but often dream of an opposite condition like stupid tramps who lie in gutters and think that they are millionaires.

It was easier for me to feel sorry than to feel forgiven. So much of what I had done was beyond restoration. Life and innocence, once lost, can never be replaced. And yet I felt the possibility now that there was a Father beyond the grave—not the rector of Lasterby but his Father too—who was waiting for my embrace, who was ready to accept it and forgive me and take me as a sobbing child into his arms.

It was in this frame of mind that my attention returned to the Irishman who knelt each night beside his slop bucket and told us with such confidence that all his sins were forgiven. I questioned him about penitence and he described the form. "And at the end of it," he said, "the priest tells you your penance, then gives you absolution, and you're forgiven."

I had begun each night to dread the remorse which afflicted me as I lay sleepless on my bunk. It was like a fever, making me giddy with sorrow and terror, but the ache of my soul was worse than any pain in the body and the yearning for that forgiving embrace so acute that at times I would groan out loud and be cursed for it by Selden.

In desperation, therefore, I had recourse to MacSweeney's remedy. I had learned from him the form of Confession and decided to try it out, for if it could clear his conscience perhaps it would salve mine. I therefore slipped in among the

Papists one Saturday afternoon (the prison authorities encouraged religious observances, thinking that they made for better citizens) and knelt in a row, waiting my turn to go behind the curtain into the confessional box. And then I was there, kneeling in the dark, my face up against a crucifix, and a square of wire mesh with a man's face distinguishable behind it.

"Bless me, father, for I have sinned," I said, repeating the words MacSweeney had taught me. The priest grunted. I went on. "I have sinned first—that is, the reason for which I'm in prison—I seduced a girl of fifteen."

"And do you intend to marry the girl?" asked the priest.

"No."

"Don't you love her?"

"No. I did it deliberately . . . to deprave her."

The priest paused and then said, "That is, certainly, a serious sin."

"I have done worse," I said.

"What have you done that is worse?"

"I have seduced and depraved a dozen other girls. I have killed a man, and a child, a baby, in front of its mother's eyes."

"How did you kill the man?"

"I was robbing a jeweler's shop. He surprised me. I hit him on the head."

"And the child?"

"The mother worked for me as a prostitute. The child would have been a nuisance . . . and I hated it. I hated the idea of the child and so I drowned it."

"And did the mother do nothing?"

"No. She did nothing."

The priest was silent, as if incredulous.

"She was very much under my influence," I said.

"And what other sins have you committed?"

"I have stolen," I said. "For the past ten years I have lived off theft."

[323]

"And prostitution."

"Yes. And prostitution."

I continued to list my sins, blurting them out in no order, some with explanations and others without—bald accounts of disjointed incidents which welled up out of my conscience like acrid vomit. And the ear behind the wire mesh listened to it all—the maiming of Billy, the humiliation of Freddy, the impoverishment of Mark—like a doctor listening to a patient recount the symptoms of a disease.

When I had finished, when the last wisp of bile had been thrown up from my memory, he sighed and asked if I was sorry for what I had done.

"Yes," I said. "For most of it."

"Not for all of it?"

"I find it difficult to be sorry for stealing . . . from the rich at any rate."

"But for taking life and innocence?"

"I'm sorry for that."

"You should be sorry for stealing, too."

"It seemed only to be taking from one man what he himself had stolen from another."

"In some cases," said the priest, "it may be so. I have had thieves in this confessional who have stolen out of real need, for their wives or for the children. But you were never in need . . . in real need. You had your ability and your intelligence. You had no need to steal at all. You robbed only from the hatred in your heart."

I said nothing.

"You must understand that and be sorry."

"Yes," I said, with a certain reluctance.

He paused again. "Why are you sorry for any of your sins?" he asked.

"Because I'm ashamed and I'm afraid."

"Well might you be ashamed," he said. And then he asked, "Are you afraid of Hell?"

"Of Hell and of death."

"Fear is the meanest reason for being sorry."

"What other reason can there be?"

"Love."

I said nothing.

"Love of God," the priest went on, "and love of your fellowmen for his sake."

"I can't say," I said, "that I have had much affection for my fellowmen."

"So it would seem."

"Nor for God. I hardly know him."

"No. You hardly know him."

"And yet now . . . I do feel and see the need to love him and should like to feel that he might forgive me."

"If you are sorry," said the priest, "even if it's just because you are afraid, God will forgive you, for he knows you and he loves you, whatever you may have done."

"I would like to believe that," I said.

"You must believe it," he said, "for that is why God sent his only Son down onto this earth—not for the good men but to call sinners to repentance."

"Yes," I said.

"God will forgive you, but you on your part must determine to make amends."

"Yes."

"Of course you can't give life back to the man or the child, or the use of his legs back to your friend . . ."

"No."

". . . but you must return what you have stolen."

"Yes."

"And what you cannot return, you must give to the poor."

"Yes." I hesitated and then asked, "But must I give away what I haven't stolen?"

"No. What you haven't stolen, you can keep."

"Even if its source is . . . irregular?"

"Your paintings, do you mean?"

"My paintings and my speculations on the Stock Exchange."

"Well," said the priest, "from what you have told me, I

would judge that you never forced anyone to buy your paintings or to sell their stocks and bonds. And so absolution would not depend on giving that money to the poor. But it is possible, isn't it, that your spirit of penitence may grow—that you may wish to divest yourself of your wealth and dedicate your life to the service of others?"

"Yes," I said, "it is possible."

"After all," he said, "you have offended God through harming others and so you can only really repay him in a like manner. That is why, for your penance, I shall not ask you to say one or a hundred decades of the rosary but shall rather leave it to God to show you a way to repay him."

"But what if he does not make it clear?"

"Then you may be grateful that your sins have been forgiven with no penance at all; but if your heart remains contrite, I do not doubt but that some opportunity for sacrifice will present itself. . . . And now, before I absolve you, let me ask you one thing."

I waited.

"Are you a Catholic?"

"No."

"I thought not."

"I was baptized as an Anglican."

"Then why come to a Catholic priest?"

"Because I believe that you can forgive me."

The priest paused and sighed and then said, "I shouldn't absolve you, but I will. Would you be here if you weren't sorry? If somewhere within you there was not a belief in Christ and his church, nurtured by the grace of God? It may be that your penitence is a flash in the pan, that as soon as you are out of prison you will return to your sins, for you do not understand what led you into sin and what has pulled you out of it. But in all our weakness and confusion, one thing is sure: if you pray to God and learn to love him, all else that is good will follow. . . . And now make your act of contrition while I give you absolution."

The last weeks of my sentence were among the happiest of my life. Superficially the conditions of the prison remained as bad as ever—there was the irritating proximity of Selden and MacSweeney, the all-pervading smell of urine, the snores, the groans, the hawking of the other prisoners—but this foulness of the fringe of existence could not touch the peace I felt at the center. The priest in the confessional had indeed worked a miracle, for while I was still conscious of the evil I had done, and knew that I was to be punished for it either before I died or after, I felt that like the Prodigal Son I was forgiven and that my soul, diseased and decrepit though it might be, had time now in which to recover and grow in preparation for eternity.

The fear which had driven me to repent was, in these weeks, replaced by a confidence in God and then love; and the restitution which I envisaged—not only giving Mark back his money but giving all I had to others—would not be to placate an angry deity but to please one who regarded me with affection.

I had few specific plans as to what I should do with my life upon my release; I accepted the word of the priest in the confessional that God would make my penance clear to me. I envisaged, I think, a monastery or some more secular form of self-abnegation, such as work in a madhouse or among the senile and incontinent. But no man should look into the mind of God, or predict his actions.

It came to the day of my release. I took my leave of Selden and MacSweeney and went down with an escort to the Governor's office, where I was commended cautiously for having been a model prisoner. Then, still with an escort, I was taken to exchange my prison denims for the clothes I had come in.

My watch and wallet were taken out of an envelope and returned to me, after which I was free.

I stood still for some time after the prison gates were closed behind me. It was nine o'clock in the morning on the thirty-first of October. There was pale sunshine. The air was warm. It smelled different outside the walls—fresh and free from any trace of cabbage steam or urine. I began to walk away from the gates. My legs felt a little weak, as if I had been in a hospital for the two months. The traffic and the people in the street looked strange and intimidating; after the drab order of the prison, all seemed chaotic and difficult. It took me some effort of mind to decide how to get back to my house in Kensington.

I walked on to the left and came eventually to a bus stop. There I waited and took the bus when it came. It did not take me to Kensington, but it went at least to a part of London where I could get my bearings; indeed, by the time it had reached Westminster, I was sufficiently in possession of myself to get off and take a taxi. I was home by a quarter past ten.

Immediately upon entering my house I was aware that something had happened to it while I was away. I smelled a difference; I sensed the presence of another. I went down to the kitchen, where there were signs that someone had eaten breakfast there that morning. Nothing had been washed up; the coffee was still warm in its pot.

I went upstairs again. Everything in the drawing room was disarranged but nothing gave away the perpetrator of the disarrangement. I went up to the bedroom, and there everything was made clear. A familiar suitcase lay open on the floor, familiar cosmetics were on the dressing table and the wardrobe had been left open by the owner of the clothes that were in it.

My reaction to this—the presence of Martha in my house—was one of dismay. I had somehow assumed that with my sins I would lose the victims of them. It was true, perhaps, that Martha's belongings reminded me of some happier moments in my previous life; all the same, her presence was inconsistent with the solitude that I imagined was to be my lot.

It was also that, having served one sentence on her account, I did not want to serve another. As I thought of this I heard the key turn in the lock of the front door. I went to the top of the stairs and saw her come in with a bunch of flowers in one hand, a bottle of champagne in the other and a key held in her mouth.

Her appearance was unchanged except for her belly, which stuck out like a ball. Her hair was still thick and black. Her shoulders bent forward. At first she did not see me. She put the bottle under the arm which held the flowers and with the hand thus freed tried to put the key back into her handbag. This proved too much for her so she put the flowers and the bottle on the hall table and was thus able to use both hands on the key.

I came down the stairs. She looked up, startled, and said "Oh."

I did not say anything but smiled at her.

"I didn't think . . ." she began. "I mean . . . I had meant it to be a surprise."

"It is a surprise," I said.

She looked at me with an uncertain expression. "I hope you don't mind my moving in. I got a key from Mrs. Partridge."

"Not at all," I said. "Your clothes were here."

"Yes," she said, "and . . . well, I had to leave home."

"Do your parents know you're here?"

She nodded. "Yes."

"Then we can expect another call from the police," I said.

"Oh, no," she said, tossing her head back. "I'm sixteen now."

I smiled and said, "That's just as well. I wouldn't particularly like to go back to prison."

"No," she said.

We were standing facing each other in the hallway. I glanced down at the flowers and the champagne.

"It's to celebrate your release," she said.

"That's very kind of you."

"It was the least I could do . . . I mean, after getting you in."

I smiled again. "It was an interesting experience."

We went into the drawing room.

"Was it awful?" she asked.

I shrugged my shoulders. "Not so awful."

As if she did not want to hear more, Martha said, "I'll just go and put this in the fridge, and the flowers in water." She turned and went down to the kitchen, her heavy body creaking the boards of the stairs. I sat down in an armchair and stretched back, wondering what I should do now with her in the house. All I had in mind, such as a bath and then the complicated unraveling of my stolen property from the rest, were not occupations in which she could participate.

She came back up the stairs and into the drawing room. "How long have you been here?" she asked.

"About ten minutes."

"I thought of meeting you at the prison gates, but then I thought I might miss you."

"Yes, you might have done."

There was a long moment of silence; then she said, quite quietly and firmly, "Would you like me to go?"

"No," I said, "but I think I might have a bath."

"Yes, of course. I'll fetch you a towel." She was about to leave when I asked her to wait.

"Sit down a minute," I said, "and tell me what's happened."

She did as I asked, sitting on the sofa five or six feet from me. "Well," she said, "I've been living here for about ten days."

"Isn't your mother worried . . . about that?" I pointed to her stomach.

"I don't care if she is," said Martha. "Anyway, there's a

perfectly good doctor down the road and he's booked me into Queen Charlotte's."

"Dr. Wilson?"

"Yes. And Hattie comes over to see that I'm all right."

"How is she?"

Martha blushed. "She's fine," she said, and then, "By the way, I didn't mind about that . . . I mean, about you having had an affair with her, but I rather wished you'd told me."

"I'm sorry," I said.

"Did you love her?" she asked.

"Not really," I said.

She hesitated, then blushed yet again, more deeply—most deeply of all. "And did you love me?" she asked.

"Yes," I said. "Always. From that first time in Harriet's house."

She seemed to sigh; then tears came to her eyes. "They all said you didn't. They all said that you'd done it . . . I don't know . . . out of spite."

"But you knew, didn't you?" I said, standing and crossing to sit next to her on the sofa and taking her into my arms.

"I knew, yes," she said, sniffing, "but sometimes . . . when I was alone . . . I wondered a bit."

I kissed her on her cheek and said, "Never wonder about that. I always loved you and will always love you."

"I knew," she said, tears rushing out of her eyes. "I knew, I knew. . . ."

Later in the morning I lay in my bath and wondered why I had said that I loved someone whom I did not love when I was now so committed to the truth. It was extraordinary how decidedly I did not love her, and extraordinary how clear it had been to me that I should say that I did. If anything, I loved her less than I had loved her before because her previously pretty body was now gross with the child she carried—her back curved, her stomach stuck out. There was about her, however, a most explicit expectation, and a greater

[*331*]

truth was indisputably served by my meeting it. To have told the strict, mean truth at that moment would have been worse than to strike her; and so I had lied, quite conscious of what that lie would entail. God had wasted little time in providing my penance, and though it was not what I had expected, I accepted it. I vowed that whatever it might cost me, I would protect Martha's innocence and happiness. It was as if I stood in a room full of porcelain I had myself smashed in a fit of madness and held in my hand the pieces of one fragile vase. If now I could glue them together, I could preserve a remnant of the collection.

The food which Martha cooked for lunch that day was better than prison food, and we drank the champagne she had bought that morning. She chattered at the beginning and chattered more as she drank more—about her mother and my mother, Mark who had married, and Sir Edward who was trying to save Lasterby from going up for sale. "Poor Daddy," she said. "He didn't really want them to prosecute you, and Mummy didn't in the end, but once the police know about it they just go ahead."

"I don't blame them at all," I said. "We did behave in an irresponsible way."

"It wasn't irresponsible if we loved each other," said Martha quickly.

"Perhaps not."

"And anyway it'll all be for the best in the end, because if I hadn't got pregnant, they'd have made us wait for years before letting us get married."

"Will they let us get married now?"

"Oh, they'll have to. I mean, they know I won't give up the baby and they hate the idea of it being illegitimate. It's not as if everyone in Yorkshire doesn't know about everything anyway, but somehow nothing's so bad if it ends well."

"Did they say they'd let us marry?"

"We didn't discuss it, really, because they were so sure

that you were a vile seducer who wouldn't marry me—especially as we're broke, now, as a family. Even your mother said you wouldn't."

"They don't know me. They were quite wrong."

"I knew you, didn't I?"

"Yes."

"That's what love is, isn't it? Knowing someone better than anyone else?"

"Yes."

"I knew that you did love me. It was impossible that you didn't. But you were so odd when your father died. . . ."

"I know. I'm sorry."

"No. I'm the one who should be sorry. I mean, I was a little tactless, I suppose." She peered at me. "I say," she said, "you've got awfully thin."

"Prison food," I said.

"Was it disgusting?"

"Like school."

She screwed up her nose. "Poor you. Never mind. I'll fatten you up."

Prior to that there were some details to be seen to, and while I began my calculations Martha wrote to her parents, a dignified letter asking them for permission to marry. She then came to me at my desk and asked me what I was doing.

"A few sums," I said. "I've got to make sure that we've enough to live on."

"Oh, don't worry. If you haven't enough, I'll get a job . . . as a typist or something. I don't want to be a burden to you."

"There'll be enough," I said.

She smiled.

I asked her whom Mark had married.

"That girl friend of his called Carol. I've never met her. None of us were asked to the wedding. Hattie says she was a . . . well, a kind of call girl."

"How exotic," I said.

"Isn't it? She must be quite noble, anyway, to marry Mark,

because he's all set to become a bank manager and the most boring man in the world."

"I dare say she loves him," I said.

"It's wonderful, isn't it," said Martha, kissing me brusquely, "the way people do love each other."

In the evening we went out to a film and after that to a restaurant. That night we slept in the same bed, chastely, like brother and sister or, rather, like long-standing husband and wife.

The next day I did my accounts. They were not as difficult as might be imagined because I had each year entered my profits from different sources under their appropriate headings. These were the conclusions I came to: I should have to return my entire collection of paintings and other works of art to their owners; I should have to give the sum of £680,000 to the poor, being the money equivalent of what I had stolen over the years, plus £127,000 representing five percent compound interest. From the money I had derived from the sale of my pictures (£110,000) I subtracted £50,000 as the appropriate tax that I had paid out of other funds and added this, together with my profits from Westbourne Grove, to my gift to the poor, making a grand total of £885,000.

This left me with £60,000 from my paintings, £800,000 from my share in Eric's club, and £926,000 in accumulated dividends and capital growth on my investments in the stock market. The grand total was around £1,800,000. I remained a rich man.

As will become apparent, my purpose in securing this sum was not as selfish as it might seem. I intended to divest myself of much of it, but meanwhile I began to pack up the pictures and statues. It was difficult to buy the materials for doing this in a way whereby I could not be traced afterward. The shops I chose had to be far from the house and my appearance in making the purchases had to be disguised. All the time I was doing this, Martha remained at home, cooking lunch and supper and talking to Mrs. Partridge. There was one occasion when she questioned me about what I was doing as I knelt on the floor wrapping my German diptych in cotton wool.

"I'm afraid I have to return them," I said. "They don't actually belong to me."

"Were they lent to you?"

"Sort of."

"Who by?"

"Various collectors."

She went off and asked me nothing more about the denuding of my walls—from discretion, I think, rather than stupidity, or perhaps she was preoccupied with her baby.

That afternoon she received a letter from her father and mother saying that in view of all the circumstances they gave their permission for her marriage to me. We took out a special license the next morning and were married later that day. Harriet and Eric were the only witnesses. We went back to the house to celebrate with the bottles of Krug that I had reserved for another occasion, but before we had even toasted our future Martha's contractions began. At nine we drove her to the hospital; our child, a boy, was born at ten the next morning.

While Martha was still in hospital I drove down to Croydon. By the time I had found the street of modern semidetached houses in which Mark and Carol were now living, it was five in the afternoon. I rang the bell and Carol opened the door. She saw me and started back, then made half a gesture to close the door again.

"Don't," I said, and she could tell from my tone of voice that I had not come to harm her. The look of fear cautiously left her face and she backed away from the door and let me in. I followed her into the house—into the small sitting room decorated with no taste, scrupulous in each detail of its suburban character.

"I came to see how you were," I said. "Both of you."

"We're all right," she said; then she added quickly, and with self-conscious pluck, "We're all right so long as we're left alone."

"No one's ever left alone by their relatives," I said. "I was married to Martha last week."

"Why?" she said. "They haven't any money."

"I know," I said. "That's why I'm here."

"Why . . ."

"I thought Mark might like what he lost at Eric's."

"He lost half a million pounds."

"I know."

"And you want to give it back?"

"Yes."

She shrugged her shoulders. "I'm making some tea," she said. "Would you like some?"

"Yes," I said.

She went into the kitchen which—because of the small size of the house and its thin, modern walls—was within earshot of the sitting room.

"Did you buy this house?" I shouted, looking around again at the details of the room, the plastic suite of furniture and the reproductions on the patterned wallpaper.

"No," she answered. "It's rented."

I then waited until she returned with the tea on a tray.

"What time does Mark get back?" I asked.

She looked at her watch. "Any time now."

"Does he know about . . . about me . . . about West-bourne Grove and all that?"

She looked at me. "No," she said.

"Why does he think you left him?"

"Because he'd lost his money." She answered without hesitation.

"And why does he think you came back?"

"Because I discovered I loved him."

I nodded.

"Why did you marry that girl, Martha?" Carol asked in her turn.

"She was pregnant," I said, smiling.

"Huh," she said.

I shrugged my shoulders. "I followed your example. It's time I settled down."

She looked at me again with an even greater expression of skepticism. "And why do you want Mark to have his money back?"

"Conscience," I said.

"And what about Billy?" she asked.

"What about him?"

"Are you going to give him back his legs?"

"I can't."

"No, you can't." She drank from her tea.

"He'll take the money, won't he?" I asked.

"I don't know," she said. "I don't think so."

"Why not?"

"He's . . . he's happy here, I think."

"As a bank manager."

"He's not a manager yet."

At that moment we both heard the front door open, and in a moment Mark appeared in the sitting room. He looked first at Carol and then at me and appeared equally delighted to see us both. "My goodness," he said to me. "How did you find us down here?"

"Harriet gave me your address."

"Well, it's nice to see you . . . after all that dreadful business." He took off his overcoat. Carol rose to take it from him.

"I'll bring another cup," she said as she left the room.

"Yes, do, darling," Mark shouted after her.

He looked well—better than I had seen him for several years—and I told him so. "Oh, yes," he said. "I'm marvelous. A regular life, no drink except an odd glass of sherry. . . . Would you like some?"

"No, thanks."

"And you've got married to Martha. Mother told me. It's too extraordinary, but I must say, I'm awfully glad. The whole trial was the stupidest thing Mother's ever done, and she's done quite a lot of stupid things."

He laughed and went on talking at a greater speed and with more enthusiasm than I had ever heard him talk before.

"Lasterby's going to have to go, of course, which is a pity for poor old Father," he said eventually.

"Don't you mind?"

He shrugged his shoulders. "Not really . . . well, a little, perhaps."

"It's about that that I've come to see you."

Carol returned with a cup.

"I've mentioned it to Carol," I went on. "It's about the money you lost at Eric's."

"That's all water under the bridge," said Mark, blushing a little.

"I've arranged for it to be paid back to you."

"To be paid back?"

"Eric owes me a favor or two, and now that I'm one of the family, as it were, it strikes me that it might be best if . . . er . . . the money went back to you."

"That's frightfully generous of you," said Mark in a disappointed, uncertain tone of voice. "The only thing is . . . well, I'm so well set up here—I mean, I like it here. I don't really want to go back to . . . to that sort of life." He glanced at Carol. "Do you?" he asked her.

"No," she said. She turned to me. "We'd rather not have the money."

"Don't think I don't appreciate what you're doing," said Mark. "I mean, it would be marvelous to pay off the mortgage on Lasterby—perhaps you could get Eric to do that? I mean, if he really wants to pay back some of the money. I don't really see why he should, though. The game was quite genuine, wasn't it?"

"Yes," I said.

"Well, anyway. I leave it to you, Hilary. I'd much rather not think about it, if you don't mind. The thing is, they keep me rather busy at the bank."

"All right," I said. "I'll see to it."

About half an hour later, I rose to go. There was one further matter I wanted to discuss, so I turned to Mark and said, "Have you heard from Billy?"

"No," he said. "I haven't. Not really. I mean, I get secondhand reports. He's evidently not too bad."

"I want to tell you something," I said, "and I want you to accept it."

"What?"

"That accident. It was my fault. It wasn't yours."

He said nothing.

"It wasn't your fault," said Carol. "It was Hilary. I was in the car. I know."

Mark shook his head. "All right," he said, "but why? Why did you do it?"

"I didn't like him," I said.

Mark turned down his mouth. "Well, in that case, I'm glad you never took against me."

I glanced at Carol; her eyes met mine. Neither of us said anything.

There was still time, when I got back to London, to go to the hospital to visit Martha and the child; when I entered the room where they lay, Lady Clare was there too. At my entrance, Martha looked alarmed and Lady Clare almost afraid, but her look, like Carol's that afternoon, became less timid when I smiled and shook her hand. Nor was I hypocritical, for I felt no rancor toward her—indeed, I had reason to be grateful.

The child lay in his cot asleep. Around his wrist, protruding from the blanket, was a label with his mother's name, his sex, the time of his birth and "normal delivery" affixed in ink.

"We must think of a name," said Martha.

"Have you got any ideas?" I asked my mother-in-law.

She blushed. "I . . . I haven't thought about it."

"I'd like one of his names to be Ernest," I said, "after my uncle."

Martha looked doubtful. "His second name, perhaps."

"I always liked your father's name, Miles," said Lady Clare, looking uneasily at me.

"I prefer the name Edward," I said.

"Would Daddy like it if we called him Edward?" asked Martha.

"I'm sure he would," said Lady Clare.

"Edward Ernest Fletcher," I said, looking down at the child.

When Martha was let out of the hospital, I thought it best that she should go north to Lasterby, where there would be better facilities for her recuperation and the child's care. I promised to follow her in a week.

By the time I did so, I had deposited my art collection—all carefully packed—in the left-luggage offices of three London stations and sent the tickets to Scotland Yard. I left it to them to return each piece to its owner; after all, I had paid my taxes and could expect some service from them. Three days later I read in the paper of an "unprecedented find of stolen paintings" and hoped to myself that if Martha read the same story she would not connect it with me.

Meanwhile I arranged the sale of stocks and shares for the realization of £885,000 cash. When this was done I had bankers' drafts sent to various charities without the identity of the donor being made known to the recipients. My secret was as safe with the manager of my bank as it would have been with any priest in a confessional.

I also got in touch with the brokers who held the mortgage of Lasterby. They were surprised but quite content that the mortgage should be paid off in full. The rights to the property and the income of the estate were thus returned to Mark.

By the time I went north to Yorkshire, I felt that I had done as much as was probably possible to make up to those who had suffered from my wrongdoing. There were still many unrecompensed, but in their cases restitution was beyond my powers and would have to wait for the next world.

Martha met me in York, and that evening I sat down to dinner at Lasterby Hall to the right of Lady Clare and to the left of my mother. Martha smiled at me across the table, and when the women had left the dining room Sir Edward came and sat next to me, filled my glass with port and put his arm on my shoulder.

"I'm awfully glad that you're here," he said, "and that everything's turned out for the best with you and Martha. She may be young, but I've always said it doesn't matter when, it matters whom."

I thanked him for the compliment.

"And when all's said and done," he went on, "it's better for a girl to marry a man who's been through it all, than some young chap who does it all later."

I agreed. "I hope I can make her happy," I said.

"I'm sure you can," he said. "You'll need to be firm with her, though. She's very stubborn when she wants to be."

"I know."

"To tell the truth, Clare and I are both quite frightened of her."

When we rejoined Lady Clare, my mother and Martha, all three women met me with a smile. Such an expression may have been understandable enough on the faces of the second two, but to see it on the face of the first—my mother-in-law—seemed strange in view of her determination a few months before to have me incarcerated. But like many irate parents, she had been softened by the birth of the child. The daughter's seducer gave way to the father of her grandson, and the older our boy grew, the more cordial, almost affectionate, she became toward me.

It was when he was a little over two and learning to talk that we had a second child, which further assisted my reconciliation with the Metheralls, though shortly after its birth Sir Edward had a heart attack and went with Lady Clare to live in the dower house. Lasterby Hall was then empty for some months because Mark could not be persuaded to leave Basingstoke, where he had become a branch manager of his bank. Nor could Carol be persuaded to take up a position as chatelaine of Lasterby Hall.

It was Mark's idea that the estate should be made over to Martha, or to our son Edward, and that we should take it on. "After all," he said, when he came to see us in London one weekend, "you don't seem to need to live in London and you can afford to run Lasterby."

"Certainly," I said, "but I don't see myself in the role of a country gentleman."

"Why ever not? You'd be frightfully good at it."

He persisted with his idea and wrote letters to his father and sisters. He drummed up opinion in the family to accept the plan while I did my best to douse it. I loathed the thought of living at Lasterby; my soul still yearned for solitude and self-abnegation and I chided God for not permitting me to serve him in this way. I had kept my money for Martha's sake—she would not have been happy without it—but my private income was more painful to me than any flagellation, and the comfort and privilege of our life itched more acutely than any hair shirt.

I counted on Martha to save me from the punishment she could now unwittingly inflict upon me. I knew that she liked London, for while I had nothing to do there, and found the days too long, she ran about and saw her friends and films and art exhibitions.

It turned out, however, that when she heard that Lasterby could be made over, and that our son Edward would be the heir, a change came over her. "It would be a pity," she said, "if nobody took it on. It's such a wonderful place, and think how nice it would be for your mother to have you there."

On another occasion she said, "It's not as if there's much to keep us in London. I mean, we can always have people to stay." And on yet another occasion, "It would be so wonderful for the children to have all that space and fresh air."

I advanced no arguments against what she said—and thus it was that two and a half years after our marriage we left London and went to live at Lasterby Hall.

The study of Lasterby is now my hermitage. To this day I would rather the whitewashed walls of a monk's cell to these shelves of vellum-bound books; and to be one of an anonymous religious community than an upstart among the landowners of the North Riding. Even the Catholic church is embarrassed to accept me, a spiritual parvenu, for I am known to be a parson's son and my conversion is an affront to the spirit of reconciliation which is fostered by the two religions. But into the pit of frustrated penitence God has sent me the consolations of nature. First there are my son and daughter—their small hands which cling to me and their smiling, imperious eyes. And then there is the change that has come over my feelings for Martha. From the first the spirit of contrition with which I had bound myself to her had contained some affection, and as she grew into someone both humorous and beautiful I came to feel admiration and respect. But it was only in Yorkshire—as if God had taken pity on me—that these feelings became love, and the love eventually passion, until all her words, glances and movements now fill me with delight.

Certainly, there are moments when a nostalgia for my earlier days comes over me like a wave of pain. I long to see Qazvini again and am tempted to run to London to find Rosamund or Alice or some other whore and wallow in their company. It never happens. I remain in my study in Lasterby Hall, dressed in a tweed suit, writing this account of my past life.

"Why don't you go back to painting?" Martha said one afternoon as she sat by the fire wrapping Christmas presents. "You were good at that."

[*343*]

"I've told you before," I said. "It was a fraud. In this"—I pointed to the manuscript—"in this I am trying to write the truth."

"You may think it's the truth," said Martha, who has read passages over my shoulder. "If you ask me, half of it's your imagination."

"You can think that if you like," I said, tapping my pen against my teeth.

"I simply don't believe you got all those girls to do all those things."

"You may not want to believe it."

"And why didn't they go to the police?"

"You were the one to do that."

She blushed. "And Mark losing his money was nothing to do with you."

"I prayed to the Devil to make the ball land on red."

She looked at me queerly. "I think you're slightly mad," she said. "It's all that Catholic mumbo jumbo you picked up in prison."

She crossed to the window to see if it was raining. "Or perhaps it's being a rector's son which makes you so obsessed with good and evil and guilt and redemption."

The rain had stopped. She went out without waiting for an answer.

It is now January. To all outward appearances nature is entirely dead. At Christmas Martha's brother and sister and their families came to stay; and at dinner we were joined by their parents and my mother. I sat at the head of the table and poured out the wine. In the afternoon there was a tenants' party to which the rector's daughter and the doctor's son were both invited. There were also my cousins Sam and George with their wives and families. My feelings at that party cannot be difficult to imagine, but Martha was happy and I felt that God approved.

In the New Year our guests departed and we are now

alone again. Each morning I see to my son's estate and each afternoon I sit at my desk. My eyes move from the paper to the darkening landscape of trees and fields and then back to the paper. Soon it will be five o'clock, when I shall go up to the nursery and have tea with Martha and the children. And in time I shall die. Between these two appointments there is nothing of importance.